FIRST
DAUGHTER

FIRST DAUGHTER

MARLIE PARKER WASSERMAN

First published by Level Best Books/Historia 2026

First Daughter is a work of fiction. Incidents, dialogue, and characters, with the exception of select historical figures, are products of the author's imagination and are not to be construed as real. Where real-life historical figures appear, the situations, incidents, and dialogue pertaining to those persons are entirely fictional, and are not meant to depict actual events or to alter the entirely fictional nature of the work. In all other respects, any resemblance to actual persons, living or dead, events, or locales is entirely coincidental.

Author Photo Credit: Gretchen Mathison

First edition

ISBN: 979-8-89820-153-1

Cover art by Level Best Designs

This book was professionally typeset on Reedsy.
Find out more at reedsy.com

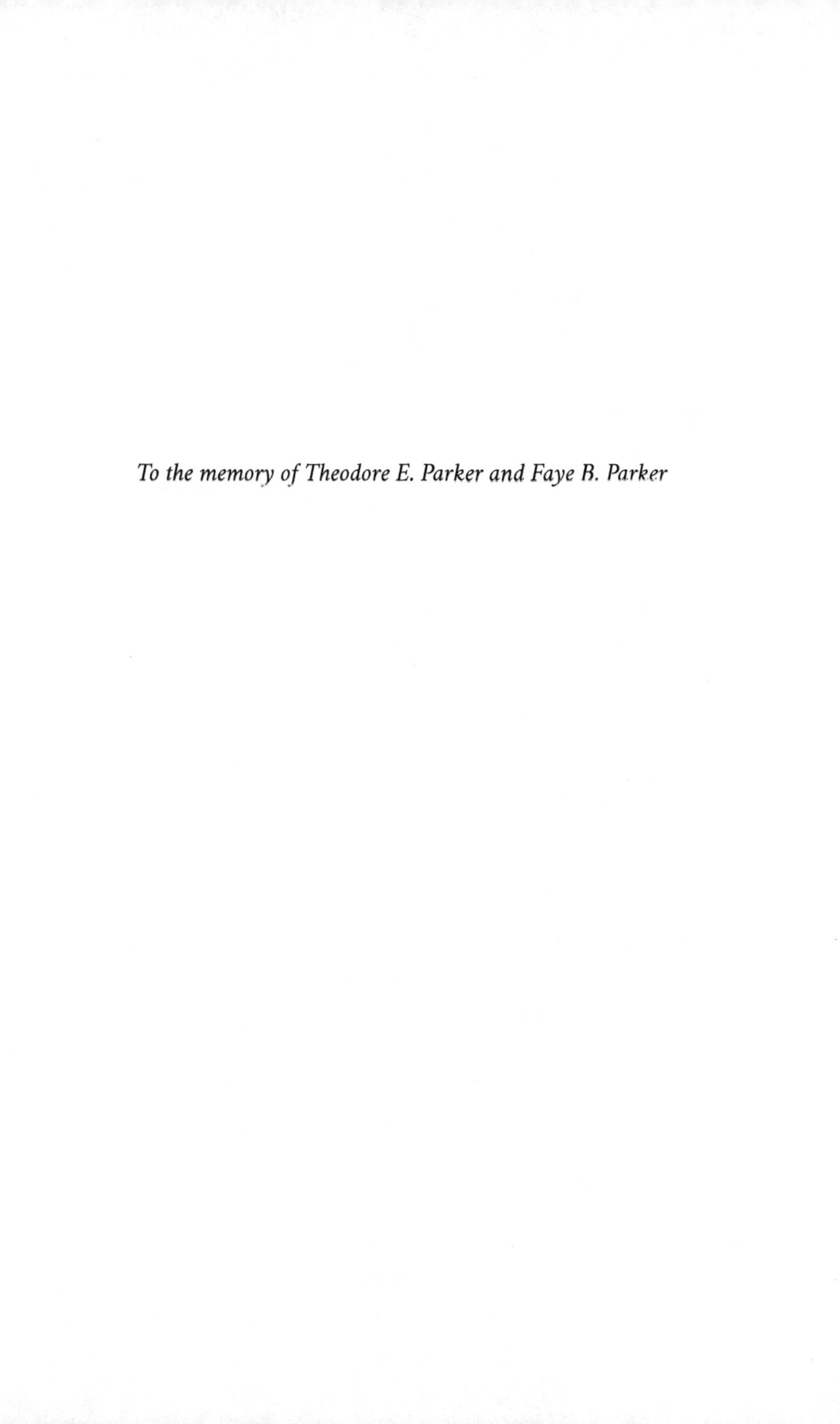

To the memory of Theodore E. Parker and Faye B. Parker

Praise for FIRST DAUGHTER

"Arresting, brilliant, emotional! Marlie Wasserman's *First Daughter* had me hooked from the very first page. Like her other works, fact and fiction are delightfully blurred by the fantastic level of historical detail, creating an exhilarating ride through the kidnapping of President Grover Cleveland's first child and his obscure misdeeds."—**Jane L. Rubin**, author of the award-winning Gilded City series, *Threadbare, In the Hands of Women* , and *Over There*

"In this masterfully woven historical thriller, the past comes alive with rich detail and taut suspense. In the summer of 1895, President Grover Cleveland and his wife retreat to their Cape Cod estate, seeking respite from political turmoil—until their three-year-old daughter vanishes. A ransom note surfaces, but is the culprit a political enemy or someone in their household? Seamlessly blending fact and fiction, this novel delivers a riveting tale of betrayal, resilience, and a mother's relentless quest for truth."—**Maryka Biaggio**, award-winning author of *Gun Girl and the Tall Guy* and *The Model Spy*

"A parent's worst nightmare unfolds for President and Frances Cleveland— their daughter is kidnapped. And no one knows why she was taken. The real motive behind the kidnapping may lie closer to home than anyone dares to imagine. *First Daughter* is a thrilling tale that clutches your heart and won't let go. This haunting historical mystery steeped in vivid period detail explores the cost of secrets and the burden of public life, wrapped in a mother's relentless instinct to protect her family—no matter the consequences."—**JF Tanner**, author of *The King's Collar*

"Grabbed from the very first page, Wasserman's tale of the abduction of President Grover Cleveland's young daughter Ruth (Baby Ruth) delivers Gilded Age details, tense characters and no bigger problem than a child in danger. With the deftly structured combination of Frances Cleveland's determination to bring justice to her family and a parallel hard luck tale, readers will forget this is non-fiction."—**Chris Keefer**, author of *Find Your Way to My Grave,* a Carrie Lisbon Mystery

"*First Daughter* is an intriguing and intricately-plotted historical mystery novel. I loved the depth of research and the evocative setting of President Grover Cleveland's summerhouse Gray Gables at Buzzards Bay. I look forward to reading more from Marlie Parker Wasserman."—**Margo Laurie**, author of *The Anarchist's Wife*

I

Part One: Frances's World

Chapter One

At the western edge of Cape Cod, in the grandest bedroom in the sprawling residence known as Gray Gables, Frances Cleveland couldn't stifle the rising sound of her own screams. Between pains, she rested. The late morning breeze drifted across the lawn from Buzzards Bay, fluttering the lace curtain and cooling the sweat on her forehead.

Even at this moment, Frances felt grateful that Grover chose to spend summers away from Washington's heat, away from the prying public. Here, in this secluded haven, she needn't fear strangers hovering near the windows of the Executive Mansion for a glimpse of their president—or, more likely, of his wife and daughters. She could concentrate her fears on her pains and pray for the safe birth of her third child, in the same way she had for her first and again for her second. Frances expected from experience that her suffering would soon recede, replaced by the joy of motherhood. She did not know that before the day was over, her bodily misery would end, yielding not to joy but to overwhelming terror.

The previous February, after sensing a flutter beneath her gown while greeting a crowd of visitors at a reception, Frances guessed the baby would be her third girl. Practiced at keeping confidences, she never mentioned her prediction to her preoccupied husband. When she gave birth to another girl, the blathering journalists would have their say. They would try out their jokes about the president's little harem. Most days, Frances ignored the journalists. Most days, she trusted Grover to love each of his babies.

The image of a trio of girls was far from Frances's mind now, as she suffered in bed. She cried out, too loudly. Dr. Bryant reminded her that she'd survived labor pains before. "Don't you dare say that again," she said, in a shrill tone that surprised her.

At last, Frances heard the newborn's cry, faint but lovely. Dr. Bryant chuckled while he clamped and cut the cord. "Mrs. Cleveland, should I bring the president upstairs to see his new daughter? He's pacing on the front porch. Once he sees this one—she's beautiful—he won't regret it's not a son."

"Yes," Frances said, with the strongest voice she could muster. A girl, as she'd guessed. For an instant, with the last of her contractions, she'd ignored her prediction and hoped for a boy. Now, she didn't linger on that momentary weakness of character. She let a surge of pride swell over her, above the exhaustion. She'd done it. Again.

Frances turned to the local midwife hired to assist. "Tell the steward, his name is Sinclair, to get Ruth and Esther. I want my daughters to see their new sister."

Frances raised herself a few inches, enough to see the midwife slip into the hall. The woman returned and gave Frances a nod. The girls would come shortly. Frances sank back and watched the midwife wipe down the infant and swaddle her. She did look beautiful. "Here," Frances said, crooking her arm to make room for Marion, the name Grover chose that would serve for a girl or a boy. The same name as a town across Buzzards Bay, where many of their friends lived. Frances appreciated Grover's decision to buy an estate on the outskirts of a different but nearby town, Bourne. The family could escape Washington's heat and busybodies.

And escape the threats.

Hours earlier, Frances gave thanks for the breeze blowing through the open window, reminding her that Gray Gables was perfectly located on a point overlooking the Bay's east side. But now she blocked the sound of wind and waves. straining to make sense of other sounds, to hear what Grover would say about a third daughter. The doctor scurried downstairs.

The midwife remained stationed over the bed, tending to Frances and crooning softly to the baby. Frances ignored the woman, mindful only of the voices wafting in through the window. First, low tones as the doctor talked to Grover. They were friends. Dr. Bryant saved Grover's life two summers ago, removing the cancer eating away at his palate. Now, Frances imagined the doctor patting her thickset husband on his shoulder and shaking his hand. She hoped Grover would offer the doctor a contented smile. Seconds later, Grover clomped upstairs. The doctor followed behind, with lighter steps.

"So happy, Frankie." Her husband used one of her nicknames. After their wedding, she asked Grover to call her by her more dignified name, Frances. He still used Frankie or Frank in private moments. She let him—the nicknames added tenderness to his gruff voice. "The doctor tells me you're fine. You managed without chloroform this time, too. And the baby's healthy. Marion, right? Three girls. They will enjoy each other's company."

He said the right thing. She didn't need to feel anxious about another girl. He was a good man, kind to her, whatever others thought. He wouldn't hold the baby, rarely did. But he wiped his chubby hand on a cloth, then touched Marion's forehead. He stood there for a few minutes, cherishing their third child. For him, it was a fourth, but no matter. His eyes shifted to gaze at her. He wouldn't see the tall, slender belle he married nine years ago, the one the reporters called lovely. He'd see a tired, sweat-drenched woman who looked every day of her thirty years.

"Ruth and Esther?" Frances asked again, eyeing the midwife. "Did you send Sinclair for them?"

"Yes, ma'am. The steward went a minute ago." The midwife spoke quietly, carefully. She'd feel nervous in the presence of the president.

Still almost flat in bed, Frances clutched Marion, admiring the infant. Perfect features. Ten fingers and ten toes. Another blessing from God.

A familiar sound at the door. Sinclair knocked softly. His usual pattern—soft, loud, soft—keeping to the household code. Another sound, when the midwife opened the door. Next, Frances would hear four little feet rushing toward the newest baby.

No feet. Only hushed words.

"Sinclair found Annie," the midwife said. "She's your older daughter's nursemaid, right? He tells me she needs another minute to bring Ruth and to tell your younger daughter's nursemaid to bring Esther." The midwife stood far from Frances's bed, speaking almost in a whisper.

Grover didn't look concerned. His rough mustache skimmed Frances's cheek as he kissed her lightly on her damp forehead. She was too tired to return the kiss. She heard him drop into the nearby rocking chair.

"Joseph," he said, addressing the doctor, "you're certain Frankie is fine? No complications?"

"Just fine, Grover. Ready for the next one before long."

Four years earlier, when Ruth was born, Dr. Joseph Bryant told Frances how to manage her family. "Breastfeed for six months." He looked straight at her, with no awkwardness. "You'll not get in the family way, and the baby will stay healthy. After six months, well, you and Grover can proceed to another." And so they had. Esther after Ruth. Marion after Esther. A daughter every two years.

Frances closed her eyes, relying on her ears. Dr. Bryant thanked the midwife for her assistance. The woman tidied up, gathering soiled sheets and opening a chest, hunting for fresh linens. The room went silent, except for the soft, repetitious squeak of the rocking chair. Grover leaned up, then back, up then back. Frances sensed herself drifting off.

Another soft knock, barely a sound, followed by a pause, and two more soft knocks. Not Sinclair. One of the nursemaids. Annie? The midwife opened the door. "Ma'am." Annie's voice came out as a croak. "I can't find Ruth."

Frances bolted upright. The palpable pain of terror replaced the soreness in her womb. The room was airless. She gasped for breath.

Grover moved faster than Frances could remember. He bounded to the bedroom door. Later, when she grew irritated with him, she'd struggle to recall his speed and his yell for his steward.

"Sinclair, run. Get Agent Hazen. Tell him Ruth is missing. He'll grab Agent Donnella."

Frances's right arm, cradling Marion, went limp. The midwife, her mouth open in horror, exchanged a frightened look with Dr. Bryant. They turned their eyes to Frances and the baby. In two seconds, Frances repositioned her arm, almost too tightly. She kept gulping for air.

Grover would know what to do. His broad back shook as he towered over the terrified nursemaid.

"Annie," he yelled, "stop whimpering. What happened?" Silence. "Damn. Tell me what happened." Frances cringed at Grover's "damn." She'd never heard him swear at anyone except the politicians who stood in his way daily.

"Sir." Annie choked. Coughed. "You know, with the window open, we could all hear Mrs. Cleveland." Annie glanced at Frances, at the baby. "Anyone would scream. She did less than most." Annie hesitated. She always talked slowly. "Even so, Ruth and Esther got scared. They didn't understand what was happening. I told Bonnie to take the girls from the house, so they wouldn't hear."

"Who's Bonnie?" Grover yelled. He didn't remember the name of Esther's nursemaid. Frances winced and struggled to take a breath. She tried to say "nursemaid." No sound came out.

"She's nursemaid for Esther." Thank heaven Annie answered.

"Around noon, I walked Ruth to the Wylies—you know—the house-keeper's cottage. Bonnie carried Esther. I thought that was all right since it's close to your porch. Mrs. Wylie wasn't in her cottage. She helped Susan cook, here, in the residence." Another irritating pause. "I set Ruth down in the cottage." Annie would guess that her trembling voice dropped too much to be heard. She repeated herself. "I set Ruth down. I gave her pans to play with."

Grover moved his hand in a circle to demand Annie hurry up. She locked her eyes on the far wall and choked out the rest. "Bonnie carried Esther up to the staff rooms—the bedrooms on the second floor—and set her down on a bed for her nap. She fell asleep. Then the screaming stopped. I didn't know if that was good or bad. I didn't hear a newborn's cry, must've been soft, so I got worried. I didn't want Ruth to know I got worried. I went to the front of the cottage and walked toward the main house to see if I could tell what was happening."

While Annie mumbled, Jeffrey Hazen slipped in through the half-open door. Frances shifted her eyes to the head Secret Service agent. She respected him, trusted him. Nothing bad had happened under his watch. He averted her gaze, uncomfortable in the birthing room with the president's wife in a nightdress. She supposed he was deciding to push propriety aside. He leaned against the wall, listening to Annie stammer. Frances followed the agent's eyes as they shifted to Grover's raised right hand. Grover yanked his mustache, a sure sign of his anger at Annie's drawn-out rendition.

"From the lawn, I saw Sinclair." Annie pointed to the hall where the steward must be standing, waiting, scared. "He came out on the porch and looked around. He spotted me and beckoned with his arm. I ran to him, and he ran to me. We met halfway. He told me the baby was born, a healthy girl, and to bring Ruth and Esther. He said it pretty loud because I know Bonnie heard, upstairs in the cottage. He said he'd wait on the lawn, and I should get the two girls." Annie turned away from the president, toward Frances. "Ma'am, I asked him if you were all right. Then I turned around and went back to the cottage." Annie raised her hands, hiding her face. She sobbed.

"Get it together. Keep going." Grover roared. He half-raised both arms and closed his hands into fists, as if he were about to kill Annie. She stared again at the wall beyond him.

Somehow, Annie found her voice. "Ruth wasn't in the cottage."

Frances felt the blood in her head plunge down, toward her feet. She trembled. The midwife stepped up to hold her shoulders, but Frances couldn't control her body.

Grover thrust his chin toward Annie, raising his arms again.

"I went to the second floor of the cottage." Frances tried to stop shaking. She must focus on Annie's quivering voice. "Bonnie sat there, knitting, calm. She'd heard Sinclair's news. Esther was asleep. I ran back to Sinclair and told him to say I needed a few more minutes. I searched better, in each room in the cottage and in the garden. Bonnie woke Esther and searched too." Annie's slow voice dropped to a murmur. "Ruth was nowhere."

Frances saw Agent Hazen stare at her, take in her fright, and glance at the baby. He raised both hands, palm out. Frances understood. Don't worry. I'll find Ruth. He lowered his arms and spoke, moving his head slowly across the room to address everyone. "Annie, come with me. Mr. President, stay with your wife. Agent Donnella and me, we'll find Ruth."

Frances sucked in air until she was almost breathing normally and could slow her trembling. Keeping her eyes on Grover, she heard Annie and Agent Hazen walk downstairs and out the main door. Stretching an arm and pointing a finger, Frances signaled to the midwife to open the window further.

The midwife raised the window as far as possible, then turned back to Grover and Dr. Bryant. She whispered to them. All three looked at Marion. The midwife walked to the bed. "Mrs. Cleveland, while your husband's bodyguards find Ruth, we must think about the baby. I'm going to do my job, to help you care for this beautiful girl." Frances felt the midwife's hands adjust Marion, hold her tiny head, encourage her to latch. Feeling nothing but pain, Frances shook her head. She would not nurse this third daughter until her first daughter returned. The midwife shook her own head, moved Marion another inch, and caressed Frances's wet cheek. "Mr. President," the midwife said.

He caught the beseeching tone and walked toward the bed. "Frances, you let Jeffrey Hazen and the others find Ruth. Your job is to care for Marion." Though his voice sounded stern, his eyes spoke love. Frances honored the command, as she usually did. She took a deep breath and put her hand over Marion's back, next to the midwife's hand.

"Grover, I will, but I will not be left out. Join the search, even though Agent Hazen told you to stay with me. I can manage. You will report back?"

He flinched at the word report. She should know better.

She changed the timbre of her voice. "I mean, please tell me what is happening." Grover's face softened.

"Of course. You nurse Marion. I'll find Jeffrey and keep a watch on the search."

Grover called Agent Hazen by his first name, Jeffrey—a good sign, Frances thought. The agent would work hard for a congenial boss.

"If you don't find Ruth soon, come back upstairs to me. Let me tell you what I'm thinking." Now her body was torn in pieces—her sore womb, her busy breast, her broken heart, and her active mind.

Chapter Two

July 7, 1895

"The front lawn—at once." Agent Jeffrey Hazen, his voice urgent yet controlled, raced outside to round up the servants. He motioned for Annie and Sinclair to wait near the porch.

He ran around the residence, stepping on the flower beds encircling the lawn. With a shout, he grabbed Bud Wylie from the shed where he kept the president's fishing gear and snatched Agent Sky Donnella from his patrol around the property. Hazen spotted groundsmen trimming shrubbery near the outbuildings and grabbed them, too. He darted back to the lawn in front of the porch, where a dozen familiar faces already gathered.

Hazen allowed himself two seconds of irritation. When he was assigned to Gray Gables, he thought he'd be protecting a president. No rebel like Booth, no madman like Guiteau, would get to Cleveland. Not under Hazen's watch. Now, instead of saving the president, Hazen hunted for a child. He tried to restrain his thoughts. No time to linger on the affront.

The servants and staff formed a half circle around him. The women, whispering to each other, might be useless. Then again, the cook or the maids or the laundress might know little Ruth's habits. Did she have secret hiding places in the rambling house? The groundsmen would certainly be useless, just lads from town who kept the property neat and helped with security. But the gardener, a muscled fellow, was fast on his feet. And the steward and the coachman had brains. They knew the household and learned easily. And Bud Wylie, the caretaker who spent most of the summer skippering the president's boats, looked after the property long before the Clevelands bought it. He'd know of hiding places on land and around Buzzards Bay.

Hazen stood at the center of the gathering, all eyes on him. Even though these people weren't soldiers, they stood at attention, awaiting orders. He had made an effort to get to know them. Just not too much. He boarded with them in the servants' quarters in the cottage, but unlike the servants, he often met privately with the president and the missus.

Hazen straightened his jacket and tie. He dressed better than the servants and more formally than Cleveland, who wore a rumpled suit in the summer. Hazen's fiancé told him he looked the part of a presidential guard—tall, brawny, with handsome features. He fixed those features into an expression of confidence.

But he had to reach for that confidence. Three-and-a-half-year-old Ruth could have run away on her own, though she was a sweet child, not mischievous. One-and-a-half-year-old Esther would more likely hide than Ruth. Was he right to concentrate on hiding places? Thinking back to threats against the Cleveland children, he tensed his neck.

Maybe not hide-and-seek. Maybe abduction.

He'd give Sky Donnella the most dangerous assignment. The man wasn't big for an agent, but he was fast and smart. "Agent Donnella, hightail it to the train station. Make sure no one's leaving town that way. You're armed?" Hazen put his hand on his own Colt revolver, hidden under his jacket. Donnella nodded and hurried off.

Bonnie, the sturdier of the two nursemaids, stepped into the spot where Donnella had stood. She held tight to Esther, who wriggled and fussed. "Bonnie," Hazen said, "take Esther down the road to the closest neighbor, probably the Parkinsons." Uncharacteristically quiet, Bonnie seared her eyes into his, looking for answers, or maybe assurances. He had none to offer, but nodded his head, a modest but sufficient gesture.

As Bonnie turned to leave, Hazen worried about Esther, now the middle child. Could this tot be in danger, too? Hazen scanned the crowd for a suitable bodyguard, stopping at the gardener. "Walk to the Parkinsons with them." With a surprised face, the gardener strode to Bonnie. The two walked away, the gardener slowing his steps to match hers. Bonnie clasped both arms around the whining girl.

"Bud, you're next. Check the president's boats. We hope Ruth is simply lost, but if she's been taken, we don't want some culprit escaping with her into the Bay." Cleveland's skipper ran to the dock with more of a lope than a bolt. Hazen could count on Bud to stay coolheaded in emergencies.

Hazen pointed to the steward. "Sinclair, hunt along the shoreline in case Ruth went off on her own." Sinclair nodded, proud of the assignment. The two men played poker after hours and got along. Hazen didn't care about skin color. He was grateful for a poker partner. Sometimes Hazen won, sometimes Sinclair.

Scanning the servants and staff still on the lawn, Hazen saw that the uniformed coachman, a tall, broad-shouldered man, was fidgeting. He'd know the stables and the nearby sheds.

"Nolan. John Nolan." Hearing his name, the coachman raised his head, ready.

"What can I do?"

"The outbuildings. Go through each one." Nolan peeled off, running behind the residence.

The faces in the crowd swung to the side all at once. The president rushed out the main entrance. The big man's fingers stretched his mustache, signaling—what? Distrust? Hazen worried as Cleveland opened his mouth to talk. But then he seemed to change his mind and listen. Moving his head up and down, likely in agreement with the directives he must have heard from the hall, the president planted himself just behind Hazen.

"Sir, best if you stay with your wife." Hazen spoke in a low voice. "Most likely, Ruth is hiding somewhere. But if she's been abducted, you could be in danger too. Remember, we've seen threats against you as well as your children. You should return to Mrs. Cleveland or to your study. I'll come to your side as soon as I can."

"I'll go. Only here for a minute to lend support. I know you'll find Ruth."

Good, Hazen thought, he trusts me, though God knows why. He'll let me do my job.

Hazen turned back to face the household staff. He sent the groundsmen to search the backwoods. Then he looked over the women. A few wiped tears away. "Those of you who tend to the house, check every spot inside." Although he doubted the girl had squeezed into a hiding spot, he had to cover all possibilities. "Lena," he said to Mrs. Cleveland's lady's maid, "check the bedrooms, the wardrobes, the lavatories, the attic. Wherever a small child might hide." Shit. He didn't know the names of the two chambermaids. "Lena, take all the maids with you. Then check those places a second time. Fast."

While the three maids rushed back to the house, Hazen called on the cook. "Susan, check the pantries, the cellar. Then check a second time."

He saw the laundress and managed to remember her name. "Ingrid, check the basins and the drying room. Behind every pile of laundry. Twice."

Only two women remained on the lawn—Mrs. Wylie, the housekeeper who boarded the staff and the agents in her nearby cottage and helped Sinclair manage the maids, and Annie, the pint-sized nursemaid who just haltingly told how she took her eyes off Ruth for thirty seconds. "Mrs. Wylie, go to your cottage. Take Annie. Look everywhere, again."

Hazen watched Effie Wylie turn away. She was a sensible woman, married to Bud, and mirrored his calmness. Annie, head down and sobbing, followed in the housekeeper's wake for a few steps. Then Annie said something to her, pivoted, and stumbled back toward Hazen.

"This is my fault." Annie's voice quivered. "Please don't jail me."

The poor woman sank into herself, as if the sky had fallen on her.

"No arrests. Let's just find the girl." The nursemaid bobbed her head and swiped her tears. Hazen watched her slink off toward the housekeeper, already close to the cottage. Annie couldn't fathom that the fault was not hers.

The fault was entirely his. Or if not the fault, the responsibility.

In recent assignments, Hazen tracked down counterfeiters and infiltrated gangs of criminals. That's what he would still be doing if his brother William, chief of the Treasury Department's Secret Service, hadn't needed to assign a senior agent and a junior agent to protect the Clevelands at Gray Gables. Jeffrey Hazen fit the bill of senior agent, and Skylar Donnella, of junior agent. Hazen thought Will wanted to give his younger brother a prestigious post in a safe, pleasant town, far away from the crazy people who threatened Cleveland. What would Will think when Jeffrey couldn't even keep track of a child? Hazen hunched his shoulders. He'd failed. Failed his brother, failed the Treasury Department, failed the president, failed Ruth. Hazen shook out his shoulders and told himself to remember his task.

He was alone on the lawn now except for the president, who stood there, seemingly unable to move, stretching his mustache as far as it would go. Hazen approached, hesitated for a second, then patted the president's shoulder and guided him back toward the house. Judging from the shadows on the grass, it was mid-afternoon. Hazen checked his pocket watch. 2:05.

Chapter Three

July 7, 1895

Frances tried to control her shaking. She stilled enough to fix her mind on listening. Doors opened and closed, and the maids congregating on the lawn mumbled to each other. Then the official voice of Jeffrey Hazen carried up and through the bedroom window. He was giving orders.

Frances caught Bud Wylie's voice, with the thick accents of the region. She could count on Bud. She heard Bud's wife, Effie, speak with the same accent, in a soothing tone. Maybe trying to comfort Annie. Then the familiar voice of their steward, William Sinclair. The other voices sounded less familiar—too many to sort out—maybe the cook, the coachman, the groundsmen, the maids, the laundress, the other Secret Service agent. Then Agent Hazen's voice again, telling the gardener to take Bonnie and Esther to—a breeze carried away Hazen's words—maybe a neighbor's house. Then silence. The staff must have spread out.

Dr. Bryant left the bedroom, assuring Frances he'd return to check on her. She didn't thank him. The midwife stayed, sitting on the edge of the chair Grover had abandoned, with her feet planted so she didn't rock. She stared at the traditional, flowery wallpaper as though it merited attention. Every few minutes, she stood up to adjust Marion's position, to wipe Frances's brow, or to tidy up more. Neither Frances nor the midwife spoke.

The midwife broke the tension first. "Mrs. Cleveland, I'm sure your daughter is hiding. Isn't that what girls do at that age?"

Bristling at the platitudes, Frances let her frown speak for her. The midwife looked down, realizing she overstepped.

"Well, I'm sure that agent will find her."

Frances said nothing.

The woman tried again. "Mrs. Cleveland, would you like me to sing? A lullaby? The newspapers say you like music."

"Yes, I do. But not now. Just sit still. Let me think."

With each passing minute, Frances imagined increasingly horrific scenes. Ruth trapped under a fallen tree. Ruth in the attic, bitten by a bat. Ruth enshrouded in mucky eelgrass, sunk into mud. Ruth kidnapped. Ruth murdered. Frances shifted her eyes to the side. That pesky midwife should stop staring. Through the open window, Frances smelled Buzzards Bay, briny, stinking.

She lost track of time. From the bed, she couldn't see the clock. "How long has it been?"

"About an hour," the midwife said.

"Not longer?"

"Maybe a bit longer." The midwife stood up and took Marion from Frances's arms. The woman adjusted Marion's swaddling blanket and placed her gently in the cradle at the far end of the room. Frances was supposed to sleep. Both she and the midwife knew that. Both she and the midwife knew that was impossible. The midwife returned to her chair, slumped forward, her head in her hands.

Through the still open window, a whoop, then a hurrah.

Frances locked eyes with the midwife. The woman ran to the window and leaned out. The cheers moved from the dock, across the lawn, in different voices. The midwife raised both arms, elbows bent. As she flapped her hands, she shouted. "They found her! They found your daughter!"

Frances raised her own arms, spreading her fingers wide. "Thank the Lord." The words came out as a wheeze through the onslaught of her tears. "Thank the Lord." Clearer this time. The midwife turned away from the window, beaming. Reaching out, Frances forgot forever her irritation at the unsuitable words of comfort the midwife had offered. The two women, strangers that morning, embraced.

They looked toward the cradle. "Mrs. Cleveland, Marion's slept through it all."

Ten minutes later, Ruth rushed to her mother.

Frances crushed her oldest daughter into her arms and with her fingers lightly caressed Ruth's blond waves. "Are you all right? Oh, Lord, thank you. Sweetheart, what happened? You must tell me before you see the baby."

"I can tell you more quickly," Grover said. He and Dr. Bryant had followed Ruth into the bedroom. "A woman—a stranger—"

Frances put one finger to her lips and pointed to the cradle, though Marion still slept. Grover lowered his voice to a whisper.

"She must have hidden near the housekeeper's cottage. Ruth said that after Annie walked out to talk to Sinclair, the woman entered from the back and told Ruth to come that way, that the new baby was born and was at a pond, one of the ponds where I fish."

Ruth, usually a chatterbox, said nothing. Now, a soft whine. "I wanted to see the new baby."

Frances patted her head.

"The woman put Ruth in the rowboat we keep in the Bay, the one Bud pulls halfway up to the shore, with the red "C" painted on one side. The "C" must have been on the far side, or the woman might have thought twice. She rowed Ruth out. Then, a miracle—Joe Jefferson rowed by." Frances cocked her head in surprise. "Yes, Joe, our neighbor. At that very moment. Too late for fishing. He just wanted some exercise. He saw a strange woman in our boat with Ruth, well into the Bay, and thought that was peculiar. The woman struggled against the currents, though she kept going. She turned the boat around after she saw him stare. He moved after her, faster. She reached the dock and hopped out of the boat. Then she put Ruth on the rocks and ran. When Joe got to Ruth, he checked on her first. Didn't want to leave her to go after the woman. A minute later, Sinclair found Ruth and Joe. Meanwhile, Bud noticed the rowboat was missing and thought he spotted it in the Bay. He knew he couldn't get the sailboat moving fast enough, so he ran down the shore to borrow another rowboat. Then Sinclair and Joe yelped, 'found her.' That was around 3:30."

"The woman?" Frances said, with a tense whisper.

"No one recognized her. She's still on the run. Jeffrey Hazen and some of the others are hunting for her."

"Where do they think she went? How did Joe describe her?" Frances sputtered out questions, ignoring Grover's impatient look. He gave short, useless answers. Dr. Bryant hovered, ordering Frances to rest.

A knock—soft, pause, soft, soft. Frances barely registered the nursemaids' code. Bonnie came in with her charge, little Esther, who toddled over to the bed, climbed up, and joined in a cuddle, bouncing against her mother and her sister. "The gardener came to fetch us at the Parkinsons," Bonnie said. "To tell us the good news. I ran back with him and Esther."

Frances, still hugging Ruth, moved her fingers from Ruth's hair to Esther's darker curls. After a minute, Esther settled down.

"Now, girls, you can see your new sister. She's sleeping in the cradle, so be quiet."

"Sister?" Ruth said.

"Yes, dear." Frances sighed, drifted off to sleep, and forgot the ideas she was holding far back in her head to share with Grover.

Chapter Four

July 8, 1895

The next morning, Frances turned her head in bed—no Grover. Then she remembered. For a month, he would sleep on a large and comfortable cot Sinclair set up in the book-lined, first-floor study. The nursemaid could bring Marion into the bedroom for a nighttime feeding without waking the president.

A single tap on the door—it would be the cook, Susan. She entered the bedroom with a breakfast tray. Frances smelled toast and oatmeal. She craved her first meal since giving birth. Grover followed Susan into the bedroom, then snagged a piece of toast, pushing half of it into his mouth with one bite. He wore his business attire, not the floppy hat and rumpled brown suit he wore almost daily each summer, designed, he thought, for fishing. The servants belittled that suit behind his back. Frances had caught them snickering at what they called the "cut of his jib."

"You look well," Grover said, pecking Frances's cheek. She chose to ignore the crumb that fell from his mouth onto her pillow. "How is my newest daughter?"

Frances smiled. Before she could answer with words, he spoke again. "I rose early and ate breakfast, hmmm, my first breakfast, with Henry." Grover and his private secretary often started the day going over business.

"No fishing today, dear?"

"Maybe in an hour or two." He shoved in more toast and turned his head to watch Susan leave the room. He pushed the rocking chair a few inches closer to the bed, with a scraping noise, then sank into the chair and bent forward. "Frances, we must reach an agreement." The timbre of his voice changed. Pleasantries were over. "The entire household staff knows what happened to Ruth yesterday. They helped find her. They must not talk about it."

As heat rose through Frances's sore body, she willed herself not to react dramatically or quickly. She'd start with a quizzical look.

"Henry and I don't want the story getting to the press. Those vultures will write about the abduction in all the papers. I don't want to give anyone ideas."

Grover pulled his droopy mustache, stretching it out, letting it recoil, then pulling it again. Frances cringed at Grover's choice of the word abduction, at his pronouncement, and at his gestures. He noticed.

"I'm serious. I don't want that woman—or anyone else—to try again. And there's more." He picked up steam. "Reporters will dig for blame and realize that thirty-four policemen guard us in Washington and two Secret Service agents guard us here. Some will write that we're careless. Others will write that those agents were hired to apprehend bank robbers and counterfeiters, not to guard a president on Cape Cod. Or his family."

He was reminding her, not so subtly, that she was the one who insisted on agents at Gray Gables, even though Congress made no allowance for security at a president's summer home.

"And Frances, critics who don't follow the threats will blame us for treating Gray Gables like a fortified castle. We can't win this gossip war. The less the public knows, the better."

Gray Gables. Grover bought it as a summer home, a place where his children could frolic around Buzzards Bay without gawkers peering at the girls or asking for locks of their hair. He paid $20,000 for one hundred acres of oak and pine, farmland, pastures, and marsh, with a fine home, dock, and outbuildings.

Gray Gables' unpainted shingles and gabled roof gave the residence its name. With twelve rooms, the house accommodated the family and the nursemaids, and Grover added a wing with a playroom, nursery, and lavatory. Still, no observer accustomed to elegance would pronounce the house grand, though every observer would find the setting impressive. The house sat on a point jutting into Buzzards Bay, on the western side of Cape Cod. When Frances took coffee on the porch, gazing through the pillars, she could see the sprawling lawn, ringed with her beloved marigolds and bachelor buttons, and beyond, the waterfront, with Monument River to one side, the Bay to the other. Grover chose Gray Gables for privacy—the nearest neighbor was half a mile away—and for the mingling of ocean water and freshwater. He could fish in Great Sandy Neck Pond, Long Pond, Little Pond, Red Brook Pond, Scraggy Neck, or Abiel's Ledge. A different place each day. Leaving her alone.

Frances snapped her attention back to her husband's grousing. She dug her teeth into her bottom lip, contemplating what to say. She could listen to him fuss, soothe him, and coax him to her aim, as usual. That worked when she wanted a new piano or to host an expensive reception. But now she must protect a child. She would not stoop to cajoling.

"Grover, I don't care about the press blaming us for having too few guards or too many. I need—no—we need to find that woman and protect our daughters." She dragged out the word *we*, intending the mild insult, but unsure Grover would hear it.

"Of course," Grover said. "We need to protect the girls. But you know, people copy the actions of others. If scoundrels learn that some woman pulled off an abduction, we could see more attempts. Either against the children or against me."

Frances tried another direction. "Does Henry agree with secrecy about what happened?" Grover's secretary usually took a sensible approach to problems. "If we told others, if stories ran in the papers, Henry and you must see that we could get leads on that horrid woman."

"No, Frances. We'd get every unhappy husband saying it was his wife. Those false leads would distract us. And Henry always advises keeping troublesome matters away from the public. Don't fret—Jeffrey has ideas about how to investigate."

She moved her hand under the quilt covering her to pinch her right thigh, a signal to steady herself. "Jeffrey Hazen is a good agent. Skylar Donnella, too. Really, though, how will they find that woman without help? We shouldn't waste any time, right?"

Grover's eyes roamed. He had scant interest in her thoughts. She pressed her thigh again. Before she could add to her plea, he rose from the chair. "No, Frances. Let's settle this—we will keep the abduction to ourselves."

"Abduction? Or perhaps a kidnapping."

"Not a kidnapping. It cannot be a kidnapping without a ransom note." He watched her, then paused for a long second, at last registering her frustration. "But all right, Frank, we can revisit all this if the woman isn't apprehended quickly."

Her nickname—Frank. He'd offered a meaningless concession to show her he was listening. In his restrained way, to show his love. Frances nodded in acknowledgement. She made do with so little—she would rethink her deference later.

"I'm gathering the servants and staff to issue a warning. They can't talk about what happened. Not to anyone. They must keep the abduction a secret. Henry will pass along word of this to the midwife and to Joe Jefferson. No need for you to join us. Rest here."

He pecked her cheek again and left the bedroom.

She should take this opportunity to rest, to nap. But the phrase Grover used, "keep a secret," bounced around in her head. Frances had grown good at keeping secrets, very good, matching his skills.

Before she could decide on her next step, the house filled with voices. "Form a circle, and quiet down." These words wafted from the parlor up the stairs, through the half-opened bedroom door. They came from William Sinclair, Grover's steward. The household staff, even the servants not used to his color, respected Sinclair and immediately hushed.

Next, Grover's voice, gruff yet high-pitched for a man his size. He didn't let his private secretary, Henry Thurber, talk for him. Or his chief of security, Agent Jeffrey Hazen. No, Grover spoke to the staff himself, demanding secrecy, demanding loyalty. She couldn't make out his words. She did catch his tone. The next voices were murmurs of agreement. The maids and other servants admired Grover. They would honor his wishes. If Agent Hazen disagreed with the orders, he wasn't saying, or she couldn't hear.

Then quiet. The staff resumed their daily tasks. Frances turned to her tray. The remaining piece of toast was limp, and her oatmeal was cold. She sipped her lukewarm coffee, then gave up on breakfast. Did Grover think that sharing the story of the abduction would bring out more scoundrels? Or was he falling into his habit of secrecy for some vague political purpose? Most days, he managed the conflict between his role as a devoted father—she never, not once, doubted his devotion—and his role as dutiful president—she never, not once, doubted his sense of duty. But most days, the conflict Grover managed centered on how he spent his time, not on how he reacted to the abduction of his first daughter.

Frances rubbed the tension at the back of her head. She heard a familiar sound, the nursemaids' code—a soft knock, a pause, two more soft knocks.

Since yesterday evening, Annie, having begged and been granted forgiveness, took charge of Esther as well as Ruth, as Frances planned for months. Bonnie, now responsible for Marion, entered the bedroom carrying the infant. Frances gave one last rub to her head. She took a calming breath and reluctantly shifted her mind from her headache to her new daughter.

While nursing Marion, Frances mulled over how to talk to Ruth. Time to comfort, or to question? Frances had decided not to grill Ruth the day before, and she'd discouraged Grover and Agent Hazen from doing so. They wouldn't use the right words, the right manner. And she certainly couldn't expect Annie to talk to Ruth about what happened. For the past three—nearly four—years, Frances relied on Annie to help care for Ruth, and she still trusted the nursemaid despite everything. But Frances, and Frances alone, might succeed at eliciting information from Ruth. Who was that woman? What did she look like? What did she sound like?

When Bonnie came to carry Marion back to the nursery, Frances asked for Ruth. Ten minutes later, the girl curled up on the bed. Frances cuddled her and eased into a question.

"Did you peek at baby Marion?"

"I thought she was a boy."

"What made you think that?"

"She said a boy."

A boy? Frances stared at Ruth, unable to think what to say, what to ask. The woman wouldn't have known one way or the other. She guessed wrong.

"No, sweetheart. Another sister. Do you think she looks more like you or like Esther?"

"Dunno."

"Do you feel better today than you did yesterday?"

No answer. The pressure in Frances's head returned.

"You aren't afraid, are you?"

Still nothing.

Earlier that summer, when Frances clanked the piano keys as she practiced, Ruth sat on the floor, looking bored. She pulled on Frances's dress for attention. Frances tried something new. She put down her classical music in favor of the lively vaudeville tune, "Where Did You Get that Hat?" Ruth looked up, smiled. When Frances reached the second chorus, Ruth laughed. By the third chorus, Ruth sang along with the last line—"where did you get that hat?"

Now, Frances thought she remembered the lyrics. She began to sing, capturing the jilting sounds of the melody. Ruth, curled up on the bed, didn't sit up or squirm. Frances sang the third chorus. Ruth moved an inch, then muttered the last two words, "that hat," out of tune but on time.

Frances smiled and patted Ruth's hair. What? Not possible! Frances raked her fingers through the waves. She raised a shock of Ruth's hair and stared. At the back of Ruth's head, Frances saw a nearly bald patch—an uneven stubble—as though a lock had been hacked off.

"Annie!" Frances screamed, ignoring the bell she used to call the nursemaids. Ruth teared up but said nothing. Within a minute, Annie arrived, looking frightened and carrying Esther.

"Do you know about this?" Frances didn't hold back her accusing tone. She pushed down Ruth's jerking head to expose the patch.

Annie gawked, then gasped. "I brushed Ruth's hair. This morning. I didn't see that." A maddening pause. "I planned to wash her hair tonight. I would've noticed then."

Frances released Ruth's neck. "Did that woman cut your hair?" Ruth rocked up and back and wailed.

Through Ruth's cries, Frances heard "yes."

II

Part Two: Mary

Chapter Five

December 30, 1874

Twenty-one years before the turmoil at Gray Gables, neither Mary Brinski nor her employers, the Potters of Pontiac, Michigan, had heard of Grover Cleveland, then a lawyer in Buffalo, New York. They had not heard of a town named Bourne in Massachusetts, or of an estate called Gray Gables. Mary had spoken once of living in Buffalo, but she doubted the Potters gave that a second thought. Their minds, like hers, were set on the next three days.

Wearing her black dress and white maid's apron, Mary held open the ornate front door of the Potters' fine mansion, letting in frigid air as the three Potters walked out onto the flagstone driveway. "Have a happy new year," Mary said.

Mrs. Potter, who must feel warm in her furs, nodded a thank you. "You have a good celebration yourself. We'll stay with my sister until Saturday." Mrs. Potter narrowed her eyes. Was she trying to remember Mary's tasks? "Don't forget to take in the sheets before they freeze on the line and make sure to bolt the doors before you leave."

Mr. Potter hurried to the waiting carriage without a word. Son Jack, bundled in a warm jacket, followed, hurrying into the comfort of the carriage. He waved goodbye to Mary.

"Yes, Ma'am, I will remember the laundry and the door. See you in a few days, in 1875." Mary named the coming year with a smile.

She stood in the entranceway, shivering and waving. The minute the driver pulled off, Mary slammed shut the mansion's door.

She had two hours before the evening train took her the short distance from Pontiac to Detroit for her three-day New Year's break, her longest in a year. She washed the Potters' lunch dishes, then went upstairs to straighten the bedrooms.

Over the eight years she worked for the Potters, she and their young son Jack grew chummy. Who else could she talk to? He knew her husband worked in a railyard in Detroit, and he wanted to learn every detail about engines, about tracks.

As Mary dusted, she stared at the map of Detroit the Potters had hung on the wall and ran her cloth slowly along the walnut frame. Jack loved that map, and even now, at age thirteen, asked Mary to point out Orleans Street where she stayed each Sunday when she visited her husband, and to point out the railyard where he worked. Jack could be a spoiled brat, but he knew Mary had a life beyond the mop.

In the largest bedroom, Mary picked up the silk frock crumpled on the canopy bed. Mrs. Potter must have tried on the dress and deemed it unsuitable. Mary held it up in front of her then peered in the mirror tilted against the wall. Not right, she thought. She removed her white cap and pulled free some of the brown ringlets she'd pinned back that morning. Now the young woman gazing back at her wasn't a maid, but a fashionable society lady. Mary glided her hands over the smooth fabric. Mr. Potter manufactured wool in a local mill while he happily paid for his wife's silk dresses. This one would become hers next year, handed down. She'd take in the seams a few inches and have a pretty dress to wear for George.

After restoring order to the mansion, Mary had another hour before leaving for the train, enough time to follow the story she learned of from the Potters' dinner chatter. She picked up the newspaper on the side table, smelling the wood polish she rubbed on the day before. The sad story, on everyone's mind, began at the end of June and still had no end. Four-year-old Charley Ross disappeared off the face of the earth.

Little Charley and his older brother had been playing in front of their home near Philadelphia. Two strange men befriended the boys and gave them candy. The men offered treats for five days straight. A week before the Fourth of July, they enticed the boys into their buggy and drove them to a store. One of the men handed the older brother money and sent him inside to buy firecrackers. When he returned with his purchase, he couldn't find the men or young Charley. They'd disappeared. The kidnappers demanded $20,000, which Charley's father did not have. No one could find the boy, not in July, not in August, not in September. Now, finally, at the end of December, a bit of news.

Reading stories about Charley, Mary laid eyes on the word kidnap for the first time.

* * *

After the cold walk from the train station, Mary welcomed the warmth of the Detroit boarding house. That comfort lasted only a minute. "You're late for dinner. Your husband, he vashed up already." The landlady's German accent thickened when she was irate. "He's at the table. I vaited dinner on you, like he asked, but the young ones are hollering for food."

Mary expected that disagreeable greeting from Mrs. Weber, the widowed shrew who owned the boarding house. George would have told her that his wife, who usually stayed with him only on Sundays, would stay for three days and need meals. His *wife*. Mrs. Weber had no reason to question that word.

With her surly expressions, Mrs. Weber made it clear she wasn't thrilled to board such an odd pair—Mary, thirty-one, comely it was said, with her brown waves and Irish looks, and George, forty-two, short and rough-looking, with his Polish accent—but the landlady needed the steady rent. Thanks to George's pay at the railroad yard and Mary's pay from service, Mrs. Weber always got her money on the first of each month. And the landlady was happy her boarders added no more children to the two noisy ones squabbling in the dining room.

At the dinner table, before sitting, Mary leaned over to put her hand on

George's shoulder. Mrs. Weber wouldn't stand for more than a shoulder tap. Mary learned to bear with the fusspot's rules. After all, the meat smelled tasty, George had scrubbed the railyard soot from his cheeks, and the kitchen stove warmed the first floor.

"Pot roast for you? I suppose you'll vant meals for the next few days?" The children at the table turned to their ma and took in her face, then mirrored her pout. The sour looks gnawed at Mary. Did the children think she'd take food from their mouths?

"Yes, meals." Mary answered quickly, then swooped in with a stab of her own. "You've seen the newspapers? About Charley Ross?" Mary learned her letters in an orphanage, but the Webers couldn't read. No papers in their home. Not even the *Detroit Abend Post*, in German. But they'd followed the story of Charley Ross. Everyone across America knew that two men kidnapped Charley. The family might resent feeding her, but they'd welcome the latest news.

At the mention of Charley Ross, Mrs. Weber's eyes moved from stretched narrow to wide open. Again, the children mirrored her expression. George turned his neck to look at Mary.

"Two burglars broke into the house of a rich judge in Brooklyn." Enjoying the attention, Mary picked up speed. "The judge wasn't home, but the judge's brother lived next door and heard the commotion. He got his shotgun, and he brought his son and servants. They all carried guns, and they went to the judge's house and shot the burglars." Mrs. Weber bent her head to the side, waiting for the connection to Charley. "You know how dying men sometimes confess? Well, one burglar pointed his finger at the other for kidnapping Charley Ross, then they both died before either one of them said where Charley was. Or if he's alive."

"You mean the little boy might be wandering alone somewhere, freezing in the cold?" The Weber daughter directed her question to Mary.

"Or maybe he's locked in a box somewhere." The Weber boy tried to outdo his sister.

"Or left in the forest for wolves." The girl spat her newest entry at her brother.

"Shut your maws." Mrs. Weber kept the accent of her native German tongue while picking up the slang of the Irish. As a child, Mary heard warnings to shut her maw every day, usually by sots sloshing their words.

The landlady's voice dropped low. "Think of poor Mrs. Ross. She must be dying of fear." Mrs. Weber's face went slack when she spoke. Even the hag had a heart.

The sad news about others lightened things up, just as Mary figured it would. She took her time to cut herself a thin slice of apple strudel, sure Mrs. Weber would notice the size. "Swell dessert. I know better than to try to make your strudel for my missus in Pontiac." Mary forced a smile. She put down her fork and wiped her mouth on the less than pristine napkin.

The children, paying no mind to their mother's warning about their maws, kept up their banter and snapped at each other, filling the silence. George barely spoke. That was his way since he regretted his Polish accent, even though it was mild after twenty years in America. Mary had relayed the news about Charley and praised the meal, but other than that she too talked little. Maids should limit their chatter, a habit that stuck with her.

Mary carried her plate and George's to the sink, then said her standard "g'night." She climbed upstairs to George's two small rooms. He followed, holding onto the banister. Mary felt a prickle at her back. The landlady must be staring at George's slow gait. She would worry about his health and whether he could keep his job.

In the attic rooms, away from the warmth of the stove, Mary shivered. She spotted the Sanders chocolates, loved by everyone in the city, that George always bought the day before her visits, for them to enjoy together. The chocolates rested in a silver dish George found discarded on the train tracks. She ate one piece, finishing it off in two bites. With a weak wave of his hand, George motioned that he'd eat his later. Mary waited for an embrace, for George to put his arms around her, cupping her rump or her breast. Instead, he slumped on the bed, scrunching his pant legs and mussing his sleeves. She caught sight of the tattoos on his arms, a remnant of his sailor days. She fixed her eyes on him.

"Mary, it's my back. My hips. My right hand too. I'm in pain every minute on those tracks. Not sure I can keep this up."

"Like I said last week, love, we'll find you something else. Where you can sit."

"I said I'd think on it, but men gotta read to get those sitting jobs. Mary, I'm no good to you. Or anyone. Can't even give you children. Remember, years back I couldn't keep the coal fires going on that freighter in the lakes and this week I could hardly bend on the rails."

"Same thing, every week. Stop it already." Mary plucked a strand of hair from her bun. She wound it around her finger. George didn't like when she did that. This time he didn't notice. "We'll find you something. I'm sure."

George gave up answering, except for a faint nod. He closed his eyes. Mary sat beside him on the bed. She rubbed his back and sang Aura Lea until his hardened features eased. Years before, he told her that tune drifted through the hospital tents when he worked as an orderly during the war. Aside from that, he never spoke much about those days. Mary rolled onto the bed and curled up beside him, straightening the thin blanket over them both. She remembered Mrs. Weber's stare ten minutes earlier while she watched the couple climb to their rooms, George barely able to put one foot in front of the other. She'd wonder how Mary could have wed this unattractive, broken man. This broken man loved her. She'd care for him as he'd cared for her.

Chapter Six

May 21, 1876

Keen to see George after a week with the Potters, Mary dropped her satchel in the boarding house's attic bedroom. The Sanders chocolates were not in their regular place in the silver dish on the dresser. She ran out to the backyard. The landlady, standing beside piled-high laundry baskets, hung sheets to dry in the warm spring air.

"Mrs. Weber, have you seen Mr. Brinski?" The woman didn't look up. Mary raised her voice a notch. "Most Sunday mornings he waits for me upstairs. Or out on the porch if it's warm enough, like today. I can't find him. I don't see his work boots. Did he step out?"

The landlady raised her chin, with an expression of anger or disgust. Or maybe a hint of worry?

"I ain't set eyes on your man since Tuesday. He never came back from vork. Thursday, I looked in your rooms—that's my right. I saw his clothes. If he took off, he vent empty-handed. You still owe me rent, mind you. He can't leave with no notice."

Mary skipped a breath, jumping past her usual polite manner, clenching her fists. "For God's sake! We've been here, in your rundown house, with your brats, for years. Paying you on time, keeping our rooms clean. Mr. Brinski fixes the boiler when you ask. And all you worry about is your rent, not my man?"

The woman threw a hateful look.

"I'm off to the railyard to ask, something you might've thought to do yourself."

Mary stormed away. George had worked on ships on the Great Lakes, stoking engines on rough waters. He'd lifted patients in Union army hospitals. He'd suffered injuries in wagon accidents. He survived all that, only to disappear in Detroit? He'd never run out on her, never gone on a drinking binge. Her own mother left her in an orphanage, not looking back. George would never abandon her.

Mary stopped strangers and asked for directions. She found the yard, then wandered until she found a foreman. "I'm looking for my husband, George Brinski. He's on your crew. You heard anything about him?"

The man gawked at her. She knew what he was thinking. How could a pretty woman like you marry that ugly runt? Today she didn't feel pretty, just frantic.

"Hah. Your man's trouble. We never saw Brinski after the lunch break on Tuesday. He'd been coughing all morning. Claimed his back was killing him. Then he disappeared. The crew thought maybe he'd fallen behind some equipment. See, we pile up ties and rails. Spikes, too. Sometimes the piles fall where they shouldn't. No one found your husband. He didn't come back the rest of the week. We replaced him already."

The foreman spit out tobacco, barely missing Mary's dress. "But, dearie, don't think of asking for his back pay." As he said "dearie," his eyes roamed over her, pausing at her waist, her bust.

Mary glared at him. He was useless. She'd move on. "Give me the names and addresses for some of the other hands. I'll talk to them myself."

The man looming in front of her grunted, probably realizing "dearie" hadn't gotten him anywhere. "Hey lady, I'm Sean Regan, a railroad yard foreman, not a clerk."

Sean Regan, Mary thought. Maybe a good Catholic. "Mother of God, have compassion. I'm in a family way and I need my man." Ahhh, if only it were so.

But she did get two names and found the men at home, willing to talk. Same story. George disappeared.

Mary had planned to take the early train on Monday back to Pontiac, as usual. Instead, she sent a telegram to Mrs. Potter. "Family emergency, back Monday night." Then another. "Back Tuesday night." If she delayed longer, she'd lose her position. On Tuesday at noon, she boxed up George's things, mostly work clothes, asked Mrs. Weber to stow them in the cellar, and quit the dingy rooms for good.

"That fool lit out on you?" The landlady sneered when Mary handed her the last of the rent and walked toward the door. "He caught a pretty one like you, who knows her letters, and he bolts? Count your blessings. You can do better."

"No. I can't. If he comes, you tell him I need him."

Mary could think of nothing else to do. George had no family, aside from those left in Poland, with names and addresses she didn't know. He had no friends, and his workmates had given up on him. America abandoned George.

III

Part Three: Frances's World

Chapter Seven

July 8, 1895

Secret Service Agent Jeffrey Hazen had never heard of the maid Mary Brinski or of the railyard worker George Brinski, missing now for nineteen years, when Grover Cleveland lectured the servants and staff in the parlor of Gray Gables on the morning after his daughter had gone missing. Hazen stood at attention, watching the big man, with his beefy shoulders and barrel chest, command the room. As Cleveland called for silence about events the previous day, Hazen nodded in agreement. Months later, he would question why he honored the president's demand for secrecy, but for now, he remained the obedient guard.

Moving his eyes downward, Hazen saw Agent Sky Donnella stiffen at the president's words. The minute Cleveland dismissed the gathering, Donnella looked up to his boss for a sign of response.

"In my office," Hazen said. "Let's talk."

The agents crammed into the little windowless room at the back of the residence. Donnella didn't wait to begin fussing, barely lowering his voice.

"Demanding we ignore what happened? What's that about?" Hazen put his finger vertically across his lips. Donnella toned down a notch and half closed the office door. "Shouldn't we spread the word, to track the woman who took Ruth?"

"Shit. If it was up to me, that's what we'd do." As Hazen spoke, he took his seat behind his desk, and Donnella took the smaller chair. "I'd wire reporters and all the police in Massachusetts. But think about this from the big man's point of view. He knows, like we know, that reporting on a crime can inspire more crimes, similar crimes. And since the press loves baby Ruth—well, she's no longer a baby—the reporting would turn sensational. Imagine the wording: 'Blond-haired, blue-eyed daughter of president cries as female villain snatches child, breaking her parents' hearts.' Isn't it possible that kind of story would stir up other fools to try? They'd say if a woman can get that far, I can get farther."

Sky Donnella scrunched his mouth. Hazen knew that look. Donnella wasn't convinced. Not yet.

"Even more likely, half the people in the country would blame you—yes, you Donnella—and me for taking our eyes off the family. Sure, we'd explain you were guarding the perimeter, and I was doing paperwork, trying to ignore the missus's screams. How do you think that would sound? We might lose our jobs, or Will might be forced to bring in someone over me."

Donnella bent his head and screwed his features into a stunned expression.

"Sure, Will's my brother, but he's under pressure too. Or maybe you and me would both be sacked if Cleveland's critics asked why the public should pay for any guards at all at a summer retreat he chose himself."

Hazen watched Donnella. He was listening, still worried. My junior agent, Hazen thought, I'm lucky to have the bloke around, as long as I remember he understands police work better than politics.

"Sky, even if I'd manage all this differently, remember, Ruth's back home. What's to gain from shouting to the public? I'd like to find that damn woman, to bring her to justice. But odds are low she'll try again."

Judging by Donnella's softening jaw, Hazen thought he'd made headway.

"Maybe you're right. She's most likely holed up somewhere, not a danger anymore. I can tell you don't think we have a choice."

"You got it. We need to make a list, follow protocol." Hazen could shift Donnella's attention by putting him to work.

An hour later, after Hazen asked the gardener to take on temporary guard duty at the residence, the two agents walked to Bourne to see what they could learn from shopkeepers and villagers. "A woman no one recognized,"

Hazen said to the local milliner, "entered the Gray Gables property, nosing around. We want to question her. Have you seen someone new to town? Maybe wearing a straw bonnet?" The milliner looked skeptical. "Hmmm, I suppose half the women here wear straw bonnets. But I need to ask. We always patrol to keep an eye out for strangers who might be up to no good—just a regular part of our guard duties."

Hazen and Donnella moved down the street to the postmistress, a woman who loved to pry into everyone's business. She looked even more skeptical than the milliner and came up with nothing. The same with the grocer and with three villagers strolling through town.

The agents walked on, muttering to themselves. "No luck here," Hazen said. "Damn. We better not risk raising suspicions by asking further." Donnella returned to complaining about the big man's demand for secrecy, this time in a low voice.

Their route drew near the Bourne police station. They met each other's eyes and chuckled. "Yeah, we'd rather chase counterfeiters," Hazen said, "but no avoiding our next move. Time to talk with the constables. The chief's an oaf. His deputy's a better copper, but not by much. Sure, they've prevented a crime or two, but I doubt they ever solved one." The agents buttoned their suit jackets. They knew from previous visits that the station had a sparsely furnished room in front, occupied by Chief Nate Sullivan and Deputy Julius Combs, and a filthy jail in back, occupied by drunks. Hazen and Donnella had learned the town's running joke from the president's cook. Were there more drunks in the front or in the back?

Chief Sullivan, dressed in work pants and a wrinkled shirt, rose and signaled to his deputy to grab two spindly chairs. "We won't sit," Hazen said. "Just a quick question." He saw no reason to change their story. "A woman entered the Gray Gables property, nosing around. We want to question her. Have you spotted a woman lately who's not from here?"

Sullivan didn't spend much time thinking. Hazen heard him, then took a few seconds to translate his rambling answer and thick New England sounds, with their broad "a's" and nearly silent "r's." Hazen boiled it down to *No, sir, Julius and me, we observed nothing out of the ordinary.*

Deputy Julius Combs scratched his chin, mulling around Hazen's question. "Nothing I remembah. If I do, sir, I'll send word." Hazen felt the pressure ease from his ears. The deputy was slightly more intelligible than his chief.

"We'll go on our way then. But first, we need to hire more men to help patrol Gray Gables. A few fellows from Bourne already work for us. Any ideas how we can find more?"

Although Hazen preferred trained agents, here in Cape Cod, far from cities, he would be flexible. Up to now, he had only Donnella and part-time workers he shared with the gardener to patrol one hundred acres—ridiculous! Last night, while tossing in bed, Hazen wondered how much money he could siphon off from allowable expenses to increase patrols on the dead line—a line of posts and ropes he'd set up the previous year to separate the president's property from adjoining land. Before Ruth went missing, he and Sky and two local lads patrolled the dead line every hour in daylight—a show of force, albeit modest, to discourage intruders. Going forward, they needed patrols around the clock.

"The boys at the lumbah mill cover three shifts, so that'll be your best bet. The boys with night shifts might want extra work during the day, and the boys on day shifts might want night work. Go to the barbah's porch. Sometimes the boys dawdle there between shifts."

The agents left the constables and found the barbershop porch, where three millhands sat, smoking and jawing. They all knew Walter Breen, who took a part-time shift at Gray Gables in May and reported back that the work was fine. Two of the millhands seemed eager for work. Donnella, looking at Hazen, moved his right hand in circles, as though writing on paper. "Thanks for the reminder, Sky. Lads, give us a list of people from town who can vouch for your character." The agents had skipped that step once or twice.

It was six o'clock, the end of a long day. "Time to call it quits," Hazen said. "We haven't found the woman, but maybe we'll learn we triggered some memories.

Chapter Eight

July 9, 1895, and Earlier

Frances Cleveland stood at the mirror, wincing. Wearing one of the loose frocks she'd worn for the past few months, she glimpsed her thick-bodied profile, almost the same shape as two days earlier, the day of Marion's birth. The woman in the mirror remained tall, but no longer slender. How different she looked nine years ago on her wedding day. She posed for a photograph then, wearing her ivory satin dress trimmed with orange blossoms, from Maison Worth in Paris. Her maid piled her hair high and twisted it into an elegant chignon. Even then, Frances's brows were a bit heavy, but that flaw didn't detract from what others called her beauty. The evocative photo—she looked younger, rested, untroubled—sat on Grover's bureau, next to the mirror, a daily reminder of her former slim figure.

Her wedding day in 1886 was the first time a president married in the Executive Mansion. Frances withstood the idle tongues and blowhards who sniped at Grover, then forty-nine and two hundred and eighty pounds, for marrying a woman of twenty-one and—then—one hundred and twenty pounds. She had a harder time ignoring the political cartoons picturing Grover as loathsome. One memorable cartoon portrayed him with sagging folds of flesh, mooning over a lovely young woman with a slender waist. The implication was clear. What could she see in him? Everyone knew the question behind that question. How would the couple make love, the fatty atop the beauty? Grover likely had more experience in that area than Frances first imagined. They succeeded, she thought to herself, awkwardly at first, and less awkwardly as the years went by, pregnancy after pregnancy. No one would guess that the corpulent president, with his stubby hands and bulging belly, caressed her tenderly and bedded her gently.

Ashamed of focusing on her changed silhouette, Frances turned away from the mirror and the wedding-day photograph. She let her mind drift to the beginning of more serious worries—her first sign of trouble, a decade earlier.

* * *

After her wedding and before her pregnancies, Frances joined Grover for an official visit to the West. On their return train trip, near Memphis, the engineer headed over a bridge. Just in time, he saw the trestle on fire and backed away. Following that scare, Frances paid attention to hushed talk around her. She learned of attempts against Grover's life by disgruntled men carrying revolvers, pistols, shotguns, bombs. The threats came from men throughout the country—Humboldt, Nebraska; Albany, New York; Denver, Colorado; Boston, Massachusetts; Springfield, Illinois; Boise, Idaho; Indianapolis, Indiana; St. Louis, Missouri; Butte, Montana; New York City. Sometimes the police found the culprits before they could do damage. Other times, the police considered the threats empty and didn't investigate.

Reacting to the scares, Grover's private secretary, Henry Thurber, asked for more guards at the Executive Mansion. By the time the Clevelands departed Washington for Gray Gables, they left behind doorkeepers, ushers, sentries, guards, plain-clothed police, and mounted officers, all assigned to regulate the flow of visitors and guarantee the safety of the president.

Her mind still drifting, Frances thought back to the years she worried only about threats to her husband, with no idea how those worries would expand. Between Grover's nonconsecutive terms, Frances gave birth to Ruth. When the family returned to the Executive Mansion for Grover's second term, visitors there spotted a child toddling around the reception rooms. With glee, the public named her Baby Ruth. Frances and Grover forbade photographers from approaching Ruth, so journalists painted a picture with words, describing her blond waves and beautiful eyes.

Early in Grover's second term, Frances gave birth to her next daughter, Esther—the first baby of a president to be born in the Executive Mansion. Americans went wild again. They couldn't get their fill of the little girls. While Frances enjoyed her daughters, she held at bay her fear of prying strangers.

Until the morning of January 10, 1894.

For the rest of her life, Frances would consider that day, eighteen months before Ruth went missing, a turning point, a turn from uneasiness to dread. That winter morning, she sat at the piano in the family quarters of the Executive Mansion, tapping out the sonata she'd practiced for years.

Nursemaids Annie and Bonnie bundled up their young charges and took them out for a stroll in the cold Washington air, giving Frances an hour to herself. Missing a piano key for the third time, she frowned at her lack of improvement.

"Frances, I need to speak to you." The minute she heard her given name in a man's voice that wasn't Grover's, she knew it must be Henry. Good. She had an excuse to raise her fingers from the keyboard.

Henry walked toward her, carrying a pile of newspapers and frowning. Most days, with his shock of white hair and matching mustache, he looked older than his forty years. Today, he looked much, much older. Henry had left his law practice to work as Grover's secretary—a post more responsible than the title suggested. Henry was a dear family friend. He had a right to use her given name.

"Why so glum today? Ah, let me guess." She raised her lips to a tiny smile. "This morning, I read that Lexington, Massachusetts, installed the world's first battery-operated switchboard. It's fast. You must be jealous you didn't get it first, for the Executive Mansion." Henry, an expert at repartee, would respond with a clever tease of his own.

"I wish it were only that."

Frances took a breath and rose from the bench. With luck, Henry's concern would amount to little more than another political fracas, maybe a debate about the silver standard or a labor strike. Henry would acquaint her with what occupied Grover's days, why he spent so little time with her or the children. Or maybe Grover asked Henry to fill her in because both men respected her interest in political affairs and trusted her to hide that interest.

Carrying the newspapers with just his fingers, as though the ink would dirty his hands, Henry gestured with his chin to the parlor. "Can we move there? I want to spread these out."

A minute later, they sat across from each other at the library table. Sinclair, Grover's steward, followed them. "Ma'am, would you like me to ask the cook to bring tea?" Before Frances could answer, Henry flapped his right hand down to signal no. Oddly rude, she thought.

Henry seemed unaware of his bad manners. He tapped his finger lightly on the *Abilene Weekly Reflector*, dated December 21, 1893, again as though he were afraid to touch the paper. He moved his finger cautiously to a column headlined "Scheme to Kidnap Cleveland's Daughter."

As Frances absorbed the headline, air rushed from her body. Clutching the arms of her chair to keep from sinking, she read on.

"A letter was picked up on the street yesterday that has all the evidence of being a fake, yet may be evidence of a crank's scheme to commit a crime. Part of it is written from Minneapolis and part from Topeka. The former outlines a plan in which the writer, signing himself R. F. Rock, tells some person to whom the letter is sent to be ready at the sound of the bugle to march on Washington. There are five in the scheme, he says, and they can send Grover Cleveland to the infernal regions on short notice and get $20,000 besides. The Topeka letter says the scheme has been modified and Grover will be allowed to live while his daughter Ruth is to be kidnapped and held for a ransom."

No air remained in Frances's body.

The second her eyes reached the bottom of the story, Henry fumbled in the stack for another newspaper. After he found what he hunted for, his finger tapped on *The Evening Star*, from Washington, dated a day after the *Reflector*. The *Star* reporter quoted a letter sent from Topeka on December 10. "We will take the oldest child first; we can get her all right. Molly will get her and hand her over to us, and we will keep her until the reward is offered. It means thousands to us to get this child, Ruth, and we will get her, in January."

Frances couldn't focus, but she sensed Henry's glance. He realized she'd stopped breathing. He put his arm on her shoulder. "Frances, take in some air. The threats are empty. Read this paper from the next day, from New York." He gestured to *The Evening World*.

She snatched it and read quickly. *The World* considered it ridiculous that a gang from Kansas would go to Washington to kidnap Grover and Ruth. The reporter told his readers not to worry.

"And here," Henry said, gesturing to the *Goodland Republic*. "This Kansas paper thinks we're overreacting."

Frances read to herself. "Somebody is going to be made ridiculous through the nonsensical fright which has recently made its appearance in Washington. A foolish telegram printed several days ago about an alleged plot to kidnap the Cleveland children is actually seriously discussed by men who ought to have more sense."

Henry jabbed his finger at other papers and read aloud a few passages. Most reporters dismissed the threats as the ravings of a crank.

Frances pushed the papers away. Henry stared again, waiting for her to speak, or maybe to faint. He would not expect anger.

"Henry, what were you thinking?" Jutting her face toward him, she made no effort to control her rage until she saw Henry flinch. She moved her hands from the tabletop to her lap, then tightened her right hand around her thigh. She pulled her head back and attempted a more moderate tone. "The first story is three weeks old. You didn't tell me. Grover didn't tell me."

"Grover and I discussed it. You know, we're all unhappy that the public wants endless details about Ruth and Esther. How do they look? What are they wearing? All those prying women coming close to the house, trying to peek at the girls, and the photographers perched on trees nearby. Scaring the nursemaids. Shameful. I hired more police. We locked the gates to bar the gawkers. We keep out the busybodies and the cranks. Frances, we're doing everything we can. Grover and I chose not to worry you. There is no plot. None."

She pushed her face forward again. "Henry, this reporter from Kansas wouldn't consider it overreacting if it was his family." Henry shrugged, half acknowledgment, half dismissal.

And then, just months after what she thought of as the Kansas threat, when the family traveled to Gray Gables for the summer of '94, Frances learned of intruders on the property. She insisted on more security even though she lacked power to make that demand. William Hazen, head of the Secret Service, sent his brother, Agent Jeffrey Hazen, and a more junior agent, Sky Donnella, and promised to post them at Gray Gables every summer. Two seemingly vigilant agents.

* * *

Now in her bedroom, standing with the mirror behind her, Frances snapped back to the present. Her full breasts told her it was time to nurse again. First, she did the math. Eight years since the burning train trestle near Memphis, eighteen months since the threatening letters from Topeka, twelve months since the intruders at Gray Gables. All the threats came to nothing, so she had let her guard down.

As she walked to the nursery, she thought once more about the dangers surrounding her household. She and Grover did not follow past practice when they chose a distant location for their summer retreat. Lincoln used the Old Soldiers' Home, close to the Executive Mansion. Grant, Arthur, and Garfield favored the Jersey Shore for their summers. She and Grover searched farther. Most good-for-nothings intending to harm their children would never find Bourne, Massachusetts, on a map. Most.

Chapter Nine

July 10, 1895

Neither Jeffrey Hazen nor Sky Donnella had tangible results from their investigation so far. They searched in vain for shoe prints or other physical evidence, talked to townsfolk in Bourne, and heightened their scrutiny of the endless throng of visitors and tradesmen who called at the residence. One agent patrolled the porch while the other, or a part-time guard, paced the dead line perimeter, wearing down weeds and grasses along the path.

Three days after the abduction, the agents met for lunch in the snug kitchen in Mrs. Wylie's cottage, where they and a few servants boarded. Hazen gobbled down a cheese sandwich and drained his coffee cup. He mindlessly prepared a second sandwich, then bolted down that one too. He barely tasted his food.

"Nothing," Hazen said.

Donnella understood the meaning of that single word. "Right. It's like she vanished."

"Ha. You're barely eating. Not me. All this worry makes me hungry." Hazen patted his belly. At least it was still smaller than the big man's.

"I can see." Donnella laughed.

Hazen let the jab pass. "Time to get serious." He locked eyes with Donnella and pressed his lips together. "Need to interview the servants and staff."

The protocol was awkward. Such questioning would set the household on edge, so the agents didn't mention their plans in the days immediately following the abduction. On Hazen's list of Gray Gables employees, one man and one woman attracted his concern—John Nolan, the able coachman, and Jennie Schultz, the likable governess. When Hazen sent Nolan to check the outbuildings the day Ruth went missing, he seemed a logical choice— strong and experienced.

But Hazen soon learned he didn't know everything he should about Nolan. In the days after the abduction, the servants' overactive grapevine buzzed. Nothing like a missing child to loosen tongues. Hazen didn't consider eavesdropping a lady's purview. He used all available tools. Hearing murmurs in the hall, he hovered near the linen closet—that site and the kitchen of the Wylies' cottage fueled gossip. While organizing sheets, Frances Cleveland's maid Lena and laundress Ingrid, usually rivals for the attention of the handsome gardener, put aside their animosity to replay every detail of the search. They chattered about which servants were trusted to check which sites, competing over their mastery of details.

When they got to the coachman, they lingered over a tasty morsel. The coachman and governess did their best to hide their flirtation, Lena said, but they were amateurs at subterfuge. Didn't they know that Mrs. Wylie could see them spooning from her attic window, which offered a view just beyond her vegetable garden? Who could blame the new governess? The coachman was almost as easy on the eyes as the gardener.

Hazen, a trained detective, spent one minute thinking about the romance, and many minutes thinking that Jennie Schultz was the only servant connected with Gray Gables who was not present on July 7th.

Chapter Ten

July 10, 1895

John Nolan watched from his raised driver's seat on the landau as the president stood on the porch, bidding goodbye to Dr. Bryant and pumping his hand. "Good of you to attend to Frances again. And with such beautiful results. Regards to the family."

"I'll return in a week or so, Grover, to check on Frances." The doctor turned slightly so Nolan couldn't listen in. Useless maneuver. Surely the doctor was saying that he'd check on Grover, too.

These men thought servants were clueless. Two summers back, the president kept to his bedroom at Gray Gables, looked after only by Dr. Bryant and Sinclair. Although Sinclair mostly minded his own business, nothing could stop the cook and the lady's maid from sharing stories with him, and he'd chime in. Susan sent up strange meals to the president's bedroom—puddings and soups, not his usual chops. And Sinclair couldn't hide the dressings and ointments he carried to the large bedroom. And Lena knew the missus spent hours at the president's bedside. Nolan heard all this from Lena, the upstairs blabber. Although the servants loved to gab, they kept these stories to themselves, never muttering the word cancer. In Bourne, Massachusetts, home for Nolan and Susan, and a handful of others like the laundress and the gardener, a position at Gray Gables was a good job, not one to trifle with. As for the servants who traveled up and back from Washington to Bourne, their loyalties never wavered.

Dr. Bryant turned back to where he stood before he hushed his words. Now, Nolan didn't need to strain to hear. "I can't miss all that good fishing you provide."

Nolan drove the doctor to the train station, then returned to the stables. He spotted a note on the wooden shelf near the landau's bay. He grabbed hold of the landau's door handle to keep from passing out. Then he picked up the paper, slowly. Not again, he said to himself, hoping this new note had no tie to the one he picked up in the stables three days before, on the day Ruth went missing.

Thank God. Different handwriting. Different color ink.

7:00. Usual. No signature, as they'd agreed. He laughed at his groundless fear. This note was—ha—a horse of a different color.

Jennie wanted to meet him at their usual spot before he had to head back to his folks' home in town for the night. He and Jennie had kept company for six weeks. For Nolan, the best six weeks of his life. With her position as the Clevelands' new governess, Jennie Schultz was above his station, but she didn't put on airs. Maybe because even though she had schooling, lots of it, she didn't have much money. She sent what she could back home to her sick ma. Jennie liked horses and didn't wrinkle her nose much at the stable odor clinging to his uniform and his body. Even so, he removed the double-breasted overcoat, too warm for July, and found water to wash the smell of the stables from his chest and neck before he pulled on a fresh shirt.

Nolan started for the meeting place. With his height and muscular build, he could be spotted easily, especially because the sun hadn't set. He did the best he could, skulking behind the outbuildings, dodging open spaces. He and Jennie had found a half-hidden swath of tall grass at the center of a stand of trees, not far from the vegetable garden Effie Wylie and her son Ned tended, beside the cottage she managed. Jennie boarded there, so the spot suited her. And it was out of sight from the dead line that one of the groundsmen from town guarded each night. Probably far from prying eyes. Jennie wanted to be careful. Like most employers, the Clevelands wouldn't take kindly to two of their servants passing time together.

Nolan caught sight of Jennie ahead, leaning against the broadest tree, waiting, watching him approach. She shifted her weight from one foot to the other. He bent down for a kiss and moved his hand toward the back of her neck, thinking, as he had every day since he met her, how lovely she looked. She waved to shoo him away.

"John, later. Let me warn you what's coming."

Warn? he thought. How could she have bad news? Joe Jefferson found Ruth. Bonnie said the infant was well. Mrs. Cleveland was up and around.

Jennie caught his puzzled expression. "You know, Agents Hazen and Donnella board in the cottage too and take meals there. Lunch is informal. Mrs. Wylie leaves food on the table, and everyone helps themselves. The agents fixed their sandwiches today when Mrs. Wylie was out hanging laundry. I came in to grab a sandwich myself. Before I got to the kitchen, I heard the agents talk. Softly, just not softly enough." Jennie scrunched up her face. "John, they're going to interview all the servants. That includes me and you. They suspect one of us of abducting Ruth, or they think we might know something."

He backed up a step so he could see her face better. He'd never seen her so worried.

"What do you feah?" At first, Jennie joshed him about his New England talk, and he joshed her back about her New York talk, but over the last few weeks, they grew used to each other's voices. "Jen, come on, neithah of us took Ruth. And we don't know who did. Christ's sake—you weren't even heah. You were in New Yawk visiting your ma."

"Yes, but these agents, they were police or detectives before. They have ways of, well, of questioning people, scaring them. I've read about what they do. We won't like it."

Nolan caught that Jennie bumped up "interview" to "questioning." His shoulders went tight. If she saw, she'd think he'd bristle at being prodded by men in charge. That he'd rattle easily.

"Right. I won't like it. Not one bit. But don't fuss. I'll get through their questions." He'd better return to her neck, or Jennie might wonder about his flagging desire. "Ready for a kiss?"

"First, let me tell you what will happen. They'll start with simple questions.

Lots of them. Like how long you've been working for the president and what you did before that. How long I've been governess here and where I worked before."

He nodded his head, slowly. "How do ya know so much?"

She started to laugh, caught herself, and lowered her voice. "No, I haven't been in trouble before." But I worked in New York, remember? And I read the papers there. Murder. Mayhem. And detectives, coppers, Pinkertons. The front pages covered it all."

Nolan read the weekly Bourne newspaper, mainly about socials and dances and land sales. He also kept up with politics, sometimes from the papers, more often from the talk he overheard while driving the muckety-mucks around. Was Jennie reminding him that she was from the city and he was a country boy?

"Before too long," Jennie continued, "they'll ratchet up the questions, to scare us. You should prepare yourself. Don't take their questions as insults, even if they are, and don't show any anger, please."

He nodded again.

"One last thing, John. The less they find out about us—us together—the better. We've been careful. We need to continue that."

John brushed his hand across her neat topknot and drew her head to his. She made it easy for him to push aside his panic.

Chapter Eleven

July 10, 1895

The faint sounds of Ruth and Esther playing and of Marion whimpering drifted through the hall, into the bedroom. Not the sound of news. When Frances wasn't resting or nursing Marion, she brooded. Why hadn't Jeffrey Hazen come to see her, to bring word of the search for that woman? Was he holding back information?

After discovering the damage to Ruth's hair, Frances asked her a question or two. Ruth said little, lowering her eyes. Was she struggling with the memory of the abduction, or was she sulking over yet another sister to divert her mother's attention?

Frances's temple throbbed. The agents avoided her, Ruth shunned her, and Grover deserted her. She contemplated the irony. Here she was, three days after giving birth to a beautiful daughter, surrounded by dozens of kind souls, with not a single confidant.

Grover did look in on her, but briefly, his eyes darting to the window where he could see the dock. He spent his mornings fishing in the care of ginger-haired Bud Wylie. Bud skippered Grover's small rowboat and twenty-five-foot sailboat, maneuvering deftly through the rough currents of the Bay. Often, Grover took along Joe Jefferson, or guests who wanted to boast about time with the president. They might return empty-handed, or with bluefish or striped bass. On successful days, Grover gave part of his catch to Susan to cook and offered the rest to villagers around the Bay—one of the reasons they liked him.

Those irritating fish. Grover cared more about them than his daughters.

Frances pushed away that thought, kneading her head to ease the pressure. She knew better. He loved the girls, in his way. He claimed for years that fishing cleared his thoughts, brought him peace. Frances wished just one day he'd stay on shore and talk to her. And listen.

She could talk to only two women about the abduction. Annie wasn't one of them. Annie had entered Frances's bedroom, crumpled on the floor, and cried the night of Marion's birth, asking forgiveness that she turned away from Ruth for half a minute. Once that was over, Annie, never much of a talker, didn't want to speak about that day again.

Bonnie, now nursemaid to Marion, never feared probing. "Ma'am," Bonnie said, when she brought Marion to Frances to nurse, "Have your nerves eased?" Or "Have your jitters stopped?" Or "Your milk is good. You must be calming down."

Frances supposed she should dissuade Bonnie from such familiarity. Instead, Frances answered impulsively, happy not to ponder her answers for a change. "That day was the worst of my life," she said. Or "Praise the Lord that Mr. Jefferson was on the Bay."

Lena, Frances's lady's maid, jabbered even more than Bonnie, clearly choosing her words to encourage Frances to talk. "Ma'am, ready for a short walk today to see your marigolds? The gardener just weeded them." Or Lena might jabber about the children. "Do you want me to ask Annie to bring Ruth and Esther here? They miss you when you nap." Again, Frances supposed she ought to give guarded answers to a maid. Instead, appreciating the concern behind the questions, Frances offered honest answers. "I wake up with nightmares. I see Ruth disappearing in the Bay." Or "I'll walk with the girls, to provide extra protection."

Frances, an only child, had relished talks with her classmates at Wells College, especially when she sought their comfort after ending courtships with her beaus—courtships she never mentioned after marrying. And she relished talks with the cabinet wives she befriended in Washington. The more she talked, the better she felt. Now, she could raise her spirits after a brief minute of commiseration with Bonnie or Lena. These were good women. But the lady's maid and the nursemaid were not enough, and Frances wouldn't say more than a few sentences to them about her fears. She wanted to shout until she was hoarse. To shout to her girlfriends from college, to shout to the public, to shout to the bloody reporters. To shout to her husband. *Listen to me, help me.*

Did she just shout? No. That noise was a knock—Lena's knock—loud soft loud.

"Ma'am, Agent Hazen wishes to speak to you. Would you like to get up? Should I help you dress?"

Frances gasped. At last. Maybe that man was doing his job. "No. I won't take time to dress. I want to speak to him as soon as possible." Out of habit, she thought of the many ways she could make herself more presentable, starting with her unruly hair. Then she quickly shrank from such thoughts. *Ridiculous.* "Lena, plait my hair and fetch a shawl so I look decent. Then let him in."

Two minutes later, she was ready. She propped her head against the pillows. A shawl covered her chest, and quilts covered her belly. She greeted the agent warmly, wanting him to feel at ease in the bedroom. Her impression of him remained the same as earlier that summer and last summer—nice-looking, clean-shaven, neatly dressed in civilian clothes, inspiring trust.

"News, Agent Hazen?"

"I am afraid not, Mrs. Cleveland. I am here to report on our activities so far."

She sighed and gestured to the nearby rocking chair. He looked it over dismissively, and pulled over a ladderback chair from the far corner of the room, scraping it against the oak floor.

The agent trotted out everything he'd done in the last few days— questioning townsfolk, organizing the groundsmen, hiring help—trying to make a little into a lot. His confident bearing slowly dissolved as his tone turned defensive and his right foot twitched. Frances leaned forward, waiting a minute. Now she wanted him to feel uneasy.

"I appreciate your labors, but I gather all that work has come to naught. How do you think I feel, with my family still—still—in danger? How do you think I feel now that—I assume Grover told you—now that I know that woman hacked off a lock of my daughter's hair?"

His mouth tightened, almost imperceptibly. He caught the insult.

"You are correct to feel impatient. We have not found the culprit. Agent Sky Donnella and I are moving to the next step. When a crime occurs, we should question first those individuals who are close, who are most familiar with the setting. That means your female servants, men too, to ask where they were that afternoon, and to assess their reactions to our questions. We did not begin that immediately because you rely on your household staff. We didn't want to disrupt daily activities. Now, we must."

"You think that woman works for us?" Frances allowed her voice to turn shrill.

Hazen didn't reply. He tightened his mouth again.

"I don't."   Frances couldn't control her patronizing tone.   "Let me remind you what you already know. But you may not know the history. Understandably, you have worried about visitors more than the staff.

"We employ three groups of servants. Some work for us in Washington and travel with us here for the summer, like Annie and Bonnie. Our nursemaids are beyond suspicion. They would never harm Ruth, and we know where they were that day. Bonnie was with Esther, and Annie already expressed her guilt, misplaced guilt. Lena travels with us, too. She's been my lady's maid for years. Years. She's like family." Frances twisted a curl escaping from her plaited hair. And Sinclair, you know him—he started as Grover's steward in Albany, when Grover was governor.

"I should add the new governess, Jennie, to this group. She'll come to Washington in the fall. She's wonderful with Ruth. Of course, she was in New York for the week." As Frances spoke, she noted Hazen's brows rise at Jennie's name.

"Then we employ people from the area who work for us year-round. Like Bud and Effie Wylie. Also, the coachman, John Nolan. He cares for our horses, even in winter. Bud Wylie found him for us and vouched for him.

And the third group is villagers from Bourne who work only during the summer, like our laundress, Ingrid, and our cook, Susan. And the two chambermaids. Effie Wylie helps Sinclair assign their duties. Almost all these good people have served us for years, let me repeat, years, since we purchased Gray Gables. They are beyond reproach. Bourne is a small town, and the villages around Buzzards Bay are even smaller. Everyone knows everyone. You remember Mr. Joseph Jefferson, Grover's fishing partner from around the Bay?"

"Of course. He caught sight of Ruth in the rowboat with the woman and saw her turn around and take Ruth back to shore. I questioned him that day."

Frances raced on. "Mr. Jefferson, I'm sure you recall, is a landscape painter, and even better known as an actor. He starred in plays in New York and Washington. London too. He summers here in a cottage on the Bay. Actors are trained to master posture, gait, gestures. I took a drama class in college, and I acted in a production there, so I'm familiar with actors' professional training."

Frances realized the danger in mentioning college. The agent was unlikely to have a college education. He would resent her. He would resent her use of big words, her formal language. She could not help herself.

"For decades, Mr. Jefferson played Rip Van Winkle. He aged on stage, changing how he moved in each scene. If he knew that woman, if he'd seen her before, he would identify her from her walk or her stance. Yes, she could live around here, but I suspect she doesn't."

"Mrs. Cleveland, would Mr. Jefferson, who travels around the country performing, have visited here so often that he is familiar with the posture and gait of *all* your servants?"

Had she talked too much? Condescendingly? He must have expected her to feel poorly a few days after giving birth, and to yield to him as the authority. She would strive for a slightly gentler message.

"No need for sarcasm, Agent Hazen. Whether I am right or wrong about Mr. Jefferson, and I suppose I could be wrong, I doubt the woman who grabbed Ruth is in our household."

He took a second to manage his voice. She could almost see his brain working. After a complaint from her, he might be reassigned to watch for bad bills in the middle of nowhere. William Hazen, head of the Secret Service, couldn't protect his younger brother from the wrathful wife of the president of the United States.

"During my summers here," Jeffrey Hazen said, speaking slowly, with care, "I became acquainted with your staff. I agree they seem loyal and honest." He cast his eyes onto hers. "Do not worry that Agent Donnella or I will accuse them of misdeeds. We will, of course, follow protocol, and simply ask them what they observed, that day and the days before. If they picked up on anything peculiar."

Frances fiddled with her braid again. "Very well. Please, be respectful. These are good people."

"We will do our best." Agent Hazen did not look at her as he nodded a formal goodbye.

By using the term "follow protocol," he manipulated her. She could tell he was good at that. He was wasting time, looking at her trusted servants when he should be out hunting for a dangerous stranger. She bit her bottom lip. Why hadn't she argued with him more?

Or was she shortsighted? Could his questioning uncover a clue?

Chapter Twelve

July 13, 1895

With scant hope that the agents' interviews with her staff would lead to the culprit, Frances kept sulking. Wouldn't a word to reporters help Jeffrey Hazen find the kidnapper? Why had she promised Grover secrecy? No—she never actually promised. Grover interpreted her silence as acquiescence. And she let him.

The back of her head throbbed again. She pulled the cord on the service bell. She'd ask Lena for a cold compress and sit still to wait for relief. While rubbing her neck, Frances let her mind slip back to her history—her history and Grover's—with secrets. A long history.

Her skill began at college thanks to the drama class she mentioned to Jeffrey Hazen. For a minor part in a Shakespeare production, she learned how to breathe, how to set her features, how to react. She put those lessons to use when she became secretly engaged to Grover. She had known him forever—he'd been her father's law partner in Buffalo. Her father was the rainmaker, hobnobbing with men of means. Grover was the workhorse, attending to the business of the firm.

Everything changed two days after Frances's eleventh birthday, when her father died in a carriage accident. Grover grew increasingly dominant in her life, advising her mother on schooling and finances. She called him Uncle Cleve. Frances relied on Grover, respected him, loved him, and at age twenty-one, accepted his marriage proposal. By then, he was running for president. The public dwelled on the dumbfounding twenty-seven-year age gap between Grover and Frances. For a year, the couple kept their engagement secret, denying rumors. Frances withstood questioning from the press, never revealing the truth.

She further honed her skills at secrecy in the summer of 1893. Grover felt a mass in the roof of his mouth, the side where he chewed cigars. After a biopsy confirmed cancer, surgeons secretly operated on Grover on a yacht, out of sight in Long Island Sound. They removed part of the president's upper jaw and soft palate. A dentist fitted him with an excellent rubber jaw. The public noticed no change to his speech or appearance.

Recovering at Gray Gables, Grover disappeared for a month. Frances, along with Henry Thurber and the doctors, maintained a cover-up. They never got their stories straight. The president went on a long fishing trip, they said; he was under the weather, they said; he had ulcerated teeth extracted, he had a toothache, he had malaria, he had an attack of rheumatism. He would soon be fine. Reporters didn't pay attention to the inconsistent tales or chose to ignore them. The staff at Gray Gables? If they suspected anything, they stayed mum.

Falsehoods were necessary that year. A crippling recession hit the country. Railroad tycoons faced bankruptcy, the stock market crashed, and workers lost jobs. The Treasury was purchasing silver, fueling a run on its gold reserves. Cleveland favored the gold standard and opposed a silver standard. His Vice-President, Stevenson, favored silver interests. If rumors circulated that Cleveland might die, the prospect of Stevenson as president would move the economy from distress to catastrophe.

Aware of the potential chaos, Frances joined the liars, attesting to her husband's health. While keeping mum about the cancer, arranging her features to look unconcerned, and anticipating the birth of her second child, Frances feared Grover might not survive.

That secret of his operation two summers ago was the hardest to agree to and to keep, until now.

Three knocks startled Frances. Loud soft loud. Her maid, Lena. She could fetch a cool compress. First, Frances would ask if Grover was already off fishing—off fishing, while she wrestled with the wisdom of keeping a secret, fretted about Ruth, and worried that the culprit might return. Frances would ask for more than one compress.

Chapter Thirteen

July 14, 1895

Secret Service Agent Jeffrey Hazen sat in his cramped office at the back of the residence, waiting to start the interview with Jennie Schultz. He would question her at the same time Sky Donnella questioned her boyfriend in a different location. While the agents were busy with interviews, local lads would carry the full burden of patrolling the dead line.

Jennie Schultz earned her place on his list of suspects. Eager to visit her ailing mother, she obtained permission from Frances Cleveland to go to New York and left for the city six days before Ruth disappeared. One day after the abduction, the governess returned. That provided an alibi, a highly convenient alibi, that none of the household staff could confirm. Hazen was waiting for an agent stationed in New York to verify Jennie's visit there by talking to Mrs. Schultz's neighbors.

Frances Cleveland had reviewed the governess's references thoroughly. Before coming to Gray Gables, she worked in New York for a family that was a mainstay of society. Thanks to the servants' gossip, Hazen knew that Jennie Schultz, governess to the rich and famous, was stepping out with John Nolan, coachman to the Clevelands. Did the handsome coachman act as an evil influence? Nolan was at Gray Gables when Ruth was carried off. His sweetheart wasn't. He had helped with the search. But was Miss Schultz really in New York? Could the pair have colluded? For what purpose?

Ruth knew her governess, probably trusted her, would walk to the Bay with her. But if Jennie Schultz abducted Ruth, wouldn't the child say so? Hazen struggled to imagine the governess as the culprit.

Hazen may have said half a dozen words to Jennie Schultz since she arrived in May, after accepting the post of governess. She was slender and pretty—no surprise Nolan fancied her. Smart too.

Hazen had seen her with Ruth as they walked along the shoreline weeks ago, holding hands. "Look at the tall plants," the governess said, pointing to reeds at the water's edge. "We call them phragmites." She pointed farther to a bed of shorter grasses. "Eelgrass over there. Yes—a funny name." Hazen had not known the names of these strange plants. He remembered this lesson because the governess impressed him and because Ruth looked at the plants with curiosity. Now, when he saw the poor child, she seemed withdrawn.

Hazen checked the clock on the wall. Jennie Schultz arrived for her interview at exactly two o'clock, dressed simply in shades of gray. He directed her to the only chair. She clasped her hands in her lap, as though to keep them from jittering. Other than that, she showed no sign of anxiety. She must take comfort that she was not in Massachusetts on July 7th. Allegedly.

"I apologize that we set this interview for a Sunday. Agent Donnella and I needed to stretch out our interviews over several days, so we don't inconvenience the president and his wife."

"Of course." A somewhat clipped tone. The governess knew to keep her answers short.

"Is your mother improving?"

"I am afraid not, sir. Her doctor cannot find the cause of the pains in her chest. I left New York as soon as I could, as soon as the doctor said my mother was not in imminent danger. I am sure Annie kept a watch on the dear child, but if I had been here, we would have had another set of eyes." And she knew not to blame others.

"Yes, I must say, it's remarkable that Mrs. Cleveland employs both a nursemaid and a governess for little Ruth." Hazen didn't put that as a question or a criticism. He could see that Jennie Schultz correctly interpreted his comment as both. He could not understand the need for so many servants. He and his brother had done fine, with only loving parents. He'd keep his opinions to himself, as usual.

"I work with Ruth each morning. That frees up Annie's time because she also cares for Ruth's wardrobe—the child attends public functions, usually at a distance from the crowds. Certainly in Washington, and occasionally in Massachusetts. In the afternoon, I assist with Ruth's correspondence." Hazen raised his eyes. "Yes, people from all over the country write the child, expecting an answer. And I help organize the library here and assist Mrs. Cleveland with her own correspondence. Annie and I are always busy."

A long answer this time. Did he have her on the defensive?

"I see. Now, to the point, do you know anyone who might have cause to abduct Ruth? Townspeople who don't like the crowd—the artists and politicians and friends who visit the Clevelands each summer? Or servants who were let go and hold grudges? Or people who oppose the president's policies?"

"I have wracked my brain, to no avail. Ruth is a sweet child, and the Clevelands are kind and generous to their employees." Back to no blame.

"On the subject of their employees, I must ask you about John Nolan." He watched her jaw. Yes, a slight tightening. "Can you tell me what your relationship is with the coachman?"

Her reactions were predictable, humorously so. She blushed and crossed her arms. She looked down. If this was an act—to suggest she was guilty of love, not of crime—it was a good one.

"I do not mean to chastise you. Not at all. You're a young, unmarried, attractive woman. He's a handsome, unmarried man. But you must realize, if you're stepping out with him, we, Sky Donnella and I, as the president's protective detail, should know."

While he spoke, the governess uncrossed her arms and shifted in her chair. She forced her shoulders down.

"Sir, I admire John Nolan. As coachman, he drives the president, carefully, almost every day. He has a fine way with the horses." She stopped there. He waited.

"And what is his relationship to Ruth or to the president?"

She pushed her head back while staring directly at him. "You will not find a more loyal man. He thinks highly of the president. Mrs. Cleveland, too. And he loves Ruth. Lets her pet the horses. He loves children."

Time to startle her. "In other words, you don't think it's possible that he waited until Mrs. Cleveland was in bed, and the President was preoccupied, and then he signaled to you—not at your mother's in New York, but hiding behind the housekeeper's cottage—that the time was good?"

He watched her carefully, moving his eyes from her head to her shoes. She opened her mouth in horror, then took three seconds to compose herself. He thought he saw the nails of her right hand press into her left.

"Agent Hazen, that is impossible. And an insult to your coachman's integrity. And to mine."

Enough. Time to finish. If he grilled Jennie Schultz further, and she complained to Frances Cleveland, he'd have hell to pay. He readied his final question, a gentle one, the one he'd been trained to ask. "Is there anything else you wish to add, Miss Schultz?"

"Only to repeat what I said earlier. I regret that I was not here on July 7th."

The face in front of him was indeed a picture of pure regret.

Chapter Fourteen

July 14, 1895

John Nolan managed a bath the night before the interview and didn't think he smelled of the stables. He had to get through the next hour, had to make sure no one doubted him or Jennie. He walked to the makeshift office Agent Donnella set up at the edge of the Gray Gables property, in the small railroad station built to ease travel for the president and his visitors.

Nolan peeked through the window at the clock on the station's far wall, trying to hide from view. Two o'clock, exactly right. He knocked softly. Donnella opened the door, with no expression Nolan could read. They knew each other—Nolan drove Donnella from the station to Gray Gables when he arrived each spring, and both men sometimes joined the poker game at the Wylies' cottage on Thursday nights.

Donnella's cigar smoke filled the office. He sat at a table pulled into service and wagged his chin toward a little wooden chair. Nolan lowered his six-foot-two frame into the chair, wondering if Donnella intended to cause pain.

Jennie said that Donnella might begin with easy questions. She was right.

"Where did you work before?"

"Keenan's stables in Bawn." Nolan couldn't help the way he said the name of his town. "I was head groom." He glanced straight at Donnella, just like Jennie had told him to do. Meeting the agent's eyes was easy—Nolan only

"

told the truth. "One of the best hosses broke his leg." As with the town, Nolan couldn't change how he said the word for the animals he tended. "Had to put him down. Couldn't go back aftah that. Bad memories."

"How long have you been employed by the President?"

"I started when he bought the property in '90. He didn't come heah much until a few summahs ago."

Jennie thought that after a few minutes, Donnella would move on to questions meant to rattle. She was right about that, too.

"When you drive the Clevelands to neighboring towns, you have an opportunity to talk to them, to win their good graces?"

Nolan understood the implication, but he had no idea how to answer. He twisted in his seat and turned his eyes away.

"Mr. Nolan?" Donnella waited. For the interview, it was "Mr. Nolan," not the "John" or the "Nolan" of the poker table.

"When I drive the Clevelands, we talk about the weathah, the town, and sometimes the fish—I recommend different ponds to the president. I'm always respectful. I know my place."

"And politics? Do you have any disagreements with the president?"

Jennie hadn't warned him about this kind of question. He was on his own here. "Agent Donnella, I admit, I come from a family of Republicans. Been that way since the war." Nolan forced his mouth to say war as Donnella would expect to hear it. "Even a few abolitionists among my kin. When I vote—I don't always—I vote for Republicans. I don't follow the debates as much as I oughtta." Nolan swallowed, with difficulty, remembering Jennie didn't think he read much. She was wrong. He read just enough. "When I do follow the debates, I see both sides. Like with that Pullman strike in Chicago. I feel for the workahs—tough jobs and low pay—but I figure the President couldn't let the railroads stop running. He had to bring in troops to stop the strike. And the violence."

Had he answered stupidly? Should he pretend he couldn't read or didn't follow the news? Was Donnella another outsider looking down on the townsfolk?

No, Donnella didn't shift his eyes or his jaw in surprise. If anything, the agent's eyes stayed open an extra second, without blinking. Nolan had reckoned Donnella was a Democrat, like the president. Maybe that wasn't a requirement in the Secret Service?

"Fine." Donnella went silent for two seconds. "Now, Agent Hazen and I need to know a great deal about the staff here, to assure ourselves that they have the Clevelands' best interests in mind. Knowing about the staff means knowing about their relationships. So, I must ask, is there truth to the rumor that you're sweet on Miss Jennie Schultz?"

Feckin' copper.

The agent leaned forward, face tense, waiting for Nolan to take offense. Nolan remembered his promise to Jennie to stay calm. He eased the muscles around his jaw and moved his head closer to Donnella. Even from the small chair, Nolan looked down at the shorter agent.

"She's a real nice girl, isn't she? Pretty. Smart, too. I don't know what she sees in me. Most days, I smell like hosses." He let out a soft chuckle, and Donnella leaned back a bit. "Turns out she likes hosses. She's only been heah a short while, so we're just getting, well, acquainted."

Donnella stayed silent for two more seconds, thinking, maybe not giving up yet.

"Can you assure me that you didn't wait until Mrs. Cleveland was about to give birth, when everyone would focus on that event, and then signal to your sweetheart—who perhaps pretended to visit New York—that the time was ripe to carry off Ruth?"

Nolan jumped up and halfway raised his fists. "For Christ's sake, how could ya think that? Don't insult Miss Schultz! And me too!"

Donnella held up his right hand and flapped his palm toward the floor. "Settle down."

Nolan sat back but still glared at the agent. Donnella seemed to take a deep breath, then looked softer, almost sorry.

"Just one more question—a routine one for all our investigations. Is there any question I should ask you that I didn't?"

As Nolan took in the question about the question, he caught the air escaping from his lungs and pushed it back. He struggled to keep his eyes on Donnella. "No. If I think of anything else, I'll come find ya."

After the interview, Nolan felt easier knowing he'd asked Jennie to meet late that night, even though they ought to keep clear of each other. He was worried. It was one thing to keep his secret to himself—just holding his tongue. It was another thing to keep a clue from a federal agent. He had never lied about anything in the Cleveland household before. Serving as the president's summer coachman was an honor for a Bourne villager, an honor he wouldn't stain. Until now.

Jennie was smart. She'd know what to say. She'd know if holding his tongue would get him into trouble and if that trouble would rub off on her.

"Have you been here long?" Jennie said. At midnight, no light shone from the nearby cottage. She minded her steps in the dark.

Most nights, she got to the hidden spot first. She'd wonder why he was there already, waiting. He faced her, put his arms on her shoulders. He couldn't still his bottom lip.

"John, I can hardly see you, but from the little I do see, you look terrible. Did Sky Donnella scare you?"

"No." He felt one of Jennie's shoulders shift. She didn't believe him. "Lotta questions. That's all. I worry Hazen might've rattled *you*."

"I'm all right." Jennie stretched her arm across his shoulder and moved her hand to caress his neck. "We're going to be fine. Just talk to me."

He couldn't remember the words he'd gone over earlier that evening. He shook his head, annoyed at himself, then blurted it out. "I didn't tell Donnella everything. Worse, I didn't tell you everything." Her hand left his neck. He wanted to stop talking, but figured she wouldn't let him.

He led her to a patch of grass and helped her sit. He yanked off a blade, fiddling with it. In the dark, he sensed her stare.

"That day, the day Ruth went missing, Hazen asked me to check the outbuildings. I did. The toolshed, the coops, the stables." He lingered on the word stables. "I kicked 'round the hay, gentle-like, in case Ruth hid there. In one of the bays, not buried deep, I saw a folded note. Wish I'd left it there."

Jennie kept staring. She waited for him to say more.

"Handwriting, in black ink. The words are stuck in my head. 'If you want

Ruth back, put one hundred and fifty dollars under the horse trof in front of the Eldridge Lumber Yard, after dark.'" He did his best not to drop his r's or to stretch out his a's and o's. "'Do not involve police or officials. You know the meaning of that amount. Then you will have repaid your debt.'"

He heard no breathing from Jennie, then the question he feared. "What did Agent Hazen say?"

"I didn't show it to him."

She said nothing. Worse than anger.

Now came the anger. "What were you thinking? I can't imagine. Dear Ruth missing and you didn't say anything?" She had never used such a grating tone before.

"Cause of the amount. One hundred and fifty dollars. Didn't you tell me Mrs. Cleveland fronted you one hundred and fifty to move from New Yawk City? And you'd pay it back out of your wages?" He heard Jennie's dress rustle as she shifted her weight. She was taking in every word. "What if the missus got it into her head that you changed your mind, that you thought the money shouldn't be a loan, but more like a gift to get you to leave New Yawk? I couldn't risk her thinking that, not for a second. Then, when I walked to the other outbuildings, mulling over what to do, I heard clapping, screaming, happy screaming. Somebody found Ruth. So I slipped the note in my pocket and tried to put it outta my head."

More silence while he fidgeted and felt his blood rise. Jennie wouldn't see his red face.

"John, you made the wrong decision." He expected her to sound vexed. Instead, she sounded downcast, disappointed. "I was away in the city, and Mrs. Cleveland trusts me. She wouldn't suspect me. Also, why would I reconsider our arrangement? It seemed fair when I agreed to it, and it still seems fair. I worked for a wealthy New York family—the position was a great one. The Clevelands needed to offer enough so I'd consider leaving my mother, and they needed to cover moving costs. The amount—it is just some odd coincidence.

"And Mrs. Cleveland may seem at ease to everyone, like she's thinking about the baby and trying to get her strength back. I know better. The poor woman is frantic. When she visits my little class to check in on story time with Ruth or comes with us on nature walks, I see she drifts off. Yesterday I said, 'Mrs. Cleveland, you seem deep in thought.' She said 'Jennie, I can't rest until we find the woman who stole Ruth. What if she comes back?' So you see, you must tell those agents, now."

He should have known Jennie would say that. She was right.

"One more thing. Can I see the note?"

Nolan took it out of one pocket and took a match out of another pocket. He led Jennie farther into the woods. He struck the match and held it a foot from the note.

She read it quickly, then once again. "John, the writer spelled 'trough' wrong. Mrs. Cleveland will know I didn't write the note, and that I didn't proofread it for someone else." In the flickering light, he saw her prideful smile.

"That reminds me," John said. "Makes me think of your college days, all your reading. Donnella asked me about politics—if I was with the Democrats. I didn't see that one coming. Hazen ask you?"

"No. He wouldn't think to ask a woman. He should have."

Chapter Fifteen

July 15, 1895

Frances Cleveland stared at the paper Agent Hazen handed her. Rage and shock spiraled up from her stomach, jolting her. One hundred and fifty dollars. For her cherished Ruth. The penmanship was fine, the spelling almost fine. The woman was either somewhat educated or enlisted imperfect help. Frances took a second to sort out her anger and puzzlement. Relief too, since at last Jeffrey Hazen had brought her something tangible.

"I understand what you're telling me, that John Nolan feared suspicion might fall on Miss Schultz because I had advanced her one hundred and fifty dollars to move and accept the post of governess here. Hmmm. And that he supposed that I supposed that she supposed—" Despite her dismay, Frances chuckled at her own words. "That the advance should have been a non-refundable inducement to move from the Whitten household to our household. That's nonsense. Our arrangement was clear—we would deduct ten dollars each month from her wages, generous wages, for fifteen months. If she harbored any complaint about the money, Sinclair likely would have picked up on that through household chatter and would have brought the matter up with me. He administers the household payroll.

"Miss Schultz is all I could hope for. Remember, she worked for the Whittens for two years. They are richer than we are. And let me assure you, Miss Schultz would not misspell the word 'trough.' If she and Nolan were

76

working as a team, and if he wrote the note, she would check it, carefully, and correct the error."

Frances caught the hint of a smile on Jeffrey Hazen's face. "Agent Hazen? Don't you agree?"

"I agree that Miss Schultz makes an unlikely culprit. Same with Nolan. But I'm not sure I, or most people, can spell 'trough' correctly."

She took in the unstated. You attended college, he would think, and I didn't. Or, in this case, you and Jennie attended college, and I didn't. She'd ignore his comment.

"Also, Jennie Schultz was in New York tending to her sick mother the day Ruth went missing. You told me people in the city confirmed that alibi?"

"Yes. I asked one of my agents to call on the mother and neighbors, saying Miss Schultz thought she accidentally left some of your correspondence in the city when she visited. I did not tell my man anything more. He finally got back to me yesterday. Everyone confirmed the visit, and the dates, and said how fortunate you were to hire her as a governess."

Frances allowed herself a quick grin, then pivoted. "What bothers me is the ransom amount, not because it's the same as Miss Schultz's debt, if you want to call it that, but because it's such a small and odd amount. One hundred and fifty dollars must bear some significance. Let me ask Grover if he can think of anything. And something else. You remember those threats last year—the letters from Kansas about a plot to kidnap the girls. According to those letters, the kidnappers planned to demand twenty thousand dollars. I thought what happened to Ruth might have a connection to the Kansas scare. Now I worry it's yet another plot."

"Your husband fears just that sort of copying, and so do I. Calling attention to the threats might bring on more. That's why we're keeping quiet about what happened last week."

Frances rubbed the back of her neck. She ignored the dampness on her hand. So, she fretted to herself, Agent Hazen still believed in hushing up the abduction. She'd planned to remind Grover, this day or the next, that the morning after the abduction, he agreed to revisit the strategy of secrecy if the woman wasn't found quickly. But if the chief Secret Service agent sided with Grover, should she wait a few more days?

Jeffrey Hazen must see her eyes drift. "Mrs. Cleveland," he said, "let's come back to the one hundred and fifty dollars. In my view, as a detective—that was my job for years—the small ransom demand is the best clue we have. If you feel well enough—after—after your confinement, let's think about the amount."

Was it her imagination, or was he scanning her loose dress, checking to see if she'd shrunk? He'd see little change. She forced herself not to try to hide her stomach with her hands. She should have only more important matters on her mind.

"I'm talking to you before I talk to the president because he's fishing today. I didn't want to wait to learn the meaning of the amount. If you don't know, do ask the president, as you've offered. I will too, as soon as I see him. He might remember something. As for John Nolan and Jennie Schmidt, I'll keep my eyes on them." She frowned. "Just my eyes, Mrs. Cleveland. I will not grill them. I'll ask some of the other servants if they've picked up anything out of the ordinary about the couple. But Agent Donnella didn't think Nolan sounded guilty during his interview, and Donnella's a smart fellow, trained as a detective like me. When Nolan handed over the letter this morning and explained his misdeed, again, he didn't look guilty, just flustered. And sheepish.

"But as an extra precaution, do you happen to have a sample of Jennie Schultz's handwriting?"

Good—something she could do. She would find Jennie's letter, accepting employment.

An hour later, Frances walked to the dock to await Grover's return. In the distance, she saw Bud Wylie in the usual boat, with his nearly orange hair, rowing easily. He skippered the boat to come in at an angle. The stern, where Grover sat, was lower in the water. Grover had gone alone without guests this time. Bud pulled in and helped Grover clamber out. No fish today. Frances knew that from Grover's expression and Bud's empty hands.

"Not one trout at the pond," Grover said, giving her a quick kiss on the cheek. Despite his bushy mustache, Frances could tell that his mouth puckered. He took in her rigidity and grasped that she was in no mood for small talk. "Everything all right, Frankie?" Her nickname—a prelude to confidences.

"Let's walk along the shore for a few minutes." Once out of earshot of others, Frances slackened her pace, markedly pointing to vegetation as though she were explaining botany to her husband. "Grover, can you think of any significance to the figure one hundred and fifty dollars?" She enunciated each word carefully. As she spoke the amount, the words pecked lightly on her brain. Grover tilted his head.

"Why?"

He fingered his mustache, stunned, while she related the contents of the ransom note that the coachman had kept to himself. From fingering, he moved to scratching, then stretching.

"One hundred and fifty dollars? One hundred and fifty dollars?" He repeated the amount, slowly.

She waited. Nothing. "Grover, maybe the number of congressmen opposing a bill? Maybe a pension you vetoed? The number of federal soldiers you sent to Chicago for the Pullman strike?"

He shook his head. "I'll ask Henry. He might think of something. He's a good private secretary. Henry knows all the corners of my life."

Two hours later, as Frances sat at her desk in an alcove off the parlor, sorting through a pile of unacknowledged congratulatory notes on Marion's birth, the governess approached.

"Ma'am, may I interrupt? I would like to speak about your coachman's error in judgment."

Frances expected Jennie to look defensive, embarrassed. Jennie Schultz stood squarely, chin up.

"Of course, Miss Schultz."

"I understand from John Nolan that Agent Hazen showed you the ransom note and explained that Mr. Nolan found the note and didn't immediately present it."

"Yes." Frances used a gentle tone. Before she could find the right words to put the governess at ease, Jennie continued, still with her head held high.

"I hope you know I never had second thoughts about our arrangement. I could not move here without the money you advanced me, and the rate of repayment follows common practices. The wages we agreed on are fair. It is simply an unfortunate coincidence that the amount on that hateful ransom note is identical to the amount of the advance. And John Nolan, well, as I am sure you heard, he is a friend, even if he misjudged this time. He simply thought he was helping avoid suspicion, undue suspicion, from falling on me. He is a good man, from a good family. He would never hurt anyone." Jennie paused, then looked fixedly at Frances. "I am sure you remain worried. Can I do any more to put your mind at rest?"

Frances watched Jennie's hands, her features, her posture, with growing certainty. Neither the coachman nor the governess abducted Ruth. Their courtship was their business.

"No, nothing more to be done. We are fine. We need not speak of this again." Jennie gave the tiniest of bows and walked away, unwaveringly.

One hundred and fifty dollars, Frances said over and over to herself. What in the world?

Later that afternoon, Agent Hazen and Frances looked over Jennie's acceptance letter, agreeing that the writing, with its elegant style, blue ink, and elaborate capital R in Ruth's name, differed from the ransom note, with its black ink, cramped words, and simpler, shaky R. Hazen had asked Nolan for a writing sample, and that too, with its uneven slant, differed from the ransom note. As they were talking, Grover reported that Henry Thurber had no idea about the significance of the ransom amount. Even Henry, a master of details, a keeper of secrets, was stumped.

Frances couldn't know that later that night, Grover, alone on the cot in his study, began to fret over a distant memory.

Chapter Sixteen

July 16, 1895

Jeffrey Hazen raised his head at the sound of a woman's light footsteps approaching his office at the back of the residence. Lena, Mrs. Cleveland's maid, walked toward the half-open door. She knocked. "Agent Hazen, Mrs. Cleveland would like to see you. In the parlor."

Did he detect a slight smirk? They both knew what to expect from the president's wife. After all, he guarded her, and Lena dressed and coiffed her.

Hazen returned Lena's telling expression. He was a government official, head of the president's protection, so he had no reason to fraternize with the servants. Yet he considered them keen observers, even when he didn't face a crisis. Since arriving at Gray Gables, he made it a habit to chat each day with the household staff. Maybe more than a minute with Lena, with her loose lips, lovely lips. Not as lovely, he told himself, as the lips of his fiancée, patiently waiting for him back in Cincinnati.

He questioned Lena earlier, confirming her whereabouts when Ruth went missing. Lena had lingered in the kitchen with Susan, the family's cook, and with Effie Wylie, who lent a hand with dinner preparations. Their employer's screams reached the kitchen from both the hall and the open window. The three women trembled and prayed for a healthy baby. Moreover, when Hazen gathered them in the front yard, they followed his orders to search here and there. Lena couldn't have taken Ruth.

Hazen straightened his jacket and tightened his tie, then marched to the parlor. He guessed that Frances Cleveland wanted to discuss the ransom note again. If she couldn't figure out the significance of the amount immediately, she'd dig deeper, or hunt for other leads. Once an idea—or a fear—crawled into her pretty little head, it stayed there, grew, and took over.

He lowered himself into a wingchair in the parlor, much better than the ladderback chair in the lady's bedroom. She sat in the matching wingchair, facing him and still wearing a loose frock.

"Agent Hazen," she said, using one of her sweeter voices, "You must gather by now that neither Grover nor I can determine the significance of one hundred and fifty dollars. I had hoped that clue would set us, set you, in the right direction. It does not seem to help." She shrugged, maybe preparing to move on. "Since we spoke yesterday morning, I thought more about the fugitive who kidnapped Ruth." The lady lingered too long on the word kidnapped.

"Mrs. Cleveland, I avoided the word kidnapped because until yesterday, we were not aware of any ransom note, like the note in the Charley Ross case, in 1874. You wouldn't remember. You were just—"

"Just ten. I do remember. Everyone remembers that story. The boy who wanted candy. Who was never found. It gave me nightmares. It still does."

"I understand." He looked at the wall behind her, then thought better of that tactic and met her eyes. Would she take that as an opening? And for what?

"Agent Hazen, I thank you for all your efforts. Unfortunately, as you know, those efforts don't change the fact that you haven't found the woman."

Frances Cleveland paused, briefly. "I'm a mother, with a distracted husband, and I worry that the woman is still, how do you say it, at large. She could be hiding in the bushes as we sit here."

Hazen tightened his mouth to suppress a smile at the lady's choice of words. "Yes, indeed, she is at large. But she won't get near the house again."

If Frances Cleveland listened, she should settle her shoulders. Instead, she stretched her head high and took a labored breath.

"I'd like you to heed what I have to say. Although I'm busy with my three daughters, I still have time to think. I worry that the woman will return to accomplish whatever she set out to do before. I ask myself, who in the world would want to harm Ruth, my beautiful three-year-old daughter, the president's beautiful daughter? Who would have a motive?"

He couldn't help smiling. *At large. Motive.* What had the lady been reading?

She seemed to take his smile as an invitation to continue. Too late, he cleared the smile from his face.

"My husband has a long career in public service. Twice, he won the popular vote and the electoral college. Even when he lost the electoral college in '88, he won the popular vote. Many voters love him. But he has made enemies. In his first administration, critics harped when he vetoed pensions for soldiers. Would the aging wives of aging veterans bother to seek revenge, long after those vetoes? Then there was the massacre in Wyoming when white miners killed Chinese miners. Grover tried to protect the Chinese who survived. I can't imagine women lashing out over that episode either. Grover supported reduced tariffs. Ha, most Americans do not know what a tariff is."

Was she implying that *he* didn't know the definition of a tariff? The lady attended college, and he hadn't. But he'd been around smart, educated people his whole life, and he learned from them. She had her nerve.

She kept up her litany. "He sent troops in after the Haymarket riot, although he was not at the center of that event. He suggested returning to the South the flags captured by the North, so an aggrieved widow of a Union soldier might fuss. Now, in this second administration, Grover has made still more enemies. Half the country doesn't like his support of the gold standard. Again, I am sorry to say this, but how many women, or men, understand the gold standard? Another group condemns him for last year's Coxey's Army mess."

Ah, Coxey's Army. Here was an opportunity to remind her of the Secret Service's capabilities. "Yes, Mrs. Cleveland. Agent Donnella, the very agent who is with us this summer, infiltrated the unemployed men marching with Jacob Coxey to the capital. In spite of rumors that those men wanted to hurt your husband, Sky Donnella figured out they were harmless. They just wanted jobs. Agent Donnella spared us from a lot of bloodshed."

Hazen felt compelled to defend Donnella, and for that matter, all agents. Had he put an end to her yapping? No. Her mouth was half open. She hadn't finished. "Sorry for interrupting."

"And finally," she said, "we should include last year's Pullman strike when Grover ordered federal troops to Chicago to keep the peace. How many enemies did he make then?"

When he didn't answer, she blathered on.

"I suppose you and I can agree—most of these events are only vaguely connected with women. So I started to think again, and went back, way back."

She stared at him, hard, then said the words he'd been fearing. "Maria Halpin."

Shit. Jeffrey Hazen's face froze. The woman in front of him—the genteel president's wife—was talking about a whore, a woman on the turf. Two decades earlier, when Grover Cleveland was sheriff in Buffalo, he supposedly seduced Maria Halpin, a widow with two children, and fathered a son, Oscar. According to endless rumors, Cleveland had Oscar dispatched to an orphanage. He didn't trust Maria to raise the child. Or maybe Cleveland wanted to hide the boy. When Maria Halpin, wasted on whiskey, tried to rescue her son, Cleveland sent her to an asylum to get her out of the way. Oscar didn't spend long in the orphanage. A Buffalo physician adopted the boy, who would now be twenty-one. The long and many-sided story captivated the public just as Cleveland ran for president in 1884, almost scuttling his chances. Cleveland never denied the story, leading some voters to praise his honesty.

Now Hazen would need to talk to the president's wife about the president's former whore. The federal government didn't pay enough for this job.

"Yes, Agent Hazen." Frances Cleveland met his eyes. She showed no sign of embarrassment. Only determination. "I know about Maria Halpin. All Americans know about her, even though most of them haven't seen her name since the election of 1884. They think she disappeared. You know better. You do, right?"

"I am not at liberty to discuss Secret Service matters."

"Ha. Then if you won't tell me, I shall tell you. After years of staying quiet, Maria Halpin reappeared. She sent my husband a letter this spring, while we were still in Washington, asking for money. Don't look shocked that I know. There are few secrets in the Executive Mansion. Grover isn't always tidy with his correspondence. Servants aren't blind. I'm not deaf."

"Mrs. Cleveland, you don't really think that Maria Halpin, who is fifty-three, would grab your daughter? Remember, a few Republican operatives tracked her down in '84. She's in New Rochelle, New York. Not close to Bourne."

"Why do you discount her? Either she was a brazen woman who entrapped my husband, or she was a victim of his abuse. If the first, she has no scruples. If the second, she has a reason for revenge. In either case, she wants money. A ransom of sorts? I realize one hundred and fifty dollars remains a small and peculiar sum, but it might mean a lot to a poor woman." As she said "one hundred and fifty dollars," Frances felt the words peck at her brain again, with the same twinge she felt earlier. "And New Rochelle isn't so far from Bourne, by water."

Hazen rubbed the side of his mouth. Maria's name lodged in the far recesses of his mind and kept jumping forward despite his efforts to push it back. He hated to think so, but Maria Halpin was a sensible guess. He rubbed the other side of his mouth.

"Mrs. Cleveland, I will explore your suggestion."

She offered a slight nod of appreciation. "One more request, please. Should you decide to tell the president about checking on Maria Halpin, I ask you to present that as your idea, not mine."

Hazen tipped his chin an inch, understanding. The wife didn't want the husband to know she was dwelling on the whore.

The cheeky lady walked to her desk in the parlor and reached into her top drawer. She handed him three sheets of paper filled with neat, cursive writing.

"I've set down these events and names," she said, "the ones I just listed for you, with my thoughts. If you wish to refresh your memory."

Hazen knew he scratched his mouth when he was annoyed—a barely noticeable reaction. He knew too that he twitched his right foot or even his whole body when he was provoked—a more noticeable reaction. He was sailing toward that more intense territory. If his foot twitched, she'd see it, so he dug his nails into his palm. Would she sense his discomfort?

"Agent Hazen, if you think back, you'll agree I'm not overreacting. Surely you recall the events of last summer. You and I have some history with strangers.

Her eyes pierced his. He did recall. While alleging she was merely a wife and a mother, Frances Cleveland had used her semi-official position to get what she wanted. The summer before, in May of '94, she learned that the Bourne constables—the only guards the president had at that time—discovered rough-looking strangers roaming the Gray Gables property, claiming they were installing a new telephone line. Neither the president, nor Henry Thurber, nor Sinclair had ordered a new line. The chief constable made light of the intrusion, but the deputy constable worried. He shooed the men away. They tried to come back the next day, and the day after that. Something they said led the deputy to think the intruders were after Ruth and Esther. He told Secretary Thurber, who told Frances.

The roughnecks showed up five months after the crazy letters from Kansas about kidnapping. With one threat atop the other, Frances Cleveland panicked. She demanded Henry Thurber order the Secret Service to post agents at Gray Gables, and not to check with the president for authorization. He wouldn't agree to more agents, fearing his political opponents would consider him a coward. But he wouldn't dismiss the agents if he happened to find them at Gray Gables. Around the same time, the Secret Service picked up another threat. A detective on the federal payroll reported that gamblers in the West planned to kill the president by hiring assassins in the East to carry out the deed. Hazen's brother William, heading the Secret Service, couldn't ignore multiple threats, even though none seemed credible. That's how Jeffrey Hazen and Sky Donnella ended up at Gray Gables, on what should be an easy assignment.

Hazen met Frances Cleveland's eyes and nodded to acknowledge the memory.

He'd never met a woman like her. She loved motherhood, loved her girls, and, against all odds, loved that paunchy husband. Yet beneath her demeanor—ladylike most days, though not this day—she could get restless and mettlesome. Hazen's own sweetheart had the patience of a saint, waiting for him while he took assignments all over the country. Once he married her, would he be bound forever to a wife who second-guessed him?

Frances Cleveland at last stopped talking. He wouldn't check his watch, but he thought he'd listened for half an hour. "I thank you for your thoughts, and, yes, I will review your notes and follow your suggestion about Maria Halpin." He rose to leave, not waiting for a sign of approval. She raised her hand to stop him.

"Agent Hazen, forgive my tone. I'm sorry if I sounded irate. I'm simply worried that woman will return."

"I took no offense. You are a mother, and mothers worry." As he said his goodbye and walked away, he glanced out the window. Ruth and Esther played in the yard under Annie's watchful gaze. He glimpsed Frances staring at the same scene, then at him.

"Mr. Hazen, I think it's time you call me Frances."

"That won't come easily. I'll try. And I'm Jeffrey."

He gave a slight nod, to himself as much as to her. Yes, any good mother would press as she had, in an overbearing, opinionated manner. He couldn't let his irritation get in the way.

Chapter Seventeen

July 23, 1895

Jeffrey Hazen slumped into his desk chair, in dire need of a break. For a week since Frances rattled off her list of suspects, ranging from war widows to the Halpin woman, he'd carried out more than his share of patrols and guard duty, while Donnella was off searching for Maria Halpin. Not for much longer. Donnella's train should have reached the station twenty minutes ago. Sure enough, the landau rolled to a halt at the front porch, scraping along the gravel. Donnella would report right away, with news from New Rochelle. Could Frances have fingered the right culprit?

Hazen left the door ajar, so Donnella walked in without knocking. "Agent Donnella," Hazen said, using his teasing tone. "Made it to Gray Gables, did you? With you gone, I ran all over the grounds, checking on lazy lads on the dead line and tradesmen at the back door and bluebloods at the front. Good thing we faced no new calamities."

Donnella waved a hello. He lowered his voice to a whisper and leaned in until his face was a foot from Hazen's. "I found her. I hunted down the president's whore."

Hazen frowned and pointed to the open door. Donnella stood to close it and then sat, leaning back. "I've come a long way from my last assignments, going after counterfeiters and spying on suspicious men."

Hazen scrunched his lips—part acknowledgment, part apology.

"You're not going to welcome my report."

"I didn't think the lady solved the case, but by God I hoped she did." Hazen shrugged. "And to tell the truth, her idea wasn't nutty."

"Hey, boss, I'm not blaming you. At least this was a safe job for a change. Here's what I found in New Rochelle. No way Maria Halpin snatched Ruth Cleveland. The Halpin lady lives with her new husband in a little house. He's a carpenter. She takes in sewing. I kept watch on the house, observed them leave and enter. She's still kinda pretty, older of course. Probably harmless, almost frail. Neighbors say they know her history and think she's, well, reformed. She's been home all summer and keeps to herself. She has a dog—sends the mutt out back every morning, like one of the neighbors does with his dog. They bark together. Never missed a morning. I suppose she could have hired someone to grab the girl, but everyone in town paints a picture of a sober, law-abiding seamstress."

Hazen scrunched his lips again. Could this be right?

"I know, I know," Donnella said, with his palm out. "We both remember back in '84, when Cleveland and Maria lived in Buffalo. People there claimed she was soused all the time. Neglected her son. Acted crazy. Cagey Cleveland even sent her to a loony bin. I didn't think you'd want me high-tailing it to Buffalo to check." Donnella dipped his chin, acknowledging he understood the Treasury Department's tight budget. "I used the telephone in the New Rochelle police station to call the police chief in Buffalo, and he asked the chief who had the job before to telephone me. The older chief says Cleveland sent Maria Halpin to an asylum to dry out, and she could leave any time. I guess she did dry out. The real story isn't as bad as it sounded."

"And the son, Oscar? Any chance he's seeking revenge on the father who barely acknowledged him? And who never gave money to his mother?"

"I asked the old Buffalo chief about that. Our upstanding president did pay off the mother. Not a lot. $500. Later, he, or one of his chums, offered her $10,000 during the campaign. She sensed it was a bribe and didn't take it. Oscar, he's been raised—he's a young man now—by Dr. James King in Buffalo. Oscar wants to be a doctor. He's in medical school nearby. I asked the new chief to check with the King's neighbors. Quiet family. And everyone likes Oscar. None of the neighbors saw any sign of anger."

"All those questions…?"

"Don't worry. I followed orders. I told the two chiefs we were investigating a stranger who intruded onto the Bourne property and might have come from afar. Nothing about Ruth."

"Nice work, Sky. You'll make a good agent yet."

"I'm not finished." Donnella grinned. "Remember that Maria Halpin had children with her first husband, before shagging Grover? Her oldest son's now thirty-three, lives in Port Jervis, New York. He works as an engineer for the railroad there. You'd think he might have a grievance against the man who, maybe, seduced his ma. No hint of that." Donnella looked at his lap for a second. "You gave me the go-ahead to hire Pinkertons if I needed help. I had two of them check with that son's railroad boss and, again, with the neighbors."

"Good. Thorough. But Sky—a warning—I doubt we can expect money from Will for more Pinkertons."

"I get it. The two I talked with were fast and thorough. Everyone who knew the Port Jervis fellow liked him. Good man. Always at home. Like before, I said we were worried about an intruder. I let those Pinkertons think it was a male."

Hazen bobbed his head up and down slowly, showing appreciation. "Sky, didn't Maria have a daughter, too, before she met Cleveland?"

"The daughter died three years ago. Never married."

"So the Halpin connection's a dead end?"

"Dead and about to be buried."

"This should satisfy Fran—Mrs. Cleveland."

"Oh, so she's Frances now." Donnella cocked his chin.

"All right, she did ask me to use her given name. And," he winked, "she offered me a piece of her birthday cake the day before yesterday. Her thirty-first birthday. She didn't seem like she was in a celebrating mood." Hazen bent forward across the desk and put one open hand up, to muffle his voice. Even with the door closed, his training reminded him to stay careful. "Ruth was taken under our watch. The big man's too busy fishing to offer much help. The lady's annoying as hell, telling me how to do my job. You and me, we're on the line here." He heard himself, heard his self-pity. "Can you fault a mother for trying to protect her children?"

Donnella smiled at Hazen's change in tone. "I don't fault the lady. Whatever you call her. But how can we protect the girls, and the husband, with you and me and lads from town? And those lads, they don't even carry weapons."

"Right. Let me think. We inquired about the locals, about their reliability. When we could, we got one or two references. But we didn't ask if the lads could hit a target. Probably best not to arm them. For now, let's keep the sidearms here to two—yours and mine."

IV

Part Four: Mary

Chapter Eighteen

December 20, 1881

As Christmas approached in 1881, Mary Brinski carried on with her dreary life in service in Pontiac, Michigan. Five years had passed since her George disappeared. Still no word of him. The days blurred together for Mary, one the same as the other. She did follow news of the assassination of President Garfield—everyone did—but the name Grover Cleveland, the man just elected mayor of Buffalo, meant nothing to her then. Three more years would drag by before his name appeared in the Detroit papers, and three more beyond that before she had cause to hate him.

As usual during the holidays, Mary shifted her chores to handle the Potters' bustling social season. She stood on her feet for hours, cooking for receptions and dinners, sticking to bland Potter family recipes. The season brought one bright spot. Jack, the Potters' son who once played on the floor with toy trains while she cleaned around him, came home from college in Ann Arbor for the winter holiday. With his funny stories about classmates, he'd add a bit of cheer to the drudgery.

Her windowless maid's room behind the kitchen was always off-limits to Jack. Mary could retreat there. She flinched at the sound of a gentle knock.

"May I come in to talk?" Jack's voice sounded less lively than usual. He'd never entered the room before, not once in fifteen years. Was he in a hurry for his ironed shirts? He didn't usually pester her. No, Jack wasn't a bother.

She couldn't guess what he wanted.

When George disappeared, Jack was fifteen. Even then, the lad noticed, more than his parents, that Mary's life had shattered. Mr. and Mrs. Potter spoke kindly to Mary after she returned from Detroit, grief-stricken. But once she took up her chores again, they pushed aside thoughts of her sorrow. Mr. Potter knew lots of Detroit bankers who greased the wheels of business at his Pontiac mill, but he knew no one in the Detroit police force. For her part, Mrs. Potter liked Mary staying around on Sundays rather than hurrying off to see her husband.

Only Jack repeatedly asked Mary what happened. He'd wait until she was alone in the cellar doing laundry, as though he thought she might tell him more away from the others. She said little. George died from illness, out in the streets, she told Jack. Or he fainted and fell down and was hit by a streetcar. Mary knew Jack didn't buy those answers. He'd scrunch his face and roll his eyes. She'd remind him that the Detroit police said they were stumped. Then he'd give her one of his looks. They both understood that the Detroit police wouldn't search hard for a missing railyard worker, especially one with a Polish accent.

Now Mary grabbed her cap from the bureau, replaced it atop her hair. She glanced around the neat room. Nothing to tidy up. Nothing to hide. She opened the door and motioned to Jack to sit in one of the two wooden chairs while she sat in the other. In the narrow space, she smelled the faint but distinctive scent of aftershave. Maybe clove or cedar. No tobacco, no beer. Not like other young men who came to her room elsewhere, long ago. Jack crossed then uncrossed his long legs. The chair was too small for him? Or did he pick up on how uneasy she felt, seeing a man in her room?

"Mary, you're busy with the holidays, so I won't waste your time. Here's what I'm thinking. Hear me out. The fellow I room with at college has a brother, Nicholas. I met him last month. He works for the Pinkerton Detective Agency in Chicago. You know of them?

"Pinkertons. Of course. Didn't one of 'em roust out the Molly McGuires, some of the miners? In Pennsylvania? You," she said, stressing *you*, "might not mix with miners. Two of my uncles worked at those coalfields." She lowered her voice. "Sure you want a Pinkerton as a friend?" She and Jack had talked about strikes before. He knew she could read, knew that even as a maid, she thought about the stories she read.

"This Nicholas fellow isn't like that. He does detective work for families." Jack went silent for a long second. "He works for wives who are suspicious about their husbands. Husbands who are suspicious about their wives. Parents with fifteen-year-old daughters who never come home from a party."

Mary fixed her eyes on Jack. "That got you thinking about my George."

"Yes. I don't mean to meddle, but when I met Nick, I thought he might help. You know, one last try. I could ask him to hunt for George. Nick would reduce his payment. I could loan you money to cover the fee."

Mary fiddled with her cap. She didn't need time to think, just time to find the right words.

"Jack, you're a fine lad, looking after me. But no, George is gone, and that's that. Five years since I saw him. I keep count. He's gone, Jack. Dead. He was sick, and sick at heart that he couldn't work hard. He worried he'd lose his job on the tracks, be a burden on me. He dragged himself off somewhere and died. If he was still on this earth, he'd check in on me. I know that."

"How can you be so sure?" Jack started the question softly, then lingered on his last word. He never asked that before.

Mary shifted in her seat. He wouldn't give up unless she said more. Since entering service, she'd fallen into a habit of secrecy, to keep her job. Maybe she could say a little, a few drips of her story. Maybe no one cared about her life before Pontiac. Maybe after working for the Potters for so long, she was part of their household, like a worn-out piece of furniture. Jack's eyes were glued to hers. She stopped shifting and met his gaze.

"I'll tell you. Now you're old enough. George wasn't always a railroad worker. When I met him, he was a seaman on the *Acme*, a freighter hauling grain around the Great Lakes. He stayed in a rooming house in Buffalo when his ship was in port, and he spent time at a tavern at the dockside." She paused, fussed with her cap. "A tavern where I served beer."

He didn't turn his eyes away from hers. "I was a barmaid, Jack." He'd figure out the rest without her saying much.

"George was one of the better ones. I couldn't understand him much at first—he talked with a Polish accent. And he wasn't handsome like some of the sailors. No. George was short, stocky. Kinda' rough-looking, with those tattoos that sailors make a show of. But he wasn't all hands, like the others."

For two seconds, her mind wandered back. Two seconds was all it took for her to dredge up how George laid eyes on her at the bar, stared, tried to get her attention. How he hung around one night, until she swept the floor and the bar closed, and followed her at a distance, not in a threatening way, more like he simply wanted to keep her in his sight. How he saw two sailors stop her on her walk home. She'd seen them both in the bar. Good lookers. They grabbed her. One held her while the other pawed under her skirt. She stood still, let it start. She'd pushed men away before, one at a time. When she could. She couldn't fight two. How George charged both of them, growling, yelling in Polish. How they ran.

Mary kept her eyes on Jack. "George and I had good times then. He talked to me about his freighter, about the ports where the *Acme* picked up and delivered goods. Chicago, Green Bay, Cleveland. What he'd seen. And he talked about fights on the waterfront when the dockworkers and stevedores grumbled about wages and threatened to strike. And about the strange ways he found in America. I liked him. We kept company. That was around when the war started. He asked me to stop barmaid work. Said he'd share his wages with me."

Jack's face went tight. "Mary—"

"It wasn't like that. No, George wasn't trading. He was gentle. He liked talking. He cared about me. That was in 1860. We had a good life for three years, living in a boarding house. He'd head out on the lakes a lot, as crew. He'd stay home whenever he could. I cleaned for some of the captains' wives. Later, one of them gave me a reference for your mother. But back to Buffalo. By '63, the war heated up. George enlisted. He got close to some of the battles in Virginia. A supply wagon rolled over him, and he never really got better. Then one of his Polish buddies from the *Acme* told George he knew railroad workers in Detroit. That's how George got on in the yards there. You know the rest."

She checked Jack's eyes, his jaw. No longer tight. No sign he was about to rat on her to his folks.

"George was in pain, every day. His back, his lungs, other things. He knew toughs who'd sell him opium. He wouldn't take it. No doubt in my head—he'd had enough. He wanted to die. Poor bloke, he never got a fair shake. If he didn't come along back then, I know where I'd be, and you know too."

Still, Jack said nothing. Now he pursed his lips, as though he questioned her story, or questioned her conclusion to her story. With a sigh, he raised and lowered his shoulders, moving on. "Tell me, if you wanted to remarry, could you? I'd help sort out the problem that you don't have a death certificate."

No point, she thought, in admitting she'd never married George. "I'm thirty-eight. Beaten down."

"I shouldn't say this, Mary, but you're an attractive woman. Even Mother says so. I've seen her look at you and then try to suck in her belly." Jack chuckled.

Mary chuckled too, then looked down, startled by the compliment. She pushed it aside. "You know from my story that I had my fill of men. I work hard here, for your parents. They treat me right. I'm fine, Jack." She managed to say "they treat me right" in her everyday tone of voice. She managed to resist pulling out a lock of hair and twisting it. No adults ever treated her right. Except George.

Jack shook his head. He thought she just went along with whatever happened to her. Did she? As Jack stood to leave, Mary stood too and touched him on the shoulder. Again, the smell of clove or cedar. Unfamiliar, out of place.

"You're a dear boy." She thought for a minute, then added. "I told you about George and me so you'd understand. He made me feel safe, and I made him feel wanted. Then he went and died on me. He's gone." She saw Jack's eyes, still doubtful.

Whether her story made sense to him or not, he listened. He'd always be curious about George—the mystery of his disappearance—and he'd always have a soft spot for the maid who took care of him.

After Jack left, Mary sat thinking, not about what she said but about what she didn't say. While she had George to go to once a week, she had an anchor—a man who accepted her past and who loved her. Now she had a job, with room and board, and nothing else. Her pa had deserted her. Then her ma, deep into her cups, dumped her only child in an orphanage. Then George went missing, sucking out what little air she had. Leaving her.

Alone.

Mary removed the starched, white cap from her head and put it between her teeth. The Potters would hear if she screamed. They would not hear the sound of cotton ripped in two. That sound, soft as it was, held her rage because she had no one to pummel.

Chapter Nineteen

July 25, 1884

"I don't recall such heat in Michigan when I was a boy. What about you, Mary? You were raised in Buffalo?" Mary set down the water pitcher she carried from the kitchen and turned to Mr. Potter. He never gabbed with her when she served dinner. He'd ask for more potatoes or gravy, nothing else. None of the Potters pressed her much about Buffalo, and she didn't offer much, at least not since a few years back when she opened up to Jack about her time as a barmaid.

Mr. Potter didn't wait for Mary to answer. "Buffalo's on my mind these days, I admit. I suppose on everyone's mind." He snickered.

Mrs. Potter glared at him. "Enough, Stuart. You are sitting at our dinner table. You're not really going to talk about the…the Buffalo matter, are you?"

Mary guessed the wife would have the upper hand on manners. Yes. Mr. Potter shifted his snicker to a fake sorry look.

"I shouldn't mention the scuttlebutt. You are right, dear. Maria Halpin is no topic for a lady." He looked at Mary. "Or a maid."

Five hours later, after midnight, Mary crept to the parlor and nabbed the *Pontiac Gazette*, bringing it to her room where she could read by candlelight without anyone noticing. It didn't take her long to find the Halpin story. "If the charges against Governor Cleveland of seduction, abandonment, and brutality, of Mrs. Maria Halpin, published first in detail at his own home in

Buffalo, are true, he ought to be breaking stone in the Auburn Penitentiary instead of officiating as Governor of New York." And more—an agent working for Cleveland had snatched his bastard child from Maria, hiding the boy in an orphanage. All this happened eight years earlier, and reporters couldn't pin down the facts. Even so, the story riveted readers because Cleveland had become the Democratic candidate for the presidency.

Over the next few days, when the Potters were out, Mary skimmed through the pile of newspapers in the parlor. She read more about the Halpin woman, more about the scandal. When Mary served sailors beer in Buffalo, Maria Halpin lived in Jersey City with her deathly ill first husband. By the time Maria found herself a widow, moved to Buffalo, and shagged Cleveland, Mary was in service in Michigan. Although the two women's paths never crossed in Buffalo, Mary could picture Maria Halpin's life in that city, a city, like most, hard on any woman without a man by her side. Mary mulled over Maria's story, and the words the reporters used—seduction, abandonment, brutality. Mary's own story was different, or was it? She was seduced before she met George. She was abandoned by her ma and pa when she was ten. She was brutalized by men, by the matrons at the orphanage. She wasn't forced to place a child in an orphanage. She had no child at all.

Everyone knew Maria's story. No one knew Mary's.

V

Part Five: Frances's World

Chapter Twenty

July 23, 1895

When Frances Cleveland woke on the morning of July 23rd, 1895, her thoughts were far from Grover's long-ago indiscretion with Maria Halpin. Instead, Frances stared at the ceiling, mindful of the date and the sounds she heard exactly twenty years before. The knock at the door of the relatives' house, where she and her mother were visiting. The footsteps of the messenger hurrying off. The noise of paper ripping as her fearful mother tore open the envelope addressed to Mrs. Oscar Folsom. Then no sound as her mother stood still, frozen, and silently handed Frances the telegram to read for herself. A carriage accident, the words wailed. Frances screamed, not so much in sorrow as in anger that her devoted father abandoned her to her nagging mother. Later, Frances heard the details, the rumors. After a night of drinking, Oscar Folsom drove his carriage recklessly around a corner, hitting a wagon. He flew off the seat. He hit his head, and then his carriage rolled over him. Paralyzed with a fractured skull, he died hours later.

Half honoring the memories, half trying to erase them, Frances kneaded the tense muscles of her neck. She looked out the window at the wispy clouds over the Bay, then closed her eyes. She forced herself to remember her father's spirit. Joyful, sometimes too much so. If he were looking down over Gray Gables, he'd counsel her to push him out of her mind, to take pleasure in her three healthy daughters, his granddaughters.

And not only three healthy daughters, Oscar Folsom would think. Never prudent with money, he'd counsel her to take pleasure in having sufficient wealth to employ three capable servants to help. Three servants for three children. Bonnie now devoted all her time to baby Marion, while Annie, once nursemaid only to Ruth, took charge of both toddlers. Annie no longer let them out of her sight, not for a split second. And the third woman, Jennie Schultz, read to Ruth and offered her lessons. Frances could tell that Jennie noticed Ruth's sulks, new since the kidnapping. Jennie patiently let those moods pass.

Frances admired the governess and the nursemaids. She kept an eye on them, not from any lack of trust. She wanted them to see her concern for their well-being, to take their attention away from curiosity about her well-being. Petite Annie would tip her head up to give tall Bonnie a telling glance as they passed in the hall, sharing, not their sizes, but an appreciation of the increased duties that came with a third child. Frances would stop and add her smile of understanding to the glances. I know, she wished to signal, an infant means more work.

For months, Bonnie would be the most tired member of the household. She no longer roomed with Annie but slept beside Marion in the nursery. When the baby woke in the night, hungry, Bonnie knocked—soft, pause, soft, soft—on the Clevelands' bedroom door. Grover still slept on the cot in his study, so Bonnie could bring Marion to Frances without waking the president. Bonnie would sit near Frances, sometimes dozing off. When Marion seemed sated, Bonnie would bring her back to the nursery. Only then did Frances tiptoe to the girls' room.

She needed to see for herself that Ruth and Esther remained sleeping in their beds. She did not want Annie or Bonnie, both obsessively vigilant—and certainly not Grover—to know of her middle-of-the-night checks.

Each night followed the same rhythm. One or two feedings, then a secret peek. Each day, too, followed the same rhythm. Frances gaining strength, trying to squeeze into the looser of her regular frocks. Walks along the jagged shore of beautiful Buzzards Bay. Grover off fishing, or busy at his desk. Pleasant family dinners cooked by Susan, featuring the simple, heavy beef and potatoes Grover favored or the bass he caught. Grover drinking the beer that began to fatten him decades ago in Buffalo, and Frances abstaining as usual, following her longstanding temperance pledge. Grover expounding on the highlights of his political tussles. To all around her, she must appear as the contented mother of three, skillfully supervising more than sufficient help with the children and the household.

Appearances.

She couldn't get a deep breath. Couldn't sleep, even between feedings. She continued her habit of counting—sixteen days since Ruth went missing, since that woman who was still out there butchered Ruth's hair. And Grover—Frances's anger rose—worried that the woman's near success would give ideas to others. Or he worried that his enemies would learn about the agents and say Americans were paying for palace guards. Or not enough guards. Or was Grover simply too busy with political matters to care?

When she peeked into his office in the afternoons, he looked preoccupied and rarely noticed her in the doorway. He sat huddled with Henry, both puffing on cigars. Grover thumbed his mustache while Henry rubbed his shock of white hair. They addressed business passed along from Congress or the Cabinet, although in the past few days, they had the coming presidential campaign on their minds. Chatter from Washington floated easily to Bourne, Massachusetts. After beating Blaine in '84, then losing to Harrison in '88, then beating Harrison in '92, would Grover run for a third term on his beloved Democratic ticket, or would his newest adversary, William Jennings Bryan, snatch the nomination? Frances heard Grover on the telephone, fielding questions, still smoking as he snarled into the mouthpiece.

She dwelt on the fugitive. Grover moved on.

Frances's mind shifted between Grover's inattention and her dear father's memory, finally settling on the inattention as she lingered in bed on the twentieth anniversary of her father's death. Hearing heavy steps, she lowered her eyes from the ceiling to the door. Grover came to check on her.

He plopped down on the coverlet. She rolled toward him, as she had other times. She chuckled, expecting him to do the same. Not this time. He fiddled with his mustache and bobbed his leg. These gestures were not about Ruth because he looked away, not at Frances. When he yanked on his mustache, she knew that although he might have the prospect of another term on his mind, his anxiety more likely hinged on a dismal topic. The hangman. She'd kept up with the stories.

Grover suffered under the weight of hundreds of pleas for pardons and commutations. He spent hours agonizing about convicted murderers sentenced to hang if he didn't intervene. It was the hanging that got to him.

"Thomas Taylor," Grover grumbled. "Killed his wife. He discovered her with another man and went crazy. The details aren't fit for a lady's ears." Frances shrugged. Old story, she thought. "Anyway, Taylor's crime wasn't premeditated. That doesn't seem to matter. He'll hang in four days unless I commute his sentence. He gets the same noose as a murderer who planned his crime for years."

"A Negro, right? Good, you're taking his petition seriously, as I guessed you would."

"Then there's Cephas Wright. This one killed a white man. Wright will hang on September 13th."

"Wright's a Choctaw Indian?" Grover showed no surprise that Frances followed the stories. He liked her to keep up with events, as long as she didn't jabber around others.

"Yes. And last, we have Clyde Mattox. Surprise—sentenced to hang. October 11th."

"Mattox is white for a change, right? He shot a Negro?"

"Yup, Frank—three tough cases."

Grover used her short nickname, reserved for a moment like this. He wanted to talk to her about these petitions, even though he wouldn't burden her with details that were not right for a lady. He wanted her to listen. And yet, she thought, when she wanted him to listen, he did not.

Henry Thurber, trained as a lawyer, could review the legal elements of the cases. According to rumors in Washington, Henry was a hard worker and smart, while Grover was simply a hard worker. A plodder, the public called him. For Grover, the cases' legal elements were only the beginning. Hangings haunted him. When he served as sheriff in Buffalo at the start of his public career, he did the deed himself, pressing the lever that released the trapdoor. Frances knew he replayed the grotesque motion of that lever again and again, often in the middle of the night.

She could help him. "Would you consider reviewing the cases in order of the execution dates? Begin with Thomas Taylor?"

Grover gave another stretch to his mustache. For the next two minutes, he did all the talking, clarifying the difference between first-degree and second-degree murder. Frances paid attention, with an occasional nod. By the third minute, if Thomas Taylor could overhear, he would calm himself.

Frances patted Grover's shoulder, conveying the wisdom of his thinking. "We can talk later," she said, "about the Wright and Mattox cases. They still have time."

Sitting up in bed, Frances sipped the coffee she'd started earlier. It was cold. She gathered her thoughts. Grover worried about three convicts, all murderers. She'd listened, not to help the men, but to settle Grover, hoping that at last he might shift his thoughts from what was on his mind to what was on her mind. No movement. She'd try a more direct approach.

"Grover," she said, with her hand still resting on his shoulder, "have you had a chance to speak with Agent Hazen? Any news?"

"News?"

She bit her lip to keep from lashing out. Twice in the last week, she'd reminded Grover that the kidnapper was still on the run. He always changed the subject. She hadn't gone so far as to remind him of his promise to revisit his demand for secrecy, not after realizing Jeffrey Hazen advocated the same questionable strategy.

"Yes, Grover. News about the woman who grabbed Ruth." Frances strained to keep the anger from her voice, with partial success. "She's a fugitive. And we can call it a kidnapping now that we've seen the ransom note, right?"

Grover pulled on his thick mustache, a yank this time, revealing irritation yet again.

"As I told you, Jeffrey's searching, Sky Donnella too. No news. If I did have news, I'd tell you. I know better than to try to hide anything from Frances Folsom Cleveland. Just turn your attention to Marion, dear."

Grover rose from the bed. Frances rolled back to the center. He pecked her cheek and walked toward the bedroom door.

"I'll find Henry, to tell him to telegraph the attorney general. I'll commute Thomas Taylor's sentence."

Grover smiled as he left, knowing she'd appreciate his decision.

With her eyes on his back, she understood that for the rest of the day, he'd give little thought to the fugitive. Frances was on her own.

She'd prepared. She rang the bell for Lena and asked her to tell Agent Hazen she would see him in his office. Lena returned five minutes later. "Mrs. Cleveland, Sinclair tells me Agent Hazen is meeting with Agent Donnella, with the door closed. Do you wish me to interrupt?"

"No. Perhaps they've made headway in their pursuit." Frances didn't like to mention the search to her lady's maid, but it wasn't as though Lena didn't know what was going on in almost every corner of Gray Gables. "Ask Sinclair to watch Agent Hazen's door and see that he calls on me when they're through."

Later that morning, Jeffrey found Frances on the porch. She led him to a deserted corner of the dining room, where he reported on Sky Donnella's surveillance of Maria Halpin. Unlike the week before, when Frances spoke that name aloud, Jeffrey now fully mastered his gestures, adopting a matter-of-fact tone about Maria Halpin's circumstances and whereabouts.

"As you suggested, when I informed your husband that I was sending Agent Donnella to New Rochelle to investigate, I presented the trip as my idea. I'll report to the president this evening, as I am reporting to you."

When Jeffrey finished, she waited before thanking him. She expected him to offer another course of action. He didn't.

"Thank you for assigning Agent Donnella to the investigation. And I appreciate that he investigated that woman's son." No need to say which son. Jeffrey would know she meant the bastard son. "I think you can agree that Maria Halpin had a motive. She was the most logical suspect." Jeffrey gave the slightest acknowledgment with his chin. Frances pressed her right hand into her thigh as a signal to herself to erase thoughts of the whore and her child and to pivot. She would steer Jeffrey in a new direction.

"Now let me move on to another thought." The poor man couldn't hide his emotions, probably fearing she was about to send him into another blind alley. He rubbed his jaw, deciding what to say, what roadblocks to put before her.

"The Pullman strike," Frances said. "You know it was a bloody affair. The president called in federal troops to stop the violence, although he advocates for limited government most days." She avoided Jeffrey's eyes. She didn't want him to realize she understood differences in political philosophies. "My husband couldn't let the railroads come to a complete halt. We don't need to rehash the details. Just remember that four men, directors of the railroad workers union, went to prison, along with their leader, Eugene Debs. They were charged with inciting union workers to strike."

Frances saw from Jeffrey's stunned expression that she was saying too much, admitting to know too much, behaving in an unladylike manner. She tried to slow down. She couldn't.

"Is it possible that a woman somehow connected to the strike, or related to the men in prison, decided to take out her anger on Ruth?"

Frances heard him cough. A stall.

"Do you have a particular striker in mind?"

"I thought *you* might."

No cough now. Only seconds of silence.

"We're ridiculously short-handed. But I will make inquiries."

He stood up, nodded a goodbye, and left without looking at her. She bristled at the slight. Was this to be his usual pattern after they talked?

Chapter Twenty-One

July 23, 1895

Had he just walked away from a hysterical lady? After listening to Frances Cleveland's nonsense, Jeffrey Hazen pouted in his office. He saw no choice but to talk to the big man, directly. Sinclair said the president was off fishing, expected to return soon. Hazen walked to the dock. He paced in the glaring sun, eyes on the water, looking for the boat. He fixed on the rapid current and let his mind drift. Before long, the president's floppy brown hat came into view, a short distance across the Bay. The servants made fun of that hat. Bud Wylie, the dependable skipper with sun-weathered skin and ginger-colored hair, rowed to the shore. He wore no hat.

If Hazen continued with protection detail every summer, he ought to buy a hat for himself. At the sound of the boat hitting the dock, Hazen forgot his musings on haberdashery, which he knew was a way to avoid his real problems.

Most days, Jeffrey Hazen felt confident about his skills and ability to manage people. Today, for the first time, he feared for his job. His fiancée waited back in Cincinnati, expecting him to switch to an assignment closer to her once Cleveland's term ended. But what if he lost his position as a senior agent, either because he couldn't please the president or the president's wife? Hazen rolled his shoulders to try to relax. He turned to the unpleasant task ahead.

Holding a string of scrawny fish in one hand, Bud Wylie helped his distinguished passenger off the boat.

"Hardly worth going out today," Cleveland said, frowning and gesturing to the string of fish.

Hazen pursed his lips in a look of sympathy to mask his feeling of envy and annoyance. Must be nice to spend a day just worrying about the size of your catch.

"Can we speak for a minute, sir?" Hazen gestured to a spot away from Bud.

"A problem, Jeffrey?" Cleveland's fat jowls sagged more than ever as he grimaced.

"No, not at all. Only a question." Hazen led Cleveland to a spot toward the side of the residence. "I want to discuss Mrs. Cleveland's latest thought about the kidnapper. Your wife wonders if the woman could be related to one of the men involved in the Pullman strike." Hazen spoke each word slowly, distinctly, avoiding the president's eyes in an obvious manner.

The president took a minute. He scratched his hairy cheek. "This Pullman idea sounds improbable to me, and I can tell from your expression to you as well."

"Sir, let me speak directly. I am sure you realize we're short-handed here. Only me and Agent Donnella and a few local lads. I've been charged with guarding you as well as the family. I can't look into every activist connected to the strike. Besides the enormous effort, sir, this idea strikes me as, well, a stretch."

The president resumed scratching his cheek. Underneath his fingers, a smile?

Hazen cocked his head in a questioning manner. "Your advice, sir? How seriously should I take Mrs. Cleveland's suggestion?"

The big man chuckled. "I've tried to ignore her, Jeffrey. I really have. Tried just this morning. So she went around me. Here's what you do. Tell her you're looking into it and will need time."

Was the president really winking?

"Once we return to Washington, with the balls and dress fittings, she may forget the whole matter." Cleveland's voice, almost playful, suddenly turned serious. "Oh, one more thing. I realize you're stretched thin, trying to protect everyone here. If you do get a lead on the kidnapper, give it all your attention. Don't shortchange the children to guard me. Steve can always replace me." Adlai Stevenson was Cleveland's vice-president—the pair were known as Cleve and Steve. "No one can replace Ruth."

Hazen nodded in agreement. While he dreaded misleading Frances Cleveland, he felt relief. Cleveland hadn't blamed him for mentioning Frances's insane idea. As a matter of fact, the big man admitted that he, too, suffered from her obsessions.

Frances Cleveland's latest guess about the kidnapper's identity was the most far-fetched yet. A woman related to a labor activist? Next, Frances would blame the great-aunt of Maria Halpin's second husband's brother-in-law. Yet, in the mid recesses of his mind, Hazen knew that he, a trained detective, was stumped.

Chapter Twenty-Two

July 28, 1895

John Nolan lay on the grass close to Jennie Schultz near the Wylie cottage and vegetable garden. They were inches from each other, half propped up by their elbows. Trunks of three oak trees hid them from the view of anyone peculiar enough to take a late-night walk around the property. Checking the windows of the cottage, Nolan saw no light from kerosene lamps. The Wylies and their borders were asleep.

The moon shone enough light for Nolan to glimpse the tendrils of Jennie's blond hair that escaped her topknot, and then to glimpse her ankles, peeking out from her dull gray dress, suitable for a governess. Leaning forward, he plucked a blade of grass and used it to lightly stroke her legs through her stockings. She drew in a breath and kept talking.

"John, I worry that I'm not helping Ruth. Mrs. Cleveland follows what I teach and approves. Sometimes she even offers ideas for new lessons. Good ideas. But every day she pays attention to what Ruth and Esther wear, always telling Annie to dress them in this frock or that one. To make sure their hair is brushed. Their shoes polished. As if how they look matters as much as anything else."

Nolan barely heard Jennie's words. He kept stroking, while trying to listen. She remained still, unfazed by his silence.

"I think about Mrs. Cleveland while I read that book I ordered from New York. It was in one of those packages you fetched from the post office yesterday. The book has a funny title—*The Woman's Bible*. I read a bit of it, after the household quieted down last night."

Nolan almost forgot his stroking. He was thrown off that Jennie—she didn't go to church—was reading a Bible. An odd one. How could he ask? He fumbled with words in his mind, then slowly eased into questions. "A Bible for women?" She didn't laugh at him. "You like it? How's it different from a Bible for men?"

"Dramatically different. The author's Elizabeth Cady Stanton." Jennie lowered her voice. "She's a suffragist too. She has it right. She explains how the Bible, the real one that the missus and some of her friends think is the first and last word on everything, says on page after page that women are inferior to men. Mrs. Stanton created a fuss, questioning that."

Again, what words could he pull together? What words were right? "Well, I dunno about the Bible, old or new, but I can tell you this—anyone sitting through your lessons knows you're top-notch, not inferior."

"John, most men don't want to hear me speak about books." He felt her hand move over his hand. "You are a good man.

"Let me tell you about those lessons. Ruth used to listen to them. She doesn't anymore, except sometimes when we sing. Her mind wanders. When I first got here, back in May, she paid attention. She asked about the birds—those whistles from ospreys. And she laughed at the honks from the geese. She sat close when I read her stories. Even *Black Beauty*, though that's for older children. Oh, that reminds me. She loves horses."

Now, safer ground. He didn't have to think what to say. "I see her with them. No fear. Last week, when I drove the carriage out front, Annie headed off on a walk with Ruth. I saw the girl smiling at the—" He moved his lips, trying to say the word right, but he couldn't. "At the hosses. Her first smile in weeks." As Nolan spoke, he dropped the blade of grass and slid his fingers up from Jennie's knees, skimming over her thighs in small circles. She slowly eased her hand away from his.

Jennie lowered her body into the grass and went silent. After a while, she raised herself back up on her elbows and spoke.

"That gives me an idea. I could make a suggestion to Mrs. Cleveland. She should ask you to spend an hour with Ruth, letting her pet the horses or brush them down. It might give the girl some fun, change her mood, and show the missus what a help you are to her household. I bet she'd agree if Annie or I went along—I think the missus trusts you, but I'm not certain."

In the moonlight, he thought he could make out Jennie wince, then drill her eyes into his.

"We can't just go along with how things are, if we can do more, if we can help Ruth."

He caught her tone—preachy. But maybe she was right. Since he kept the ransom note hidden until she pressed him to show it, she seemed worried he was slow to act, too ready to stand back. Sure, he was handy with horses and carriages, proud of her schooling, just not the sort to take an extra step.

Well, he could fix that.

He'd show Ruth how to groom the horses, maybe teach her about animals, same way Jennie taught her about books and plants. He slid his hand away from Jennie's leg, swung toward her, and pressed his chest against hers.

"Yes," Jennie said. "Let me plan a day of fun in the stables. And a pony ride?"

She leaned back and slid her arms around him. He felt her body nuzzle into his.

Chapter Twenty-Three

July 30, 1895

Thoughts of her three daughters took over Frances's brain. Baby Marion needed to nurse every few hours, day and night. Was she nursing enough? Too much? And Esther, she had more energy than anyone else at Gray Gables. Her mouth, open as she tried to form words, lit up her face while she grabbed Ruth's dolls. As for Ruth, well, Ruth had always been happy and talkative. Now she was serious and quiet. Did she cling to Annie and Jennie before? Frances tried to remember. Were the older girls busy enough? Were they playing and learning? Were they overdressed in the heat of the day? After a while, worries about the fugitive snaked into Frances's brain, mixing with worries about the girls.

Better to dwell on her daughters than that loathsome woman. Frances sat on the floor in the playroom, alongside Ruth and Esther, giving the nursemaids time to attend to the girls' wardrobes. Frances twisted her legs to the side and sat on her voluminous skirt. She shrugged off the discomfort. She watched Ruth stack wooden blocks, always putting on top the cube with a horse on one side. Esther knocked them down, with a shriek of delight. Again and again. Ruth saw what was coming and pushed Esther's hand away. Frances steered the girls to a new game. She stacked playing cards in the shape of tables and tents. Ruth tried to balance the structures while Esther knocked them down. Again and again.

The children's game was boring, mindless. Frances's legs fell asleep while the sound of the falling cards distracted her. A soft thwack. A giggle. Another effort to build. A thwack. A giggle. Lost in the repetition of falling cards, Frances let her mind drift.

She mused over one idea, unrelated to her previous guesses about suspects—an idea that required dispensation from her implied promise to keep mum about the kidnapping. She would meet Grover at the dock to put the scheme in motion. Ready to stand, Frances rearranged her numb legs. Glad to have a course of action, she ignored pricks of pain.

She settled the girls back in Annie's care, then walked to the dock to watch for Grover. She waved as the rowboat came into view, headed to shore. Grover saw her, waved his floppy hat. Vigorously. He was in a good mood.

Frances would bide her time, not show her hand too soon. Bud Wylie helped Grover off the boat. With self-satisfied looks, both men pointed to the haul of fat bass. Frances waited to speak until Grover pecked her cheek, and she could feel his turned-up lips beneath his droopy mustache.

"Looks like a good day." She nodded approval at Grover's catch, watched him smile at her smile.

"A fine day. Bud had live worms and found the best spot—a deep drop-off where the young bass schooled. If we got out earlier, I could catch twice this many. For a few hours, Frankie, I didn't think about the hangman or a third term, only about bringing home a good haul. Bud'll offer a few to Effie for the staff tonight. And a few to Susan, for us."

"I'll stop watching my waistline and enjoy dinner." Frances saw her opening. This was as good a time as ever to bring Richard and Helena Gilder into the conversation.

The Gilders.

Richard and his wife Helena had been leading lights of the summer colony—a salon of sorts—of artists and writers clustered in Marion, a nearby town that was their new daughter's namesake. Richard edited the celebrated *Century* magazine, and Helena was an accomplished artist. The Gilders had moved to the Berkshires, but they visited often with the Clevelands.

"If the fishing stays this good, you might want to take Richard out with you when he and Helena visit next week." She spoke lightly. No need for

Grover to know she'd planned for days to ask for help from Helena.

Frances watched the lines on Grover's forehead, lines that shifted when he worried. As usual, she detected no irritation when she mentioned the Gilders. Grover, glory be, remained oblivious to her attraction to Richard. Or his to her. Part of her own attraction, Frances knew, resulted from Richard's love of the arts, in sharp contrast to Grover's disinterest. Part of it was deeper, different from her comfort in Grover's presence, in his embrace.

Years ago, Frances learned of rumors linking her with Richard. Awkwardly, she warned him. From that time on, they spoke solely in the presence of others. Just the slightest of smiles between them, almost imperceptible, hinted at their connection. Only occasionally, only at night, did Frances allow herself to indulge her imagination in what might have been.

Richard Gilder wasn't the only man gossipmongers linked to Frances. Reporters searching for love interests pointed to a fifty-five-year-old newspaper editor from Kentucky and a youthful suitor from Buffalo. Those stories added to Grover's scorn for the press. Frances had favored many men, but only Richard Gilder might have competed with Grover.

As Frances stood on the dock, Richard was less on her mind than his wife, Helena. At forty-nine, after giving birth to seven children, Helena still worked as an artist. Frances sought that talent now.

"Grover, you remember that Helena paints. You've seen her work?"

He grunted a yes while admiring his bass. Bud Wylie collected the rods and carried them toward the tool shed.

Frances watched Bud walk away, giving herself a second to try for an easy tone of voice. "I want your thoughts, Grover. What if we ask Helena to speak to Ruth and Joe Jefferson? They're the two who saw that woman."

Grover narrowed his eyes. "Why?"

"Do you remember the stories from England about artists helping to solve crimes?"

Grover tilted his head, partly in acknowledgement, partly in annoyance.

Frances never liked to mention England or any European country. She had toured Europe for a year, and Grover, busy earning a living and politicking, never traveled abroad. An embarrassment for him. She rushed on.

"Police there have used artists to sketch portraits of criminals on the run, based on the memories of witnesses. I read that in at least one case, a sketch led police to the criminal."

Grover turned away from his beloved bass. "Frances, that is cockamamy. Joe barely saw the woman. You'd need to tell Helena what happened. She'd tell Richard. I don't like that. I know you're still worried, but Ruth is safe now. If she wasn't, I'd grab at every possibility too. But hear me, she's safe. The time has come to let all this go."

Frances locked her eyes on his. She felt her hands go to her hips. He'd see that, so she pushed her hands down to her thighs.

"Grover, I won't rest until I try everything. You should be relieved that I'm not asking Jeffrey to hunt for fingerprints on the oar." She forced a chuckle. "I understand that in England, some scientists suggested those prints can point to a criminal." Another chuckle. Grover would see a drawing as less ludicrous than a fingerprint, especially since prints would be smudged by now, and Jeffrey caught no suspect who could be fingerprinted for comparison.

Seconds passed. She waited, with her eyes still set on him. In the quiet, in the stillness, he'd sense her determination, as he had many times over the years.

"All right. But you stay out of it. Let Jeffrey Hazen take the lead when the Gilders come."

She gave a slight bow of appreciation, even though she had hoped to conceal from Jeffrey this experiment with art. If he thought she was mad as a hatter before, what would he think now?

Chapter Twenty-Four

August 5-6, 1895

Jeffrey Hazen knew the pattern. After four to six weeks of confinement, recovering from childbirth, Frances Cleveland would pick up where she left off, with carriage rides, teas, and luncheons. She'd do so, he guessed, while continuing to stew and squawk about the woman on the run. Now he would need to protect Frances and the children on their outings as well as on the grounds of Gray Gables.

Jeffrey Hazen couldn't do his job without more help, but he was running out of money. He had to pay the villagers helping with patrols, as well as the fee for the Pinkerton detectives that Sky enlisted for the Halpin investigation. The money for summer protection would soon be exhausted.

He prided himself on appearing competent and independent, not desperate for funds. He rarely drank while working, but then again, he rarely needed to beg. As soon as Cleveland was closeted with Henry Thurber for a late afternoon of work, Hazen opened the locked cabinet where he hid a small supply of liquor next to the ammunition for his revolver and Sky's. He took a swig of warm whiskey to ease his nerves, leaving a bit in the glass. Surely the president's demand for secrecy exempted communication with brother William Hazen, head of the Secret Service. Unless Will knew about the kidnapping, he wouldn't authorize additional expenses.

Hazen shut himself in his office and telephoned his brother. The much-used telephone line to Washington was clear.

After the usual niceties about Hazen cousins and other kin, Will listened to the story of the kidnapping and released a torrent of profanity. "You're silent, Jeff, while I swear up a storm. Don't worry, I'm not blaming you. You're the best agent we have. Who could imagine anyone would snatch that pretty little girl? We guard Cleveland and now the whole family—a man, a woman, and three children. Protect them from a woman? Damn crazy."

"Will, I told you about the kidnapping, even though Cleveland wants to keep it secret, for a reason. My job here isn't easy. I guard the girls, a president who's out of the house for hours at a time, and a wife who's running around in circles. She wants me to find the kidnapper, and she won't let up. She's entering society again and entertaining, a month after giving birth. She started taking carriage rides with tubby hubby." Hazen trusted the workman who laid the phone line the previous year and insisted that this particular line was securely private. "I think she uses those outings to peep around town, to see if she spots suspicious-looking women. Sky Donnella's great—thanks for assigning him here—but just two of us? That's not enough."

Jeffrey Hazen took another sip of the remaining whiskey, paid no heed to the sweat dripping down his neck, and plowed on. "I need another agent, or more money for the lads I hire from town, or both. I hate to call you like this. Hate to beg."

Exactly three seconds of silence.

"Jeff, I'm already in trouble for sending two agents up there since Treasury never received authorization to guard anyone besides the president. You remember, I only sent you and Sky because the wife insisted when she panicked about some roughnecks pretending to lay telephone lines." Not quite the full story. Will had learned of other threats as well—something vague about vicious gamblers in the West targeting the president—but of course Frances's panic had stuck in his mind.

"Naysayers in Congress will want my neck if I give you more funds. They claim Grover's acting like some royal who demands a palace guard. They think any danger is overstated. Carlisle and the rest of the brass here in

Treasury won't appreciate the expense." Jeffrey Hazen needed to answer to brother Will and Will needed to answer to John Carlisle, Secretary of the Treasury.

Hazen stayed quiet, waiting out Will.

"All right. Another $1000."

When the call ended, Hazen closed his eyes and let relief sweep over him. He'd survived the telephone call with some semblance of professional integrity intact. His big brother was under stress, too.

Hazen rolled his shoulders and stretched his arms. He opened the door and saw Sinclair standing in the hall, just far enough away to avoid the appearance of eavesdropping. He would be waiting for the muffled sounds of the call to end, so he could deliver a message. "Jeff, the missus wants to speak with you." Sinclair didn't use formal language, yet his voice sounded a shade ominous. He knew more than he admitted. What could the lady be up to now?

Five minutes later, Hazen joined Frances Cleveland for coffee on the porch. Was he misinterpreting, or was she showing a sly smile?

"Jeffrey, don't worry. I have no more names to offer you, no more ideas about the president's enemies. I can offer another idea, though, of a different nature. Have you followed the story of the sketch that allowed British police to capture a murderer a few years back?"

Hazen struggled to control his features as Frances related the story. Remembering the big man's wink and advice to be agreeable, Hazen assured her he would send a telegraph to obtain additional details. Once he turned to leave the porch, he let his brows furrow. At the front door, Hazen saw Sinclair register that furrow, then glance away, probably hiding a knowing look.

As Hazen opened the front door, he felt a welcome breeze. He headed toward the Wylies' cottage. He'd be in time for Effie's dinner, and, best of all, he'd find ice there to cool his second whiskey.

* * *

The following day, Hazen watched John Nolan pull up a pair of draft horses to the front of the house, with Richard and Helena Gilder in the landau, its hood folded down. Nolan had fetched them from the railroad station. Hazen had never met the Gilders and would let Frances make the introductions later that afternoon. Helena grinned, happy to arrive at Gray Gables after a long trip from western Massachusetts. She most likely had no idea yet of Frances's latest scheme. Sinclair greeted the couple and helped them down from the landau as Hazen ambled to the side of the house, preferring to stay out of sight.

Frances approached the Gilders, two steps behind Sinclair. Hazen recalled the gossip, so he watched carefully as Frances embraced Helena and spoke warmly to Richard, not touching him.

Two hours later, at the appointed time, Hazen donned a more formal jacket than the one he wore for guard duty. He entered the parlor. Most official meetings took place in the president's commodious study. Hazen had never been invited to meet in the parlor itself, with its massive cobblestone fireplace, unused all summer, surrounded by cozy seating. He sensed the style to be more country house, or maybe hunting lodge, than Victorian. At one of the Thursday night poker games, Sinclair provided Hazen and others an accurate description of the summer quarters. "All for comfort, not for show."

Hazen arrived last. Richard Gilder and Frances sat on a settee, with three feet between them. Ruth sat on the edge of one of the child-sized chairs the Clevelands brought with them from the Executive Mansion. She held a pencil, pressing it down on a pad of paper on her lap. Joe Jefferson, the actor who summered nearby and viewed the fugitive from his boat, sank into the well-cushioned wingchair. Helena Gilder perched on a slat back chair, with a wood board angled on her lap and drawing paper tacked to the board. Glasses of lemonade sweated on the side tables. Frances Cleveland set the stage to relax her visitors. The president was out of sight. Admiring his fish?

When Hazen looked over the cluster of people, he realized he should separate Ruth and Jefferson so neither's memories influenced the other.

But that approach, required in a police station, would hardly work in the president's parlor.

Frances smiled at Hazen, then turned to the Gilders. "Let me introduce you to Agent Jeffrey Hazen. He is the experienced agent responsible for our protection at Gray Gables. Grover asked him to take charge of this exercise."

Yes, Hazen thought. And what an odd request. Actually, Frances made the request, and an hour after that, the big man peeked into Hazen's office, asking him to humor the missus and exchanging a grin, as though the two men had partnered in the business of humoring.

"And Agent Hazen, meet Mr. Richard Gilder and Mrs. Helena Gilder," Frances continued. "Please join us." She pointed to an armchair and then to a glass of lemonade on a nearby table, ready for him. She smiled, a tad too long. An afternoon party for all.

"Mr. and Mrs. Gilder, Mr. Jefferson, Ruth—as Mrs. Cleveland said, the president asked me to manage our exercise today." Hazen looked from one Gilder to the other. "I assume you know of the disturbing events at Gray Gables on July 7th?"

The Gilders nodded a yes. "I filled them in," Frances said. "And of course, Mr. Jefferson was a witness."

All eyes rested on Hazen, waiting. He'd get through this farce. "I see from Mrs. Gilder's board that you understand we are here to try a composite sketch. Following Mrs. Cleveland's recommendation, I telegraphed Scotland Yard and can report on the history of that concept. In 1881, a man shot and stabbed an elderly corn merchant on the Brighton Railway. The British police detained a suspect, but he escaped. Then they created what they call a composite sketch and turned it into a wanted poster. The poster helped the public find the murderer. He was tried and hung."

As Hazen said, "hung," he immediately regretted using that word. He looked at Ruth. She was busy scribbling with pencils.

"Mrs. Cleveland asks if we can learn from the British. Mr. Jefferson, you observed the woman. And Ruth..." She didn't hear him. "Ruth," he said louder. "You saw that lady, too, the one who took you on the rowboat the day Marion was born?" Ruth gave a faint bob of her head. "If you will both describe what you saw to Mrs. Gilder, she can try to create a drawing of the woman."

Helena Gilder, frowning, turned her head from Hazen to Frances and back to Hazen. She didn't like any of this. "I have never drawn from descriptions before. I draw from live models. And occasionally from photographs. And *en plein air*. Not from descriptions."

Frances jumped in. "But Helena, I hope you agree it's worth a try." Frances, mouth half open, seemed about to add to her plea. She stopped herself and looked to Hazen.

"I understand your reluctance," Hazen said. I certainly do, he snickered to himself. "But let's try. Mr. Jefferson, can we start with you? You provided a description that day. Can you repeat it for Mrs. Gilder?"

Hazen considered the old codger spry and alert, even at sixty-six.

"As I said then, I never got a great view of the woman. At first, I just saw the rowboat, with that big red 'C' on one side—the side facing me. Then I spotted Ruth and couldn't figure out why she was boating with a stranger, a stranger who couldn't steer the boat."

Hazen saw Frances smile and wave with a beckoning motion at the same time that he got a whiff of fresh baking. Susan arrived with a tray of warm cinnamon cookies, adding to the party atmosphere Frances must want.

Joe Jefferson was the first to grab a cookie. His chewing didn't impede his continuing story. "The woman had blond curls and a large straw bonnet. Possibly spectacles. She was much too far away to be sure." Helena began to sketch, slowly, while Jefferson kept talking. "The woman's dress was either blue or gray. Nothing that made an impression. I do paint when I'm not acting, but landscapes, so I pay more attention to the colors of water and sky than to the colors of clothing. I only stared at the woman because I wanted to make sure she really was a stranger, and not one of the housekeepers or nursemaids. Like I said, I'd peg her at forty or fifty."

While the Gilders kept their eyes on Jefferson, Frances looked at Hazen. He caught her meaning. She wanted him to concentrate on suspects of that age.

"Nothing about her features stuck with me," Jefferson said. "Just regular-like. But as I said, she was far away, so I can't be certain. When she turned the boat, I only saw her back. She seemed average size, a little shorter than Mrs. Cleveland and Mrs. Gilder. When she scrambled onto the wharf, she carried Ruth in one arm and a basket in the other, so I couldn't tell much about her gait. I could tell she was a woman—certain of it—not a man in women's garb."

"Shoulders?" Helena asked. "Broad or narrow?"

"Hunched too much to tell. She struggled with the basket and the child."

"Bonnet? Made of straw or fabric? Ribbons? Bent brim?"

"Hmmm. A lady would ask that. I don't know. The brim might have been bent down, over her face. That's a guess." Helena moved her charcoal stick tentatively up and back over the drawing paper.

"Anything more to add?" Hazen asked.

"Sorry. No."

Hazen mumbled thanks, then turned to the child.

"Ruth, can you tell us what you remember about the lady who took you on the boat?" The girl kept scribbling, eyes on her paper. "When I talked to you that day, I asked if you could remember her voice. If she said I'll take you to your new brother—she thought the baby was a boy—or if she said I'll take you to your new brothah—with a Yankee accent." The Gilders chuckled and Jefferson guffawed. "You couldn't remember. Today I want to talk about what you saw, not what you heard. Mr. Jefferson told us she had blond hair and curls. Does that seem right?" Ruth raised her head an inch.

"Blond."

"Curls too?"

Ruth didn't answer.

"Let's move to her clothing. Do you remember the color of her dress?

"Pink."

"Pink?"

"Pink." Hazen stared at Jefferson. The man shrugged. He wasn't about to argue.

"And her bonnet. What do you remember about that?"

CHAPTER TWENTY-FOUR

"It was pretty."

Helena jumped in. "Ruth, dear, was there a ribbon on it?"

"Pink."

Another shrug from Jefferson. Helena grimaced as she held her charcoal in midair.

Hazen took over again. "Ruth, is there anything else you remember about the woman? Was she larger than your mother or smaller?"

"Smaller." Hazen wondered if the woman was smaller than the pregnant Frances or the not-pregnant Frances. He wouldn't ask. He already suspected the woman was small. She hadn't trampled the grass.

Helena piped up again. "Ruth, you sat across from her in the rowboat, so you had a good view. Let's talk about her features. Was her nose wide or narrow? Long or short? Were her eyes close together? Was her chin…"

The child squirmed.

"I suppose you don't remember?" Ruth resumed her scribbling.

Hazen understood. Ruth didn't want questions.

Frances knew enough was enough. She looked at Helena, acknowledging defeat. Helena returned that look and put down her charcoal. She held up her board. Two empty ovals—a horizontal oval for a hat atop of a vertical oval for a face.

Gilder, who sat silently, closed the exercise with three words. "A valiant try."

Chapter Twenty-Five

Frances loved Helena Gilder. The woman was the mother of five living children, as well as an artist and a teacher. Helena followed her interests while she raised a family, like some of Frances's schoolmates at Wells College.

Frances occasionally felt a flicker of envy. Only a flicker. Most days, she embraced her role as the president's wife, serving as a model for womanhood. The women of America loved her. They loved her children. They loved her elaborate gowns, her choice of bright colors, her rhinestone embellishments, her capes, her feather boas, her flamboyant hats. They secretly loved her low-cut necklines, while publicly condemning them. They followed her attraction to bustles, and then her aversion to that accoutrement. They copied her updo with short hair at the neck and temples.

This attention had a dark side. Frances bristled when businessmen appropriated her image in advertisements for their products, implying she recommended their plates and their playing cards and their tonics. Grover too railed against those unscrupulous men. Or maybe, if Frances was to be fully honest with herself, she merely gave the impression of bristling, to satisfy Grover. Maybe some part of her was pleased that her image could attract customers.

Yet, she knew the attention sprang from her youth and her beauty, not from her accomplishments. Helena, slightly plainer in appearance, received praise for her art. Now, a month after giving birth to Marion, Frances felt pudgy, and fretted that she'd fallen short as a mother. She thought of Helena with admiration. And a renewed twinge of jealousy.

Helena also had the good sense to marry Richard, a man who echoed and from time to time surpassed his wife's accomplishments. When the Gilders visited, the two couples gathered in changing numbers. Sometimes all four dining together. Sometimes in threes with the Gilders and Frances discussing a book. Sometimes in twos with Richard and Grover fishing or drinking or smoking those deadly cigars, or Frances and Helena walking or sewing.

Or Frances and Richard talking. Those were the best times. Frances and Richard kept them to the least times, and always in the daylight, and always with others in view.

On this second day of the Gilders' visit, Frances asked Nolan to drive her and Helena to Marion, an hour away. Helena wanted to visit what everyone in the area called the Old Stone Studio, the cottage where she'd painted and hosted friends before she and Richard moved to the Berkshires for more space for their family. The Gilders owned the cottage and the house behind it, and kept both buildings, unsure about using them again. The two women would check to make sure the studio remained in good condition, then lunch in town. If they moved along, they would be back in time for Frances to nurse Marion.

Nolan helped the women climb into the landau, onto the upholstered benches that faced each other, with Frances looking forward as she wished. He never turned his head to see her. She could see him, on the high driver's seat, grasping the reins. He always kept the horses, whether a pair as today or four, under control when he drove her. She guessed he'd heard the gossip about how her drunk father crashed his carriage through the streets of Buffalo and died. Today, Nolan seemed to drive with greater care than ever. He must remember his mistake—withholding the kidnapper's note. She tried to put him at ease, certain he'd acted with honest intentions.

"John, thank you for folding the hood down. The weather is unseasonably hot for Bourne. At least with the top down, we can catch a breeze—a faint breeze."

Frances sensed sweat dripping from her scalp, under her wide hat, dropping onto her shoulders. Helena, hatless, tapped at the sweat on her own forehead, smiling at Frances in solidarity. The women tried to dry themselves with swipes of their handkerchiefs.

Walking from the landau into the cottage, Frances and Helena eyed each other with pleasure when the damp, cool air hit them. They hovered in front of the massive fireplace, admiring it as they had many times before. Richard enlisted his friend Stanford White to design it, knowing it would be an attraction.

"I do paint in the Berkshires," Helena said. She must be remembering the artists and writers who gathered around that hearth. "But I miss our days here in Marion, and the company of other artists. Writers too. I loved the heat from that fireplace on chilly days—and the cool air on hot days like today—and learning what others were painting."

Frances circled the room. "Helena, the studio looks in good shape. No evidence of squatters, and no one made off with the andirons or the Windsor chairs. I suspect the townspeople—they liked you and Richard—keep an eye on the cottage. You know, I miss the company of that crowd, too. When I visited here, I always returned to Gray Gables with my spirits lifted. Grover knew I loved this area and your circle of friends. That's why he bought property here. Well, that and the distance from Washington, and the weather, and the fishing." Frances laughed at her words, the first time she'd laughed in weeks.

"Does the president fish most days?" Helena spoke with a solemn voice, and her eyes moved from the fireplace to Frances. "Do you miss his company?" A pause. "Do you feel alone with the girls?"

"Yes, he fishes most days, though he also manages the government's business—he usually goes back to his desk after the girls are in bed—and he gets on well with them in the evening. And he's available to us more than you might think." Frances heard her clipped tone. She found herself defending Grover. She took a second to calm the muscles in her face. "Why do you ask, Helena? Grover's a dear. He's the least of my problems."

Helena wouldn't give up. "Frances, you seem down. Is it Ruth? Do you worry about her? She showed no interest yesterday in the questions about the kidnapper. I must say, reflecting back, I'm rather ashamed of myself for questioning the child. I should've advised you to leave it be."

Frances tried to ignore the coming tears, until they gushed down her face. Before she could turn away, Helena's arm guided her to a bench against the cool stone wall.

"Dear, dear, I'm sorry to upset you. Or maybe I'm not. Let's talk?"

"I can't stop thinking about that woman. How close she came to stealing my Ruth. I'm the only one who seems intent on finding her before she can try again." Frances choked out the words while sobbing, as Helena gently rubbed her back.

"I'm sorry to fall apart like this. You see, Grover wants to cover up the whole matter. He won't talk about it. And Jeffrey Hazen thinks I'm a hysterical nag. Sometimes I feel like one when I push him. And the nursemaid—Annie—just wants to forget what happened. And I don't know how to talk to Ruth. Whether it's better to persuade her to talk or hope she moves on."

"A month ago, you gave birth to a baby, which upsets your body—believe me, after seven children I know—and can upset your mind." Helena's hand, still circling on France's back, stilled at the word seven. Two of the Gilders' children did not survive.

"Many women feel downcast after childbirth. And then, this awful thing happened to Ruth. It makes sense you're worried." Helena's voice slowed. "That you feel you can't protect your family." Frances understood what was unsaid. She and Helena had confided with each other about how they managed their husbands in unseen ways. Helena's voice returned to its usual speed, and her hand moved again. "If a stranger grabbed one of my children and then disappeared, I'd agonize too."

Frances could hardly see. "Let me help," Helena said, as she used her damp handkerchief to dab Frances's eyes.

"I'm afraid that both our handkerchiefs are wet from perspiration after that ride. Sorry my dear. You haven't asked, but here's my advice. You can do two things at once. You can. You can tend to your girls and your husband, and make sure that officials continue to hunt for that criminal. And something else. I know you start out even-tempered, then you think you're too overbearing, then you pull back, then you start up again. Just don't let your fears overwhelm you. Find an even keel."

Frances nodded.

"Now, Mrs. Cleveland, let's leave this cool haven and ask your coachman to drive us to the café for lunch, so you get back in time to that babe of yours."

Chapter Twenty-Six

August 7, 1895

After driving Helena Gilder and Frances Cleveland back to Gray Gables, John Nolan walked the draft horses around the paddock to cool them off. He added water to their pails, washed dust off their coats, and brushed them down. Next, he polished the landau and fed treats to all the horses. Hearing a knock on the open stable door, he raised his eyes.

"Nolan, can we talk?"

Richard Gilder, with his fine gray hair and mustache, looked out of place in the stables. What could he want?

"Yes, sir. Should we sit outside? Smells better there." Nolan pointed through the door to a rough bench, in a spot shaded from the late afternoon sun.

Once Gilder sat, Nolan sat, tensing his shoulders. Was this dandy about to chew him out for hiding the ransom note for days? Didn't he know the Clevelands forgave him?

Gilder began, with no ire in his voice. "Thank you for driving my wife and Mrs. Cleveland to Marion today. The route must be familiar to you—you often drove the Clevelands there to see us before we moved."

"Yes, sir. I know the route well. I hope the ladies enjoyed themselves."

Gilder didn't say one way or the other. Seemed like his mind was on something else.

"Nolan, I understand that the president is keen to keep the events of July 7th confidential." Gilder moved his eyes across Nolan's face. "I see your alarm. Please do not think I question your actions around that day. No, the Clevelands seem to trust you. So I trust you. Also, let me explain how I know about the kidnapping, since at the president's orders, the story should not go beyond his household. I know only because Mrs. Cleveland, with the president's approval, told my wife." Gilder rolled his eyes, then smirked.

"Are you married, Nolan?"

Nolan shook his head.

"Well, if you do marry one day, you will learn that even the best of wives, and mine is the best, rarely keep secrets from their husbands."

Nolan lowered his shoulders. The dandy seemed friendly.

"You may know that Mrs. Gilder is an artist. Mrs. Cleveland thought that if Joe Jefferson and Ruth could describe the mysterious woman—the fugitive—then my wife might create a sketch, a portrait, to help officials or townspeople locate the woman. I'm afraid that didn't work. Now, on my initiative, all mine, I'd like to try a different approach." He paused. "You reside in town, in Bourne, that is, correct? I'm interested in your local connections."

"Local connections?"

"You've lived here a long time?"

"Yes, sir. Spent my whole life heah. Twenty-foah years."

"I've spoken with Agent Hazen. He tells me that he's in touch with the Bourne police, but that the station consists of two constables whose primary duties are guarding drunks and thieves in the local jail. For a while, the constables also patrolled Gray Gables when the president was in town. You might already know what I learned from Mrs. Cleveland. Early last summer, she complained that two constables, with limited training, were inadequate, and that's when the Secret Service sent Agents Hazen and Donnella. Hazen tells me the constables are able men, just not up to investigating the kidnapping of the president's daughter."

Nolan tipped his head in agreement. "Yes, Nate Sullivan and Julius Combs. They keep the peace in town."

"Let me tell you what I think. Someone around here must have seen the kidnapper sneaking around, but no one's talking. Hazen and Donnella spoke to the stationmasters at all the nearby train stations. They weren't aware of any unfamiliar woman coming in by rail. They spoke to the manager of the Norcross House and the boarding houses in Bourne. No strange woman registered as a guest on July 7th, or any time shortly before that. Bourne is a small town. People would notice a strange woman."

Nolan gazed into the far distance, across the grass, toward the residence. Gilder noticed.

"I sense you already know what I've said."

"I keep my ear to the ground, sir. I shouldn't say this, but a lot of chattah floats 'round the household staff."

Gilder bobbed his head an inch and narrowed his eyes. He must wonder what else the Cleveland's coachman caught wind of.

"Your powers of observation lend more weight to my idea—what I want to talk about. Since I bought our cottage in Marion years ago, and since I've been visiting the Clevelands in Bourne, I've come to recognize that relations between the local townsfolk and the many guests swooping in from Washington and New York aren't always ideal."

True enough, Nolan thought, trying not to laugh.

"Part of it is language. You stretch out some words differently. When a maid says she's straightening out a drawer, we think she's telling Helena to draw." Gilder chuckled, more in good humor than mockery. "So you sound, ahhh, irregular to us."

Nolan held back his thought that it was the Gilders and the rest of the high and mighty set who sounded irregular. Funny though, Gilder picked up on that notion.

"And, yes, I'm sure we sound irregular to you. But it's more than language. You think, mistakenly, I assure you, that we see you as rustics." Nolan smiled. Gilder smiled back. "And you see us as snooty and useless. I believe that when Agents Hazen and Donnella ask around, the townspeople think of them as, well, you might say, invaders." Gilder set his eyes on Nolan, waiting to see what he'd say to that.

"You've got it right, sir, mostly." Nolan dragged his boots across the dirt under the bench, buying time. Should he say more? "Lots of people in Bawn, and in Marion too, gripe about posh people swarming the place in summah." Nolan studied Gilder's face. Yes, the man caught that Nolan's Bawn was the same as the fancy crowd's Bourne. "Townsfolk don't fuss about the president or the missus—the Clevelands are nice to everyone. But my buddies, they think visitors to Gray Gables see Bawn like a one-hoss town. They talk down to the locals." Nolan checked Gilder's face again. The man didn't look riled.

Nolan rushed on. "There's another side. The folks who call on the president, they fill up Bawn's hotels and cafes. And the Clevelands hire near twenty townspeople each summah. And me, my family thinks I have a swell job, working for the president. Some of the locals line up with the president's way of thinking, about politics, I mean, and they all say Mrs. Cleveland's a beauty and treats the maids and other help real good. But you're right, people in town won't go outta their way to lend a hand."

"Nolan, that's why you can help. In Washington, the agents command respect. They don't realize the animosity here. I believe you, born and bred in Bourne, can ask around. You'll get more information than the agents. Ask your buddies, the lads you grew up with, your sisters. Just don't tell them why. I can invent a story for you. Say that Mrs. Cleveland invited a friend from New Jersey—that's where the family used to summer—to visit her, and that the friend was to arrive in Bourne last month, but never sent word that she arrived. The friend is unreachable. Mrs. Cleveland wonders if the woman became confused and remains here, alone, in Bourne."

Nolan screwed up his face.

"I see you're skeptical. You think the story is a stretch? Right. But it doesn't matter. Let your neighbors think you confused the details. Again, no matter. The story will start them talking. You may learn more than you realize."

Nolan expected blame. Now this instead. Richard Gilder, a rich magazine editor, was asking a poor coachman to lie and to investigate. What would Jennie make of this? Nolan couldn't forget how she'd snapped at him about keeping the ransom note tucked away for a week. Would she think that by helping Gilder, he could make amends? Too much to sort out quickly.

"Sir, I gotta say, I'm dumbstruck by this." He scratched his head under his cap and rubbed his boots in the dirt again. "But ya might be right. There's some bad feeling between the town folks and the city folks. And I do know nearly everyone in town. I can snoop around.

Gilder stuck out his hand. Nolan did too, hoping Gilder wouldn't feel his calluses as they shook.

"Yes. Please report back to me. If you discover any useful information, we will take it to Agent Hazen. He's a good man, and trying his best but getting nowhere, and I don't think he'd approve these methods."

Nolan tried to push back the quip that came to mind, but couldn't. "You mean the government doesn't exactly want Secret Service agents watching the president to go looking for help from a foolish coachman?"

"Foolish?" Gilder asked.

"Some think that, 'cause I didn't tell Agent Hazen about the ransom note right away."

"Don't berate yourself. You were trying to help the governess. As I'm trying to help Mrs. Cleveland."

For the next few weeks, John Nolan would take satisfaction from Richard Gilder's support, while figuring he was simply on a mission to curry favor with Frances Cleveland. One thing Nolan knew for sure: word traveled from lady's maid Lena to governess Jennie to coachman John that the most Gilder could hope for from the lady was thanks, nothing more.

Chapter Twenty-Seven

August 9, 1895

Knowing what time Jennie Schultz started her nature lesson, Frances summoned the usual participants to the front porch at ten. She walked out the front door, holding Ruth's hand. Next came Annie. Despite her short stature, the nursemaid carried Esther easily. Jennie and Helena followed. Walter Breen, a fellow from the village, waited on the porch. He'd watch over the group on their walk. Jeffrey Hazen stood on the crowded porch, too, taking his turn with front-of-house guard duty.

Frances looked squarely at Annie, lowered her head slightly, and chatted about the lovely weather. She wanted to avoid meeting Jeffrey's eyes. She knew he'd lost patience with her.

Glancing for an instant to the side, Frances realized that Jeffrey's gaze was not on her, but on Walter Breen. The agent looked over the lad, from his toothy grin, down his tall and lanky body, to his shabby work shoes. "Walter, stay close to the ladies and children." He nodded yes, seemingly proud of his new duty. Frances didn't know the lad well, just that he was a mill hand hired for part-time help with patrolling and gardening.

Grover exited the house, ready for his outing to a bait and tackle shop in Barnstable, twenty miles away. The proprietor had sent word of a new shipment of rods. Jeffrey would accompany the president, Sky Donnella would take over front-of-the-house duty, and the Breen lad would shadow the women and children. Frances saw Jeffrey scramble each day to provide security.

She heard a crunching noise as Agent Donnella hurried to the porch. The two agents talked for a second—their usual changing of the guards exchange.

"We both need to stay vigilant, Sky," Jeffrey said. "No telling who hangs out around the tackle shop. And no telling who thinks the women and children are alone here, unguarded." Hazen spoke softly, his face turned away from the cluster of women. But Frances, on alert, heard.

She understood that Grover needed time away. A few days earlier, he brooded over the Clyde Mattox capital punishment case, rereading the file Henry gave him, the file from the Attorney General that stayed open on the bedroom bureau. First, Mattox killed a deputy marshal in Indian Territory and got off, claiming self-defense. Then he killed a Negro who was supposedly protecting two little girls. Mattox was tried multiple times for that case, with disputes over evidence. In the end, he was sentenced to die on October 11th. Peeking at the file, Frances read pleading letters from Mattox's widowed mother, asking Grover to commute the death sentence and telling him she was sending her pleas far and wide.

As Nolan drove off with Grover and Jeffrey, Frances gestured to Jennie to begin the walk. The group fell into line, with Jennie taking the lead and Frances following. She stared out at the shoreline, barely aware of the others with her.

She didn't care one way or the other about Clyde Mattox. Three of the letters she'd peeked at the night before claimed he was an outlaw and a gambler and had committed crimes besides the two murders. A dozen other letters vouched for him or railed against hangings in general. No wonder Grover stewed over this case. But she stewed over its effect on him. He worried about the *wrong* criminal. Thirty-three days after the kidnapping, the mysterious woman—*their criminal*—remained a fugitive.

Frances knew she should observe the plants, the color of the water. She looked at Helena's profile and remembered her words in the stone cottage, urging Frances to find an even keel. Helena set a good example. She carried her sketchbook for later but now simply admired the scenery. Jennie's look mirrored Helena's admiration. "Beautiful path, right Mrs. Gilder?" A minute later, Jennie stopped and pointed out to the Bay. Frances stopped too and turned her eyes to follow Jennie's raised arm.

"Ruth, see that huge clump of eelgrass. Those narrow leaves, the ones like ribbons. Those plants feed the fish that your father catches. Eww, that clump might be rotting already."

Annie held her nose. "Are those leaves the reason I smell rotting eggs?" she said.

Esther, still in Annie's arms, looked at her nursemaid and then held her nose too. Annie laughed. Helena and Jennie smiled. Frances didn't join in. She stared at Ruth. Her older daughter neither looked at the eelgrass nor pinched her little nose. Frances knew the child hadn't lost her senses—she simply didn't respond to the odor. Frances hated the stench, and before the summer ended, would remember it, connecting it forever with a different kind of decay.

"Ma'am?" Frances heard Jennie's voice—deliberate, kind. She must have noticed Ruth's sullenness and Frances's stare. "You remember, the coachman plans to let Ruth spend time with the horses, the pony too, this afternoon after he returns from Barnstable. A good change for her, I hope. Annie and I will come along. Bonnie says she'll look after Esther so Ruth can have all the attention. John—the coachman—he'll let Ruth pet the horses, show her how he grooms them. He'll let her feed them."

Frances nodded and walked on, eyes back on the shoreline. Jennie had said little about the coachman recently, still embarrassed he hadn't rushed to hand over the ransom note, yet today she didn't shy away from saying his name.

Late that afternoon, Ruth returned from two hours in the stables. "The coachman knew how to interest her," Jennie reported. "He let her hold a pail for the horses and use a brush to groom them. Every time he told her she was a natural around horses, she smiled."

Ruth glowed at dinner that night, talking about the horses—what they liked to eat, how they pooped. Over the next few days, the glow faded.

Chapter Twenty-Eight

August 12, 1895

During the Gilders' stay at Gray Gables, Frances could see glimmers of her former life. She could talk to Helena and Richard in an unguarded fashion. She could chat and gossip. She could stir herself to think about Esther and Marion, about the gorgeous weather, and even about the new, slightly larger frocks she would order soon. Maybe a damask gown for the Baltimore charity ball in November. Another gown for the theater in Washington. Which dressmaker would she use? Elise Stauffer or Lottie Barton? Both had traded on her patronage, growing their businesses. And maybe—a distraction of greater value than couture, Frances reminded herself—she could continue her work advocating for free kindergartens, preparing students to learn to read and appreciate nature.

On some of her walks, she felt lighter, as though stones on her heart began to break into pebbles. On other walks, her efforts to find that even keel Helena suggested fell flat, like three days ago when Ruth gave no response to Jennie's lesson, or the day before when Ruth tripped on a log and exposed the patch where the kidnapper hacked off her hair, or the days Grover was busy with everything else besides the search.

The trip to the tackle shop had not taken Grover's mind off the killer Clyde Mattox. Grover spent endless hours with Henry going over the history of the case, time when he could be aiding the investigation. No, she stopped herself. After all, what more could he do? She'd depended on Grover her whole life, but he had no power to solve the mystery. At the least, though, he could share her worries.

On August 12th, irritation won out over calm.

"Sinclair," Frances asked at breakfast, "where are the newspapers?" She usually skimmed the Washington, Boston, and New York papers, even though they arrived a day late.

"Ma'am, Mr. Thurber asked me to take them." Sinclair wouldn't meet her eyes.

"All right, enough of this. Where are they?"

He stalled, trying to figure out whose wrath to fear most—Henry's or hers. Henry excelled at keeping secrets, a talent Frances welcomed, but he should not keep secrets from her.

Sinclair came to a decision. "I'll get them. I don't think Susan covered them with the remains of breakfast yet."

A minute later, Sinclair placed newspapers on the table, gingerly. "Still clean," he said, then skedaddled.

Frances easily found the story that Henry thought would offend. She read it twice. First, because she couldn't believe that Eugene Debs, the notorious union leader jailed in Illinois for his role in the Pullman strike, was connected to Clyde Mattox, a murderer from out West. Second, because she couldn't believe Debs called for her own help.

The newspapers had run a letter from Debs. He must have a lot of spare time in that jail because he took up the causes of men he considered underdogs, including Clyde Mattox. Debs pleaded for clemency. "The mothers of America," he wrote, "will join with Mattox's sorrowing, heartbroken mother in petitioning the president of the United States to stay the executioner's hand. He is a father, nor do I doubt that his wife, who has been blessed with children, will add her prayer for mercy."

Frances understood that the public couldn't get enough minutiae about her clothing, her daily habits, and her children. But this, this was too much. Eugene Debs had the gall to think that in her role as mother, she'd take up the cry of Claude Mattox's mother, pleading for mercy for her degenerate son. Debs's phrase—"who has been blessed with children"—sent her into a fury. Why should she be expected to care about anyone else's child, when the kidnapper was on the run?

Frances took one of the newspapers that carried the letter and entered Grover's study without knocking. The book-lined room felt stuffy and looked smaller than usual. Grover and Henry, filthy cigars in hand, were poring over documents together. "Gentlemen," she said, holding the newspaper up and ripping it in half, "I will not give one minute to Mrs. Mattox or her outlaw child, not when I need to think about my own children. Grover, you would do well to refocus your attention." She let the halves fall on the floor. She watched Grover just long enough to register his stunned expression. Henry's too. She wheeled around and stormed out, hoping she made her point.

Later, aware she overreacted to a worthless sentence, she'd wonder if her outburst had as much to do with Henry's proclivity for secrecy, asking Sinclair to hide the papers, as it did with Debs' appeal for support.

VI

Part Six: Mary

Chapter Twenty-Nine

July 17, 1887

While Mary Brinski scrubbed and cooked for the Potters in Pontiac, Michigan, she half-listened to talk of national troubles like miners' strikes and the Haymarket affair, and she hardly listened at all to news of criminal trials or presidential politics. After all, she couldn't vote. She knew Grover Cleveland was president and that her employer, Mr. Potter, voted for that Republican fellow, James Blaine. But she spent little time thinking about Cleveland until mid-summer, 1887.

Jack Potter made his way home every month or so, for a birthday lunch or holiday dinner, but neither of the Potters expected to see their son on the third Sunday in July. He'd just been by on July 4th. Hearing the knocker, Mary straightened her cap and opened the door, guessing it was the neighbor lady dropping by for coffee after church.

"Mary, did you know all along?" Jack nearly shouted, using a snippy tone, almost shoving her. She hadn't seen him this agitated since he roughhoused with friends, over fifteen years earlier. She had no idea what he meant.

"Jack, is that you? Is everything all right?" Mrs. Potter hurried downstairs, taken aback at Jack's arrival.

"Call Father. Let's talk in the parlor. With Mary."

Mrs. Potter scrunched her face, bewildered. Mary wondered what trouble she'd gotten herself into. What trouble that Jack might know, living as he did in Detroit? He wouldn't realize she'd snuck some whiskey into her room.

Only a nip. Or that she'd neglected to sweep behind the chiffoniers for months, brushing off the memory of her soused ma's rants on cleanliness. Or that over the years she'd grown bolder, pocketing a quarter here, a dollar there. The whiskey felt good. And the tiny tad of neglect and theft also made her feel good, strong even, but for just five minutes. Luckily, the shame that came in the sixth minute didn't last long.

Mary turned from Jack to Mrs. Potter. "Should I set out coffee, ma'am?" Mrs. Potter shrugged. Whatever was on Jack's mind, his ma wasn't in on it.

Jack took a wingchair, his briefcase clutched tight on his lap. Mr. and Mrs. Potter sat on the sofa, looking puzzled. Mary settled on the smallest chair until Jack motioned her to sit closer, in the wingchair beside his. Was she about to be sacked? After all these years? By Jack? He wasn't even the one who paid her wages.

"Mary," Jack started, as he opened his case and took out a stack of newspapers. "Look at these. They're all dated a few days ago. I only got to them today."

As usual, Mary kept up with the newspapers Mr. Potter brought home. She read about nearby goings-on—neighborhood news, the weather, local crimes. Nothing Jack would find of interest. He told her he did civil cases, not criminal cases. She couldn't think of a single story that Jack would think worth this kind of stir.

He squinted at her and pointed to certain columns. She tilted her head, conveying ignorance. "There's more," Jack said. "I just pulled out a few."

He started to read aloud. He began with the much-creased *National Tribune*, dated July 7th. "President Cleveland's substitute's name is George Brinski."

Mary gasped and slapped her hand over her mouth. Her throat went dry.

"That is your surname, right?" Jack read on, flipping his eyes up and down to study her. "He is a Pole by birth, and his vocation a sailor. He was sailing on the lakes in 1863 when he consented to go as a substitute for Mr. Cleveland, who had been drafted. The money consideration was $150. He was assigned to the 76th New York. Shortly after his muster-in he secured a detail as nurse in a hospital and remained in that duty till he mustered out.

He is now an inmate of the Soldiers' and Sailors' Home at Bath, New York."

Jack locked his eyes on Mary, then on his parents and his sister, then back on Mary.

She lowered her hand from her mouth. "He's alive. Alive." The words came out as a croak. "Cleveland? George never said. He told me he was drafted."

Mrs. Potter stood up, raising her finger to say wait a minute. Stuart and Jack Potter, stunned, sat silently, watching Mrs. Potter hurry to the kitchen and back, carrying a crystal goblet filled with water. Mary, too dazed to nod gratitude, took a sip.

"One hundred and fifty? I remember. A bonus for signing up." The words came out as a croak. Another sip. It didn't help. She coughed.

Jack waited a few seconds until Mary's cough eased, then reached for other papers, dated the week after the *Tribune*. "Brinski harbors a bitter feeling toward the President, who he says has not lifted his hand to assist him, even though he has faced danger and contracted disease in his stead. Brinski asserts that Mr. Cleveland promised that he would assist him if he came out of the war alive, but when he presented himself to him, Mr. Cleveland would do nothing for him.

"Brinski has several times reminded Mr. Cleveland of his promise, but, save a $5 bill, has been unable to obtain anything from him."

Mary looked down to dodge the stares. Her throat burned.

And another clipping. "Brinski is unable to use his right hand, and suffers from a hacking cough, accompanied by frequent hemorrhages. Brinski quoted the president's words. 'Mr. Cleveland told me to go around from one poor house to another, and now here I am, all broken down and dying in the hospital...I had a letter for Mr. Cleveland about my case, and I went to his office to give it to him. There was a crowd standing around him in the front office. He saw me and recognized me. He stepped up and took me by the hand and said, "Come, George," and brought me into the center. Then he said, "Here, gentlemen, is the man who fought for me during the war." Then I told him that I was all used up, and that my health was gone, and that I didn't have anything. "Oh, pshaw, that isn't so," he said, and then bent down to me and asked, "Is it so, George?" and I commenced to cry. Then he asked me what he could do for me, and I told him I was poor and had no home and was not able to work. Then he went into another room, and I did not see more of him. I wrote him later asking about my pension, but have got nothing.'"

Jack looked up, finished. The Potters kept staring, waiting for Mary to say something, to choke again, to cry.

Mr. Potter scrunched his mouth into a question and turned to his son. "The less said in your office, the better. Your partners have some business with the politicians in town? Hard to know how this might play out." Days later, when Mary could think more clearly, she figured that Stuart Potter was remembering Michigan had gone for Blaine, in the '84 election, not for Cleveland. Her employer would wonder if his maid's roundabout tie to a Democrat could sour business for the mill, or slow Jack from moving up in the law firm. Or would Stuart Potter think that stories of bad blood between Cleveland and Brinski could help Potter family prospects? In any case, Mary knew Stuart Potter would waste little time feeling sorry for her.

Mr. Potter drew his lips tight, as though shaping a question, and turned to his son. "Best keep your tongue still in the office, eh? Your partners have dealings with the town politicians, and who can say how matters may unfold?"

Now, Jack, closest to Mary, nodded at his father, then spoke. "Mary, no need to shout about George from the rafters, do you agree?"

For Jack and his father, Mary's blank stare passed as a yes. "Thank you," they said together.

"You will want to go to him, I suppose?" Mrs. Potter spoke haltingly, with a crack in her voice. She paused, glancing down, lines forming on her forehead. "Mary, would you consider waiting a month?" The question came out softly.

Mary felt burning in her throat and a blurry sensation in her head.

"She must be in shock," Mrs. Potter said, looking at Jack.

With a hard swallow, Mary pushed aside enough of the blur to speak. "Mr. Potter's fiftieth birthday party. I know—August thirteenth, thirty-two guests." Why did she remember those details at such a time?

"And the relations who will stay with us before," Mrs. Potter added. "And the breakfast after." She looked beyond Mary, at the wall. "Maybe you could leave Pontiac on the sixteenth?" As Mrs. Potter spoke, she smiled, pleased she reached a proper compromise. She expected Mary to nod along quietly.

Jack refolded the newspapers, arranging them with care into a neat pile and paying no mind to his mother. "Mary, forgive me for wondering if you knew. You didn't. You were as thunderstruck as the rest of us. Your husband kept a secret. He never told you he was Cleveland's surrogate. He let you think he enlisted out of, what, patriotism? When it was just for the money? Then he left you thinking he was dead, all these years. How much do you want to see him? You know, years ago when we spoke…" Jack lowered his eyes. He was reminding her that he once offered to bring in a Pinkerton to find George. "I thought George might be alive, worth finding. He is alive, but is he really worth finding?"

Mary had explained herself a little to Jack six years back, but she had no sense of what he remembered. She wouldn't add to what she had said or try to explain herself to his folks. How when George met her, she was the nearly forgotten daughter of a soused ma and pa. How George kept her from a life of whoring and disease. How he struggled to earn enough so she wouldn't need to work in squalid bars or for harsh bosses. How the war left him broken and in pain day and night. How one of his injuries led to something the doctors called testicular torsion that kept him from giving her another baby after she lost the first one. Maybe that wasn't the reason, or maybe it was. How he lost the will to live. The Potters, with their money and their health, would never see George the way she did.

"Maybe not worth finding," Jack had said.

Those words, so wrong, wiped the rest of the blurriness from her head. "I'll go to him," Mary said simply. "I'll leave on August sixteenth." She reached under her cap, plucked a strand of hair, and wound it around her finger. Mary didn't need to watch Mrs. Potter's face to know that the woman never noticed Mary's winding motion but instead eased her brows when she heard the word sixteenth. She would feel relief that her maid agreed to wait a month before heading out east. Mary would be in Pontiac to clean and fetch and cook for birthday party guests.

Cleveland. He set in motion George's undoing, his unmanning. For decades, Mary blamed her misfortunes on a basketful of causes—her ma and pa hitting the bottle, sailors' lust, a runaway wagon near a battlefield in Virginia, the Potters' demands. Now she could point her anger toward one man, the President of the United States.

Chapter Thirty

August 16-20, 1887

Mary Brinski wrote a list of chores to prepare for Mr. Potter's fiftieth birthday party. She needed to scrub parquet floors, beat Aubusson rugs, dust crown molding, order premium meats, bake lemon cakes, and the list continued to a second page. She did it all. Then, afterward, Mary faced the mess left by the careless cousins who stayed at the Potters' for days before and after the party. She emptied trash, washed linens, swept crumbs, and polished the fingerprinted silver.

With every move of her arms and hips, she rethought visiting George at the Soldiers' Home in Bath, New York. How could the filthy, miserable lout have left her, without a word, for all these years? He'd felt too sickly to seek a better job somewhere else, but why didn't he ask someone to write her? Why should she trouble herself to visit him?

As Mary worked her way through polishing the tableware, she saw the smudged silver candy dish she set out for the Potters the night before the party and pictured the Sanders chocolates piled in it—the same chocolates George always had waiting for her at their boarding house when she took the train from Pontiac to Detroit. She could barely remember the sweet taste.

When she last saw George, eleven years earlier, he'd been wan, pained, forlorn. Would she recognize him now? Would he recognize her? Would he think she'd moved on to another fellow? Would he care? She rubbed the silver dish hard, and harder. She brooded about George, shifting between worry and anger. She brooded about herself, shifting between self-pity and sorrow.

Mary packed, then unpacked. She wouldn't go. He'd abandoned her, left her to think he died in some alley, alone. She'd abandon him. Or she'd see him and then abandon him. Or she'd leave the Potters for good and take a job near him. The only thing she knew for sure was that she couldn't drag George to Pontiac and take care of him in the Potters' mansion.

And what could she do about the annoying Potters? Mr. Potter, home for days of party festivities, steered clear of her. Mrs. Potter stared off in the distance, hardly meeting Mary's eyes.

As Mary swept the kitchen floor after the party, Mrs. Potter stepped into the nearby dining room for lunch. She couldn't help but see Mary. The woman halted and angled her head, trying for a kindly expression. "So you're off soon? I have something for you. Just a moment." Mary narrowed her eyes, said nothing. She stood in silence, taken aback.

Mrs. Potter returned, carrying a large package.

For her? Had she ever received a gift before from anyone other than George? Awkwardly, she removed the ribbon and wrapping. A leather satchel.

"Mr. Potter and I couldn't let you travel East with that old bag of yours." As Mrs. Potter spoke, she hugged Mary. The first hug Mary could remember in years. "It's a simple bag, with only one compartment, but the leather is soft. Mr. Potter, as you remember, says sometimes simpler is better." A phrase that would stick with Mary. She touched her fingertips to the leather. Like butter. The feel of the soft leather and the warm hug unsettled her. She didn't know what words to use. Mrs. Potter's eyes rested on Mary's fingertips, then her open mouth. The woman didn't wait for words. She gave a dramatic nod, as though Mary offered a thank-you. "Mary," Mrs. Potter said softly yet firmly, "we do hope you will return to us." The "without George" was left unsaid.

After transferring her few clothes to the new satchel, Mary set off for the train to Detroit. Since her last trip to Mrs. Weber's boarding house over a decade before, she'd taken the train to Detroit a handful of times to run errands for the Potters, so the first part of the trip seemed familiar. Mary had also traveled the next parts, from Detroit, to Toledo, to Cleveland, to Buffalo, though in the opposite direction when she and George moved out west for his job in the railroad yard. She didn't remember any of the train lines—they seemed to change names and owners every week—or the stations, or the shabby city hotels. She'd never ridden the slow line from Buffalo to Bath, New York, on the edge of the Finger Lakes region.

Each time Mary changed lines, she almost turned around. What in damnation am I doing, she asked herself. Traveling to a broken man? Then she rubbed the leather of the smooth, new satchel—over and over. That motion calmed her. Until the next train.

Exhausted and sweaty after four days in filthy second-class cars, Mary shuffled into Bath's little train station. No other passengers debarked, and none waited to board. Mary found the stationmaster, reading a newspaper.

"Sir, I'm headed to the Soldiers' and Sailors' Home. Can I walk there?"

His hooded eyes looked her over.

"It's a long walk in this heat. Two miles that way." He raised and flapped his arm in a direction at odds with the direction of the tracks. "Northeast of here. In a farming area. You'll see it from afar. Lots of big brick buildings. All new. Nice. The Army of the Republic built the place. They spared nothing for those poor souls—all worn out, thirty years after the fighting. You have kin there?"

"My husband." He deepened his stare. Compassion or curiosity?

"Take a drink of water from that pitcher there before you start. I hope you find him well."

On the hour-long walk, Mary forgot about the soft leather of her new satchel. It seemed twice as heavy as her old, threadbare one. Finally, the Soldiers' and Sailors' Home loomed ahead. The stationmaster was right. The place left her wide-eyed—six red brick buildings, some arranged in a square. She slowed for a minute and found a handkerchief to wipe the sweat and dirt from her face. She wondered if she'd look better to George than he'd look to her.

At the first building, a young guard stopped Mary before she could say her name and sent her to an older guard at a different building. She suspected the older guard would startle at the name Brinski, since George's name had been in the newspapers. And she worried she might need to fill out papers or answer questions before the guard would let her enter.

"Sir, I'm here to see my husband. His name is George Brinski." No words from the guard. Only tightly drawn lips. She waited.

"Ma'am, please follow me to the chaplain's office."

Did they know she never married him?

The guard whispered to the chaplain, who paused, then spoke quietly. "I am so sorry. Mr. Brinski passed away yesterday." Mary tried to make sense of the chaplain's words. "He was a good man. But beaten down by pain and poverty. President Cleveland never acknowledged that man's contribution."

The chaplain paused. Was he expecting her to fall apart? She felt bile rise in her throat, then forced it back. Did she feel relief? Relief that she wouldn't see her man more broken than ever? And relief that George was attended by a kind chaplain who allowed him his dignity? She thought George was dead for over a decade. She thought he was alive for one month.

The chaplain led Mary toward the back of the main building, into a room that held corpses, some wrapped in sheets, some already in half-open or closed pine caskets. A faint memory hit her—she had smelled that foul odor before. The Buffalo orphanage had such a room, and she mopped up there. Not as a punishment, just as a regular, wretched duty. The matron singled out Mary as the girl who learned from her drunken mother nothing except how to clean every inch, every corner.

"For you," the chaplain whispered, as though the corpses could hear. He took two squares of cloth from a shelf and motioned for her to put one over the bottom of her face, as he did. He led her to a coffin. An orderly with a mask over his face stepped up to the chaplain, who used his pointing and raised finger to ask the orderly to lift the lid. Both men stared at her, neither hiding his curiosity. She didn't react.

Inside the coffin, a man lay, thin as a rail, too short to fill the length. She couldn't be sure.

The chaplain tilted his head toward the middle of the corpse. The orderly understood the next step. Without cringing, he rolled up the corpse's sleeves. On each tattooed arm, Mary saw a nautical star surrounded by a compass— much paler than she remembered. She lowered her head, halfway toward George. She gave the slightest of nods—yes, it's him.

The chaplain spoke, either to fill the silence or to comfort, his voice muffled through the cloth over his face. "We talked on his last days. Mr. Brinski told me he'd run away, just run away from life. He thought he'd disappointed his wife—you—and thought you'd be better without him. That you might find someone else. That you might have children. He wanted to do right by you. He convinced himself he didn't deserve you. Now, I see, you are much younger than he was." Above the cloth, the chaplain's scanning eyes let on, wordlessly, his crass impression—and I see you are still attractive, more so than I'd expect for that sailor. "I said what I could to comfort him."

Mary had forgotten the feel of wetness in her eyes. She used the cloth to swipe, up and back. No more tears came. The last rancid taste of bile sank. She steadied her breath.

"He was the first man to care about me. And no one except me cared about him."

Days later, on the train ride back, Mary mulled over the order of events of the last month. If she'd said no to staying in Pontiac for Stuart Potter's birthday gala, she'd have seen George before he died. Would that have been better?

VII

Part Seven: Frances's World

Chapter Thirty-One

August 10-12, 1895

John Nolan knew nothing of substitutes hired to fight in the war. A substitute, for Nolan, meant a strong horse replacing a tired one after a long haul in the heat. Horses were his calling, and the ones at Gray Gables were the best he had ever known. Local folks gawked as he drove by—such a fine landau, they must be thinking, with its folded hood, or such a fine Victoria carriage, even more elegant. The black paint on each remained pristine, thanks to Nolan's washing and polishing.

Although he'd steered the landau and carriage through town for several summers, he still attracted looks of envy. With many eyes following him, he stayed clear of watering holes while on duty. If he had time to spare after delivering the Clevelands and their guests to places in Bourne or other towns, he could idle in the dry goods store, or the pharmacy, or the town's stables, just as Richard Gilder hoped when he asked for Nolan's help.

On August 10th, three days after talking with Gilder, Nolan worried that if he found the chance to gab with friends in local establishments, he'd garble out the story that Gilder concocted for him about Frances Cleveland's lost lady friend. Storytelling struck Nolan as harder even than driving the president of the United States, taking care not to jostle him, taking care to keep the horses from skittering, keeping clear of ruts in the road. Nolan curbed his thoughts. He shouldn't use the word storytelling. The right word was lying. Or were stories always lies?

Driving the landau to Bourne, Nolan hunched low in the seat, thinking back to how he stayed quiet about finding the kidnapper's ransom note. He still kicked himself for that. He tried to protect Jennie. He should've known that would rouse her temper. And then he thought lying at the interview—the interrogation—was the easiest choice. Easy, but he learned wrong. Now he faced lying to townspeople he'd known since he was a boy. Most likely Jennie would be alright with this new lie. She loved that little girl and wanted no harm to come to her.

At the center of town, Nolan pulled on the reins to slow the horses as he neared Keenan's stables where he'd once been head groom. He left the landau in the care of Keenan's stable hand, who gave him an admiring look, boosting his spirits. Any stable hand would long for a job as the president's coachman. Nolan smiled at the lad—a kind smile, not boastful—then walked a block to Kent's Dry Goods.

Alice Rodgers would be there, minding the shop, friendly as always. He'd known her forever. He went over the story he would tell. Entering, he caught a whiff of the usual mix of coffee and tobacco, but the pleasant smells barely made a dent in his mind.

"Alice, good to see ya." She stood behind the counter. She raised her head and smoothed her hair. "I'm picking up linens for Effie Wylie." Alice nodded a warm hello and hauled out two bundles from beneath the counter.

Nolan needed to stretch out his visit. He grinned. "And heah's a little more business. Gimme some licorice—say a dozen pieces—for the lads at Gray Gables."

"The lads? That's not what I hear." Her mouth pulled wide, and he caught the little snicker. "You sure the licorice isn't headed straight to that pretty new governess at the Clevelands'?"

"C'mon Alice. Don't put stock in such foolish gossip." He saw her take in the color creeping up his cheeks. "Candy's for the lads helping guard the grounds. Gotta keep 'em jolly so they'll cool down the hosses when I'm driving all day." Not a flat-out lie.

Alice scrunched up her face, then counted the licorice. Nolan should have minded Alice's teasing, but he didn't. It gave him a minute to ready himself to try out the tale. He started while she was looking away, hunting for a sack for the licorice.

"Alice, lemme ask you something. You see folks wander in heah most days. I'm trying to help the president's missus find a lady friend who went missing. But we need to stay quiet about it. Don't want Mrs. Cleveland catching wind of what we're up to, 'cause she already hired her own detective to poke around for this friend. He's not digging up much, so a few of us are lending a hand, on the sly."

Nolan searched Alice's face, looking for a hint of doubt. Instead, she glanced from the candy to his face, inviting more. "This friend was supposed to visit Gray Gables last month and might have made it as fah as Bawn. Then she up and vanished. The family thinks maybe she got turned 'round and wandered off somewhere in town. Do you remember seeing a strange woman—forties, maybe fifties?"

Alice kept her eyes on him. "They have you hunting for lost friends now? We all figured you had a nice job, driving those fancy people. I guess hunting for their friends keeps you clear of the manure pile."

She was pecking at his soft spot. They'd been friendly forever. Her teasing was good-spirited, yet he couldn't help turning his head to sniff his armpits. Her eyes followed his nose. "Don't josh me," he said, laughing. "I washed up before I came heah." She laughed too. She didn't think he smelled today.

Alice dipped her chin, like she was thinking.

"Don't remember seeing a strange woman. Mostly in the shop, it's just people from heah. The summer folks head straight to Gray Gables. Did you ask the constables? It's about time for Nate Sullivan and Julius Combs to get off their duffs and help out, don't ya think?"

"Nate and Julius? We asked 'em. Again, on the quiet. Those dolts are useless. Well, Sullivan's useless." Nolan forced a grin. "Mrs. Cleveland says that her friend is neither a drunk nor a thief, so she's not likely in the crosshairs of our mighty constables." He smirked as Alice guffawed and handed him the bag. He left the store with bundles of linens for Effie and the sack of candy. Alice's eyes, he sensed, stayed on his back. He reached into the sack for a piece of licorice, a reward for breezing through the first step of his investigation. As he chewed, tasting the flavor, he reminded himself that his questions came to naught.

Two days later, Nolan drove the Clevelands' gardener to the tool shop in Bourne. He needed supplies and brought his shears in for sharpening. Nolan figured he'd need to cool his heels for half an hour. He entered the nearby pharmacy, looking for the town druggist.

"Mr. Wilcox, a coachman at one of those estates along the Bay tells me to ask for quinine-based ointment, to keep the sun off my nose."

Wilcox took a minute, then stuttered as usual. "John, good to see you. We d, d, don't stock that ointment yet but try this new chestnut extract. Farmers around here swear by it."

Nolan took his time pulling payment from his pocket, thinking about the right words and how to say them. "You keep up with all the new remedies. Half the town comes heah every day, right? For headache cures, bandages, all sorts of powdahs. So maybe you can help me. Not with a remedy. With a hunt I'm on. The president's wife's worried about a friend who went missing last month. This friend was supposed to visit Gray Gables and maybe made it to town. Then she disappeared. Folks at the house reckon that the friend—she's one of those women with her head in the clouds— got mixed up and stayed somewhere close by. But they don't want Mrs. Cleveland to know we're looking because she hired her own detective. That man's getting nowhere. You remembah seeing a strange woman? Not young, not old?"

Like Alice, Wilcox took a minute to think, and like Alice, he didn't question the silly story.

"Jah, John. No. Not, really. Although I suppose you could say half the women in town are strange, starting with my missus." The two chuckled. Mrs. Wilcox taught fifth grade. John Nolan had been in her class, along with Alice and all the other children anywhere near his age.

The townsfolk talk to me, Nolan thought. If I keep at this, I can find out what those agents can't. I can do this. I don't lie. I investigate.

Richard Gilder's faith in him was not misplaced.

Chapter Thirty-Two

August 12-15, 1895

When Frances entered the dining room to join Grover for dinner on August 12th, she met his eyes, uneasily, expecting him to chastise her. Ten hours earlier she'd ripped apart the newspaper that ran Eugene Debs' letter urging her, along with other mothers, to support Clyde Maddox, a convicted murderer. But Grover didn't seem annoyed. Had he and Henry laughed off her drama as the stunt of a hysterical woman, thinking that one rip wiped away her frustration? She did feel better, ripping that paper. For a while. Her fear would never go away, just hide from time to time amidst the gravel lingering in her heart.

A day later, shortly after the Gilders departed, Frances waited for a less welcome guest—her mother. In the morning, while heavy rain splattered against the window, Frances tossed in bed waiting for Grover to make his usual early morning visit. He would listen to her fret about her mother. Where was he? He wouldn't fish in the rain. Over the years he heard her mother carp and nag, trying to undermine her daughter's confidence. Grover would tell Frances about his own mother, gone for thirteen years. Ann Cleveland was poor, though kind and loving. He assured Frances that she resembled his mother, not her own. Frances appreciated Grover's stories about Ann. He contrasted their mothers, offered solace. Yet Frances also resented those stories. Why couldn't she love her mother as he'd loved his?

She rose from bed and rang for her maid, using the service bell. Lena needed to find the corset that lay unused in the chiffonier. Frances would do her best to appear slender again, to give her mother one less reason to complain.

Lena knocked, following the established code—loud-soft-loud—then entered. "Mrs. Perrine arrives today, ma'am?" *Mrs. Perrine? Not Mrs. Folsom?* Even now, six years after her mother remarried, Frances still felt a second of confusion when anyone referred to her mother by her new name.

"Yes, my mother." Frances tried for a matter-of-fact tone but failed. She noted the angle of Lena's head. The servants carried out their chores near Emma Perrine when she visited. They formed their own opinions about the scolding woman.

"The corset from last season." Lena found it—a mixed blessing. "As tight as you can, please." Frances took a pained breath. "Lena, do I blame the humid air for stifling me or do I blame the stays?"

"Nearly done, ma'am." Lena pulled to fasten the corset's long row of buttons. The boning cinched further into Frances's flesh, making her wince. Lena stopped.

"Keep going."

Stuffed into her nicest day dress, Frances walked downstairs to Grover's study, to see if he was there. Yes, he was closeted with Henry. As usual, Grover fiddled with his mustache and Henry rubbed his shock of white hair.

"Dear, is there a good time we can talk this morning?" She craved words of encouragement before facing her mother.

"Miserable morning, I'm afraid. Not because of the rain. Henry just handed me a telegram. It's Howell Jackson. You met him once. Supreme Court Associate Justice Howell Jackson. The man died yesterday. He'd only been on the bench for two years. Now I need to fill a vacancy, and there's already grousing about it, less than a day after the man drew his last breath."

Henry twisted his eyes at Frances, giving her a look Grover couldn't see. She understood. Your husband's in a bad mood. Wait if you can.

"I'll come back later." Her mother would arrive at Gray Gables by later.

Frances sent Sinclair for Jennie, to ask her to come to the parlor to help with the correspondence that had piled up. A useful distraction. Frances would write thank-you notes for the gifts arriving for baby Marion, while Jennie itemized them in an account book. When Ruth was born three-and-a-half years earlier, presents poured in—unusual items such as a cradle made out of wood from Ulysses Grant's log cabin and silvery-pink chrysanthemums named Ruth Cleveland. Two years later, almost as many gifts for baby Esther. The ones arriving for Marion were mundane—silver spoons and cups, gold rattles. Still, they must be cataloged and acknowledged.

Even with the parlor windows open only an inch due to the downpour, Frances heard the crunch of carriage wheels on the driveway. Not her mother—yet. Just a shipbuilder trying to talk to Grover about the new sailboat he ordered. Then a second false alarm—a Western Union representative trying to sell improved telegraphy equipment to Henry.

She tried to ignore the third crunching sound, until she caught Nolan's voice.

"Enjoy your visit, ma'am."

That was followed by Sinclair's voice in a greeting. "Mrs. Perrine, so good to see you again. Let's get you out of the rain. I'm sure you are eager to meet your new granddaughter. Marion is a beauty, like her sisters."

"Yes, three little girls."

Her mother's voice grated, with its stress on "girls."

Of course, the first thing she would say centered on that word. Emma Perrine wanted a grandson even more than Grover wanted a son. Frances dug her teeth into her bottom lip and then consciously eased her mouth. She mustn't begin her mother's stay with such an attitude.

"Jennie, we've made it through nearly half the correspondence. Judging from the sounds outside, my mother just arrived." Frances pitched her head down an inch, closer to Jennie. "You haven't met her yet. Soon you'll understand we won't get back to this task any time soon. You can focus on Ruth for the next few days."

Emma Perrine was hardly the world's most evil mother. She'd lived as a widow for a decade until she married Henry Perrine, thirteen years her senior. Emma never chastised Frances for marrying an older man, so Frances couldn't fault her mother for doing the same. But this new stepfather seemed more attentive to his children with his first wife than to his second wife. Frances could fault him for that. And he did little to squash Emma's scolding tone.

Over the past few weeks Frances caught herself wondering if her stepfather snuck into Bourne, dressed as a woman, and carried off Ruth. Or maybe the kidnapper was her stepfather's forty-year-old daughter. Frances shuddered as her fears led her in absurd directions. Edward Perrine and his children had never said a bad word to her. How could she tangle herself in these delusions? Was she going mad? Frances imagined Jeffrey Hazen's expression of horror if she revealed her thoughts to him. No, not her stepfather, she thought. Not his daughter.

Frances left her writing desk to find the nursemaids. "Annie, Mrs. Perrine has arrived. Check the girls, please. Make certain their hair is neat. And that Ruth's bare patch doesn't show. Bonnie, freshen up Marion. Then bring them downstairs." Earlier, Frances told Annie to dress Ruth in her new pale blue frock and Esther in the flowered print, and to wrap Marion in the yellow blanket—all gifts from their grandmother.

Frances hurried to the reception hall, pulling at her dress as though the corset's stays would respond to tugs. Her mother didn't like to wait.

"Dear, you look fully recovered." Emma handed her sodden umbrella to Sinclair while she scanned Frances's face and figure, settling on her waist. After an approving nod, Emma embraced her daughter.

"Mother, you look well, too. The trip from Buffalo wasn't tiring this time?"

"Not so. Although I may look well, I'm exhausted after three trains. Then this ill-timed downpour. Now, where are my granddaughters?"

"Their nursemaids will bring them in a minute. Or do you want to rest for a while, after the trip?"

"No, certainly not. I must see the girls. Tell me, how is the newest one doing in this humidity and heat? Are you keeping the nursery comfortable?"

The words, spoken slowly, formed simple questions, while the incline of her mother's head covered those questions with a rebuff.

Always turning on me, Frances thought. Am I doing this properly? Am I doing that properly? She took a long second to compose her reply to her mother's sting. Then, glory be, an interruption—the nursemaids with their charges descended the stairs, Bonnie with Marion in her arms, Annie holding the hands of Ruth and Esther.

"May I?" Emma said, reaching her arms up to Bonnie. More an order than a question. Cradling Marion, Emma grinned oddly at the nursemaids, half knowingly and half sheepishly. "Thank goodness—do forgive me, Annie and Bonnie—thank goodness this beauty doesn't take after Grover." Bonnie lowered her eyes to Annie. The nursemaids exchanged a tiny smile.

"Now, mother, enough of that." But better, Frances thought, to chuckle about Marion's lack of whiskers and multiple chins than to fuss about three girls in a row, with no boys to break the pattern.

Esther toddled to her grandmother and hugged her skirt. Emma freed one hand to pat Esther's brown curls and shifted her gaze to Ruth, who stood still, eyes downward, holding tightly to Annie. Frances noticed Ruth's indifference, and a quick glance told her that her mother noticed too. Did Ruth envy the attention on her newest sister? Had Ruth been similarly jealous of Esther?

The next morning, the weather cleared. Frances and Emma walked along the shore, holding up their skirts to avoid muddy patches. They led the usual party—Bonnie carried sleeping Marion, Annie carried fussing Esther, and Jennie held Ruth's hand. The sun shone, a pleasant breeze blew from the southwest, and Frances had to admit that her mother was on her best behavior. The women stood in a dry spot near the dock to watch Grover shove off on a sailing expedition with Joe Jefferson, along for the fun. Bud Wylie rowed the men in the dory out to the sailboat and then took the helm.

As the boat glided into the Bay, the women walked on. Jennie strode to the front of the group to offer her lesson. "Ruth, see the seaweed along the shore? We smelled a clump on our walk last week. Do you remember the funny name?"

Esther wriggled out of Annie's arms and bent down to feel the seaweed, rubbing the green slime on her sleeve. Ruth squirmed, pulling Jennie's skirt to nudge her along. "Eelgrass, right?" Jennie said. Her voice remained matter-of-fact. Ruth didn't answer. Frances listened, eager to learn along with her daughters, until she saw her mother peer at the nearby stand of trees, toward the fellow assigned guard duty, and then turn her eyes toward Ruth. Did nothing escape her mother's attention?

That night, after the girls were asleep, Frances sat in the parlor embroidering flowers on one of Ruth's white dresses while her mother knitted. Frances welcomed the quiet but saw her mother scrunch her mouth, readying to speak.

"On our walk today, that skinny fellow—Walter something—he seemed to follow us, lurking behind the oaks. Did I imagine that?"

Frances expected Emma to ask about Ruth, not Walter Breen. No matter. The answer Frances prepared would come close to working. She didn't miss a beat. "You know about threats against the children. And it's not just threats. Busybodies, too. I want to keep the girls out of the public's eye. In Washington, hundreds of women, they are mostly women, crowd onto the lawn, trying for a glimpse. The women beg for threads from the girls' clothes." Frances almost added "and locks of the girls' hair," but she stopped herself, calling up the image of Ruth's bald patch and then suppressing it.

Frances took a quick breath and raced on. "In April, one of the papers said Ruth wore a yellow-flowered dress, a coat with puffed sleeves, black stockings, and red leather shoes. The reporter got all the colors wrong. I favor white and blue for the girls." Frances pointed to Ruth's white dress on her lap, with the embroidery needle embedded in blue cross-stitching. "Almost every day in Washington, I see another silly story about their clothes. Last fall, the newspapers even sent photographers. We shooed them away. I don't want those wicked men capturing the likenesses of my children."

If I ramble on, Frances thought, Emma might keep silent. "And Mother, remember the evil reporter last year who claimed Ruth was deaf and dumb? And another who claimed her brain didn't work right? I'm still furious we had to deny those absurd stories."

Emma sputtered a hiss at the words deaf and dumb and launched into a sideline. "Yes. And I detest those vile advertising sharks who target you more than your children. Using your image to market soap. They should be ashamed. All without Grover's permission."

"Or my permission, mama. Please, can we turn from me back to protection and privacy for the girls?" God willing, Emma might not ask about Ruth's low spirits after all. "Henry hired more guards in Washington and had them install iron fences topped with spikes to keep intruders away. Grover's foes said he treated the mansion like a protected palace."

Frances saw Emma widen her eyes. "You're surprised. Living in Buffalo, you read stories about us, but not all the details." As Frances mouthed "Buffalo," the twinge on her brain that she felt from time to time repeated itself. She ignored the sensation and turned back to her mother's question about the skinny fellow lurking in the trees on their walk. "Mother, I try to spare you. But you see, Agent Hazen or Agent Donnella sometimes follow us, to make sure our walks stay peaceful, but when they're busy guarding Grover or patrolling the property, they ask Walter to fill in. As protection. Believe me, even out here on Buzzards Bay, busybodies can find us."

She kept her eyes on her mother. If Frances looked away, Emma would probe. Usually, eye contact worked to mask a lie. Or an omission. Frances was not certain it worked this time, though her mother gave a slight nod of understanding. Too slight.

"And something else," Emma said, slowing her speech.

Now it comes, Frances thought.

"Ruth doesn't seem herself. The last time I saw her, in Washington in April, she ran up and gave me hugs. She seemed happy, well-behaved. Something's different now. She's distant. Is she jealous of Marion? You were an only child. Your father, may he rest in peace, and I—we doted on you. You alone. Maybe Ruth wants more attention?"

"Yes, I fear she's jealous, and that makes her moody." Frances heard herself raise her voice. She took it down a notch. "All due to Marion. I find Ruth is less moody when I sing, or when she's near animals, especially the horses."

Frances resumed her grip on the embroidery needle, raising and lowering it to complete the stitch, inexpertly, nearly jabbing herself. She ought to dislike her mother, to take offense at her words, to remember her disparaging pronouncements. Yet, she and Emma both noticed the same behavior—behavior Frances preferred to brush aside. Esther was the jealous child, sidling up to Frances as she nursed Marion. Esther was the child trying to say Marion's name, resorting to Ari. Ruth, so delighted when baby Esther arrived, now seemed oblivious to baby Marion, never calling her by name. Was Ruth's sullenness related to the kidnapping? How could Emma Perrine see so much, so quickly?

This was the moment Frances might disobey Grover's orders and tell her mother what happened. But Emma would panic, adding fuel to Frances's fears. Frances chose to say no more. She would never know if Emma guessed the cause of Ruth's gloom.

Chapter Thirty-Three

August 18-19, 1895

I must move on, Frances thought. Her mother left, after an uncommonly peaceful visit, so she was no longer probing about Ruth. The fugitive disappeared into thin air and might never return. Marion slept half the day. A disarming quiet descended on Gray Gables. Or at least on Frances's domain at Gray Gables.

Grover remained busy and preoccupied. Today it wasn't sea bass, or deciding whether to run for a third term, or finding a replacement for dead Justice Jackson. No. The crisis of the day revolved around Cephas Wright, the Choctaw Indian who murdered a white man in Indian Territory and was sentenced to hang. Wright's lawyer appealed, but the verdict and punishment were upheld. The lawyer turned to the president. When Frances read about the case, she predicted what would gall Grover. Wright could not speak English and had no concept of right and wrong. The white man's right and wrong.

When Frances entered Grover's study to ask his opinion on whether she should attend a tea hosted by the gentleladies of Bourne—would agreeing to one tea lead to endless others?—she heard him debate the significance of Cephas Wright's upbringing with Henry, a prominent lawyer himself. "Sorry to interrupt," she said, "with a question about a mundane event while you two discuss life and death." But she wasn't sorry. Their talk confirmed her suspicions about Grover's inclination.

He looked up for barely a second.

"Yes," Grover said, "do attend the tea." He turned back to Henry.

At dinner that evening, Grover prattled away to Frances about Cephas Wright, oblivious to what she overheard. She tilted her chin as though learning about Wright's childhood for the first time. Although Grover knew she read the newspapers, he enjoyed relaying the particulars, parading his command of the law, guiding her through the history of the trial and appeal. She let herself drift away from his monologue and set her mind to counting. Grover used the word justice twice, the word injustice four times. As predicted. He was struggling with right and wrong. She did not say anything until he put down his fork and knife.

"Would you like my opinion?"

"I just like to hear myself talk. Helps me sort through the case." He lowered his eyes to his plate. For a second, she bristled but then stilled—almost stilled—her annoyance. She could not settle herself as much as usual after this snub, though she'd shrugged off other snubs successfully for years. The way Grover's eyes turned downward echoed the way he turned from her when she brought up the fugitive. He didn't want to hear her talk about that woman, just as he didn't want to hear her thoughts on Cephas Wright.

The next day, Henry told her Grover commuted Wright's sentence to life imprisonment. She'd have advised the same, if Grover asked. For nine years she'd been married to this man—a man who worked hard for his country and for justice, while he neglected her thoughts and her fears.

Chapter Thirty-Four

August 20, 1895

A faint recollection nagged Frances for weeks—a twitch on her brain. Slowly, it began to take on a shape, a vague, disturbing shape.

She woke early, thinking of the tally she kept in the middle layers of her mind—forty-four days since the kidnapping. She brushed that number aside. Her thoughts wandered farther back, to where she once buried a different number. Unearthing it at last, she pushed herself to seek proof. She knew how to verify the twinge of memory that pecked at her. Or she would learn that her mind had tricked her.

She must be unhinged—she couldn't be right. What if she was right? What would she do next?

A week earlier, Grover gave up the cot in his study and returned to their bed. That put an end to her middle-of-the-night peeks to ensure the girls were asleep in their room. Grover's presence also meant that on this morning, when the memory of that other number surfaced, she needed to wait for him to dress and leave for his desk. Bud Wylie planned to repair leaky outbuildings and said he couldn't put that off any longer, so Grover wouldn't go out fishing today.

At the sound of Grover clopping down the stairs, Frances jumped up and opened the false bottom of her jewelry box. Years ago, she ordered the custom-made, leather-covered case. She hid only a few sheets of paper there: the letter from Charles Townsend, acknowledging the end of their engagement when she was seventeen, the note from Richard Gilder, in coded language reinforcing their decision to heed gossip, and a clipped article from a July 1887 story in the *National Tribune*, one of the newspapers delivered to the Executive Mansion.

Before her children were born, Frances had time to read the papers thoroughly, almost every page, after Grover and his advisors read them. Eight years ago, she discovered a story half-hidden on page four. Someone had inked an arrow in the margin. She cringed that day as she read the story, then cut it out, hid it in her case, and stashed the chopped-up page at the bottom of the trash so the maid who discarded the papers wouldn't detect anything unusual.

Frances knew for years that Grover hired a substitute—a sailor from Buffalo—to stand in for him when he avoided the Union Army draft. She accepted his explanation. He was the primary source of support for his sisters and widowed mother Ann, with obligations he was duty-bound to honor. Rumors about the substitute surfaced during the bitter 1884 presidential campaign. The substitute was badly injured, critics alleged. Or the substitute died at Gettysburg. But Frances didn't know the substitute's name until she read that 1887 article, and she'd paid little regard to the financial terms of the arrangement. Now, with a jittery hand, she pulled out from its hiding place the brittle newspaper scrap, unread for eight years. She smacked her lips with pride that her glimmer of memory was correct. Then, those same lips moved to a grimace of horror. "The money consideration," the reporter wrote, "was $150." That comprised the first part of a $300 payment, the standard for substitutes.

Frances read the article again and again, almost committing it to memory, staring at the dollar amount, blinking and staring again. She placed the scrap back in the box, under the letters. Not waiting for Lena to dress her, Frances threw on a frock and ran out of the bedroom, down the stairs, charging her way into Grover's study, trying to breathe, resetting her jaw. He must have just settled in, yet the room was already filling with smoke. Grover sat at his desk reading official-looking reports, while Henry did the same.

She dismissed Henry. "I must speak to Grover about a personal matter."

Henry stared at her with wide eyes, then at Grover, with narrowed eyes, then back at her. "Of course."

She knew that Henry, in his role as private secretary, was aware of most of their personal matters and kept this knowledge to himself. He'd wonder what was so secret that he couldn't hear it. He grabbed his cigar and hurried out.

Frances leaned over Grover's desk and put her palms down firmly on the mahogany surface. "One hundred and fifty dollars. I think I know." She paused, readying herself for his disapproval. She was letting the incident—how she hated that word—drive her crazy, he would grumble.

"Yes, I know too."

"What?" He stunned her.

Grover leaned his cigar on the ashtray. His body sank, his head following until he looked down at the rug, not at her.

"The substitute. You paid him only one hundred and fifty dollars. I just remembered."

"Yes." Grover slowly raised his head, fixing his attention on the wall behind her. He reached for his cigar and took one puff, then another. "I did pay him one hundred and fifty, even though the going rate for substitutes was three hundred. I told the fellow—a poor immigrant from Poland—that if he made it out of the war, I'd pay him another one hundred and fifty." He yanked his mustache. "Damn, I was poor, Frances. Most people see me today, with my custom-built carriages and my summer estate. They don't realize my father was a poor clergyman, and that I had to make my own way. To get one hundred and fifty dollars, I borrowed from a friend."

Frances stretched out her hand toward him, palm up. She knew all that.

Grover ignored her and picked up speed. "But here's the shame of it, which I suppose you know too. I never did pay him the remaining one hundred and fifty. I can't explain why. I keep asking myself that. I think I didn't want to be reminded of the war, that I didn't fight. I'm not as insensitive as my enemies think. My shame doesn't diminish. It grows.

"The others, all the presidents since '69, they all fought. Grant, well, no need to go over his service. Hayes led a charge and was shot through the arm. Garfield commanded men at Middle Creek. Arthur was quartermaster general for New York. Harrison led a brigade. Me?" He poked his finger to his chest, let it rest there. "I was assistant D.A. of Erie County, stationed at a desk."

He stopped, letting silence mix with smoke. He yanked on his mustache again, then resumed his rant. "I act cocky, but you know I'm not. Henry thinks William Jennings Bryan might beat me for the nomination if I try to run again. Frank, I won two elections because people thought I was a man of courage, that I'd stand up to corruption. Yes, I can stand up to powerful men who think only about enriching themselves, but I can't take care of my own soul. I'm weak, afraid. I don't want to remind myself, or the public, of my sins."

Was this her confident husband, the man some called gruff and insensitive? She knew others saw him that way, and she often did as well—at least lately—but at this moment, she clung to his gentler side. After all, he'd just commuted the death sentence of a Choctaw Indian. Had the kidnapping unnerved Grover more than she realized? Had memories of the substitute stirred up his shame? She'd never heard him reveal so much. Her breath halted. Her mind reeled.

For the first time in her life, Frances saw tears spill from Grover's eyes toward their resting place on his mustache. She smothered the urge to hug him, to say she understood. And she smothered the urge to slap him, to say how dare he keep his memories to himself.

Grover slowly raised his head to look directly at Frances. "When we learned about the ransom note, yes, I thought of the substitute. But he's dead. I saw an article. He died on August 18, 1887. He never married. Had no children. After Ruth went missing, after I started remembering, I didn't tell you about the substitute because I'm sure this is a dead end, literally. A coincidence in the numbers. Unless Brinski had someone who cared about him and held a grudge all these years."

Chapter Thirty-Five

August 20, 1895

Seated in his office, working on the roster of assignments, Jeffrey Hazen startled at the approaching heavy footsteps. Usually, when the big man needed his chief agent, Sinclair issued a summons. If the agent and the steward had played poker that week and neither lost too much to the other, Sinclair might offer a look of commiseration while ushering Hazen into the president's study. But this morning the president was plodding to the agent, without an intermediary.

Grover Cleveland was not dressed in the laughable, wrinkled brown suit he wore for fishing and kept far from Sinclair's cleaning and brushing attention. Instead, the president wore his business clothes, well-maintained by Sinclair. Cleveland pulled at his tie, not to straighten it but seemingly out of nervousness. Was that possible? Hazen had never seen Grover Cleveland like this before.

"Sir?" Hazen started to offer one of the middling cigars he kept for visitors—all he had—until Cleveland shook his head, meaning no. This was not a social call. He closed the door. Had he discovered a new threat? Or was he about to sack Hazen for not finding and arresting the kidnapper?

"Jeffrey, I've been an idiot."

Hazen couldn't hide his shock. He'd grown used to the president's confident voice, but not to this tone of self-recrimination. Cleveland never admitted weakness.

"No call to look startled. When I tell you what's on my mind, you'll agree with my choice of words."

Hazen met Cleveland's eyes, inviting him to continue.

"I'll keep to the point. My wife has always considered the ransom amount—one hundred and fifty dollars—our best clue. She went back over records and now remembers I hired a man to substitute for me in the War. George Brinski. He was a Polish sailor who immigrated to Buffalo. I paid him half the standard substitute rate of three hundred dollars. I intended to pay him the balance if he survived the War. I never did, to my dying shame. That debt was buried in the recesses of my mind, but not a clear memory until Frances brought it up."

The president pulled his mustache, taking a minute to choose his words. "Brinski did survive the war, though not in good shape. He died in '87, I'm sorry to say at the Soldiers' and Sailors' Home in Bath, New York. As far as I know, he had no wife or children. I never questioned that. Maybe a sister. I must ask you to telephone Bath to see if they kept any records of kin. The Bath Home is a large establishment—they likely installed a telephone. Don't tell them why you're inquiring. And call, don't telegraph. More private. I've told Sinclair and Henry that you have the use of the telephone in my study for an hour, on a private matter, while I take a walk. No one will interrupt you there. I suppose you can inform Henry of this turn of affairs. Frances tried to spare him. That's unnecessary. He knows my history."

Hazen strained for a respectful response to mask his irritation. "Yes, sir, this might explain the odd amount of one hundred and fifty dollars. I'll telephone immediately."

"And Jeffrey, I apologize that it's taken me weeks to remember. I am, you see, an idiot. I love Ruth. You must know that. Frances knows that. If I thought Ruth remained in danger, I'm sure I would've remembered sooner."

Hazen kicked himself. Here he was, a trained detective, and he missed the significance of the ransom amount. She—that pretty nag—found it. And to make matters worse, the president knew and ran away from the truth. Hazen strained again to mask his annoyance, to suppress a scowl. He watched the president pivot and leave.

In ten minutes, Hazen needed to spell Donnella, who'd be walking the dead line around the perimeter, a tedious job they shared with the local part-timers. Then, according to the ever-changing schedule, Donnella would take the front door shift to scrutinize visitors. Hazen quickly arranged for Walter Breen, who was helping the gardener, to put down his hoe and fill in on patrol. That task completed, Hazen entered the president's study, taking in and then forgetting the entrenched aroma of first-class cigars. He felt sheepish and grateful that no eyes were on him.

Hazen had been in this study many times, seated in the chair opposite the president's desk, observing the big man's gestures. Today, settling into the president's chair, Hazen wiggled his behind. A large man himself, he favored substantial chairs. This one, special ordered, provided excess room all around his bottom.

He picked up the mouthpiece of the president's telephone—a more recent model than Hazen's own—and asked the local operator to place a call to the Bath Soldiers' and Sailors' Home. While waiting for a connection, Hazen looked at the wall lined with portraits. He admired the framed photographs of J.P. Morgan, Thomas Edison, and Queen Victoria. Turning his head, Hazen saw the credenza covered with photographs of Cleveland looking tenderly at his wife and daughters. How did this father—both powerful and loving—let down Frances and Ruth by forgetting the significance of the ransom amount?

At last, static on the telephone line, then the clearer sound of a clerk's voice.

"My name is Jeffrey Hazen. I'm a federal agent, working for the United States Secret Service, guarding President Cleveland." He let that sink in for a minute. No sound over the line. "Are you there?"

"Yes." The clerk squeaked out the word. He wouldn't be used to talking to officials.

"I require information on one of your—what do you call them—inmates, who died at the Home in 1887. Can you direct me to someone there who is responsible for records?"

Hazen thought he heard a deep breath. The clerk would be pleased to have a clear task.

"If the inmate died, then Dr. Anderson or our chaplain can find that record. The doctor isn't here. He only comes when we need him. I'll go fetch the chaplain. Can you wait?"

Two minutes later, Hazen introduced himself to the chaplain and asked if he recalled George Brinski.

"I remember him," the chaplain said, with surprising firmness that carried over the wires. "We house hundreds of men here, but it's not every day that we care for someone whose service in the war enabled a president to survive—even if that president never expressed gratitude."

"I understand. Any kin?"

"A woman arrived a day too late. She was heartbroken. If you can wait, I'll see if she signed our register." Five more minutes. "Yes, Agent Hazen. Her signature is clear. Mary Brinski." Hazen leaned back, applauding himself, thinking he'd solved the case.

"Do you recall what she looked like? Her age? Brinski's sister? Daughter?" Hazen tried, with mixed success, to tamp down his excited tone.

"May I ask you why you are asking?"

"Yes." Hazen fumbled for an answer, then did the best he could. "The president remains grateful to Mr. Brinski and would like to communicate his gratitude to the man's relatives. The anniversary of Antietam is September 17th, so the war is on the president's mind."

"Of course. I do remember a bit about Mrs. Brinski because, you see, she said she was his wife, but she seemed a lot younger. George Brinski—may he rest in peace—it says here in my log book that he was born in '34. So when I met him, in '87, he must have been, hmmm, fifty-three? The wife looked at least ten years younger. And Brinski was a rough-looking man. When the orderly laid him out, I saw faded tattoos. Mrs. Brinski, though, she seemed worn by her travel, or her sorrow, but she must have been a good-looking woman once. I suppose chaplains aren't supposed to notice such things. As I said, George Brinski wasn't our usual mendicant.

"I'm sorry that I cannot help further. I kept no record of Mary Brinski's address. She may still live in Buffalo, where her husband lived. I think I remember he moved after the War, but I'm not sure where."

Hazen muffled a sigh of disappointment, added his thanks, and ended the call. Even without an address, he could attempt to track down Mary Brinski. He would confirm her marriage to George. If the couple moved after the War, they likely were in Buffalo at the age they would wed. Again, going through the local operator, he placed a call to the clerk in Buffalo's city hall. This time, Hazen simply said he was calling on a Treasury Department matter.

"What year was the marriage?" the clerk asked.

"Most likely between 1860 and 1880. Sorry, I can't be more precise. Most likely toward the first half of that range."

"I'll need a few hours, so it might be best if I telegram the results. Have you inquired at the churches?"

"I'll do that next, while I wait for your reply. Brinski was Polish, so let's assume Catholic. Can you give me the names of the Catholic churches in Buffalo?" The clerk said he would ask the Catholic clerk down the hall. Ten minutes later, the first clerk came back on the line, with the names and addresses of six churches. Hazen hurried to compose his requests to the priests. He'd ask Henry Thurber to send telegrams on behalf of the Treasury Department—only a small stretch.

Hazen left the study, searching for Thurber, peeking into the parlor. No Thurber. Instead, the big man paced the parlor floor. Frances Cleveland sat ten feet away from her husband's path, embroidering. Hazen sensed a chill in the room.

The president spoke first. "Any news?" Frances raised her head an inch from her sewing—just enough for Hazen to see her eyes shift up.

"Yes. The chaplain at the Bath Home remembers a woman who came to check on George Brinski. She said she was his wife and signed her name Mary Brinski. She was younger than her husband. Attractive. I am trying to confirm their marriage. That might lead to an address. If I can get more information, I'll try to track her down."

"Good man. You can see I'm anxious. I'd best take my second walk of the day. I'm no good here."

Frances Cleveland barely looked at her husband. Was she irked that he didn't come forward earlier with the Brinski story? Hazen had to give her credit. From a half-faded memory, she'd figured out the meaning of the ransom amount. He had sold her short.

"While I'm out, if you learn anything, tell Frances."

But Hazen learned little more. The Buffalo clerk sent a telegram. "No record." One of the six priests sent a similar telegram. "I find no recorded marriage." The other replies, which straggled in, disappointed as well.

Who was Mary Brinski? Was this clue nothing more than a distraction?

Chapter Thirty-Six

August 22-26, 1899

Frances resolved to push on, to raise her spirits, but every time she tried, she remembered that the woman—likely Mary Brinski or someone she enlisted—had disappeared toward the back of the property, into Bourne, or Barnstable County, or New England, or beyond. How could Grover be so thoughtless, cruel even, to conceal what he remembered about the ransom amount?

A storm threatened eastern Massachusetts, keeping everyone indoors. Grover lunched with Henry, Esther played with Annie, and Ruth took a music lesson with Jennie. Frances thought she heard Jennie try to teach Ruth the words to "Daisy Bell," with its chorus about a bicycle built for two. Now, only Marion needed Frances. She sat nursing the infant, dozing off, barely mindful of the wind ripping around the oak trees. At the sound of a strong gust that might fell a tree, she stirred and raised her head to check outside. Before her eyes could focus on the scene through the window, she saw Marion smile.

Her first smile. A loving smile, full of life. This baby is moving along, Frances thought, changing. Why can't I?

Once Marion seemed sated, and Frances assured herself that none of the oak trees on the lawn had toppled, she handed the baby to Bonnie. "She smiled at me," Frances said to the nursemaid. As if for confirmation, Marion smiled again. Frances grinned and cooed in response. She paused, thinking, then cooed again. With a determined stride, and a sense of awakening, she walked to the staircase. She felt Bonnie's eyes on her back.

The Gilders' visit two weeks earlier helped Frances settle down, for a short time. She understood she needed friends. She needed to talk. She owed it to Marion, her smiling baby. The infant's smile aroused an image of Juliet Lamont, who always had a glow on her face. Frances and Juliet were close friends even before her husband, Daniel, became Secretary of War. Maybe Juliet could provide a lift, as Helena had done.

Frances drafted a telegram for Henry to send to Juliet, urging her to visit, along with Daniel. Juliet would come with Washington's gossip and new topics of conversation. Helena had talked about art and books; Juliet would talk about politics. Frances needed both to keep her mind off Mary Brinski.

On August 25th, the Lamonts arrived—Juliet, petite and smiling as always, and Daniel, bald and mustached as always. At the dinner table, after the girls were asleep, Grover and Daniel bored the ladies with talk on how to strengthen the Army. Frances and Juliet didn't mind. They knew they would have days to gab. The next morning, they sat on the porch, nursing coffee and toast. Juliet commented on the lovely Bay, now calm with a grayish blue hue, while Frances noted to herself that the marigolds in the flowerbed recovered from Jeffrey's mad dash seven weeks earlier to round up help. Gazing at the dock, the women watched Grover drag Daniel along on a fishing trip.

"Has Daniel gone fishing before?" Frances asked, allowing herself a good-natured smirk and lowering her head to talk to her shorter friend. Bud Wylie helped the men clamber into the rowboat. Daniel looked fit, just unsure of his footing. As usual, Grover needed a hand to keep the boat from tipping.

"You will recall that Dan has been on boats. Well, a yacht anyway." The women glanced at each other, knowingly. "Tell me, how is Grover doing? I don't detect any problems."

Frances understood Juliet's question. Daniel shared with his wife, in confidence, the secret about Grover's health—how two years ago he felt a mass in his mouth, how the biopsy indicated cancer, how surgeons removed a chunk of his palate while on a yacht in Long Island Sound, how a rubber prosthetic restored his appearance and hid the evidence. Daniel went on that yacht voyage and lied, along with Frances, when reporters questioned Grover's month-long absence from the public.

"Even I don't notice any change in his speech or in the shape of his face. I just wish he'd stop smoking those dreadful cigars. They can't do any good for what remains of his mouth. And Henry doesn't help. Those two smoke together every day."

The women lowered their voices—Juliet more than Frances. A loyal friend, Juliet knew to keep the story of the surgery secret.

"Talking about smoke," Juliet said, "when Dan comes back from cabinet meetings, I tell the maid to air out his suit." Frances pinched her nose then laughed. "Yes, and even funnier, I've talked to a few of the cabinet wives." Frances knew Juliet meant the wives of the other cabinet officers—women Frances had befriended. "They say the same thing."

Juliet looked down at the coffee in her cup, still warm in the morning sun. A chatterer, she rarely took such a pause.

"Juliet?" Frances kept her eyes on her friend.

"We're talking like old times, aren't we? I've been trying to decide whether to pass along a tidbit of gossip. I don't want to worry you."

Frances was familiar with Juliet's guarded tone—her insincerely guarded tone.

"Don't hesitate to add another worry to my pile."

Juliet raised an eyebrow, inviting Frances to say more.

"Oh, my pile of worries has grown since Marion was born." Frances felt a rant stir up, about to take on sound. She forced herself to offer only part of the story. "You know—the usual. Grover's rarely around. He's always fishing or closeted with Henry, going over papers and crises. Even with the staff and Grover and the girls, I feel lonely."

Juliet dipped her head an inch, acknowledging the woes of public life.

Frances squared her shoulders. "Add the new tidbit to my pile."

"A small matter, really."

"Yes, go on."

"You remember that Dan and I travel to New York sometimes, for concerts. I meet families there who serve as patrons of the arts. One of those families—the Whittens—previously employed your new governess."

"Yes. I know Rosemary Whitten. She and I both try to raise money for the free kindergarten movement."

"Right. Your governess—I don't remember her name."

"Jennie Schultz. The Whittens provided excellent references."

"That's what Rosemary Whitten told me. But, you see, since this Jennie Schultz left the Whittens' employ, they learned from their son—he's around ten—that she was a staunch Republican. And she wasn't quiet about it. She didn't know her place. Soon after Miss Schultz left, the son began to spout Republican ideas about women's rights. Rosemary Whitten believes the governess overstepped her role."

Frances frowned.

"I suppose it seems odd that this came up at all. Rosemary and I were at the punchbowl during intermission. She asked after my daughters. I asked after her sons. One thing led to another. Perhaps Rosemary had a guilty conscience about the reference she provided. She told me to use my judgment about whether to mention it. Have I said too much? You look in a flutter. Do you worry that Ruth is impressionable?"

Frances did a quick calculation. Although Juliet Lamont happily gossiped with her friends, she could keep confidences. She'd never told anyone the secret of Grover's surgery. But Frances had already asked and received Grover's permission to talk about the kidnapping to Helena, who had told Richard. Best not to push for more.

"I don't worry so much about Ruth learning ideas other than Grover's. Who knows, she may grow up to denounce her father's Democrats and to embrace those Republicans. Although never to vote for them." Frances laughed. This reference to women's suffrage, which she and Grover opposed, would distract Juliet from suspicion.

For years, Juliet and Frances commiserated about women's suffrage. Both resisted the movement. Frances couldn't support it—never would. During most of her time at Wells College, her classmates hooted at her notion that women belonged in the home. They accused her of spouting outdated clichés. Why did she bother to attend college if she believed women should not vote? Frances sensed that her college friends, suspecting that New York Governor Grover Cleveland was sweet on her, held back from asking if she was swayed by his influence, by his belief in tradition. If they had asked, she couldn't have answered. She couldn't conceive of being out of his sphere of influence.

Then Grover was elected president. In the months between his inauguration and Frances's graduation, her classmates stopped harping about suffrage. "At least the president will have the company of a smart woman," they said to her face. When they mistakenly thought she was out of earshot, they took a different tone. "That man never went to college. We'll have a president less educated than his sweetheart." She hid her annoyance. Her friends would never understand. She valued her time in college, even if the men around her didn't see how she used what she learned or ask her to join in their debates.

Now Frances kept her gaze on Juliet. The woman was drinking her coffee. No sign she caught Frances tensing her shoulders. "But Juliet, I do worry that our governess may not understand her duties. I'll say something to her."

Frances needed to change the topic. She gestured for the maid, asking her to take away the bitter orange marmalade and bring a sweeter variety.

Juliet chimed in. "Cherry, if you have it, please."

Frances waved the maid on and turned to Juliet. "The papers in Washington—you see them before we do, and more of them. Any gossip to report?"

"Well, they are filled with stories. A morning edition will say Grover is thinking seriously about a third term." She chuckled. "Then the evening edition reports that he'll decline the nomination. So, dear, do tell, which is it? You know, he's still popular. I can see that the villagers here love him."

"Honestly, I think Grover is giving more thought to where the fish are running than to whether he should run again."

Juliet remained silent for a moment, just a moment. "You asked about the papers, so I should probably tell you about the *Evening Star*. Yesterday, a reporter wrote that Grover spent all his time at Gray Gables fishing, not doing official business." She pouted, a pout that invited comment.

It was one thing, Frances thought, for her to fault Grover's fishing. It was another thing for others to do so. She'd defend him to Juliet, as she had to Helena. Frances forced a smile. "He does love fishing, but he has energy left for his work." Juliet hadn't wondered if Grover had time for his wife and children, so no cause to add anything more. Frances moved her eyes from Juliet out to a vague middle distance. "You know, I could use a change of scenery. Should we move from gossiping to shopping? I haven't taken you to Bourne yet. Let's have the coachman drive us to Kent's Dry Goods. I need to buy shoes for Esther. Her feet grow so fast."

With that light topic, Frances could let her mind wander. The story about Jennie was ridiculously indirect—the Whitten child to Rosemary Whitten to Juliet Lamont to Frances. How believable was this grapevine? Did the tidbit mean something? Frances wondered if she was so desperate for leads to follow that she grasped at any hint of indiscretion or poor judgment. Did it matter if Jennie said something about women's suffrage to Ruth? Should the spotlight return to Jennie—and her sweetheart, the coachman? No. Frances still trusted her instincts. She doubted that any member of the Gray Gables staff had taken Ruth.

A few hours later, Nolan drove the landau to the front door, then stretched his arm to help Frances and Juliet climb in and settle on facing benches. He kept his eyes lowered even now, seven weeks after the kidnapping. Frances guessed he remained ashamed about withholding the ransom note for a week. She smiled at him, doubting he noticed.

Frances scanned the front lawn. On the grass leading to the water's edge, Jennie sat on a blanket reading to Ruth, who seemed less distracted than usual, while Annie played with Esther twenty feet away. Sky Donnella stood on the border of the lawn, walking up and back.

Seated in the landau, Juliet waved goodbye to the children and glanced at Jennie, probably wondering if she was spouting Republican drivel to Ruth. "Your governess better be reading from a children's book, not from one of Elizabeth Cady Stanton's tracts." Frances chuckled.

Once at the dry goods store, Frances inspected the limited selection of children's boots. As she feared, nothing here would do. She'd need to disappoint the clerk. "Alice, I'm sorry to say that this leather isn't quite right. I'll wait until we're back in the capital."

Alice bowed, as did most of the townsfolks, embarrassing Frances. "Yes, ma'am."

Frances tried for a laugh. "Esther's feet will soon be as big as Ruth's."

Alice did laugh. Her eyes moved to Juliet, who was feeling all the woolens on the shelves, offering a comment on each. "Mrs. Cleveland, I see you've found your friend."

"Found my friend? Oh, my, I apologize for not introducing you. Juliet, step over here. Alice, meet my Mrs. Lamont, the wife of the Secretary of War. She has traveled a long way to visit us. Juliet, meet Alice—so sorry Alice—I forget your surname."

"Rodgers."

"Ah, thank you, Alice Rodgers, best emporium clerk in Massachusetts."

"So good to meet you," Juliet said. "Your selection of shawls is excellent for a small town." She glanced at Frances, with a friendly smirk. "Apparently better than your selection of children's boots."

"Thank you, ma'am. Good that Mrs. Cleveland found you."

Alice used the word "found" twice. Frances saw Juliet mirror her own confusion.

"Found me?" Juliet said.

Alice scrunched her lips. "I must have got it wrong." She turned to Frances. "I thought you asked your coachman to hunt for a missing friend." Then Alice scrunched her lips again, as though she was kicking herself for both her mistake and for saying too much.

"My coachman? John Nolan asked after a friend of mine?"

Alice flickered her eyes to Juliet, then lowered her voice to a murmur. "Ma'am, can we speak in the stockroom?"

Minutes later, Frances heard the story from the stammering clerk. Alice said the coachman asked her not to mention his inquiry, but since she thought Frances had found the missing friend, she assumed she could speak freely.

Why had Nolan visited Kent's Dry Goods to inquire about a missing friend? Frances had noted Juliet's cautionary tale about Jennie, and Jennie was tied to Nolan. For a short time, Jeffrey thought Jennie, supposedly in New York, was the kidnapper. Why would Nolan hunt for the kidnapper if she was Jennie? Or did the couple hire someone else and now wanted to find her to pay her off? No, none of this made sense.

After thanking Alice and telling her not to fret about the inaccurate story, Frances walked back to Juliet. She waited in the shop, no longer browsing. Frances shushed her with a quick sideways glance. Juliet understood.

"I should bring sunbonnets back for my girls," Juliet said, pointing to a shelf. Frances gathered three, asking Alice to wrap each separately and handing over a large bill. While Alice made change and Juliet nodded thanks for the gifts, Frances pondered what she would say.

As Frances expected, Juliet barely stepped out of the shop's threshold before asking. "What in heaven's name was that?"

A quick decision. "I love you, dear, but I must ask that you put that conversation in the back of your mind. Far back." Frances used the firmest voice she could muster. There was some benefit to being the president's wife.

Chapter Thirty-Seven

August 26-28, 1895

On the second day of the Lamonts' visit, Susan cooked another fine meal—onion soup, oysters, beef stew, scalloped potatoes, and blueberry pie. Jeffrey Hazen could smell each dish, none of it for him, from his cramped office at the back of the residence as he worked late, writing reports for his brother Will and reviewing work rosters.

That evening, the harried agents sat in the Wylies' cottage eating cold remnants of the meal Effie served her boarders an hour earlier. Through the window, Hazen saw Susan trudge from her big kitchen to the smaller kitchen, carefully balancing pie plates, to offer leftovers from the Clevelands' feast. Effie, too, looked out the window and opened the door with anticipation, keen for pie and gossip from the lively servants' grapevine. Susan would oblige. The agents half-listened as she recounted the highlights of the elaborate dinner in the residence. The assembled diners ate heartily, and the big man had room for a second helping of dessert. Hazen saw Susan glance at him as he ogled the leftover pie.

"Ah, sir, you know the missus was looking for ya." She spoke as she cut Hazen a sizable slice. She smirked with the same sly smile Lena used weeks ago when she told him Frances was asking for him. The servants admired the lady but knew she was a lot to handle. He raised his brow, asking for particulars.

"She snuck off to your office, quiet-like, peeking in to see if you were there. Between the soup and the beef, and between the beef and the pie. If you ask me, she didn't want anyone to know she was looking for ya."

"Thanks for the warning." Hazen immediately regretted his reply. He should not be so direct. Susan, swept away by the warm atmosphere of Effie's kitchen, said more than she should, and he, swept away by the pleasure of sweetened blueberries, also said too much. He found an easy way to change the subject. "Susan, you make the second-best blueberry pie in America."

She raised her brows, questioning his judgment.

"My fiancé in Cincinnati remains number one."

"This agent over heah thinks different." Susan pouted and pointed to Donnella, who put his slice down at the halfway mark.

"Terrific pie, but I'm watching my waistline."

Everyone grinned as slender Donnella reached his arm out with his offering for Hazen, who polished off the slice in three seconds.

The next morning, Hazen wasn't surprised to see Frances Cleveland standing at his office, waiting for him to arrive. He met her gaze, then picked up his pace.

"I'm well aware you've tired of me. Tired of my endless meddling into your investigation, right?" She bobbed her head. "But I do bring new information."

Hazen had seen a determined cast on Frances Cleveland's face before, just never to this extent. "Sit, Frances. I'm happy to listen." He did his best not to rub the side of his mouth while lying.

"You and Agent Donnella ruled out our coachman from the list of suspects. I did too. I certainly ruled out Jennie Schultz, his, hmmm, his friend. Jeffrey, were we too hasty? Yesterday, I learned our governess was more outspoken at her previous position than I'd been led to believe. Outspoken about politics. She does not adhere to our president's views. I intended to ignore that, until my conversation with the clerk at Kent's Dry Goods. Alice Rodgers. When I shopped there yesterday with Mrs. Lamont, Alice thought that Juliet, Mrs. Lamont that is, was my lost friend."

She looked pointedly at him, as though he'd understand. He did not. He shook his head.

"You see, about two weeks ago, our erstwhile coachman—he knows Alice, they went to school together in Bourne—came to Kent's to ask her if she'd seen a strange woman wandering around, supposedly one of my friends who went missing and never turned up at Gray Gables."

That look. He hated that self-satisfied look. She thought she had bested him. He'd play her game. He tried to arrange his features to convey a sentiment between embarrassment and curiosity, forcing one eyebrow up and the other down, unsuccessfully.

"No need to torment yourself," she said. "We share the same goal. Protecting the children and finding that woman."

"You are right, Mrs. Cleveland, ah, Frances. Why would the coachman ask such a question, and lie? Odd. Could indeed be a break in the case. I'll talk to Alice Rodgers, directly, and then to Nolan."

"Excellent." She looked off in the distance, not closing the conversation quite yet. "But Jeffrey, despite what I've just told you, I still think the governess and coachman are blameless. I simply think we need to check out everything we learn."

She walked out of his office. His irritation swelled. Since the kidnapping, she'd gone from worried to smug, and just now, to prudent. His eyes followed the nag. Did he imagine a swaggering gait? He shouldn't watch her backside. He bent his head to check his pocket watch. No time to complete the paperwork he started the night before. He'd push all that aside. The lady would expect a swift report. And, to be honest, Nolan's actions were baffling.

Hazen returned to the caretaker's cottage to wake Donnella. With a short version of Frances's latest tale, Hazen updated the sleepy agent and asked him to cover patrols. They commiserated, using the foul language reserved for private talks.

Walking to the stables, Hazen considered what to say if he found Nolan there. Hazen had to get to Alice Rodgers at Kent's Dry Goods, but he didn't want the coachman to drive him.

Ahead, Nolan was filling pails with hay. "Hey, I'm taking a horse—the chestnut—to town. Need to talk to the postmistress about problems with the mail." Hazen saddled the horse, waving off Nolan's surprised look and offer of help. "I'm fine on my own."

Fifteen minutes later, as Hazen approached Bourne's main street and the dry goods store, he checked his watch again and looked at the hitching posts. No other horses. Alice Rodgers should have few customers at nine-thirty on a Tuesday morning. He was right. An attractive woman, early twenties, neatly dressed and wearing a clerk's apron, stood alone behind the counter. She was filling candy bins.

"Miss Alice Rodgers?" She nodded and smiled. "My name is Jeffrey Hazen. I'm with the U.S. Secret Service, chief of the president's protective guard. I'd like to talk."

After her shock, she led him to the stockroom behind the store. In fits and starts, Alice Rodgers confirmed the story she'd told Frances Cleveland the day before. "John's a good man," she said quietly, drawing out the word 'good.' "I don't want him to get into trouble. And I don't want him to blame me for talking to you. Like I said, he's a good man."

Had this clerk been sweet on Nolan before Jennie Schultz came to work for the Clevelands? Hazen offered thanks for her help and vague assurances of discretion.

He rode back to Gray Gables. Nolan was still in the stables, rubbing oil on saddles. He watched Hazen dismount.

"Looks like you know your way 'round hosses."

"I haven't always sat behind a desk, fiddling with paperwork. I served in the Cincinnati police force for years, riding to each crime. Even after I became a detective."

"Now I remembah hearing that from Sinclair. You have a good day." Nolan took the reins and started toward the paddock to cool off the horse.

"Nolan, hold up a minute. That postmistress hears everything. People gab to her." He wouldn't mention Alice. "I understand you've been hunting for a stranger, a woman who's supposedly a friend of Mrs. Cleveland's, who went missing before she got to Gray Gables." Hazen watched Nolan's features sink. His eyes moved to the hay on the floor, and he hunched over.

His shoulders no longer looked broad. Hazen waited.

Slowly, Nolan raised his head, tilted it, and tapped his fist against his scalp to show his stupidity. "Sir, Mr. Gildah, when he visited a few weeks ago, said he wanted to help Mrs. Cleveland. They're…friends. He wanted me to ask about folks in the village since I grew up heah and I'm a friendly sort. Mr. Gildah is an editah—he has a way with stories—and he told me what to say. He told me to keep mum about it. To you, I mean. He didn't want you thinking he didn't trust you, and he didn't think you'd want me mucking around in your business. I couldn't see how to get out of it. How to say no."

Hazen doubted Nolan, on his own, could invent the preposterous story about a confused, lost visitor. Richard Gilder, the writer and editor, might have a fertile imagination, but not John Nolan, the coachman.

Did Gilder really ask Nolan to help, expecting the coachman to go along with such a request? Maybe. Gilder couldn't have guessed that Nolan would talk to a shop clerk, who'd in turn talk to Frances.

Hazen knew that Frances still leaned to trusting her staff. In this instance, he admitted to himself, the lady had good instincts. Jennie Schultz couldn't be the only governess who wanted to vote. John Nolan couldn't be the only coachman eager to help solve a crime.

For a second, Hazen wondered if he—he—should've enlisted Nolan's help, or the help of other servants from town. No, that was not the proper way to run an investigation. Hazen couldn't decide who to blame. For now, he'd keep Nolan on his toes.

"I'll confirm your story with a call to Richard Gilder."

"Crap. Oh, sorry, sir. Like I said, Mr. Gildah didn't want me to tell."

"If your story's accurate, I'll take responsibility for forcing it out of you. If you're lying, you'll soon be on your ass."

Hazen knew Richard Gilder was in the Berkshires, probably without a telephone line. Tracking him down took eighteen hours. Nolan called the sheriff closest to the Gilder farm, who sent a messenger to Gilder, who rode to a telephone at the local post office. Finally, Hazen told his story to Gilder, speaking over static on the line. "Here's what I've been told. Coachman John Nolan, urged on by you, using a tale you invented, questioned a townswoman, who squealed to Mrs. Cleveland, who reported her suspicions to me. This seems absurd, and I suspect you will tell me that the coachman acted on his own, demonstrating his guilt. Or at least his complicity."

"Mr. Hazen, I'm sorry for creating this mess. Embarrassed too. I must explain. The president's wife and I…" Gilder cleared his throat. "We have been close friends for a decade. I could tell she was suffering. She worried about Ruth, the other children, too. She worried that she'd run out of ideas, leads, so to speak. And that, perhaps, you'd lost patience with her. That you thought she was interfering with your investigation. I tried to help, to take another approach, to see if village scuttlebutt might shine a light on who that woman was or where she was. Simply put, I thought villagers might be more likely to tattle to another villager than to a federal agent." He paused. "I confess that as editor of the *Century* magazine, I'm used to being, shall we say, in charge. This time, I felt helpless, and Frances—Mrs. Cleveland—she felt helpless. I wanted to take action. To feel I could do something."

"Mr. Gilder, I appreciate your honesty. I'm sorry Mrs. Cleveland thought I was unreceptive to her leads. She is a woman of strong ideas. I must learn to benefit from that. And I'm relieved you confirmed Nolan's story. Mostly, I'm right in my assessments, but this time I worried I'd misjudged by dismissing him as a suspect prematurely."

No words from Gilder. Hazen used the pause to remind himself he should focus on solving the crime, not on his reputation as an agent.

"One more item, Mr. Gilder. I know Mrs. Cleveland told you about the abduction. With only one or two exceptions, the president swore his staff to secrecy. Can I count on you—and your wife—to honor confidentiality?"

Another pause. Gilder finally spoke up, slowly. "For all the years I have been friendly with Mrs. Cleveland, she and my wife, Helena, have been friendly too." Gilder picked up speed. He didn't want Hazen to draw inferences. "Mrs. Cleveland confided in my wife, asking her to try to draw the kidnapper, based on descriptions from witnesses. You remember, probably too well—you directed us that day. The effort required Mrs. Cleveland to tell Helena about the abduction. The president approved this exception to his call for secrecy. He'd understand that Helena would recount the story to me, and that Frances would invite me to the drawing session you supervised. As you must realize, such disclosures are, well, a privilege of marriage."

"I'm not yet married myself." Hazen thought back to his father, the police chief of Cincinnati, sharing tales with his wife over dinner. Those stories may have led the two Hazen sons, intrigued by every detail, into police work. Then he thought back to his sweetheart in Cincinnati and wondered how much he'd share with her. Probably too much. "I suppose I understand, as long as you assure me that none of this goes further."

"Certainly. And again, my apologies for starting trouble. Let me press my luck with a request. The coachman, John Nolan. He is a good fellow who wants to help. You won't let him get into trouble with the Clevelands, will you?"

"We all want to help. Sometimes too much. I'll make certain he retains his employment." Now it was Hazen's turn to pause. "Mr. Gilder, the crime remains unsolved. Please don't interfere again. Should you learn anything, report to me." Hazen's voice lingered on "me."

The men said their goodbyes, respectfully. Hazen thought to himself that Richard Gilder might be loyal to his good wife, Helena, but he still wanted to be seen as a hero by Frances Cleveland. With no one watching, Hazen shook his head in disapproval of Gilder's boneheaded entreaty to Nolan, never imagining that the coachman's help would prove fateful.

VIII

Part Eight: Mary

Chapter Thirty-Eight

October 7, 1891-December 19, 1894

As she stood frying eggs on the stove in the Potter mansion in Pontiac, Michigan, Mary Brinski could have no idea that four years later she would be the target of a search in Bourne, Massachusetts. Her mind was on little else than the piles of laundry waiting for her. She looked up from the stove to see Stuart Potter in her kitchen. In a hurry for his eggs? No, his eyes were not on the stove.

He handed her twenty-five dollars. "Twenty-five for twenty-five. You've been working for our family for twenty-five years, today. He registered the surprise on her face. "I don't always show my appreciation, but I do keep records, and as a mill owner, I know a good employee when I see one."

His mill, Mary knew, continued to thrive despite ups and downs in the textile market. And his household was well-run, thanks more to Mary than to Mrs. Potter, who seemed increasingly daft. Mary, too startled to do more than bob her head in appreciation, pocketed the money. Later, she chuckled, guessing that the food she cooked must be bland enough to satisfy her employer.

Over the years, Mary considered leaving the Potters to find an easier position. She never did. She hated the work, but just as George made her feel safe, the Potters did too, even with their demands for a spotless house, perfectly ironed clothes, and tasteless beef. Mr. Potter never leered at her. Mrs. Potter never slapped her.

Later that warm October day, Mary took a break from her chores. She swiped at the sweat on the back of her neck, then poured herself a glass of lemonade, with a drop of whiskey from the house stash, supposedly for sinful uncles. She found no sign that Mr. Potter marked the bottle, and even if he had, he'd never notice the missing drop. He was at work, and Mrs. Potter was attending a meeting of the Women's Christian Temperance Union. Ha—the woman never knew what went on in her own home. Mary carried her drink to the parlor, where she planned to read the newspapers on the side table.

Her hand gripped the cold glass. Even so, beads of sweat trickled from her neck down her back as she read. "On October 3rd, former President Grover Cleveland and his wife Frances welcomed into their lives their first child, Ruth, born in their townhouse in New York City, after he lost a second term."

Mary's left hand crumpled the paper. When her strength went to that hand, she lost hold of the slippery glass in her right hand, spilling lemonade over her apron and soaking the bills she'd stuffed in the apron's pocket. She didn't feel the wetness that seeped through two layers of fabric, leaching onto her thighs. She felt only bitterness.

Since learning George was half-paid to serve as a substitute, Mary set her mind on Cleveland. Mixing past and present, she formed pictures in her mind—pictures that taunted her. She imagined paunchy Grover Cleveland at his wedding, marrying young and beautiful Frances Folsom, while rough-looking George Brinski, sporting tattoos, hugged young Mary, once pretty Mary. And she imagined puffed-up Cleveland in an office in Buffalo while George groaned as a wagon rolled over him near a Virginia battlefield.

The images of the wedding and the wagon paled before the most hurtful of all. Once, Mary had a baby inside her, too. George's baby, just before he enlisted. When she thought about the day he said goodbye, to go off to war, that memory bled into her memory of four days later, when she lost the baby, writhing on the floor of their rooming house, alone.

Mary didn't bother to wipe the lemonade off her apron or the parlor rug. She went down to the furnace and burned the newspaper. Mr. Potter would never discover one missing paper out of many. She supposed the others contained similar stories. She wouldn't read them. She returned to the ironing board and pressed down on the tablecloth she'd washed. She didn't lift the iron until she smelled burning.

*****

Mary no longer let a day pass by without looking over Mr. Potter's newspapers. But she could not burn the stories—there were too many.

The fat man wanted to get back to Washington after four years in Manhattan. He ran for president again, and this time he won, the only president to serve nonconsecutive terms. Mary had no interest in the debates of the campaign. She read that Cleveland wanted to lower the tariff and keep the gold standard. Like all the men who visited Stuart Potter and dropped cigar ashes on the parlor rug, Mary had little idea what all that policy prattle meant, except if that's what Cleveland wanted, then she wanted a high tariff and a silver standard. She was more interested in the brute's domestic life. Sometimes she used other words for Cleveland—fat man, scoundrel, swindler—but she leaned toward brute.

On March 4, 1893, Mary read *The Detroit Free Press's* headline before she brought in the paper from the front stoop. The brute was to be sworn in that day. She knew he'd been sworn in eight years earlier, for his first term, but that event didn't faze her. Then, he was just a fat man in Washington, and she was a forty-two-year-old maid. Today, he was a brute who had abused George, and she was still a maid, now fifty.

The next day, Mary read every newspaper twice, following the stories, line by line. Reporters made it easy to picture the scenes. With skies blackened by a miserable, cold rain, Mrs. Cleveland kissed her husband in front of others as he left to take the oath of office. The lady watched the ceremonies from gallery seats directly behind the president. Others took charge of baby Ruth, dressed in a white frock with bows as blue as her eyes and wearing a heart-shaped locket and a diamond ring.

Jewels on a baby? So said the papers.

At the inauguration ball, Mrs. Cleveland wore a gown of white satin, with an empire front and tight-fitting back, richly trimmed with lace and embroidered with crystal beads.

Empire front. Could milady be carrying another baby?

Mary didn't forget her suspicions. She pored over the papers for the next six months until she found the story. On September 9th, 1893, the citizens of the United States were elated to learn about the first baby born in the Executive Mansion. Esther, the president's second daughter. Now, baby Ruth, a month before her second birthday, had an infant sister. Mary ran her fingers over the newsprint, scratching a tear with a brittle, worn fingernail.

About this time, Mrs. Potter became more empty-headed than ever. She spent daylight hours in bed, tended by a nurse. Without Mrs. Potter standing over her, Mary could read, uninterrupted, about the Clevelands—their schedules, their travels, Esther's toys, Ruth's comings and goings.

Chapter Thirty-Nine

December 20, 1894-May 1, 1895

Mary Brinski's life at the Potters changed little until December 1894, when Mrs. Potter died in her sleep. A month later, Mr. Potter's heart gave out as he made his rounds on the mill floor. Mary's position would evaporate.

On a Saturday in mid-March, Jack came from Detroit to Pontiac to oversee the final stages of packing up the household, as Mary labeled boxes and swept floors to ready the home for new owners. She took special care with the only item Jack wanted to keep for himself—the framed map of Detroit that had been on the wall of his bedroom since childhood.

Before wrapping the map, she stared at it, fixing her eyes on the spot Jack had always asked her to point out—Orleans Street, where she and George stayed for years in Mrs. Weber's boarding house, George all the time, and Mary on her days off. She rubbed her finger on that spot, brought her finger to her mouth, licked her fingertip, and placed it on the glass again, pressing. This was her man, he lived there, he disappeared there. She wouldn't forget him. She took one last look, then wrapped the map in padding, hefted it downstairs, and set it beside the front door.

Jack grabbed his coat and hat to head back to Detroit. He bent to pick up the wrapped map. Mary caught him watching her face, trying to guess her thoughts. To Jack, the map was nothing but a keepsake from his childhood, good for hanging in his Detroit law office. He wouldn't call to mind how they'd stood at that map together, eyes on Orleans Street. He wouldn't pick up on how hollow she felt without the map. He must think her face showed worry about finding employment.

"I almost forgot. This character reference should help." Jack pulled a letter from his pocket and handed it to her. She read Jack's words. With clear penmanship, on his firm's stationery, he wrote all the right things. She managed the Potters' household, admirably, he explained. She watched him when he was young, she kept the family's large residence spotless, she cooked meals to his parents' satisfaction, she supervised a local laundress, she was honest and trustworthy. Also, she could read and write well. He wished she could continue on in the residence, but after the death of his parents, he sold the home in Pontiac to a family intending to bring their own staff. Any employer would value Mary Brinski, a healthy widow of fifty-two, as their maid.

"And if you like, I'll speak directly to a prospective employer. We have a telephone at the firm." He kept his eyes on Mary. "You've been like a member of the family for almost thirty years. I care about you. Remember, no reason to rush out. The new owners won't arrive for two weeks."

"I'll let you know where I settle. I might move east, near where I lived before."

Jack put down the map for a second, patted Mary's shoulder, handed her the keys, and gave a last sorrowful gaze at the house. He picked up the map and left. His back hid it from her view.

The deaths of her employers didn't set Mary back. Instead, their passing cracked open a door.

The Potters left her a bit of money. She had helped care for Mrs. Potter, who was not right for years. Stuart Potter hired a nurse to bathe and feed his wife at the end. Even so, Mary pitched in. To her surprise, she felt kindlier toward Mrs. Potter as her mind failed. The first time Mary sat by her side, the woman said, "Call me Eunice." She smiled as she asked Mary where she was buying meat these days. And asked again. Mary listened. And listened again. Days after Eunice Potter's death, Stuart Potter told Mary he wouldn't forget her help. She thought little of those words at first, so it came as a jolt when Jack told her his father left her a bequest. The amount was small—nothing to live high on—but added to her savings, she didn't need to hurry back into service. Not unless a new position suited her purpose. She could steady herself, shape her plans, strike out east. Not to Washington. She read the papers. The Clevelands no longer summered there. They'd bought a home in a place named after buzzards.

Chapter Forty

March 25-April 3, 1895

Mary pieced together the best route, using maps and timetables at Pontiac's public library. A jumble of different railroad lines would carry her from Michigan through Ohio, Pennsylvania, New Jersey, New York, Connecticut, and finally to North Union Station in Boston. From there, she would take the Old Colony Division of the New York, New Haven and Hartford Railroad to Falmouth. The trip would stretch to five days—even longer than her trip to Bath, New York, eight years earlier.

She packed her meager possessions, along with three of Mrs. Potter's dresses, taken in at the seams, two rings, and a pearl necklace, all set aside on the quiet the night the woman passed. Jack's clueless wife spent more time with her parents in Detroit than with Jack's parents in Pontiac, so she wouldn't remember those jewels or think to claim them.

Without hesitation, Mary bought second-class tickets. She had money for the first-class car but didn't care about upholstered seats. The long train ride east, on wooden benches in cars just behind the sooty engine, sped by. Mary bought newspapers at each stop, searching for political news. A little on the aftermath of the Pullman strike, preparations for the Kentucky Derby. Not much to chew on. Mary could think about how she might extract her pound of flesh from Cleveland. Ha. She surprised herself with a chuckle.

Mary muddled over one plan after another. Each had some catch that gave her pause.

She set the planning aside for a while and busied herself dreaming up new names. She'd read somewhere that when folks tried to make themselves over with a new name, they shouldn't stray too far or they might trip themselves up. She'd keep to her own initials. She sifted through some choices—Maria, Maeve, Maggie, Mattie, Martha, May, Mabel—until she landed on Margaret. That settled, she tackled Brinski, leaning her head back, looking up to the heavens she didn't believe in to ask George for forgiveness. She'd keep the two first letters again. Something short. Brown, Bryant, Brooks? As the sun rose one morning in Pennsylvania, streaming into her train window, she came up with Bright. Yes—Margaret Bright.

She reached to the car's window to lower the shade, brushing her arm across her hair. She fingered her waves. Four days without a maid's cap to hold down her wavy hair. Mary hadn't gone four days without a cap since her time in the orphanage.

Nearing the end of her journey, Mary spent one night in a run-down hotel in Boston. She ditched her sooty clothes, dressed with care, and then bought a first-class ticket for the women's car headed to Falmouth. She sat across the aisle from a chatty mother and daughter. A perfect place to try out her new name. The words came easily. Then she inquired about suitable hotels.

"The Tower House," the mother said, with the daughter nodding in agreement. "A clean, respectable hotel. An unaccompanied woman such as yourself should feel perfectly comfortable there."

An hour later, on April 2nd, Mary signed the Tower House registry as Margaret Bright, a widow seeking a change of scenery. Dressed in the finest of Mrs. Potter's dresses, Mary—or Margaret—called little attention to herself.

Although she could idle at the Tower House for weeks, she was in no mood to waste time. Falmouth wasn't her true aim, but Bourne, another town in Barnstable County. She could go up and back between the towns in forty minutes by train. When she settled on her route east, she skipped past Bourne on purpose. No one was likely to trail her, just as no one was likely to hunt for Mary Brinski. But since her plans were unsettled, she'd leave nothing to chance.

The hotels in the area were sure to staff up for the summer. Chattering with the Tower House maids, Mary learned that the Norcross House, in Monument Beach, off Buzzards Bay, was the largest and most popular hotel near Bourne. Donning one of Mrs. Potter's simpler dresses and armed with Jack Potter's reference, Mary rode the train to Bourne, then walked to Monument Beach. She hardly gave a thought to the scrubby plants along the path. In the coming months, the maids she met, young women who lived in Bourne their whole lives, would point out the violets and the huckleberry. She'd nod and smile, keen to fit in. But now, all that mattered was finding her way. Ahead, the path split. A narrower path headed to the Bay. That one might take her to Gray Gables, later.

Mary had made it East without a hitch. She couldn't count on good luck forever. You can turn around this minute, she thought. Take the train back to Pontiac. Search for a new position there. Forget the rest. Or stay here and find a position, but again, forget the rest. No one will ever know what you've been thinking.

At the crossing with the smaller path, she looked right. Nothing but bushes and pines. And mist. She smelled water, half foul, half fresh. Buzzards Bay. Could she see Gray Gables? Not through the morning fog. But this place, this was where she wanted to be, not Pontiac. She would stay on the main path to reach the Norcross House. For now.

After a long walk, Mary saw the hotel, an impressive, five-story white building, rising tall at the edge of Monument Beach, on the shore of the Bay. Balconies wrapped around the second and third floors, looking fancy. The Tower House girls had steered Mary right. A hotel this grand would need a large housekeeping staff.

The hotel manager—Mr. Maurice Bolton, according to the brass nameplate—sat at his desk in an alcove off the lobby, wearing spectacles and staring at ledgers. Mary walked toward him, stepping just hard enough for him to hear. He pushed his spectacles down over his nose and slowly passed his eyes over her. He waved her in.

"So good of you to make time for me, sir. I am Mrs. Bright. Like the sun." The name felt good as it left her mouth. "I recently lost my position of thirty years, as maid for a wealthy family in Michigan. My employer—both the husband and the wife—died this year. I'm a widow, so I came to Falmouth to spend time with my sister, who lives there. She knew I was seeking a position and recommended your establishment."

"Yes."

That one word, drawn out, sounded like an invitation to go on.

"My employer's son, he's a lawyer in Detroit, he wrote a reference for me." She handed over Jack Potter's letter, dry now. The night before, she'd smeared the ink on the last four letters of "Brinski" and, to imply an accidental tea spill, on two nearby words. Jack had referred to Mary only as Mrs. Brinski, so her first name never showed up.

Bolton raised his spectacles and read Jack's letter. Every word. Mary waited. Bolton's eyes returned to her bosom and her spotless frock.

"I'm hiring for the summer. Two of my maids from last season found themselves in, well, they had to leave." His darting eyes told the story. They were pregnant. "I need two additional maids." He paused. "Also, the housekeeper who managed the maids struggled with a bad hip and left our employ, so I need to hire a new chief housekeeper as well. Preferably someone a little older than the maids, to keep them in check."

He needs a woman old enough not to get in the family way, Mary thought. Then she fixed her attention on a word he used—manage—turning it over in her mind. She would tip up her language a bit.

"This letter is fine, Mrs. Bright, but this Mr., ah, Mr. Jack Potter, he says nothing about managing."

"Ah, an oversight, Mr. Bolton. You see, although Mr. Potter knew me, he was away at college for years and didn't always see the women I managed. Besides the laundress, who he did mention. I also managed Mrs. Potter's seamstress and two more maids we brought in for extra cleaning in the Christmas season. I made sure they kept the house spotless. Oh, and also the fellow we hired to paint the carriage house. The gardener and the arborist, too." Yes, he'd think, if she knew the word "arborist," then surely she could manage a gaggle of maids.

Bolton's eyes stayed on Mary. He might be picturing her ordering around a staff on a grand estate, not a single maid slaving away in a city mansion, keeping to the only thing her soused ma taught her—cleaning. He put his elbow on the desk, bent his arm, and with his palm out gave a wave. She'd said enough.

"And how do I reach this Mr. Jack Potter to confirm what he wrote?"

She'd talk like a chief housekeeper, not a maid. "Mr. Potter offered to speak to a prospective employer by telephone or telegram. I suggest a telegram because he spends much of his time in court and might be hard to reach."

Mary didn't worry that Jack would question a telegram asking him to confirm his recommendation. She didn't think she let her new first name slip out to Maurice Bolton, and even if she had, with every word costing money, he was likely to use only her new last name. Jack would think that Bolton couldn't get his head around the foreign-sounding Brinski. And if Jack noticed that the telegraph came from Monument Beach, he'd be unlikely to connect that location with Gray Gables. Reporters usually wrote that the Clevelands' summer home was in Buzzards Bay, which must sound more dramatic and suggestive to them than the gentle sound of Bourne. Jack might question why she'd traveled to Massachusetts, but not enough to fuss.

"If this Mr. Potter repeats his enthusiasm, you can begin next week." He mentioned the pay—a quarter above her wages in Pontiac.

She smiled, though she didn't care about the money. "Thank you, sir. You can send word to me at the Tower House in Falmouth. Another fine hotel." She ducked her chin and studied her hands in her lap. "But if you send word there—you know messages are hardly private in hotels—the clerk will see I'm looking for a position, and I don't want him to think I may struggle to pay my bill. I have savings to cover it."

Should she trouble herself about the Tower House clerk? Mary couldn't be sure because her plans weren't firm yet. But if anyone tracked her to the

Tower House, she didn't want them to learn enough to also track her to the Norcross House.

"Instead, sir, for the sake of privacy, may I telephone you in a day or two?"

"Hmmm. Yes, tomorrow afternoon."

At four o'clock on April 3rd, Maurice Bolton offered Margaret Bright a position. He required her to provide her own black dresses, but understood she might want a few weeks to arrange that. She could have Tuesdays off. If she wished, she could board in a tiny room in the hotel cellar—reserved for the occasional worker who didn't live in town—for modest rent.

Just that easily, Margaret Bright became chief housekeeper at the Norcross House. Was it her reference? Her still-fine figure and thick brown hair? Her post-childbearing age? She could hardly believe she had done it. She had passed the first hurdle.

* * *

Mary reported for duty, carrying her old, timeworn bag and the butter-soft leather satchel the Potters gave her nine years earlier. Mr. Bolton handed over a chatelaine with keys and ran through her responsibilities—assigning rooms to eight maids, checking their work, ordering supplies, and cleaning some rooms herself, as needed.

A maid sweeping nearby kept her broom close to the floor, probably to lessen the noise of bristles against the parquet. She must want to listen.

"Violet," Bolton said. "Here's Mrs. Bright, your new chief housekeeper. She'll stay in the cellar room. Show her there."

Violet wore the usual maid's outfit—a dark gray dress, white apron, and white cap—almost the same as Mary's garb for the last thirty years. Mary stared, then clutched the chatelaine now clipped to her waist. She might never wear a maid's uniform again. Never cover her wavy hair with a cap. Even the higher pay hadn't hit her this way. She was moving up in the world. But what pushed her on was a chance to even up accounts, or, if she said the word straight to herself—retribution. She had not traveled to Cape Cod for a better position. Could she have both?

Mary followed Violet down the cellar stairs. Once out of Bolton's hearing, the barrage started. "I've been at Norcross a yeah." Violet spoke with pride, and a heavy accent Mary found unfamiliar. "Best hotel 'round heah. Best location for the summah tourists. Bolton's not bad. A little too much with the eyes, if ya know what I mean. Thank the lawd, only the eyes. Sure happy to have a new housekeepah. Sorry about the last one's hip, but me and the other girls, we weren't sorry she left." Violet took her first pause as she opened the door to the dark, meager room. "Mrs. Bright, Bolton said. Is that what ya want us to call ya?"

Mary stiffened, unaccustomed to her new name and to the chatter. She mumbled an answer while fiddling with the jumble of keys at her waist. "Call me Margaret. My missus called me that when I worked as housekeeper at her mansion in Michigan."

"Michigan! I thought ya talked different. What are ya doing *heah*?"

"I've been widowed for years, and my missus and her husband died a few months ago. My sister lives in Falmouth, so I came to visit her and look for a position."

"No children?"

"No children. My sister is my only living relative."

"Maybe I know her. I have kin in Falmouth."

"Not likely. She moved there herself only last year."

Mary's short answers seemed to satisfy Violet. Thank God, she didn't ask for details. She kept up her chatter, moving to a preview of the other maids: money-grubbing Polly Pearson, who was stepping out with a millhand named Walter Breen, a cross-eyed maid who wouldn't find a beau, a scatterbrained maid. Mary didn't try to remember all the names.

When Violet finally left, Mary's shoulders eased for a second. Then she thought about what Violet had said. The maid ragged on the other maids—with good humor, not malice. These girls chummed around together.

Mary took stock of what she'd done already. She picked a name and landed a job. She figured out how to walk from one place to another. She put money by if she needed to hire helpers. But she hadn't thought much about shifting from a quiet life, where she was the only servant, to stepping into a circle of maids. Yes, she was their manager, and they'd have to mind her. At the same time, she'd need to find her own place in the friendly gaggle of women Violet spoke of, women who knew each other's loves and troubles.

In the Buffalo orphanage long ago, Mary made friends with the girls who came and went. In the Buffalo tavern, she had fewer friends, except for a bawdy barmaid or two. In Pontiac, she made no friends. The Pontiac maids who worked for Stuart Potter's mill managers probably deemed her snooty since she worked for the mill owner. They wouldn't know she'd forgotten how to talk to women her age and had little to say anyway. Then those maids, the ones she met at first, married and new young ones took their places while Mary, set apart, stayed at the Potters, growing older, giving her less than ever to talk about.

From the high window above her bed in the cellar, Mary couldn't see the Bay. She stood up, twisted her head to the right, and made out the edge of the path that rambled around the Bay in the direction of nearby estates. Toward Gray Gables.

Keeping to herself wouldn't work. She needed to fall in with those maids. She might need their help.

Opening her satchel, Mary pulled out a booklet of train timetables she'd snatched from the Pontiac library. She placed the booklet, open to the page for Buffalo, on the flimsy bureau in her room. She'd leave it there, as a sign to herself, to remind her of the city where she met George, to remind her of her goal, to remind her she was no longer lonely, quiet Mary. She was genial Margaret. No one was likely to enter the shabby room. If they did, they wouldn't think twice about a booklet of timetables.

Over the coming weeks, Mary got on with the maids better than she'd expected. She even caught herself liking their company, feeling part of a little crowd for once. The few times she didn't want to gab with the maids, she slipped back to her room. She glanced at the Buffalo timetable and felt as though George was there, lifting her spirits.

Mary learned that tea breaks—Bolton allowed one short break each day— wet throats and loosened lips. The breaks allowed time for Violet and the other maids to share stories, to gather gossip. As Mary expected, Violet began to press for details.

"What did your husband do while you managed the mansion in Michigan?"

"He was a railroad foreman in Detroit. I saw him every weekend." Somehow, the word "foreman" rolled off her tongue easily.

"You looked aftah the whole mansion?"

"The cook pitched in. And the scullery maid." Ha, Mary thought, no scullery maid or cook ever crossed the Potters' threshold. "Ya know, before I moved up to housekeeper there, I was a chambermaid. I know what it's like to clean up filth. How hard it is to get every speck of dust and grime."

"So *you* understand what we do. The housekeepah before you, she was nevah in service." Mary began to like Violet, gab and accent and all.

Mary had seen immediately what that old housekeeper missed. Mary knew all the shortcuts—not cleaning behind dressers, not dusting the tops of picture frames, not washing every coverlet. She could call these girls out for their lapses, but that didn't suit her plan.

"Let's keep Bolton happy if we want our jobs." Mary gave a wink. They understood—clean just enough.

Her new life was working. She could jabber. She was getting along.

Chapter Forty-One

June 1-2, 1895

Mary sensed the maids felt at ease with her, forgetting she was over twice their age. At tea breaks, thcy asked her fewer nosy questions. They told stories of spoiled food at church socials, or old boyfriends who fell in with the wrong lot, or how this one's sister was marrying that one's brother.

Mary didn't need to dig hard for what she wanted. She just had to mention the mansions along Bourne's waterfront. "So many guests this week," she said. "The season's picking up. We'll be too busy soon. Don't none of you go thinking about leaving the Norcross to work at one of those private estates. You may think you want a new position, but the devil you know is better than the devil you don't know." She forced a twinkle in her eye.

"Don't worry," Polly said with a smirk. Of all the maids Mary managed, Polly stood out. The girl was money-grubbing. She was also amiable and a hard worker, and a tad easier to understand than Violet. "I can get on with the Hacketts, if I want—if you start harping on me. My cousin Liza, she's in service there, she tells me her missus is looking for an upstahrs maid. The thing is, the pay's bad, and I'd make no tips like the ones we make at the Norcross for ironing and mending. I earn good pay letting out seams in the dresses of guests like that fat Isabel Smithson."

Mary waited for the laughter to die down. "And those other estates down by the water? They don't tempt you?"

"Well, I already picked up wages at Gray Gables this spring, before you got heah. When Effie—she's the Clevelands' summah housekeepah, Effie Wylie—needs extra hands with cleaning to get the place ready for the president, she asks me to come in for a few days. It's something to tell friends who don't live 'round heah that I work a bit on the president's estate, even if it's only for scrubbing. Bolton gives me time off if, like he says, 'occupancy's down this week.' What's really down is his eyes looking down my neckline."

Mary joined the other maids in more laughter. She'd done it, she thought to herself. She'd steered the talk to Gray Gables. She looked at Polly, inviting more. Polly didn't need any prodding.

"And sometimes aftah the season starts, when the posh visitors from Washington show up, Effie has me come in on my day off." Polly gave a wide, tight smile. Mary was to consider Polly's work at Gray Gables an honor.

"So this Effie sees what a bad job you do? Won't offer you a permanent position, huh?" Mary ended her taunt with a guffaw.

"Bull," Polly said, raising her chin in defiance. "See, every May the Clevelands bring their regulah help with them and hire locals for extra summah help—like Ingrid Mann. She's their laundress."

"Right," Violet said. "Ingrid's my cousin. Five yeahs older 'n me. She likes working there. They treat her well. Only problem is she doesn't get along with Mrs. Cleveland's lady's maid, that stuck-up Lena, the one the missus brings from Washington. It's because of the gardnah, the handsome one who tends the property. Ingrid fancies him. Then every summah Lena comes and gets in the way. Like she's bettah because she's the regular lady's maid and my cousin's the summah laundress." Violet spat out the word "bettah," defending her cousin Ingrid.

The maids bobbed their heads in agreement. They seemed to follow goings-on at Gray Gables.

"The only new local hires this season," Polly said, "are a few fellows to help with the grounds and patrols. Like my Walt. He picks up extra wages that way. He's saving up for a ring for me."

Mary set her mind to remembering the idle chatter. And some of the names.

She wasted little time working out how to use what she just learned. Polly, thank the lord, did the heavy lifting.

"Margaret, should we walk 'round the waterfront tomorrow?" The maids started cleaning early and finished by three. "We'll see if Liza's at work at the Hacketts. You'll like her. And Effie too. She always has cookies. Sometimes she'll even gab about what's happening with the Clevelands."

"Good," Mary said, tamping down her glee and forcing a tired tone. "I can use some air after the mob last weekend." She spoke slowly, finishing with a yawn.

The next day, Mary let Polly lead her along the shoreline. Mary paid attention to the twists in the rocky path and the tall oaks and pines. She couldn't tell yet if she'd need to go that way later. To keep from looking too fixed on the path, she made a show of admiring the dark blue berries along the way. Huckleberries, Polly said. She sank to her knees and picked a bunch, filling a sack she brought along, oblivious to the dirt. Polly planned to offer the huckleberries to her beau's ma, Mrs. Breen, who worked for a baker who'd pay for them. Ahhh, the girl'd do anything for money.

On the waterside, Mary saw the clusters of strange grasses she'd eyed earlier, on her first walk to the Norcross House. Some smelled like rotten eggs, so Mary raised the basket she carried, to take a sniff of the cinnamon muffins Polly told her to bring as gifts for the maids they would visit. Polly seemed oblivious to the stench. She jabbered away about Walt. He set his sights on a plot of land for their cottage. He'd need one hundred dollars for the first payment. Mary tuned out the jabber. She kept her eyes on the ground ahead, wondering how it might help or hinder. She looked toward the Bay, wondering the same thing.

Polly pointed to a break in the trees. "Come, Margaret, Liza's down a ways, at the Hacketts." Mary didn't think they'd reached the turnoff for Gray Gables. She followed Polly into the kitchen of a large estate, where Polly and Liza caught up on news. Then back to the path. After a stretch of woods, Mary spotted the same narrow path she remembered from April, when heavy fog hid her view. She squinted into the distance, in the direction of a point of land stretching toward the Bay. Her eyes fixed on a sprawling, shingled house near the water and a neat, white cottage closer to the path.

"The big house is Gray Gables. Cleveland lives there."

Mary had heard that the place, for all its size, was dull brown and shingled, but the sight still caught her off guard. "My lord. Not elegant, like the brick mansion where I worked in Michigan. Just big and rambling."

"Even the toffs like shingles heah in Massachusetts. And Effie's cottage is right by the big house. Come along. You oughta meet her. Most days, her husband's off with the Clevelands' boats or patching them up. Their son Ned might be about. He's fourteen. Cute boy."

Polly knocked on the door of the housekeeper's cottage. A plump, pleasant-looking woman in her mid-thirties, wearing a clean apron, greeted Polly warmly and turned her head to Mary.

"This heah's Margaret Bright," Polly said. "Our new chief housekeepah. She worked for a rich family in Michigan—a mill owner, she tells me."

Effie put her arm lightly on Mary's shoulder. "Come in for a cuppa tea. I have cookies in the oven for Ned and my boarders. If you wait ten minutes, you can eat the extras." Her gaze took in both visitors. "Gab to me. What's going on at the Norcross?"

"And we brought cinnamon muffins," Polly said.

"Those day-old ones you buy from the hotel suppliah, to save a penny or two?" Effie said, with a joshing tone.

"They're still good. I need every penny I can get." Soon, the three women were enjoying fresh cookies and stale muffins. Ned ran into the kitchen and waved a hello. He grabbed a cookie and headed out again.

At first, once a week or so, Mary walked to Gray Gables with Polly and sometimes with other maids from the hotel who liked Effie. Before long, Mary walked alone, sure that Effie would invite her in.

On one of those walks, looking toward the Bay, Mary saw a tall woman with a brown updo, dressed in the latest style. Even a pretty frock could not hide a big belly. No doubt, Frances Cleveland. Her face might be bloated, but she was pretty, like everyone said. The woman stood near a rowboat, watching her daughters, Ruth and Esther, and talking to the girls' nursemaids, Annie and Bonnie. Mary knew all their names, as did most Americans, from the newspapers that couldn't get enough Cleveland family gossip. But the papers hadn't reported on that belly. The brute would soon have three.

Three.

Not for the first time, Mary took a minute to wonder. Frances Cleveland married in '86. She didn't bear Ruth until '91. Then Esther in '93. Now a third. Those first five years? Had she lost a baby, too? Mary stopped herself. She must not feel anything for that woman. Frances Cleveland had birthed others.

Near the woman with the belly, the two toddlers ran around the huckleberries and skunk cabbage just off the trail and played with the small stones on the beach. Blond-haired Ruth held pebbles in her hand. She threw them into the water one at a time, laughing when they landed close to the waterline. Brown-haired Esther scooped a handful of pebbles and threw the lot all at once, almost as far as Ruth tossed her single pebble. The three women stood close by, watching. Neither child wanted to give up the game.

Mary spotted a brawny-looking man, walking up and back. Now and then, he glanced at her or at the old villagers straggling along the same path. After eyeing them, the guard turned his eyes elsewhere. Mary pulled down the brim of her straw hat needlessly. The guard didn't regard a woman or stooped men as threats. He'd let her walk close to the girls—close enough to see the pebbles.

Mary peeked out from under her brim. Frances Cleveland's bulge was low. She glanced only at her brats, not at the strolling villagers. If by chance milady looked up and out, she'd see a plainly dressed woman of middle age taking a walk, carrying a basket filled with muffins. She wouldn't see Mary Brinski, a woman who no longer gave a thought to giving up and spending the rest of her life mired in the dirt of others.

The smaller girl must be the daughter born in the Executive Mansion. Mary's thoughts were on the bigger girl. The first daughter. She'd be able to walk faster.

Chapter Forty-Two

July 1-8, 1895

Seeing that Frances Cleveland would soon give birth—again—Mary raged. Then she spotted the man keeping step with the lady and her children. Solidly built, but just one man. She whirled from rage to an idea. She toyed with a wisp of hair, working out what she could do.

Once Frances Cleveland's pains started, the lady would think only about childbirth, until she looked around. Mary pictured a place and scene—Frances Cleveland lying in a four-poster bed, shouting for Ruth. Or Frances Cleveland crying, blaming herself. Or Frances Cleveland, wondering what scoundrel stole her daughter and why. Mary caught herself. Her mind was leaping too far, too fast.

She needed to get everything right. She couldn't drop the ransom note at Gray Gables herself. If someone spotted it before she carried off the girl, there'd be no going back. And Mary couldn't mail the note from the place she'd take the girl. She needed a—what was that word—an accomplice.

She found one. Polly smoothed the way, bringing Mary to Effie Wylie. Then Polly tossed Mary another favor. The lad Polly aimed to wed, Walter Breen, worked nights in the nearby lumber mill and a shift, mostly days, at Gray Gables. Behind Polly's back, Violet whispered to Mary. "That Walt's not much to look at. Lanky, like a string bean, ya know, with a toothy smile. We call him Stringbreen. Polly pushed him into that second job to earn faster for a house."

At first, Mary saw no use for the romance between Polly and Walter—not until Polly nicked a bracelet from Mrs. Isabel Smithson, the portly Norcross guest who stayed the full season and needed her dress seams let out.

Mary stumbled on the crime. Each maid had assigned rooms to clean, and on days off, other maids, even Mary, pitched in to cover those rooms. For weeks on Polly's day off, Mary cleaned Isabel Smithson's suite. The woman kept her bracelets in a half-open box on the bureau. Six bracelets, all gleaming, all with different jewels. Mary's fingers itched to filch one, but she knew what she could get away with and what would put her in danger. She could swipe a bill from Mrs. Potter's purse in Michigan, when that bill was small and one of many. Swiping a rare bracelet would be asking for trouble. Then one day, while dusting Mrs. Smithson's bureau, Mary counted five bracelets in the jewelry box. The one with three amethysts was missing.

Smithson had left the hotel with friends around noon, all jabbering about cafes. Maybe she wore the bracelet, though it seemed too grand for daytime. Mary hovered in the hall until the woman came back from lunch. Her wrists were empty. If the bracelet wasn't on Smithson, and wasn't in the box, Polly must have nicked it. Though Mary lacked proof, she'd watched Polly take shortcuts and swipe food and dishes from the kitchen when she thought no one was looking. Besides, the money grubber always looked to make a dollar. If Polly nicked the bracelet, she'd have told her beau. She was a talker.

Polly's beau might be of service.

Late on July 3rd, Mary waited close to the lumber mill, just before the night shift would begin. Remembering that Violet dubbed Walter "Stringbreen," Mary looked around. She had no trouble spotting a tall, thin young man, hurrying to his shift, alone.

"Walter Breen, you don't know me. But I know Polly Pearson."

At his girlfriend's name, the clod showed interest, not confusion. He opened his mouth just enough for Mary to spot the big teeth Violet badmouthed. Mary blinked in relief. She'd found him.

She wouldn't waste words. "Polly steals jewels from guests."

Seeing Walter scare, Mary knew she'd guessed right. Most likely, he helped Polly or fenced the haul himself.

"If I squeal, you dolt, she'll end up in the Bourne jail with the other thieves."

Besides the big teeth, the fellow had a pathetic mug. Mary rushed on.

"If you want me to look the other way, here's what you'll do. In the next week or so, I'll send you a note. I'll send it to the mill when you're there at night, or to your ma's house in town. The note will just say 'T.' That means tonight, the first midnight after you hear from me. If anyone catches you with the note, say it means Polly can see you on Thursday. Or say Tuesday if you want. Doesn't matter. Understand?" He nodded weakly.

"You'll nab a boat and row south on Buzzards Bay, then on to the inlet to Red Brook Pond around midnight. Again, that's the first midnight after you get my note. Tell the mill foreman you're sickly."

She paid no mind to his puzzled look.

"You know that pond? Red Brook?" Another weak nod.

She wouldn't waste words telling him how she learned about the pond from the old-timer who tended the hotel's boats, or how he rowed her and Violet out there one early evening for a picnic supper, or how she spotted a lean-to near the shore—a rotting shack good for shade and hiding.

"Then walk to the far side of the pond. You'll see an old shack. If no one's there, turn around and forget you ever went out on the water. But if you see me, then I'll hand you a note. You row back and get yourself to Gray Gables and slip the note under the front door. It'll still be dark then. If a guard sees you, say you forgot your grandfather's watch when you left your shift, and you came back to find it."

"What's, what's this about?"

"That's my business. Listen up. If you ever let slip that I talked to you, or ever tell Polly, or anyone else, I'll turn her in to the constables. If you keep quiet, I won't."

His face took on a lost look, like he didn't catch on.

"Now run through it for me, just like I told you, from when you get my note, the one with 'T' for tonight. Tell me what you need to do."

It took a few minutes and no end of mistakes, with Walter whining he'd be late for his shift. The third time, he got his orders straight. Mary gave a curt nod and turned on her heel. She had no fears. Walter would do anything to keep his sweetheart, and maybe himself, out of jail.

The next day, Mary set her mind on how she would know when the new baby came. That's when the Clevelands would let go of their usual ways.

"Effie," Mary said, on a visit to the housekeeper's cottage, "Looks like Mrs. Cleveland's about to have another babe."

"Lotta excitement. Ya know, Ruth and Esther weren't bawn at Gray Gables. This'll be the first. Everyone's ready. Dr. Bryant's up from New Yawk, staying with friends in town. I tipped him off to a village midwife, to help when the time comes. Not the midwife I used." She frowned.

"In my family," Mary said, "back in Buffalo, we said a special prayer for women in childbirth. It always worked. Not a stillborn baby yet among my kin. I want to do that for your missus. Can you send your boy—Ned, right?—to the Norcross, to tell me, as soon as her pains start? I'll light a candle and stop my cleaning to pray."

How could Effie say no? Mary knew, thanks to Violet's prattle, that Effie herself lost babies, one before young Ned and one after. And Mary heard Effie wonder aloud if Frances Cleveland might've lost babies, since she was married for five years before Ruth came along. Sure enough, Effie agreed to send Ned, and four days later, she remembered.

Mary's plans were falling into place. One problem still vexed her—how on earth to snatch the child.

Her mind flashed back to the kidnapping of little Charley Ross that she and everyone in America had read about twenty years before. Two bad men used candy to lure Charley away from his home. For Ruth, the baby would be the candy. A baby boy.

On Sunday morning, July 7th, Ned Wylie found Margaret at work at the Norcross House. Mrs. Cleveland, he told her, took to bed, and Dr. Bryant had rushed over. Mary thanked Ned for the news. She'd break from work to pray.

Wasting no time, she found Bolton at his desk and asked for the afternoon off. She needed to run errands for her ailing sister in Falmouth and might need the next day, Monday, off too. Monday was a slow day for hotel business, so her absence wouldn't cause trouble. If all went well, Mary would slip back to the Norcross on Monday, no one the wiser. If all didn't go well, she'd vanish herself, like George did.

Back in her room, she scrambled into pants and a shirt left behind by a guest. Over those men's clothes, she pulled on Mrs. Potter's drab blue dress. Mary added spectacles left by yet another guest, a blond wig she lifted from a display in the town's millinery, and her own straw bonnet. For the first part of her walk, she'd look like a woman, but not like Margaret Bright, the brown-haired hotel housekeeper who always wore black.

She took one more look at the Buffalo page of the timetable on her bureau, to fix George in her mind, then nicked two ham sandwiches and a chocolate cookie from the hotel kitchen. She filled her wicker basket with hairpins, a scissors, a farmer's hat, butterscotch candy, the sandwiches, and a flask of water, placing them atop a Norcross House pillow, and left through the hotel's back entrance. She walked toward Gray Gables, taking a long, less-used path, feeling the noon sun beat down. If anyone passed her, they'd see a blond woman with spectacles, not Margaret Bright. The pants under her dress chafed against her thighs. The heavy basket scratched her arm. The grasses smelled foul, roiling her stomach.

Before Mary could make the left turn to Gray Gables, she walked ten minutes north to the Breen house. She found it with no trouble—Polly said Walter lived with his ma in a small, yellow cottage. It's in the poorer part of town, Polly said, but his ma keeps it tidy, and it's only a block from the bakery where she works. Mary twisted her eyes in all directions, spotted no one, and tossed an envelope onto the porch. On the front of the envelope, she'd written "for Walter only." On the note inside, she'd written one letter, "T." She turned around and sped back to the path that would take her along the Bay. Two hours had passed since Ned Wylie brought word of happenings at Gray Gables.

At last, the Clevelands' property came into sight. High-pitched wails? From the upper windows of the house? Mary ducked behind a shed, then peeked out. She had picked the right dress to wear. The dull blue color faded into the background. Two nursemaids, one short and one tall—the same ones she'd seen when she spotted the missus with her big belly—steered the girls across the lawn to the Wylies' cottage. Mary wanted to clap. Fortune was smiling on her today. With the girls clear of the big house, away from the brute and the guards, she had no call to sneak into the servants' entrance and hide, biding her time till Ruth was alone.

Mary darted behind trees, then skulked to the cottage, crouching beside a bin near the open ground-floor window. A woman in the cottage's kitchen talked to a child. Mary heard no trace of Yankee sounds, so it wasn't Effie. She'd want to hang around the big house, to get early word of her missus's progress.

Through the cottage's upstairs window, the words of a lullaby drifted down. Probably the other nursemaid, singing to the younger child. Mary chewed over how to distract the downstairs nursemaid. Would it work to say the midwife—

Before Mary could sort out her next move, the side door opened. She bent her neck around the bin, toward the lawn. The short nursemaid—looked like Annie—left the house alone, leaving the door ajar, and scurried across the lawn to a man with light brown skin. A butler?

One child alone downstairs. Bonnie and another child upstairs. *Pounce. Now.*

Still crouching and clutching her basket, Mary entered the side door, hidden from the butler's view by the bin and bushes. The girl sat playing with pans. "Ruth?" The girl looked up. Thank God, Mary thought, she had the right child. "Ready to see your little brother? Your mama told me to take you to the spot off the Bay where she's bringing the baby."

That was all it took. Like Charley Ross's kidnappers offering their prey candy.

The girl walked with Mary out the cottage's back door, hidden from the lawn. They neared a thicket of trees close to the dock, still out of sight of the servants who'd hang around the big house, hoping for news. Mary sat on the grass with the girl, taking a minute to talk about the new baby boy—so small, so lovable—and handing her butterscotch candy. Mary kept her eyes on the dock—still deserted, but she couldn't wait long.

She led the girl to the rowboat, lifted her and the basket into it, and shoved off. The Bay looked huge. Mary was breathing heavy, sweating. She couldn't get her bearings. She wasted time trying to find landmarks to point her to the pond. After a good while, seeing a stretch of shore she didn't know, she worked out she'd headed the wrong way. Stupid. She turned the boat around, struggling with the oars.

Now sure she headed right, she let the boat drift for a spell. She set down the oars, grabbed the scissors from the basket, ran her hand through the girl's hair to bare her scalp, and quickly snipped off a hunk. The girl flinched. "Gift for the baby," Mary said. The girl whined, then let it be. As Mary pocketed the hair, figuring she might need it if the brute went silent, the boat spun in the wrong direction.

She hadn't counted on the rough water. She grabbed the oars and rowed, twisting, rowed harder, twisting more. A man out there, far off in another boat, swung his face to her. He didn't look away.

Son of a bitch, she cursed to herself. He knows.

She turned the boat again, cursing more as she wrestled with the oars. The girl fussed. She wanted to see the new baby. Mary rowed hard. How could she be so far from shore? After what seemed like forever, she reached the dock and wrapped a rope around a piling as fast as she could. With one arm, she lifted the girl out of the boat. With her other arm, she grabbed her basket and ran ashore. The child wriggled and pulled Mary's bonnet, hollering for the baby.

Mary twisted her head toward the water. The man in the Bay—he looked old—would reach land soon. To run fast enough to get away, she'd need to leave the girl behind. She dropped her on the grass.

Gasping and dripping with sweat, Mary fled to the nearest outbuilding, the barn. Maybe the old man would look after the child, forget Mary. She heard no howls of pain from the windows of the big house, just women's muffled voices. Probably yelling to each other that this or that room was empty. The fools searched in the wrong places. Mary peeked out from the barn. Men dressed in work clothes swarmed toward the woods, away from her. Could she be in the clear?

She crouched in an empty bay. The horses lifted their heads and nickered, but not loudly. She stopped shaking long enough to stuff into her basket her bonnet, the glasses, the wig, and the dress she'd donned over men's clothing. From the bottom of the basket, she pulled out hairpins and a farmer's hat, switching her look. She started running back to the Norcross, panting, sticking to the same less-used path she'd walked hours earlier.

She looked down at her shoes. The path was dry, and her soles were flat. The shoes would leave no marks. She willed herself to slow down, to draw less attention. People might heed a small man carrying the kind of basket women filled with flowers or food, especially if he ran.

Nearing the hotel, she brooded about what to do. She would hide in a copse of trees until dusk, when she'd put back on the dress she'd crushed into her basket and sneak to her room in the hotel. She knew which windows would be open and how to dodge the clerk at the front desk. She would hit her head against the wall.

Mary was never sure how she made it back to that stifling room. Slumping onto her cot, with the smell of ham sandwiches in the basket nearly gagging her, she leaned over and drew her knees to her chest. You fool, she thought. Why did you try this? As she turned away from the sandwiches, her eyes landed on the booklet of timetables on the bureau, opened to Buffalo. George. He thought she was smart. He was wrong. As well as wronged. No one had cared about him. Cleveland cast him away like a stinking ham sandwich.

The stinking sandwiches. She'd better throw them out. Mary reached for the food, hidden in the basket under her bonnet. Her bonnet—it didn't feel right.

Before heading to Gray Gables earlier that day, Mary started to put the ransom note in her pocket so she could hand it over to Walter that night, assuming she made it to Red Brook Pond with the girl. Then she remembered she'd stuck a chocolate cookie in one pocket and should leave the other free for a lock of hair. Not wanting to dirty the note, she fastened it to the brim of her bonnet with a single pin.

Now, with sweat running down her neck, she flung everything out of the basket, onto the cot. She fingered the bonnet, the pants, the shirt, the wig, the pillow. The note she was to give Walter, the note he was to slip under the door at Gray Gables, the note that would make the brute understand he had no one to blame but himself—gone.

Cursing under her breath, Mary thought back. When she set Ruth down on land, the girl squirmed. She yanked Mary's bonnet, probably loosening the pin. Minutes later, Mary took off her bonnet and her dress in the stables. The ransom note, already half unpinned, must have dropped into the straw. Mary never saw it. The note could have fallen out when she hid in the copse of trees and switched back into a dress. Didn't seem likely. She'd have caught sight of the cream-colored paper on the grass between the trees. In the barn, though, with all that pale straw underfoot, she could have missed it.

Mary had no trouble remembering what she'd written. *If you want Ruth back, put $150 under the horse trof in front of the Eldridge Lumber Yard, after dark.*

One hundred and fifty dollars—that amount was the heart of the matter. Mary had worked it over in her head. She never asked Walter Breen to fetch the money at the lumber yard. Anyone who tried that would just draw eyes and talk. She wasn't after the money. She aimed for Cleveland to feel the sting when he saw the figure.

But that part of the plan, and the next part, were dead now. Cleveland would never see the ransom note. He would never know that the morning after snatching the child, Mary meant to—well, she'd never been sure. Maybe to leave her along the pond's shore at a grassy spot where searchers would find the girl with no trouble. Or maybe to keep the child. An eye for an eye. A substitute child for a substitute warrior. Or maybe to murder the child, smothering her with a hotel pillow. Now, no need to choose.

How could she be so stupid, so unprepared? Failing to pin the ransom note with care was just one of her blunders. She let the girl sit up in the rowboat. That nosy old man in the Bay spotted them. Then, yet another blunder, maybe her biggest one. Yeah, her biggest one. She thought of the girl as Cleveland's daughter, not as Ruth, not as a pretty, flesh-and-blood three-year-old who'd sit just inches away, with her heart bent on seeing her new baby brother. The girl wasn't craving a shiny new toy, like she was spoiled, but a baby, just like Mary had ached for a baby. How could Mary know that Cleveland's daughter would have that big-eyed look of longing?

A breeze rolled in from the Bay, through the window, clearing the air in the cell-like room. When the breeze faded, the ham sandwiches she'd not yet tossed smelled stronger than ever. She felt sick. She threw the sandwiches out the window. Shorebirds and squirrels would take care of all traces. In the left pocket of her dress, she found the chocolate cookie, half-melted, pried it free, and threw it out too. In her right pocket, she felt the girl's lock of hair and left it there. She should toss that too—it was part of his child—but it felt smooth to her touch.

Mary kept her fingers on the hair as she forced down the acid that rose in her throat and settled her breathing. Even now, she wouldn't give up. She had come close, and she learned lessons. The child was more than the brute's daughter. The child was Ruth, a little girl who wanted to see a babe. Feeling Ruth's hair, Mary accepted what she'd tried to shrug off. The girl was no more to blame for her father's sins than Mary was for her own pa's desertion. Next time, Mary wouldn't take the pillow. And she would make another change. She wouldn't bring in Walter, or anyone else. She remembered what her former employer, Stuart Potter, said when he faced a problem at his mill. Sometimes simpler is better.

Mary vowed to herself to try again, to cast a light on how Cleveland used and abused George—a reckoning long overdue. She might have one more chance. She wouldn't botch it.

On Monday morning, Mary reported to Bolton, saying she finished her tasks for her sister earlier than expected. The hotel's reception area was empty, with no gaggle of chattering guests. The maids Mary passed appeared calm. Was it possible that the brute never rang an alarm? Was it possible that no one was looking for the woman who stole Ruth for an afternoon? Was it possible that Frances Cleveland—the woman Mary pictured in her mind, wailing—didn't realize her first girl had gone missing?

Chapter Forty-Three

September 1-17, 1895

The second half of the summer dragged. Every time Mary glanced at her blue dress or the shorn lock of hair, she remembered her misery for a minute, then for hours fussed over how to snatch the girl again. Mary had wasted the commotion of Marion's birth—the baby hadn't been a boy after all—and hadn't found another chance. Effie was no help. She gabbed like usual, but only about squabbles among the servants and visits from society folks. The Clevelands would return to Washington soon, while Mary plodded away at the Norcross, with no hope and no purpose, hating her life, hating herself. But she had a hunch the passing weeks weren't all bad. By now, the Clevelands were bound to believe the kidnapper had given up.

On September 1st, Mary's luck turned.

Same as every day, she reported to Bolton. Sixteen rooms cleaned, eight half-done. Same as every day, Bolton said, "fine," as his eyes landed on the top half of her black dress. Leaving his office, she glanced at the headline in the newspaper lying idly on the sideboard in the lobby—"President Cleveland to Start Machinery in Atlanta Exposition from Summer Residence in Massachusetts."

Oh my God. A gift from the heavens?

Bolton stood near his desk, facing away from her, suffering abuse from a guest complaining that his room lacked a full view of the Bay. Mary could take time to read the full newspaper story. And then to read it again. On September 18th, Atlanta would host the Cotton States and International Exposition, showing off machinery used to produce cotton. The organizers aimed to stimulate international trade. The Exposition wouldn't be as grand as the 1893 Chicago World's Columbian Exposition, but a close second. President Cleveland would flip a switch from his summer home, Gray Gables, to start machinery in Atlanta, demonstrating the long reach and power of electricity.

So, in a little more than two weeks, on September 18th, Cleveland's big show might unsettle the Gray Gables household the same way Marion's birth did in July.

The eighteenth landed on a Wednesday. Mary's day off was Tuesday. She'd head over to see Effie on Tuesday, the 10th, and again on Tuesday, the 17th. Effie was bound to chatter about the Exposition, about how the Clevelands and the servants were setting up for it. She wouldn't think twice about Mary dropping by—the two had met up most Tuesdays in August, sharing muffins and cookies. Not once did Effie let on that Ruth had gone missing for a few hours.

On September 10th, a soaking rain drenched all of Massachusetts, blowing hard from the mountains to the coast. Mary couldn't wander around in the storm without raising questions. She grumbled to herself. She'd have to learn what she could the day before the ceremony.

The sun shone brightly on September 17th. Mary walked to the cottage, hoping for news. Effie stood in her yard, hanging sheets on a clothesline not far from the bin Mary had crouched behind ten weeks earlier.

Effie's laundry wasn't what held Mary's gaze. Three men, with cables wrapped around their shoulders, climbed the poles running along the property line closest to the cottage, then hammered at something Mary couldn't make out.

"Effie, too bad I missed you last week. That rain nearly flooded the Norcross cellars. I brought you twice as many muffins today. Your favorite, cinnamon." Effie grinned. "That racket—what in the world's going on?"

"Gimme a minute to pin up these last sheets. Then we'll sit over tea, and

I'll tell ya. Big doings."

Effie jabbered away while she ate a muffin, telling Mary what she already knew and adding more. Electricians and telephone linemen from Western Union were working to extend the electrical line that ran along the New York, New Haven, and Hartford Railroad, adding poles and wires for connections to Gray Gables. All their hammering was so the president, sitting in Bourne, could push a button to start machinery in Atlanta.

"The button's special," Effie said. "Sinclair—you haven't met him—he's their steward, that means he's like a butlah. He called the button some strange word, an annunciator, I think. He says it's black, maybe porcelain, with a gold rim, with 'Marion Cleveland, Septembah 18, 1895' engraved on it. Sinclair heard Mr. Thurbah, that's the president's secretary, say that the Atlanta folks figure Marion's gonna press it. I guess no one in Atlanta ever saw a, let me count…a ten-week-old babe before."

Ten weeks, Mary said to herself. For Effie, that was the baby's age. For Mary, that was the stretch of her wretched summer.

"Bonnie says the babe's just starting to shove her fingers in her mouth."

Mary pictured a tiny mite with nimble hands and joined Effie in a laugh.

"Effie, those Atlanta folks must think the president's children are special."

"They *are* special. Those girls have two nursemaids and a governess. Let me tell you, the girls cry and whine just the same as any farmer's brood." Effie started a second muffin, enjoying the banter.

Time to pry. "For tomorrow, think you'll get yourself an invite? Or your husband? To see the president push that fancy button?"

"Oh, no, not the likes of me. Not Bud, neither." Effie frowned. "At breakfast this morning, Jennie said—not in a bragging way—that the missus invited her and Lena."

Mary squinted.

"Jennie's Ruth's governess. She's new, nice. Lena's the missus's lady's maid. A little full of herself. I heah the nursemaids might get themselves an invite, since Sinclair says the hoopla starts at two when the girls nap. The room'll fill up, what with Mr. Thurbah and a big shot from Western Union and men from the newspapers. Oh, and of course, the president himself.

He takes up some room, ya know." Effie snickered, then took a big bite.

"Those sweet girls. Won't the missus let them go, too?"

"Don't think so. The missus holds to nap time. She insists on what she calls a regulah schedule." Effie raised her nose in the air, wiggled her head. "I nevah had a regulah schedule for Ned." She stretched out the word regular, even beyond her usual sounds.

"Ha, you need to own a watch for a regular schedule." Mary and Effie shared another laugh.

Effie kept eating, kept gabbing. "Jennie tells me Ruth made a fuss. She wants to see her papa push that button. Won't happen. Not just 'cause of nap time. The missus doesn't like her girls 'round a bunch of smoking, burping men." Mary joined in still another laugh.

Naps—a good way to turn the talk if Effie grew curious. "Nap time," Mary said, sweeping her crumbs from the table and tossing them in the bin. "Wish I had nap time. Me and the maids, we're dead on our feet. Ya know, busy season. I best rest up today—it's my day off. I need strength tomorrow to clean two rooms and keep an eye on the maids. They clean twenty-two."

"You think I'm lucky, just cleaning five bedrooms in the cottage every summah? Ya know, I cook too, and I help Sinclair manage the household staff, and I'm only a bit youngah than you."

Ha, Mary thought. Only a bit? Thank goodness she looked younger than her fifty-two years, with little gray.

Effie leaned forward, rested both hands under her chin. "By next year, I might wish for these busy summahs. Ya know, if Cleveland doesn't get a third term, he won't stay heah long. He only comes to Bawn 'cause it's cooler than Washington. Oh, and for his fish. If he sells Gray Gables, not sure what'll happen to me and Bud. Those of us from Bawn, we'll lose our jobs."

Mary took in that news. To hide her clenched jaw, she nibbled a muffin she didn't want. So stupid—she never knew the brute might sell Gray Gables. Another reason to get it right this time. "You and Bud'll keep your places, you'll just work for new owners, that's all."

"Wouldn't be the same."

Mary raised a hand in agreement and stood to go. "Be well. Maybe I'll see you next Tuesday."

"Thanks for the tasty muffins. And stay outta trouble."

Not likely.

On her walk back to the hotel, Mary paid no heed to the rocky trail or the chop on the Bay. Her mind stayed busier than her eyes. She went over all she'd picked up from Effie. Nap time—same for each girl? The big house—bedrooms all in a row? Entering—would she need a disguise? The baby's nursemaid—

Mary tripped over the spread-out roots of an oak tree and sprawled on the ground, cursing her clumsiness. She rose to her knees, then staggered up. She felt a twinge in her ankle, but she could tell it wasn't bad. No rips to her dress, just dirt she pushed away. No scrapes on her elbows. Mary was on her feet again. She smiled to herself. Yes, she was on her feet. And if she quit staring into space and scrambled to sort out one problem at a time, she might pull this off. She'd never get a third chance.

First, as soon as she was back in her room, she'd need to write Ingrid Mann, the laundress hired by the Clevelands each summer. Mary knew about Ingrid thanks to Violet, the maid at the Norcross who gabbed non-stop. The maid Mary had come to like. Violet's cousin Ingrid lived in Bourne. Ingrid's beloved sister Katherine lived in Boston, where she suffered from consumption. How to send a telegram, ha, from Boston, to coax Ingrid to Katherine's sickbed—to open the door for another laundress to fill in at Gray Gables? Mary fretted, until she gave up on a telegram and thought up another way.

She copped blank sheets of stationery from Bolton's desk, and with care wrote her note to Ingrid Mann. "Dear Miss Mann, the Western Union workers and officials tell me they require more space to set up equipment, so they will use Gray Gables' laundry room. It is best that you take tomorrow off. You should not work near those men. You will be paid in any case. Do not worry about the laundry. We will manage for one day. Yours truly, Frances Cleveland." Mary kicked herself that she didn't remember the butler's name—better if the words came from him. The lady's name would have to do. Maybe for the best, since Mary didn't know what sort of words that butler would use.

She paid a Norcross bellhop to deliver the message to Ingrid Mann that evening, when he was out of uniform. With a warning not to say who sent him, she slipped extra coins into his palm.

Once that was settled and darkness came on, Mary grabbed a lantern and borrowed a hotel boat to row to Red Brook Pond, hoping the old-timer who cared for the hotel's grounds turned in early. Of all she did to get ready, this next part rattled her the most. She had to be sure she could find the pond again, she needed to practice her rowing, and she needed to see if the lean-to she'd spotted months before still stood. No way to do this during daylight. Hours later, Mary returned from the pond, dead tired. She kneaded her shoulders, but that barely helped. Pushing aside the aches, she took up one of the sheets she'd copped from Bolton. She wrote a ransom note, almost the same as in July.

This time she added a sentence, naming a year—1863—to make sure the message got through.

Mary had one final task before she could drift off. She had to form a picture of Ruth in her mind. No—two pictures. Ruth, as a spoiled child loved by her brute of a father, maybe with a Norcross pillow pressed over her head, flailing her arms. Mary could dredge that one up from memory. Then Ruth, as a little girl, laughing and crying like any other little girl, maybe romping in a lean-to. A newer picture. The two pictures shifted and blurred as Mary fell into a troubled sleep.

IX

Part Nine: Frances's World

Chapter Forty-Four

September 9, 1895

For Frances Cleveland, the last days of summer brought a semblance of peace. She still couldn't relax, but she spent more time thinking about the girls than the fugitive. Now, if only the heat would break. She remembered the weather exactly two years ago, when she gave birth to Esther in the Executive Mansion, on a blissfully cool September day.

Frances stood beside Susan in the residence's well-equipped kitchen, fanning herself with her hand, watching the cook spread a dollop of buttercream icing on a white layer cake. Susan read her mind. "Weather shouldn't be this hot now. Not in Massachusetts, anyways. Ma'am, the icing won't stay firm for long. Want me to use a knife to carve a two into the top before I put the cake in the icebox?"

"Yes, lovely idea. Two! Hard to believe Esther turns two today."

Frances saw Susan look away—a shift of her eyes. Disapproving, like the others. Annie and Bonnie—Lena too—had asked seemingly innocent questions. "Ma'am, have you seen Esther try to run?" Or "have you seen Esther pet the new carriage horse?" Their questions were always about Esther. Did the nursemaids and the lady's maid believe Frances was deaf to their meaning? The missus worries about Ruth, they would think, and tends to Marion, but ignores her middle child. The servants talked, especially in the kitchen, so Susan would hear the gossip. Frances flapped her hand in another fanning motion in front of her face, hiding her scrunched mouth.

At least the servants cared about Esther.

"We'll have a lovely party tonight," Frances said, "with your cake and all the gifts. The dolls Henry ordered arrived yesterday, just in time. Esther will have her own dolls, and she won't need to share. She'll be the center of attention."

Smiling with approval, Susan turned back to Frances.

You're silly, Frances chided herself. Why care what the cook thinks? But the minute that thought entered Frances's mind, she knew better. The cook's a good woman, and not wrong to feel concern.

With effort, Frances had calmed down over time, at least partially. She had decided not to worry about her governess's verbal indiscretions in New York, not to worry about her coachman's poor judgment, not to rack her brain for political enemies. And better still, Frances managed to stop herself from pestering Jeffrey. Cringing, she remembered her list of suspects. All wild goose chases. She was wrong. She should've left the search to the agents. She was lucky that Grover humored her. Over their marriage, he learned to do that. She'd continue to calm down, to acknowledge defeat.

This day, Esther's birthday, Frances would mark for a short time as the day her worries eased. The kidnapper must have given up.

Chapter Forty-Five

September 17, 1895

As the Exposition drew near, the household staff prepared for visitors coming to watch Grover press an annunciator in one state to start machinery in another state. Frances asked Grover the meaning of annunciator. "Not certain," he said. "Something to do with turning on the electric circuit." Frances explained that to Lena, who probably spread the tidbit of information upstairs and down. Frances knew the servants arranged their work to walk past her often, to catch her eye. They craved invitations. The gardener, too. He staggered into the residence multiple times, arms laden with flowers for Lena to arrange. And Susan baked twice her usual loaves, casually mentioning to Frances that these precautions allowed for extra lunch sandwiches in case visitors arrived early.

Frances stood at an open window at the side of the house, peeking at the Western Union workers with their hammers and cables. They wouldn't see her frown. She saw a blur of white hair out of the corner of her eye and turned to find Henry, his weekly schedule in hand.

"Such noise, Henry. Can't the workers quiet down?"

As she spoke those words, she heard the delusion. She thought she had calmed down, but the unfamiliar men outside and the prospect of a house full of strangers the next day alarmed her. By complaining about noise, she could ignore or at least mask her true fear.

"The noise? You know, Frances, those workers fought each other for the privilege of installing equipment here. Today and tomorrow may stand as the highlight of their lives, or anyway, their working lives. They want to tell their children they supplied electricity to connect the President with machinery in Atlanta. Electricity!"

Frances squared her shoulders, knowing Henry would notice. She didn't appreciate his implication. "Henry, even though I worry the noise will ruin Marion's nap, I'm excited too. I can't say I understand the technology, but I'm not a dolt in that area. You know, Frances is teaching me—"

Henry curled his lip in confusion.

"Frances Johnston. The other Frances. The woman photographer. She's teaching me how to use the new Eastman Kodak camera."

Henry looked impressed. Offered a little bow.

"You see, I'm excited about these new inventions—Grover here in Bourne using electricity to start machines in Atlanta, and me pushing a camera to photograph a face. But not the noise."

"I'll speak to the workers." He blinked hard, a sign he was changing the subject, getting down to business. "Now, can we discuss details? The Exposition officials expect the demonstration to take place at two o'clock tomorrow. I invited Western Union supervisors and journalists. We want to give those men something to report on besides Grover's dithering about a third term. We'll have a crowd. You and the girls coming?"

Such irony, Frances thought. Henry's reaction to almost anything was to counsel secrecy—secrecy about the cancer in Grover's mouth, secrecy about threats, secrecy about the kidnapper. Now Henry sought attention. She was tiring of his efforts to shape the public's perception of their president. She'd been part of that practice. She must think about how to break from it. And above all, she must keep the girls away from strangers.

"I see. You want to make it a family affair. You think the public will like that. But one-thirty is nap time for Esther and Ruth. I like the nursemaids to keep to that schedule. And Marion still sleeps most of the day. Even if the girls are awake, I don't want them around reporters, with their smoking and spitting."

"Those reporters aren't only uncouth," Henry said, ignoring his own cigar habit. "They're slow-witted. Some of them wrote that Marion would press the annunciator to start the electricity."

Frances and Henry both laughed. He had children, too, and understood the abilities of an infant.

"I'll join if I can, after my appointment with a dressmaker, and Sinclair and our governess will come. Where is all this happening?"

"The gunroom. It's on this floor, and it's near the northeast corner, so we won't get blinded by the afternoon sun."

Frances nodded in agreement. "Should be a lovely distraction." Maybe it would be, with the girls safe in their rooms.

Chapter Forty-Six

September 18, 1895

John Nolan lowered the top of the landau, so his passenger had a clear view of Gray Gables. The young man, dressed in an ill-fitting woolen suit, didn't bother to disguise his awe as Nolan steered the horses to the front porch. "I never thought I'd visit Gray Gables," Charles Jenkins said. "I hardly ever leave Hyannis. Mostly, the *Barnstable Patriot* sends me to town halls and sometimes, if I'm lucky, to the county courthouse. I've never been in the same room with a reporter from the *Boston Globe*, let alone the president. Hope I dressed all right."

"Nothing to worry about. The Clevelands, the family, all real nice."

The reporter stumbled down from the landau. Probably not used to sitting so high up.

"Check in with the agent over by the porch. Then the steward'll let you in. You'll need to wait a few hours. Ask the cook for a sandwich—the demonstration starts at two."

Soon, other visitors would arrive at the train station, also looking for rides. The horses would shuttle up and back all day, so Nolan wanted to keep them fresh. He left the landau for a minute to fetch water and returned with a pail. Charles Jenkins had disappeared into the house. A woman stood on the driveway, carrying a laundry basket. Nolan remembered seeing her walk along as he drove Jenkins up to the residence.

"Sir, my name's Wilma Clayton." She talked to Sky Donnella, who stood at his post beside a porch pillar. "The Clevelands' laundress asked me to help out. She's on her way to Boston. Her sister's sickly. The laundress said the lady's maid or the baby's nursemaid would have a bundle for me. I'll go 'round to the servants' door."

Something about the woman distracted Nolan. Not her drab blue dress. Not her large laundry basket. Not her gestures. Something else. He tilted his head in thought. He knew the Clayton clan, but not well. The washerwoman must be from Abe Clayton's branch of the family, living on farmland to the south.

"And tell me," Donnella said, "What is the laundress's name?"

Donnella's on full alert, Nolan thought.

"Ingrid Mann," the woman said. "A good lady, and a good laundress. Ingrid said I could do the wash at my house and bring it back in a day or two. Neatly pressed and folded." Nolan thought the woman was smiling with pride as she spoke, though he could not see her face.

"Fine, then. No need to go to the servants' entrance. Not today. The cook would just send you back here for my check."

Donnella pivoted toward the entrance and knocked. Sinclair opened the door. "She's filling in for Ingrid Mann," Donnella said.

Wilma Clayton entered Gray Gables. In about twenty hours, and for years after, that scene would flash back at Nolan like lightning on a dark sky.

X

Part Ten: Mary

Chapter Forty-Seven

September 18, 1895

Mary thanked God that the guard on the porch didn't narrow his eyes when she called herself Wilma Clayton. He was sharp-eyed, knowing strangers were coming to see the show. She'd had the sense to pick up the names of large families in the area—like Clayton—families spread out over the county. And she was ready with Ingrid Mann's full name when the guard asked who did the regular laundry. Mary quashed a smile. The hard part lay ahead.

The butler opened the front door. Was he the same man with light brown skin who beckoned Annie away from the cottage in July? He motioned to the back, where Mary knew she'd find the servants' stairs, then he stepped outside, leaving Mary alone. She entered the front hall, thrown off to see such a large space inside a shingled house. She looked around. She could take the servants' stairs, but that meant walking past a maid sweeping in the parlor. To her right, a wide staircase rose to the second floor.

She started up, not hurrying, like she had every right to be there. Best not to draw eyes. The second floor should be mostly empty. Five minutes before coming inside, she'd spotted Annie and Jennie out on the lawn, minding the girls. They'd likely play there for a while, until their lunch.

The upstairs hall looked longer than Mary expected. On her right, quiet words, with the up-and-back creak of a rocker. Bonnie talking to Marion in the nursery? Bonnie would sense stirring in the hall, so no point trying to tiptoe. Sure enough, the nursemaid glanced up.

Mary raised the laundry basket for show. "I'm helping Ingrid. She's off to Boston. Her sister there took a turn for the worse. Ingrid said you couldn't get by for a day without a laundress!" Mary smiled.

Almost all the staff, Effie had said, felt for Ingrid Mann. Spry as she was, Ingrid could barely keep up with the household's laundry, what with dresses for the girls, gowns for the missus, table linens changed every day, the president with his fine clothes and his fishing togs, a heap of dirty diapers, and all the extra laundry from guests. The way Bonnie tipped her head, she must understand Ingrid's heavy workload, must remember the sickly sister. Only Lena, the jealous lady's maid, had it in for Ingrid.

"Diapers in the playroom, on the right," Bonnie said. "The girls' dresses, too. Lena, she looks after Mrs. Cleveland, she can tell you where to find the missus's laundry, but those two won't get back for a few hours. If you can't wait, try the hamper in the lavatory. Maybe the steward can help you find the president's laundry."

"Much appreciated. I'll take the wash to my house and carry it back tomorrow."

"Then just take what you can carry, as long as that includes the diapers." Bonnie pinched her nose and grinned.

Mary already knew that Lena and the missus were not in the big house. They were in town at the shop of the dressmaker, Enid Green. The week before, Enid mended draperies for the Norcross House. When Mary pitched in to help with the rehanging, Enid let word of the appointment slip. Villagers who worked for the Clevelands were glad to talk of it.

Mary pinched her nose too and angled her head in thanks.

Five more steps down the hall. Ahead and to the right, Mary picked out the doors to rooms that faced the back, probably the lavatory and the playroom that the family added the year before. Effie had shared all that. Nearer, on the left, Mary saw doors that must open to rooms facing the front. She could figure this out. The first door, closed, must lead to the largest bedroom, the one where wails sounded through the window. The second door, open, must lead to the girls' room. The third, open too, must lead to the nursemaids' bedroom—they would sleep close to the girls, or at least Annie would. Or was the second for the nursemaids and the third for the girls? Mary stopped at the second room on the left and let her feet tap out six extra steps, judging that's what it would take to walk to the playroom. Then she scurried into the second room, leaving the door open.

Yes, the girls' room. One bed and one wooden crib, close to each other. A mess of fading pink chrysanthemums in a vase—must be the ones the papers said were named the Ruth Cleveland mums when the girl was born. A pretty room with pink wallpaper, but not fancy. Mary sank down on the patterned carpet and scrooched under the bed, dragging along the laundry basket. Her shoulders and back ached from rowing the night before. She smothered a sneeze and couldn't keep herself from blaming the Clevelands' sorry chambermaid for all that dust. If Mary craned her neck just so, she could make out the clock atop the girls' bureau. 11:02. Three hours to go before the racket.

Mary couldn't see much, so she relied on her ears. In the heat of the summer's day, the window had been opened. She caught the crunch of wheels and hooves on the driveway gravel whenever the coachman pulled up his landau. He sent his passengers to check in with the agent and then with the butler. Or was he the steward? Every so often, Mary caught a name or a trade—another reporter, a Western Union man, a town official, a photographer. Strange thing—the photographer spoke with a woman's voice.

After half an hour of driveway traffic, finally, an inside noise. Footsteps leaving the nursery. Bonnie walked down the hall toward the stairs, maybe to give the baby some air.

11:58 on the bureau clock. Mary had to crawl out and stretch, or she'd go mad. She waited until she heard clatter in the kitchen. The cook serving lunch to the girls? Mary stood up. Her right arm had fallen asleep, and her legs cramped. With pain, she shook out her limbs. She crept behind the open door where she could hear better than under the bed. More visitors arrived. The butler kept up his drivel.

"Welcome to Gray Gables. Walk through the parlor. You'll see a crowd gathering in the gunroom. Our cook will put out sandwiches while you wait."

She counted. That man blathered the same thing four times in ten minutes. How many visitors fit in the gunroom? The more, the better.

She'd been out from under the bed long enough. She crawled back and waited.

1:12. More misery. She tried reaching her arm toward her back, toward the cotton of the same blue dress she wore on July 7th, now wrinkled and damp. She couldn't get to the sore place. Oh, lord, close to time for Annie to bring the girls up for their naps? She'd tuck them in, then she'd go downstairs to join the show.

1:18. Don't check the clock every minute, Mary fussed to herself. She couldn't stop. 1:27. 1:34.

Chatter from the stairs. Children, two women. Bonnie must be carrying Marion up for a nap, too.

"You each pick one stuffed animal from the playroom." Not the voice of the woman who explained where to find the dirty diapers. A slower voice. Annie?

Mary heard little footsteps toddle to the playroom. Annie must be standing in the doorway of that room, where she could watch the girls but also turn to talk softly to Bonnie, who must be standing in the hall, close to the bedroom where Mary hid. The girls wouldn't hear. The missus and Lena must still be at the dressmaker's, also out of earshot. Mary set her mind on catching Annie's words.

"He's mad, real mad. He told Mr. Thurber that those Atlanta folks are wasting his time. Seems like it's a problem with the wires. Either at this end or the Atlanta end."

Now the other woman's voice—Bonnie's. "Sinclair's mad about the delay, too. He'll need to watch the reporters and telegraph fellows 'til five-thirty, to keep the boors from flicking their cigars on the rugs."

As Mary grasped the nursemaid's words, she jabbed her teeth into her bottom lip. Damn them all to hell. At five-thirty, the girls wouldn't go down for another nap. They'd have their dinner, sitting with Annie and Susan.

While she, foolish Mary Brinsky, was stuck under the bed.

The night before, rowing to the pond, Mary had laid out everything in her head. At nap time, the girls would be alone on the second floor. The nursemaids—and the governess and Jennie too—would crowd in with the visitors, on the first floor. The agents and the village lads would steal a minute to look, paying no mind to the hall. The only eyes on the second floor would be the girls' closed eyes. And Effie and Bud Wylie weren't invited. They'd likely pout down in their cottage.

Mary would hide under the bed until she heard the racket start. Then she'd crawl out and whisper to Ruth that her mother changed her mind. Ruth could watch the show. "Come with me," Mary would say, "to see your papa press the fancy button. I'm Wilma. I'm helping Ingrid with the wash. Your mama sent me to get you." The gunroom faced northeast; the rowboat sat at the dock southwest of the big house. No one in the gunroom would catch sight of the rowboat, not even in daylight.

Mary wouldn't bother with a disguise this time. No need. The woman Ruth saw months ago, who rowed her into the Bay, wore spectacles and had curly blond hair. Mary wouldn't bother with an accomplice either. She'd heed the words of her former employer, Stuart Potter. "Simpler is better."

She'd even worked out how to deal with Esther. The tot would probably sleep deeper than Ruth. But if Esther woke, Mary would have words at the ready. "You keep quiet. I'll come back in a minute and bring you too." Then Mary would carry Ruth down the servants' stairs, out the back door.

Now, nothing would work. Still cursing to herself, Mary half listened to the nursemaids in the hall.

"This day isn't helping Susan's mood. She grumped at me even before she had all these visitors to feed."

"What's she fussing about?"

"She's scared she'll lose her job if the big man doesn't run again, or if he runs and loses, while the two of us and Lena and Sinclair—we'll go back to Washington and even if Cleveland's not president, the missus will keep us on. But different for Susan and the others from Bourne. If Cleveland's out, he'll take the family to New York and likely sell Gray Gables."

"Poor Susan. And now—smaller matter I suppose—she's nettled about not getting an invite. She says with the delay, the missus will want her and you to sit with the girls at their dinner, in the kitchen. That bloody kitchen is so far from the gunroom—you can't even get a peek."

Wrapped up in her sulking, Mary lost track of which nursemaid was talking. When she heard the word gunroom, she turned her mind back to the chatter.

The missus won't want the girls near the cigars and the coughing." Bonnie's voice? "She'll ask me to sit with Marion in the nursery. Remember how the missus follows Dr. Bryant's advice to keep babies from crowds? Bad luck for us. And she invited Lena and Jennie to the show. That's good luck for those two. We'll get the story from them."

"Damn," Mary whispered to herself. She was right. Ruth and Esther will eat dinner in the kitchen on the ground floor, far from the gunroom when the show starts. Susan and Annie will watch the girls. No grabbing Ruth. Mary bit harder on her lip, until she tasted blood.

"Time to stop throwing around those stuffed animals, girls. Make a decision. Only one stuffed animal each."

"After my nap, I wanna see the button."

Mary knew that whine and almost laughed despite her cramping limbs. Ruth wanted to join the day's fun, just as she'd wanted to row to a pond back in July to see the newborn baby. Mary's plan for this day came so close to working. It would have worked if those Atlanta idiots stuck to their schedule. Mary's mind fixed on Ruth's words, "I wanna see the button." Folks carried on as though a small black circle could open a wide new world. But for Mary, the world had shriveled to the dusty space under a bed.

"Your mother knows best." Annie's voice. "Those men aren't good company for children. Too much smoke and bad language." Another whine, probably from Ruth.

The nursemaids separated. Bonnie took Marion to the nursery and Annie brought the older girls to the bedroom. Mary wiggled her arms and legs under the bed, grateful that the sounds of Annie laying the girls down muffled everything else. First Esther. Then Ruth. She weighed little. The mattress barely sank. When Annie sat on the side of the bed to tuck in Ruth, the mattress sank only another inch.

Mary drew her finger inside her mouth, tapped the spot where she'd tasted blood. The red stain on her fingertip shattered her, dragging up thoughts of how all her fine plans came to nothing. Mary wiped her blood-stained fingertip on her sleeve. She had failed again.

The foul space under the bed smothered her.

A swooshing noise. The mattress sprang up as Annie stood and walked toward the window. Mary could see the bottom of a brown dress and white apron, set off against the pink-flowered wallpaper. Annie drew the curtains together, leaving the window open. "Stay quiet and rest well," she said, walking out and closing the door halfway.

In the hall, Annie's steps stopped. New voices came from the staircase and moved toward the bedrooms.

"Did you have a successful trip, ma'am?"

"Yes, I did. Enid Green was ready with my new gowns. She just made a few adjustments. And she did a good job of altering the seams on my older gowns. Will I ever recover after three children?" Frances Cleveland spoke softly. She didn't want to rouse her children. The lady sounded refined, and, despite her bother over her figure, she seemed at ease.

"Oh, ma'am, you look wonderful. Everybody says so." This new, soft voice must be Lena, the lady's maid.

"Thank you for saying that. I'm afraid my mirror presents a different picture. By the way, we didn't need to rush back here, did we? I was afraid I might miss the big event since the fittings took forever—Enid is meticulous—but Sinclair says the demonstration has been delayed until five-thirty. We could have stayed in town longer. Well, not much longer. I should nurse Marion."

More small talk, then the women walked on, with no sense that twenty feet away, an intruder squirmed under a bed.

Mary moved her mouth, silently spouting every curse word she heard in the bar in Buffalo. How could she flee, with the missus and Lena back? That guard at the door and Bonnie bought the story about Ingrid running to Boston to see her ailing sister. Would others? Lena would be suspicious. Mary remembered the Norcross maids jawing that Lena and Ingrid bickered over the well-muscled gardener. Even though Lena had the fancier job, that did not stop jealousy. No, Mary couldn't get in Lena's way.

Mary's whole life she felt trapped. Now, she really was trapped. She clamped her hand over her bloody mouth—a reminder not to holler. Each breath caught in her chest. Inches above her, Ruth and Esther napped. Their own breathing slowed.

A new trouble. Mary tightened her bladder. She wrapped a strand of hair around her thumb, again and again, trying to move her mind somewhere else.

At last. Annie came to check on the girls. Yawns, murmurs, rustling. Babbling from Esther. Annie seemed to be fussing with the girls' dresses.

"Are the men here?" Ruth asked.

"Yes, dear. They'll stay for a while."

Mary couldn't hold back her urge to pee. As soon as the girls left the room with Annie, Mary rolled out from under the bed and crawled toward the open door. She slowly closed the door, not all the way, just enough to block the view of people walking down the hall. She grabbed a glass she spotted on the bedside table. Squatting behind the door, she peed into the glass as best she could. The smell hit her.

The bedroom window was on the other side of the room, in sight of the partly open doorway. Mary closed the door a few more inches, crept to the open window, and spread the curtains. She set the glass on the part of the sill that stuck out. Just wide enough. She crept back to the door and eased it open a little, then crawled under the bed.

She felt better. She'd figure this out, not enough to get it right, but enough to keep on going. She'd stay under the bed until five-thirty. The girls would eat their supper then, sitting with Annie and Susan. At the same time, everyone else would crowd into the gunroom. Mary could flee down the servants' stairs. Without Ruth. If the nursemaids or the cook noticed, Mary could say she was bringing back linens early.

3:25. The cramping in her limbs was killing her. Once every half hour, she crawled behind the door to stretch. Between breaks she chewed on a slice of bread from a loaf she'd thrown into the laundry basket that morning. Along with towels and water. Along with a knife. Maybe to cut the loaf. No ham sandwiches this time. The only noises came from Lena or the missus or Jennie, going in and out of the big bedroom between the girls' room and the staircase. Mostly just footsteps.

5:16. Different footsteps, then three knocks on the missus's door—soft, loud, soft.

"Another telegram from Atlanta, ma'am. More delays. Mr. Thurber says seven o'clock." No sound. Would the lady swear under her breath? No, not this lady.

"Sinclair, those unprepared people in Atlanta disturbed this household for a full day. Ridiculous. Find Annie and Susan. Tell them to feed the girls right away, before the commotion starts. And to put them in bed early. I don't want the girls around a bunch of hungry men, puffing on their cigars and waiting for a nightcap."

"May I tell Annie and Susan that they can join in the ceremony? After the girls' supper, that is. After they're in bed."

"Ah, yes. Good of you to look out for them. Oh—you know, I asked Bonnie to stay in the nursery with Marion. If the baby is sleeping peacefully, tell Bonnie she can join us."

Oh my god. Mary lifted her head in shock, banging her forehead on the slats of the bed. Would her misery pay off? If the girls got into bed at six or six-thirty, and the entire household staff crowded into the gunroom, and the show began at seven…she had a chance.

"Sinclair, one more thing. Is Frances Johnston in the gunroom with the others?"

"The photographer lady?"

"Yes, please ask her if she'll give me another lesson while we're waiting. If she's been here for hours, she might like an excuse to step out."

A minute later, Mary heard, again, the soft, loud, soft knock. The butler.

"Mrs. Cleveland, Miss Johnston says yes, and the president says you can use his study."

The lady followed Sinclair downstairs, away from the bedrooms.

No chatter on the second floor. No need to listen. Just rest, just think.

6:35. Heavenly noises. Annie stood beside the bed, lighting the wick on the oil lamp while the girls took a last romp around the room. She dressed them in their nightgowns, tucked Ruth into her bed, settled Esther into her crib, turned down the knob on the lamp, and darted out, stopping twice in the hall before the stairs. Was Annie telling Lena and Bonnie to follow her to the gunroom? If the governess joined in too, she'd come from Effie's cottage, where she lodged, not from the second floor. The second floor would be empty!

6:50. Shuffling steps. The reporters and bigwigs took a break on the porch—Mary caught the talk and cigar smoke wafting up. Now they ambled back to the gunroom, in no rush. Their voices grew softer.

6:55. Two stragglers still on the porch, finishing their cigars. Mary looked at the clock again, praying it matched the clock in the gunroom, guessing she'd best follow the noise coming from downstairs.

A final warning from Sinclair. "One minute to go."

Now.

Scurrying out, Mary paid no heed to the cramping in her legs. She kept to the scheme she'd given up on two hours earlier, starting with a light tap on Ruth's shoulder, then a second tap.

"Your mama changed her mind. You can watch your papa press the button." Ruth half opened her eyes. Esther didn't move—still asleep. "I'm Wilma. I help Ingrid with the wash. Stay quiet. Don't wake your sister."

With Ruth in one arm and the basket in the other, Mary lumbered down the servants' stairs. Chatter rose from the gunroom, yelling and numbers counted down. The chatter became a roar. "That noise—it's because your papa asked the men to move to the train station. They're rushing there. The signals are sharper in the station."

Ruth stayed quiet on the path to the dock. But when Mary reached the rowboat, tied up in its usual spot, Ruth started to whimper. Did she know, even in the dark, that the dock wasn't the station, or maybe the sight of the boat stirred a bad memory. The clapping and racket from the house covered the girl's cries.

This time, Mary would take care of the ransom note herself. She reached into her pocket, dodged Ruth's flailing arms, and tucked the note halfway under the heavy bait box on the dock. *If you want Ruth back, put $150 under the horse trof in front of the Eldridge Lumber Yard, after dark. Do not involve police or officials. Then you will have repaid your debt. You know the meaning of the dollar amount. If you don't, remember 1863.*

XI

Part Eleven: Frances's World

Chapter Forty-Eight

September 18, 1895

Frances Cleveland stood in Grover's study, glad to be talking about photography with the lady photographer, Fannie Johnston. The two Franceses had agreed on Fannie as a nickname to avoid confusion. Frances busied herself with Fannie's camera, but even if she had concentrated instead on sounds above her on the second floor, she would hear nothing at all at 6:50 on the evening of the Exposition. Ten unremarkable weeks had passed since the kidnapping attempt, and although the fugitive was still on the run, the woman never tried again. Frances had no cause to be attentive.

Fannie glanced at the clock on the mantel. "I should move my camera and tripod to the gunroom." Frances reached out her arm to help. "No, you don't need to help. I'm accustomed to carrying my equipment. We're getting close to seven, and I want to capture your husband's finger on that button. Before we join the men, let me say this, and I mean it honestly, you have a talent for photography. I can give you another lesson this fall, when we're both back in Washington. I don't need to tell you that you have a significant advantage, knowing so many celebrated people we should immortalize with our cameras."

Frances composed her jaw. She didn't want to show how pleased she was at the compliment. Or was this the same false praise that always followed the wife of a president? No, Fannie had watched Frances's hands on the camera, had moved them an inch or two as necessary, had asked her to repeat back instructions, had nodded approval several times. Fannie wanted Frances to succeed. Yes, this could become a good hobby, better than the piano.

"I'd welcome another lesson."

Fannie looked at the carpet, then looked up.

"Mrs. Cleveland, Frances, I hope you don't mind my asking a question, since this is our third lesson. You're eager to learn photography, and you don't mind learning from me, with my reputation as, well, the pundits say a *new woman*, you know, an outspoken woman who defies conventions, and yet—yet—you're not for suffrage?

"You think it odd? So do most of my friends from college. I believe when women become wives and mothers, they use their energies in those ways. If they keep up with politics, which I can tell you from close observation, is a dirty business, then they can apply that knowledge to influence their husbands."

"I see. I suppose neither one of us can persuade the other. Forgive me for asking."

"Oh, no, don't apologize. I'm asked that all the time." Frances curled her lips. "By *new women*, that is. Admirable new women."

Fannie dipped her head, acknowledging the praise.

Laden with equipment, Fannie mouthed a thank-you as Frances opened the door of Grover's study, letting in the din and smoke from the other side of the residence. The women walked down a hall and entered the gunroom, ignoring stares from the men who kept quiet for a few seconds. The sun had almost set, so Susan carried in oil lamps to illuminate the crowded room. Frances noted the irony—her household had not switched to electricity for daily tasks.

The visitors became noisy again. Henry, with the side of his face pressed to the telephone's earpiece, sat beside Grover at a makeshift desk. Frances could tell that Henry was speaking to officials in Atlanta. He nodded at her. Almost time. Behind Henry, near the door leading to the narrow service hall, the grandfather clock showed 6:56, a tad short of the long-awaited 7:00.

Frances found a spot near Henry, while Fannie shooed men to the side and hurriedly positioned her camera. More visitors entered the room, ushered in by Sinclair, who must be clearing the porch. Surprising herself, Frances began to mirror the excitement of the spectators in the room.

"Gentlemen, ten seconds," Henry said, holding the telephone's earpiece to one ear and his pocket watch to the other ear. He began to count down from ten. The reporters joined the Western Union managers and town officials in the countdown. The youngest reporter, clutching a notebook with *Barnstable Pilot* inscribed on the front, rolled back and forth from his heels to his toes, looking like the heavens were about to open for him. Frances watched Fannie take photographs, and watched Grover flutter his pudgy thumb just over the button. He smiled—he was enjoying himself. Henry continued to count down. "Three, two, one." Cheers boomed through the residence as Grover hit the button.

Henry raised his arms, then lowered them halfway. Shush. "I'm waiting for a report." The crowd quieted. Still grasping the earpiece, Henry grinned. He turned to Grover. "Success. Mr. President, you turned on machines in an exposition hall in Atlanta, Georgia, by pressing a button in Bourne, Massachusetts." The clapping resumed, louder than ever. Frances wondered if the girls could sleep through the clamor.

She saw Grover signal with his eyes to Sinclair, and then stare at her, tilting his head one way and his hand the other. She understood. He'd asked Sinclair to serve the men a shot of whiskey, to mark the occasion. He knew Frances didn't approve, but would let it be.

When Grover stood, his audience at last quieted. "Thank you all for joining me for this momentous event, marking the power of American technology. I thank Western Union for their hard work, and I will send a telegram to the officials in Atlanta, thanking them for their hard work too. My steward is bringing whiskey—a round for all. Those of you who are here from the newspapers, make sure your stories extol the virtues of the progress we see today."

Frances clapped along with the men. She loved seeing Grover in his element—accomplishing, influencing, boasting. She should keep his talents in the forefront of her mind.

Sinclair walked around with shot glasses, followed by Susan, who passed out sweets. After a few sips of whiskey, the sound of the men's jabber only increased.

Reporters cornered Frances for quotes. She easily echoed Grover's message about progress. Glancing to the side, she saw him in high spirits as he presided over an event everyone could appreciate.

The guests began to leave, lining up on the porch for the coachman to return them to the station to catch the evening train. Frances glanced at the grandfather clock. Already 8:30. Annie glanced up at her, then at the clock too. "Ma'am, thank you for letting me and Bonnie watch." Annie craned her neck up to the taller nursemaid. "We'll go check on the children. Make sure they're asleep."

"I'll come with you. I never got to kiss them goodnight."

"Yes, ma'am." The three women left the smoky gunroom and ascended the staircase.

"Finally, fresh air." Frances took in a gulp.

Bonnie peeled off to the right, to check on Marion. Annie, with Frances just behind her, walked a few more steps, then turned left, pushing open the almost-closed door to the girls' room.

Frances bumped into Annie. Annie didn't move. Frances lowered her arm to Annie's shoulder to move her aside. The woman still wouldn't move.

Esther lay in the crib. No one lay in the bed.

"The lavatory," Frances croaked. "She must be there. Sick?"

Annie remained motionless.

"All right, I'll check myself."

Across the hall, Frances could see the open lavatory door. She checked behind the door, in the tub. She ran to the nursery. "Bonnie, is Marion here? Is Ruth here?"

The nursemaid turned from folding diapers and stared. Then she checked the infant to make sure the loud questions hadn't roused her. "Marion is fine. Ruth?"

Frances didn't answer. She ran back to the girls' room. Annie stood in the same spot, still motionless. Frances pushed past her into the room. She drew back the covers on the bed, looked under the bed. She darted to the crib and shook Esther awake.

Esther babbled nothing of use.

Frances leaned out the window to see if she could spot Jeffrey on the porch, guarding the front door. She saw him, then she also saw something else—a glass, sitting on the sill, filled with yellow liquid. She brought it inside and sniffed, then sped downstairs to catch Jeffrey.

This time, she'd push without hesitation, without apology. She'd find this woman, herself if necessary. If it was not too late.

Chapter Forty-Nine

September 18, 1895

Jeffrey Hazen took in Frances's colorless face. His own fear flared up, gripping his chest. She motioned to him to come to the side of the porch, out of earshot of the last two men awaiting a ride to the station. Frances choked out a few words. Hazen put up his palm and cocked his head toward the stairway. They sped upstairs, silent. Annie no longer stood in the doorway. The small woman was on the floor, writhing and sobbing. Bonnie crouched beside her, rubbing her back. Lena, who must have heard the sobs, entered and opened every drawer, making a racket, hoping to find a child too big to fit.

Hazen swung away from the women. He hadn't seen Cleveland for five minutes. Without taking a second to make excuses, he rushed downstairs to the gunroom, where he found the big man pontificating to Thurber about the wonders of electricity. Hazen drew a deep breath and offered a silent prayer of thanks. Whoever grabbed the child had not been after the president.

Hazen signaled that Cleveland and his secretary should come, fast. Cigars still in hand, the men followed Hazen. From the bottom of the stairs, they heard cries, Frances's atop Annie's. Cleveland didn't wait for an explanation. He bounded ahead, outpacing speedy Thurber.

Chapter Fifty

September 18-19, 1895

At a few minutes to seven, John Nolan slipped into Gray Gables, near enough to the gunroom to spot Jennie and to join in the clapping. Hours later, at nine-thirty, he struggled to stay awake. He'd made twenty trips that day, ferrying visitors from the railroad station to Gray Gables and back to the station. He'd just dropped off the last of them. He still had to return the landau to the stables and let the horses drink before he could ride back to his folks' home in Bourne for the night.

As Nolan drew up to Gray Gables, with the residence and dock in view, his pair of bays snorted and skittered. Across the lawn that stretched down to the waterfront, servants ran this way and that, swinging lanterns and yelling "Ruth!" Nolan spotted Jennie near the dock, her gray dress bright in the glow of the lantern she held. She craned her neck left and right down the shore path. Not far from her, Bud Wylie stood on the dock, peering into the Bay.

The horses were spooked. Nolan raced to the stables, unhitched them from the landau, and ran to Jennie. He saw Bud bend to pick up a piece of paper, then hold a lantern above it.

Almost reaching Jennie, Nolan slowed, mindful of her warning that no one should see them together. But she startled him—opened her arms and leaned into his chest. "Ruth's missing again." Jennie said only that, but from the feel of her arms and the touch of her hand on his shoulder, Nolan imagined her thoughts. *This time, do something.*

Ten feet away, Bud read the paper in his hand and yelled across the lawn. "Come, Hazen. Now." Turning to follow Bud's voice, Nolan saw the agents huddled on the porch with Thurber and the president. The men spun their heads toward the dock, where Bud waved the paper.

Nolan tapped softly on Jennie's shoulder. She should ease her arms. She let go and stepped back, her eyes following his. They should watch and listen.

Hazen dashed across the lawn to the dock and snatched the paper from Bud. The president followed, faster than anyone could have guessed. Donnella came next, matching the president's stride, guarding him. Thurber trailed a few paces back. The men listened to Bud say he couldn't find the rowboat, then Hazen grabbed the paper and read it, and handed it to Cleveland. "Please read aloud, sir, so Sky and Mr. Thurber can hear."

Nolan and Jennie listened to the same words the kidnapper had written on the first ransom note. Cleveland read with a shaky voice, especially when he got to the third sentence—*"You know the meaning of that amount."* The pain in his voice grew as he read the last sentence, a new one—*"If you don't, remember 1863."*

No one paid any notice to Nolan or Jennie, hovering off to the side, trying to catch every word.

"We'll search the Bay," Cleveland said. "Bud can take us out in the dory to the sailboat."

To Nolan, those words came across as an order. He saw Hazen and Bud trade glances—seemed like they agreed on something. Bud wrapped his muscled arm around the president's heft, holding him back.

"Can't see a thing in the Bay this time of night, Mr. President," Bud said. "We'll wait 'til first light." Hazen nodded in agreement.

"Don't tell me what we can't do. We have to do something."

"Right, sir. I'll round up the staff," Hazen said. "They'll search the grounds—" He frowned at the commotion around him. "In an orderly fashion."

Nolan wasn't sure if Hazen counted him among the servants now. Was the agent still stewing that Nolan waited to hand over the first ransom note? Or that he followed Gilder's hairbrained scheme to ask villagers if they'd seen a lost woman? Best to step forward or to slink away? He couldn't ask Jennie what she thought because Cleveland, Donnella, and Thurber—their eyes fixed on Hazen—hadn't budged.

Hazen stared at the bay, then muttered low, almost to himself. "It's possible the missing boat is a feint, a trick to draw us the wrong way."

The president tugged his mustache, showing his twisted mouth. "Damn," he said. "Hard to know."

Nolan watched Hazen stride across the lawn while the president plodded behind, holding fast to the ransom note. Hazen looked over the servants. They'd slowed down, waiting word on what to do. "Susan, Sinclair, everyone—form a circle near the porch."

"John, we should join the staff," Jennie whispered. "The agents might wonder if we don't. Even though I'm not sure we're in the clear in their eyes." She answered his question before he could ask.

Nolan followed Jennie to the circle, then set his gaze on the front door. The missus came out, turning her head to take in the scene. She must've been hunting for Ruth in the residence. The big man shuffled to her. He handed her the note and looked in the distance while she read. Before she finished, he left her, taking up a spot in the circle. The missus slipped the paper in her pocket. She tromped on the porch, in plain view, up and back. Nolan wagged his chin slightly so Jennie would notice too. She looked longer and harder than he had.

"We believe Ruth has been abducted again," Hazen said, scanning the crowd. "This time, the woman left three clues. First, the latest ransom note. It's similar to the one from July 7th—yes—we did eventually find one."

Nolan shrank from Hazen's glance.

"I believe the same criminal is at work," Hazen continued. "The cramped handwriting resembles the handwriting on the original note. Second, the rowboat is missing, like before. And here's the third clue. We found a drinking glass of—forgive me—of urine on the windowsill of the girls' room. And a few drops of what looks like the same thing on the floor behind the door. The liquid in the glass—forgive me again—was dark yellow, suggesting the woman was uncomfortable for a time. She might've hidden in the bedroom, under the bed, while the girls slept. Tomorrow at dawn, we'll take the sailboat and hunt for Ruth."

Then Hazen barked out orders. He named all the women but Jennie. They should continue to search the residence. He named all the men but Nolan. They should search the grounds, as they had done before. Sinclair was to wait a minute for an assignment, and Donnella was to stay close to the president.

Nolan kept his eyes on Hazen, hoping for a task. Instead, he saw Hazen catch Cleveland's sideways glance.

"Oh, before you spread out, listen carefully. Again, the president and I insist that you keep this crime to yourselves. We don't want idiots to get any ideas."

The servants scattered. Nolan watched Hazen beckon to Sinclair, then strained to catch the agent's words. "Sinclair, I need you to deliver the ransom. I'm sure you can find the funds in the household coffers. Follow the kidnapper's instructions even though I doubt she'll pick up the money if she's on the Bay." Sinclair sped off.

Once the lawn emptied, Hazen turned to Nolan and Jennie.

"Nolan," Hazen said. "I'll ask Mr. Thurber for the names of the men you took to the station and when. Then I'll check with the stationmaster to confirm your whereabouts, you know, to confirm that no visitors canceled. If I can account for how you spent all your time today, then you and Jennie will help with the search tomorrow morning."

The man's crazy, Nolan thought. While I shuttled visitors from the station, he thinks I had free time to snatch Ruth. Before Nolan could protest, Jennie shot him a look. Keep quiet. Don't make this worse.

* * *

Nolan checked on the pair of bays he had ignored for an hour, then rode in a daze to his folks' home in Bourne. He fell into a deep sleep until his mother rumbled around in the kitchen just before dawn. He bounced up, dressed, and said he was needed at the residence early. As he went to saddle his horse, he spotted Mr. Wilcox walking toward him, with hunched shoulders. The druggist lived just down the street. He glanced up.

"I'm on my way to the pharmacy. I wanted to ca, ca, catch you, but I thought you'd still be sleeping."

Ahhh, that stutter again. Nolan let himself show impatience. He had to get back to Gray Gables to make sure Hazen didn't doubt him any longer. And to help search for Ruth.

"I'm off to work."

"Just give me a minute." Mr. Wilcox looked left and right. The street was empty at that early hour. "Remember when you came to the pharmacy last month?" The druggist had softened his New England sounds thanks to his schoolteacher wife's harping. "You said you were trying to find a woman, to help Mrs. Cleveland. I told you I didn't remember a strange woman coming in. That set me to thinking you must be in the good graces of the Clevelands. See, I have a problem—a troublesome matter."

Nolan eased his pout and widened his eyes.

"You know my wife, Catherine, your old teacher, she inherited jewels, fine things, some rubies and such. And you know Walter Breen, from the other side of town. He comes to the pharmacy some days for bandages—the fellows at the mill get a lot of cuts—and he sees Catherine when she helps me out. She wears those rubies in the shop, though I tell her not to." Wilcox shook his head in disapproval.

"A few days ago, Walter came in as I was about to cl, cl, close, with a story I didn't like. He said he'd come into possession of some jewelry. Said it was his great aunt Eleanor's, and he couldn't use it. He wondered if my missus would want it. Offered to sell at a good price." Wilcox chomped on his bottom lip for two seconds.

"I did take a gander. One of the things in the pouch he brought was a silver locket. Beautiful piece. Bear in mind, I have excellent eyesight. I need to, to make sure I calibrate all the pills and potions properly. Walter might not have such good eyesight. I examined the locket, and I saw, just faint on the back, the initials FCF. I remembered that he said the great aunt, the woman who left it to him, was Eleanor. Reason I remembered is that my sister out in Brewster, her name's Eleanor. I told Walter I wasn't interested, and he should try somewhere else." Wilcox paused again, then lowered his voice.

"I wondered. Could FCF stand for Frances Clara Folsom, the president's wife? Walter wasn't much for reading—wouldn't know the name Folsom even if he spotted the initials. Can't say if he just laid hands on the jewelry or if he's had it a while and couldn't sell it fast. Then I wondered who I could tell. John, if you get on with the lady, could you ask if she's missing a locket? I don't want to get Walter into trouble, and I've known his mother, the Widow Breen, my whole life, but I don't want a thief in these parts either."

As Wilcox spun out his tale, Nolan felt a chill rise through his spine. Would Walt dare creep into the missus's bedroom on his own? Maybe he found a woman to help? The woman who grabbed Ruth? Or maybe Walt's crime had nothing to do with the kidnapping?

"Walt works sometimes at Gray Gables, but I'm busy with the carriages and the hosses, so I don't talk to him much. And he mostly keeps to himself. Mr. Wilcox, what do ya know about his ma?"

"Good woman. She helps out in the bakery."

"Does Walt have an older sister?"

"Don't think so. Just two brothers. Catherine taught them all. He does have a girlfriend. She works at the Norcross House. Why?"

The chill in Nolan's spine turned to ice.

"No time to say." Nolan leaped on his horse. Wilcox handed over more than a clue. He offered a way to patch things up with Jennie, to win back her trust.

Nolan raced to Gray Gables, pulling up just after sunrise. Sinclair stood on the porch, talking to Bud and Mr. Thurber. They looked like they hadn't slept at all. Nolan squinted at them. Had anyone found Ruth during the night? They understood the squint and frowned.

"I've news," Nolan yelled to Sinclair, while tying up his overheated horse.

"Get Hazen." Sinclair took one look at the sweat on Nolan and his mount, and then pointed to the reception hall, not the servants' door. Thank God—now Nolan knew he was no longer under suspicion. Thurber and the stationmaster must have told Hazen that the day before, the coachman spent every minute ferrying visitors up and back.

Nolan started to sniff himself, to see if he smelled, then stopped. No one would care. He followed Sinclair into the house, almost bumping into Hazen and the president and the missus. The couple kept a careful space between them while stiffly holding hands. All three were walking toward the porch, probably to make sure Bud was ready to sail.

Sinclair held up his hand to slow them down. "Sir, Ma'am, sorry to interrupt, but John Nolan wants to speak to Agent Hazen, immediately."

Hazen scrunched his mouth into a question. Nolan supposed he should wait until he could talk to Hazen alone. But the missus needed to hear, right away.

"Walt. Walt Breen." Nolan tried to control his jittery voice. "The village fellow who helps patrol. Did you or Agent Donnella question him?"

The big man and the missus stared at Nolan, then at Hazen, who snapped his head back and took a second to answer. "I did, the day after Ruth went missing the first time. That day, Walter helped the gardener trim the bushes—the gardener and the other groundsmen confirmed that—and then I saw Walter join the search. As for yesterday, even though Walter doesn't work most nights, we asked him to stay when we heard about the delays. Told him to send word to the mill that he'd be late. We wanted him to walk the dead line, so Sky and I could patrol the gunroom." Another pause. "Why?"

Nolan's throat went dry. What if Wilcox had it wrong? What if the locket belonged to a different lady with the same initials? The missus stared, hoping for news. This was the moment—he'd either blunder like before or show he could do right.

Nolan swallowed, then swallowed again until he could speak. "Mr. Wilcox, he's the druggist in town. He knows me and my folks. Knows I work heah. Caught me this morning, standing by my place. Told me Walt Breen had tried to sell some jewels that an aunt left him. Walt figured Mr. Wilcox might buy them. Wilcox didn't think the aunt was real, and when he looked ovah one of the jewels—out of curiosity—a silver locket—he saw the lettahs FCF on the back."

The missus gasped. She pulled her hand from the president's and flew upstairs, shouting as she climbed. "That's me, Frances Clara Folsom. My father gave it to me. I wore it every day until I married. The initials almost wore away." Hazen ran after her, leaving Nolan alone with the president.

"Where is this—what's his name—Walter Green—now?" Nolan bit back his irritation. The president didn't know the names of villagers who helped with the grounds, not even those who sometimes guarded his wife and children on their walks.

"I don't know, sir. Your agent sets the patrol schedule."

Hazen and the missus ran back down. The locket was missing.

"Let's think," Hazen said. "No thefts or other crimes here all summer, aside from the kidnapping. The theft and the kidnapping could be related. Or not. In any case, I'm troubled that someone snuck upstairs to steal that locket. A man—?"

A flush of excitement ran through Nolan's body. They might like this detail. He turned to Hazen.

"Sir, I picked up something else from Mr. Wilcox." Nolan felt three pairs of eyes bore into him. "He said Walt Breen has no sisters, but he does have a sweetheart."

Those three pairs of eyes fixed on each other.

"Hmmm," Hazen said. "Maybe too young. We'll see. I'll talk to Walter Breen before Bud searches the Bay. Breen's probably at his folks' house in Bourne since he's not due here 'til noon today. I suppose he could have snuck to the bedroom upstairs, but it's more likely he had help from a woman. I'll check my records for his address and go find him."

"No need," Nolan said. "I can show you. I live in Bawn."

On the way out the door, Hazen collared Sinclair. "Wake up, Donnella. Tell him to guard the president and the little ones while I'm off." Then Hazen turned his head over his shoulder to address the big man.

"And sir, like I said, don't let Bud take the boat out until your coachman and I get back."

Nolan turned aside to hide his grin. Yesterday he was under suspicion himself. Today, he was nearly a deputy, helping the president's lead Secret Service agent.

Chapter Fifty-One

September 19, 1895

On the trail to Bourne, Nolan rode alongside Hazen. The two spoke little. Nolan had let his pride swell ten minutes earlier when he stood in the grand hall of the residence, but now, back on his familiar horse, he brooded. Had he overstepped his station as a coachman?

Nolan led Hazen to the Breens' neat-looking, yellow frame house. Hazen checked his pocket watch and nodded. The family should be awake. A tall woman with a toothy grin answered Hazen's knock. She peered beyond Hazen and smiled at Nolan. As a boy, he'd fetched bread from the bakery where she worked.

Hazen identified himself, using more titles than Nolan remembered, and then barged in. Nolan followed. He smelled toast mingling with coffee and saw two boys at the table, but no Walt. Nolan nodded at the boys, who'd been a few years behind him in school.

"Need to talk to Walter. Is he here?" Hazen asked. Walt's ma gaped at him, tongue-tied.

The boys glanced at Nolan. He turned away. After a long second, the older boy muttered an answer. "Walt's asleep. He worked late last night."

Hearing a rustle, Nolan turned toward a door that must lead to a bedroom. The other faces followed his as Walt, bare-chested and looking lankier than ever, shuffled into the kitchen. He managed to get his wits about him and ask a question. "Did you find her?" He barely finished the sentence before he knew he'd said too much. "Ma, the little Cleveland girl was playing hide and seek."

"Walter, enough of that. Let's talk," Hazen said. "Privately. Put on a shirt and shoes and meet me outside, in front. Nolan—" Hazen contorted his face.

Nolan caught on. He slipped behind the house to keep watch on the back door and window. Glad to be trusted with a task, he set his eyes on possible escape routes, until he heard Walt's thin, squeaky voice drift from the front yard. Judging from the sound, Walt was too scared to bolt. Nolan strode to the front to see if Hazen needed him there.

Hazen wasted no time. "Are you in possession of stolen jewelry?"

"Joolry?" Walter dragged out the word, stalling.

"Yes, jewelry," Hazen said, angrily.

Walt's ma and her sons plastered their faces against the front window. Nolan caught the widow's gaze, heavy with fear.

Walt stalled more, taking his time to answer. "What joolry?"

The halting answers settled matters for Hazen. "I'm taking you to the constables. Do you have a mount?"

"No." The word came out faintly.

"Then you walk ahead of us. No time for goodbyes. Nolan, tell his ma we're taking him to the station to question him."

Nolan winced. This was not the kind of help he wanted to give. He mumbled a few words to Widow Breen and mounted his horse without looking back. He caught up with Hazen, who rode slowly as Walt inched forward on foot, head down.

"Faster," Hazen yelled, without much effect.

Ten minutes later, Hazen laid claim to the constables' office, sending Chief Sullivan and Deputy Combs to idle outside. At the doorway, Nolan hesitated.

"Stay. I need another set of ears."

Nolan looked to the side to hide his smile. He took Deputy Combs's chair, and Hazen took Chief Sullivan's chair. Walt lowered his body onto a wooden bench.

Hazen set his eyes on the miserable fellow. "We believe you stole jewelry from a second-floor bedroom in Gray Gables. If you found a way to sneak up there once, you may have done so again last night. Tell me, where is Ruth Cleveland?"

Staring at his lap, Walt folded without a fight. "I have joolry that's not mine. I—" He went quiet. "But the girl? Don't know." He looked down at his shoes.

Nolan winced, almost pitying Walt. The fellow couldn't even spin a good lie.

Hazen waited. He tapped his foot, loudly. Nolan guessed that Hazen learned foot tapping as part of the Secret Service method.

The tapping worked. Nolan could almost see Walt deciding to spread the blame. "There's a maid at the Norcross. Polly Pearson. Pretty girl, eighteen. We been stepping out. It's hard, me working odd shifts, sometimes nights. We get in walks when we can." He squirmed. Looked at his shoes again.

"Keep going."

"Now and then, she filches something shiny from a guest room at the Norcross. That set her to thinking. When the butlah and housekeepah at Gray Gables need extra hands for heavy cleaning for a day or two— scrubbing floors and grates—they put out a call to village girls. Sometimes Polly takes the job, up on the second floor. She might find herself some jools and take 'em home. She's a sweet girl, Polly is, and nevah knows what to do with these, um, items. So, she says to me, try and sell the jools. We're fixing to wed, want to build a place of our own, with a bit of farmland. The money'd help."

Nolan kept his eyes on Hazen, who kept his eyes on jabbering Walt. When Walt finally took in air, Hazen shook his head. "You gave me a lot of details. A real lot. More than I need. Any chance you're trying to take my attention off something else?"

Walt broke down, weeping. Nolan stared at Hazen with respect. The agent sure knew his business.

"Pull yourself together and tell me where Ruth is, fast."

Another wait. This time, not a stall. The fellow tried to catch his breath, to talk, to admit.

"Don't know where she is, but—"

"Stop looking at your shoes and talk."

"I'm sorry about what I did. But you gotta find Margaret."

Nolan watched Hazen wave his fingers at Walt in a tell-me-more motion.

"She nevah told me her name—Margaret Bright—but, I got it from Polly's talk. Margaret's chief housekeepah at the Norcross. She found out Polly cops joolry from the guests. If you ask me, Margaret knows because she nicks stuff herself. Said she'd run straight to the constables about Polly if I didn't do what she wanted." Walt's weeping turned to sobs, and his nose started to drip, but he kept going.

"Margaret told me to row out to Red Brook Pond. That was back in July. From the Bay, an inlet leads to Red Brook. She knew that. If I found her in a shack there, she'd set me a task. Something about a note, or a lettah. If she wasn't there, she said to forget the whole thing. Either way, she said she wouldn't snitch on Polly." Walt looked up, wiping the back of his hand across his wet face. "The night Margaret wanted me to row out there, that was the day the girl went missing. The first time. Then I heard the shouts—someone found her. Anyway, I rowed to the pond at night, just like Margaret asked. No Margaret, so I went back to sleep. See, I didn't figure Margaret could have anything to do with Ruth Cleveland, and I still wanted to keep eyes off Polly. And by that time, the girl was safe. I figured I'd done what Margaret wanted, and I could forget the whole thing. Walt bowed his chin, then raised it. "I didn't say nothing. But I was in the circle last night when you talked about the pee and the rowboat. The boat was gone again, on a day Ruth went missing again. Could be Margaret. She could've rowed to Red Brook Pond—seemed like she'd scouted it out good. I should've told ya last night. But I couldn't get Polly in trouble."

Twisting his head, Nolan tried to get Hazen's eye, to slip in a question. Hazen paid him no heed, looking only at Walt.

Nolan had to cut in. "Walt, is Margaret Bright from around heah?"

"No. Polly said she worked for rich folks out west."

Nolan turned that answer over in his head—Margaret Bright was not from New England.

Bloody hell.

The Clayton woman, the local washerwoman at the door, had told Donnella that Ingrid's sister was sick. She didn't say "sistah." And she said "door," not dah. Nolan wondered whether he should take a minute to explain why he asked.

Later, Nolan would realize that if the woman had talked to the household staff, they might not catch on to her speech. The ones who came up from Washington with the Clevelands were not New Englanders, so the woman would have sounded, well, regular to them.

Before Nolan could say more, he saw Hazen's mouth tighten. Something jolted him, too.

"Margaret Bright?" Hazen asked. "Bright's her surname? You're certain it's not Mary Brinski?"

"Polly said Margaret Bright. Mary could be a nickname."

"I'm asking Constable Sullivan to put you in the lockup." Hazen stood and spoke fast. "Do not talk about anything you've told me, and do not say the name Margaret Bright. Understand?"

The minute Walt lowered his eyes, Hazen opened the front window and beckoned to Constable Sullivan, who idled close by.

"Lock up Walter Breen for fencing stolen goods. I'll help with the paperwork later."

Hazen slammed the window and turned to Nolan. "Norcross House. Fastest way." Nolan tamped down yet another grin—what a perfect task for a coachman.

Riding fast to the hotel, the two men shared their stories. "Her talk," Nolan said, "she wasn't from heah. No way. I don't figure she was a Clayton."

"Her name, Hazen said. "Too close to Mary Brinski. Yeah, I'll tell you about her. And her husband George." Fifteen minutes later, Nolan and Hazen dismounted in front of the hotel.

Hazen marched into the office. "Secret Service Agent Jeffrey Hazen here, chief of President Grover Cleveland's protective detail. I met you once in

July, when I looked over your guest register. I need your help again." Nolan stood to the side.

"I'm Maurice Bolton, Manager of the Norcross House. What can I do for you?"

"Margaret Bright. Is a maid with that name in your employ?"

"Yes, why do you ask?" Nolan thought Bolton looked more worried than he should from that simple question.

"I need to talk to her about a confidential matter."

"Mrs. Bright has worked here since May. An honest woman, a hard worker." His eyes flicked to the side, as though he had another thought about her. "You don't think she's done anything improper, do you?"

"We can discuss that later. Right now, I need to speak to her."

"She's not here." Nolan saw Bolton press his lips together. "She worked for an hour or two yesterday morning. Then the maids Margaret supervised told me she went missing. I knocked on the door of her room this morning. She's not there. I'm not sure where she went."

Nolan knew he had no business stepping in, but he couldn't hold back. "Mr. Bolton, is this Margaret Bright from heah? Does she sound like she's from Massachusetts?"

"No. Somewhere else." Bolton tilted his head. "Another state, I believe. West of here."

Hazen and Nolan stared at each other for an instant. They raced out of the hotel, paying Bolton no mind, not seeing his baffled look.

Chapter Fifty-Two

September 19, 1895

It was almost ten in the morning when Jeffrey Hazen rode up to Gray Gables. He barely slept the night before, but he felt more elated than tired—finally, some progress. John Nolan rode alongside. With an ear for local sounds, he had come in handy.

The big man and Frances stood stiffly on the porch, watching the driveway, waiting. William Sinclair and Sky Donnella framed the front door, Sinclair on one side, Sky on the other. Henry Thurber paced on the lawn.

Nolan grabbed the reins, preparing to bring the horses back to the stable. "No," Hazen said. I need you with me. Sinclair, mind handling the horses?" Sinclair frowned and hurried to take over hostler duty.

Hazen met Frances's eyes, trying to signal news, then turned to the president. "Sir, there's more to Walter Breen's story. He tells us that just before July 7th, the housekeeper from the Norcross House sniffed out that his girlfriend filched jewels. That housekeeper's name is Margaret Bright." He gave a piercing look. "Close to Mary Brinski, right? An alias?" The big man winced. Frances leaned forward, eyes wide. "This woman told Breen she'd forget what she knew if he'd deliver a note for her to Gray Gables—after picking it up from her at Red Brook Pond.

"All that was in connection with the first abduction. Breen and I suspect the same woman's trying a second time. Here's my thinking. She stole a rowboat again, and asked for the same ransom, and waited for a distraction like before, so she's probably sticking to the same location. We'll search the pond."

Hazen turned to Nolan. "Mr. President, your coachman has something to add."

"Sir, when I pulled up—" Nolan's voice shook. He cleared his throat. "Up to the front of the residence yesterday, 'round eleven, a woman, maybe in her forties, talked to Agent Donnella. She toted a laundry basket and said she was heah to fill in for Ingrid Mann, whose sistah was sickly."

Cleveland narrowed his eyes. "Ingrid Mann?"

"Our laundress," Frances said to her husband, with an impatient look.

"So?" Cleveland asked Nolan.

"She told Agent Donnella her name was Wilma Clayton, and that seemed all right to me, even though I didn't recognize her. See, Clayton's a family name 'round heah. They own farms all over the county. The problem is, she didn't sound like, well, like a Yankee."

Hazen worried about this part of Nolan's story. He might imply that procedures were inadequate. Sky, still on the porch, stiffened and canted his head oddly. Then Hazen saw Nolan nod at Sky, almost imperceptibly.

"Sir," Nolan said, looking at the president, "I don't think Agent Donnella thought much about how she sounded, and he tried to check her out, he really did—he asked her the full name of your regulah laundress, and she knew it."

Hazen hadn't told Nolan to protect Donnella. Nolan could hold a grudge against Donnella after that July interrogation, but the coachman, a good man, didn't want to get the junior agent into trouble.

"Then I saw the woman who called herself Wilma go into your house."

The president and his wife said nothing, just stared at Nolan.

"Sir," Hazen said, "I'm thinking Mary Brinski uses two aliases—Margaret Bright and Wilma Clayton."

The president took a second to collect himself, then bellowed. "Red Brook Pond. Where is it?"

"I used to fish there," Nolan said, his voice steady now. "It's off an inlet on the east side of the Bay, a ways south of heah. Swampy. Lotsa places to hide."

"Hurrah. At last," the president said, pumping Hazen's hand, then Nolan's. "Bud must know the pond. He's waiting at the dory to take us to the sailboat. There's a good breeze so we can make time." Frances leaned around her husband to kiss Hazen's cheek. He wouldn't add that to his report to his brother. Or maybe he would.

"Sir, I'll meet you at the dock—I just need to run to my office for a minute. Nolan, don't go far."

At ten minutes after ten, Hazen rushed out of the residence toward the dock, followed by the president, his wife, Donnella, and Thurber. Bud was preparing the sailboat, with help from Nolan.

Hazen turned around, sizing up his followers. He rubbed the side of his mouth, almost scratching the skin. Why, he asked himself, didn't I anticipate this? No way he could bring Cleveland along. He addressed himself to the five men and one woman looking to him for guidance.

"I don't want a crowd. We may anchor some distance from the pond and wade in to sneak up on the woman. Better to keep the numbers down. We need Bud, and I want to take Nolan. He's been to the pond too." Hazen turned to the president. "You'll stay here, sir, with Sky as guard, just in case the woman who took Ruth has her sights on you as well. And Mr. Thurber, you should stay, to keep the household calm. I could see when I walked through the residence just now—everyone is on edge."

"Jeffrey, I'm joining you," Cleveland said.

"Sir, I don't know a courteous way to say this. I don't think you can sneak up on anyone." He ran his eyes over the president's bulk. The big man patted his mustache in a sign of partial recognition rather than annoyance at the slur.

Loyal Thurber stepped up to help make the case. "Grover, you know—you must know—we cannot let you go when there's even a tinge of danger."

Cleveland frowned, nodded.

"I'll stay here with Agent Donnella and Henry, praying for you."

Hazen startled at Cleveland's words. The man had never talked about praying. Or church. Or God. Even though his pa was a minister. Cleveland was indeed frantic.

Hazen took Sky aside. "I know you want to join the hunt. The problem is, the kidnapper likes distractions. If she has an accomplice, that man, or woman, if they're lurking around here, would consider—"

"I know. Your search, away from here, is another distraction. I can't take my eyes off the president." Hazen bobbed his head in thanks.

Sky and Thurber walked with Cleveland back to the residence. Frances Cleveland didn't follow. She stood still, planted on the lawn at the start of the dock. Hazen frowned at her.

"I'm coming with you." She spoke flatly, with no hint of a question.

"Not wise. Three of us on that sailboat are more than enough."

"I'm coming with you." Her tone left no room for argument.

The wind carried her voice. Partway back to the house, the president suddenly turned around. He parted from Henry and Sky and came back to use his arm to lead his wife to the house. She shoved him away. Hazen couldn't believe his eyes. The two tussled with each other. She pounded him. Hazen stood two feet away, wondering if his protection duties included separating the missus from the president. Finally, the president extricated himself, yielding to Frances. "And the babe?" he asked her, with a quiver in his voice.

"I nursed her an hour ago." Frances didn't seem to care who overheard. "I'll make sure Bud gets me back before she's hungry again." She scrunched her head into her shoulders. "I let my guard down." She raised her head. "We'll find her."

The president turned to Hazen and raised his arms in a show of surrender. "Jeffrey, you keep Mrs. Cleveland safe."

What a posse, Hazen thought to himself. An unarmed skipper, an unarmed coachman, and milady. He shuddered, then squared his shoulders. They must return with Ruth. Alive.

Chapter Fifty-Three

September 19, 1895

Frances divided her attention while she stood on deck beside Nolan and Jeffrey. She watched Bud skipper the sailboat through the rough current with his usual skill, south down the Bay. And she watched her feet because she wobbled with every wave. But mostly, she watched the shoreline. When she spotted an inlet or a cove, she expected Bud to steer toward the surrounding salt marshes and tidal flats. He must have noticed the direction of her gaze because he signaled not yet with a shake of his head and his copper-colored hair. We're not at the inlet to Red Brook Pond. Frances had no way to check the time. The Bay seemed endless.

Suddenly, a command. "Hold on," Bud yelled, as he tacked into the wind. Frances grabbed the rail to keep from stumbling. Bud narrowed his eyes, then leaned his head back slowly, as though reassuring himself. He looked at Nolan, who answered with a nod of approval, and at Jeffrey, whose face glowed with relief. At last, Frances thought—Red Brook Pond.

"We stop now," Bud said. "Too shallow to get closah." He pointed to an inlet. "A rowboat could get in with no trouble. Mrs. Cleveland, stay on the sailboat. Wait for us."

After Bud dropped anchor, the men waded ashore. Frances climbed out behind them, hiked up her dress to her knees, and fell into line. They looked over their shoulders. They looked at each other. "Nothing will stop her,"

Jeffrey said, shrugging. "Trust me." After a second, he added, "like I've come to trust her."

Nolan said he'd fished for bass here, approaching from the other side. He offered his opinion, quietly. He considered the eastern end of the pond, or possibly the adjacent woods, the most likely hiding spot. Few people ventured out that far. Margaret, or was she Mary, could stash the rowboat at that end, dodging the bogs and the clumping eelgrass closer to the Bay. If some hermit or fisherman had built a shed on the eastern end, it might still stand.

Once on land, Nolan took the lead. Frances looked at Jeffrey, expecting him to balk. Instead, he settled himself in the second position and arranged the others with Frances third and Bud in the rear. Nolan led the little crew down the overgrown path around the perimeter of the pond. He lifted his hands, palms out, and lowered his arms, then raised them again. Be quiet. Every time Frances or Bud accidentally snapped a branch, Nolan stopped and flapped the same warning.

The hem of her dress—the same dress she had worn for twenty-four hours—skimmed the swampy edge of the stagnant pond. She ignored the dampness at her ankles. She ignored the high-pitched chirp of ospreys and the honking of Canada geese. She ignored the two men ahead of her. She fixed her attention on listening for human sounds while she scanned the path and bogs. Fifteen minutes passed, with no sign of Margaret Bright or Ruth. Frances worried that the woman picked a different pond or one of the islands in the Bay.

Soon her breasts would feel full. How long could Marion last without nursing? Should Bud sail around the entire shore of the Bay? That would take hours. And again, her constant worry haunted her. Shouldn't she insist Grover notify the authorities and the public, to form search parties?

Frances's second-guessing stopped in an instant. She bumped into Jeffrey, who bumped into Nolan, while Bud bumped into her. Nolan gestured, this time with an extra flap of his arms. He put his hand to his ear, asking them to listen. Ahead and to the right, Frances caught a rustling noise. Not her own. The others caught it too.

Now Jeffrey took charge. He pointed to Bud, then to the path. Bud should continue around the pond, to look for the rowboat. Next, Jeffrey pointed to Frances and Nolan, and then to himself. They should follow him off to the right, on a narrow trail through a stand of oaks and pines. For a minute, the three walked slowly, quietly, toward the sound. The trail curved down and to the right.

"Found it," Bud yelled from the waterline path. "Found the rowboat."

Before Frances could jump with relief, Jeffrey spoke, with an unexpectedly gentle voice. "Margaret Bright?"

Ahead, Frances saw the crumbling remains of an old lean-to, with a woman in front, holding Ruth, holding her tightly. Ruth, silent, faced the shack.

"Ruth, Ruth." Frances screamed and started running. Jeffrey stuck out his arm to stop her. "Not yet," he ordered.

At the same time, hearing the sound of her name, Ruth turned and screamed too.

Jeffrey raised his voice, yelling over the racket. "Margaret, we know you are Mary Brinski. Put the child down and lift your arms."

The woman grasped Ruth tighter with her left arm and reached with her right into what must be a pocket.

With absolute clarity, Frances saw a knife.

She tried to bolt around Jeffrey. He held her back, with force.

Jeffrey spoke loudly, firmly. "You are holding a child, an innocent child. Put her down and put that knife down."

For a long second, Frances heard nothing except Ruth's screams as the woman searched for words.

"No. You get Cleveland. To hear me out and to get down on his fat knees to beg."

Frances spoke before Jeffrey could. "He's at Gray Gables. Tell me what you want him to know. I will report back. I will apologize for him."

Mary's eyes met Frances's.

"Your husband, that brute, he hired my husband to fight for him. You think George survived the war? He survived, but like a shell of a man. He hurt his whole life. He couldn't give me children." She tightened her left arm around Ruth. "The brute never paid George what he was due. Your husband sits at a desk and rides in a carriage and has three daughters. He should rot in hell."

"Mary, my husband is ashamed. He did wrong. One hundred and fifty dollars is under the trough at the lumber yard. You can fetch it, or we will get it and give it to you. Harming my child will not help George Brinski. You must know that."

"Ha. Should I harm her? Maybe. Maybe not. But I need the brute to grovel."

The woman raised the knife within an inch of Ruth's neck.

Frances shrieked and struggled to free herself from Jeffrey's clutch. His left hand tightened around her chest, while he released his right hand. She kept her eyes on the woman's arm.

Every day for the next fifty-two years, Frances would remember the worst minutes of her life. She would hear Ruth's screams, she would see a flash of orange, she would taste her own bile.

In the woods, the woman lowered the knife as Frances caught sight of a mop of ginger hair. Bud Wylie hurtled out from behind the lean-to. He charged the woman and seized the knife, letting Ruth tumble to the ground. Ruth's screaming almost drowned out the single shot from Jeffrey's revolver. Mary Brinski fell against Bud Wylie. He held her, as the blood from her chest soaked her dress, then he lowered the lifeless woman. Frances knelt on the ground, with her arms around Ruth.

Jeffrey faced the miserable scene and spoke. His voice, though quieter than usual, did not waver.

"Bud, take Mrs. Cleveland and Ruth back to Gray Gables. Use water from the Bay to wash your shirt and Ruth's nightgown." Jeffrey paused and looked out into the distance. "Nolan, you and me, we'll stay here 'til after dark. We're only a little way from the Bay." Jeffrey moved his head an inch, and Nolan seemed to follow his meaning.

"Now, everyone, listen up. No good will come from talking about what happened." Jeffrey lingered on the words no good. "My brother would have to investigate my actions. I care about that, but there's more. The President will not want any of this to get out. He has a connection to the woman that's, that's unpleasant. If he decides to run again, his enemies will have a field day. Here's what we tell anyone who knows Ruth went missing. We found her along the shore, in the care of a strange woman. With John Nolan's help, I took the woman into custody, to a prison, in an undisclosed location. If Bolton at the Norcross House asks what we learned, we tell him we discovered she was a longtime thief and, again, she's in prison. Understood?"

Frances watched Jeffrey's expression change, as he tried to speak to her with his eyes. First, a hard look of determination, then a shift to a meeker look, with an almost imperceptible bow. He would be loyal to his president, even above the law. He was pushing aside one principle to make room for another. Or maybe he was signaling that she'd been right to worry, right to review the past.

Bud and Nolan muttered their assent to Jeffrey's plan, then glanced at Frances.

"Agent Hazen, we are in your debt." She spoke calmly, deliberately. "What happened here today will remain a secret. I have three children. An evil person might think that if the oldest child can be carried off, why not the younger ones? We will protect them. I will protect them." With her last sentence, she raised her chin and locked her eyes on Hazen until she was certain he caught her resolve. Or, maybe, until she was certain she caught and held forever to her resolve.

Ruth sobbed as Bud carried her to the sailboat, past the mud, past the stench of eelgrass Frances remembered from walks with Jennie. Only the rocking of the boat and Frances's hugs soothed the child. She would remain withdrawn for another few months, until her spirits lifted as she watched Marion try to suck her fingers and listened as Esther tried to turn Ari into Marion.

Mary Brinski would never be found at the bottom of Buzzards Bay, where she rested along with the lock of blond hair remaining in the pocket of her dress. She lay two feet away from Jeffrey Hazen's Colt revolver and the extra ammunition he needlessly grabbed two hours earlier. Frances gave no thought to the whereabouts of the revolver or the ammunition, but if she had, she'd understand that Jeffrey Hazen, sickened at shooting a woman, a woman who may not have intended harm, wanted no reminders of his deed.

Chapter Fifty-Four

September 19, 1895-October 17, 1895

As the sailboat neared the dock at Gray Gables, Frances saw Grover pace on the shoreline, waving wildly. Bud tied up the boat, then lifted Ruth into the dory, and then into Grover's arms. Clasping his daughter to his barrel chest, he stared at Frances. She saw tears he didn't swipe away. She averted her eyes, not from his wet face. From his unspoken questions.

Annie and Bonnie, one holding Marion and one holding Esther, stood off to the side, giving the family a minute of privacy. The nursemaids cried while smiling.

Sinclair, Henry, and Sky Donnella stood together on the lawn, waiting. Frances ignored Donnella's raised brows. He seemed to ask, where is Jeffrey? You know we need him. And she ignored Henry's scrutinizing glare. He seemed to ask, what happened? You know I keep secrets.

Effie, Susan, Jennie, and Lena huddled in another spot, looking both relieved and puzzled. Frances ignored Jennie's probing look. She seemed to ask, where is John Nolan? Did he help?

Most of the groundsmen stood motionless on the lawn. They squinted at Bud. Frances glanced at him. He met no one's eyes as he kept busy wiping down the seats on the boat.

Good God, she thought to herself. All these questioning eyes. It's up to me.

She pressed her fingers into her thigh and turned her head from left to right, stopping for long enough at Grover to calm him. "We are relieved to have Ruth back." Frances took her hand away from her thigh and raised both arms toward the sky, gesturing gratitude. "She was taken by a woman, we believe the same woman who took her in July." Ruth was listening. "As we approached, the woman collapsed." Frances paused. Was collapsed too big a word? "She fell down. Agent Hazen and John Nolan stayed behind, to take the woman into custody. Agent Hazen says it's best if we don't know where. The woman will no longer threaten our family. The president and I appreciate your support."

Frances bowed her head in thanks, then walked to Grover and took Ruth from his arms. "Let's ask Susan for a big breakfast for you." Frances did not ask Annie to change Ruth out of her damp nightgown. No reason to call attention to any remaining stains.

As Frances carried Ruth to the residence, she glanced at Grover. His jaw moved from relaxed with relief to anger. He knew her story was a lie.

"Later." She mouthed the word, silently. "Let me settle Ruth, maybe sing to her, and nurse Marion."

"I'll be waiting."

Frances entered Grover's study an hour later. Bud Wylie sat there, moving one shoulder down, then the other, with a vacant look in his eyes. "I dragged Bud here," Grover said, stretching out his mustache. "We spend hours together each day. I like to think he's loyal, but he won't tell me anything. Just keeps repeating those lies you said to the staff. Frances, I'm the president, and I'm also Ruth's father."

Frances thought back to their earlier lies. Keeping their courtship from the public. Keeping their engagement secret. Never mentioning Grover's cancer, the surgery that saved his life. They would lie together, as always, and Bud would have no choice but to go along.

"We found the woman," Frances said, "holding a knife to Ruth's neck. She was Mary Brinski. Bud jumped on her, and Jeffrey shot her. He and Nolan will drag her to the Bay after dark, tie stones to her, and sink the body." Frances began to speak more slowly. "Jeffrey took charge. He insisted that nothing good would come from sharing the full story. Ruth is out of danger. Mary Brinski—Margaret Bright—will disappear, and no one is likely to ask after her, except for the hotel manager. Jeffrey will deal with him."

Bud's eyebrows jumped up. He must have expected a more subtle explanation.

When Frances finished, she looked from Bud to Grover and back to Bud.

Grover was quick to catch on. He turned to Bud, staring at him. "You're a fine Yankee, trustworthy and honest. Can you keep all that happened to yourself, for the good of—of my family?" He turned back to Frances, who met his eyes with an intense gaze.

Bud Wylie did keep the story to himself. As did John Nolan. As did Jeffrey Hazen. Frances knew they would recoil from their memories of that day. She knew too that they felt they took the only path they could.

* * *

Frances lingered after Bud left the study. "Grover?" She stretched out his name.

Sitting in his large chair, he looked at his cigar humidor and fidgeted. Two seconds later, he stretched out his neck and looked squarely at her. "You expect an apology. Well, you were right to worry that the woman would try again. Jeffrey and I should have paid more attention. And you were right to guess a connection to my surrogate. I married a young woman, a beautiful woman. A smart woman, too, Frankie."

A wave of calm enveloped Frances. She wanted to capture it, to reclaim it later should she ever feel lost again. "Do not forget how I helped. Do not." She barely recognized the tone of her voice. "I'm happy being a wife and mother. And the president's wife. And a college graduate who opposes the vote for women. But when someone threatens my children, I will use every part of my brain to solve the crime, even if it means a murder, or hiding a dead body. I won't shy away, or make excuses, for speaking."

Before Frances could prepare for Grover to either cower or fume, he asked a question she did not anticipate.

CHAPTER FIFTY-FOUR

"Murder? You said the woman held a knife to Ruth."

"Yes, she held a knife in her hand." Frances closed her eyes slowly, then opened them, ignoring the tears. "Mary Brinski—let's use her real name— had lowered it when Jeffrey shot her. I'm not sure if he or Bud saw that. And I need to tell you something else, just you. When I brought Ruth to the kitchen to give her breakfast, she wasn't hungry. The woman had fed her. And Ruth was clean. The woman had towels and fresh water. She wasn't going to harm Ruth. Just scare us. Mary Brinski only wanted you to apologize."

Frances and Grover locked eyes, sealing their pact. Decades ago, he set in motion the events haunting them now. She had never questioned him. They would keep their silence. She wiped away her tears.

* * *

A month later, back in Washington, Frances called on Fannie Johnston in her photography studio on V Street. Fannie had prepared for the visit, laying out eight photographs from the gunroom at Gray Gables.

"Frances, can you tell me what you're looking for? I never presented these photographs to the president or showed them to the press because I wasn't pleased with the quality. If the event had come off earlier, as intended, the light would be better."

"I'm not concerned about the quality, which, by the way, looks fine to me. I'm hunting for a glimpse of Ruth. You see, her nursemaid thinks she snuck down the stairs on her own to watch her father press the button. But don't worry, I won't reprimand her—I just want to see if the nursemaid is right."

Frances examined each photo. Fannie captured the scene well—the backs of dozens of suited men and a few apron-clad women, crowded together and all facing Grover, who sat at a desk with his finger on an odd-looking contraption. Frances studied the details behind the desk, to Grover's right. In the back corner, she could see a slightly open doorway to the short, narrow hall leading from the servants' staircase to the back door of the residence. In two of the photographs, if she looked carefully and used her imagination, she could see a blurry image of white—probably a child's nightgown since Mary Brinski wore a darker-colored dress. The dress that would become her shroud. Frances took a breath of relief. No visual evidence of Mary Brinski.

"These two, Fannie, I think I see a speck of Ruth's nightgown. Can you do me a favor—destroy these. No need for me to embarrass Ruth."

Fannie scrunched up her face, puzzled by the request. But few people contradicted the president's wife. Fannie tore up the photographs.

"I thank you. Now, can we move to lighter topics? When can you give me another lesson?"

Chapter Fifty-Five

January 14, 1904

Nine years after the summer of 1895, John Nolan sat at the kitchen table in his farmhouse in Mansfield, Ohio, enjoying the eggs Jennie served him. He could just see the sun rise, so he had an hour to idle before reporting to his job as coachman for the town's mayor. John's eyes fell on a tiny story, barely an inch long, in the *Mansfield Weekly News*.

"Ruth Cleveland, the eldest daughter of ex-president Cleveland, died of heart failure at three o'clock Thursday morning at the Cleveland mansion in Princeton. Four days ago, the child was taken ill with a sore throat, which later developed into a mild attack of diphtheria. The Cleveland family physician was in attendance, and the progress of the disease seemed to have been checked. Wednesday night, however, there was a change for the worse, and despite every effort, the child died."

Jennie stood at the sink, washing the skillet. She hummed a tune, unaware. John swigged coffee to wet his dry throat and called her over.

Five minutes later, Jennie slumped at the table, swiping her wet eyes with a napkin to keep her sorrow from her four girls playing in the next room. Four daughters, all spaced two years apart.

"Ruth never talked about it," Jennie said.

John tilted his head in acknowledgement.

"She spent fourteen hours out there on Red Brook Pond and never said a word. She was quiet those first months. Didn't pay much attention to my reading lessons. Or nature lessons. A little to music, to singing." Jennie wiped a tear while lifting corners of her mouth. "And horses. Remember, you were quiet too, at first. For about ten hours."

John knew that Jennie remembered that on the evening of September 19th, he flouted the ban on talk—but only in private. She remembered his boastful story, telling her how he led the band of men and one lady to the right place around the pond, how he helped Agent Hazen subdue Margaret Bright, how they took her into custody, how Hazen hid her in a federal prison. Jennie remembered, as he did, how they celebrated his contribution, how the straw in the stables pricked the damp flesh on their backs. And above all, she saw, as he did, that from that day on, although he might remain a coachman, he'd know he could step up, could speak up, could make his own way.

"John, you know, the women talked—Lena and Bonnie and Annie. Susan and Effie, too. They worked out what happened. They knew you were the one who connected the bits of information and got to Walter Breen and then to the Norcross House. You saved that girl. But to this day, I don't know, and none of them knows, why that woman went after Ruth."

Jennie stared at him.

"It's been almost ten years, so I'll tell you now. That woman, her real name wasn't Margaret Bright. It was Mary Brinski." He swallowed. "Frances Cleveland remembered that a sailor served as a surrogate for Cleveland during the war. The president paid him only $150 of the standard $300 surrogate fee. The sailor's name was George Brinski. No one thought Brinski had wed. No one knew he had a wife, or a common law wife, named Mary. She wanted revenge."

Jennie stiffened. Only her eyes moved. "Why didn't anyone say?" She spoke slowly, angrily.

"Cleveland was ashamed. Ashamed he hired a substitute. Ashamed he never paid the man what he was due. But mostly, Cleveland was a good man, a good pa. Once Ruth was safe, that first time, Cleveland didn't think the kidnapper would return." And I, Nolan thought, chose to obey Jeffrey

Hazen, a choice I don't regret. Not most days.

"Frances Cleveland knew," Jennie said. "She knew Ruth might still be in danger. The missus acted ladylike, but she stood up to those men who tried to ignore her." Jennie's voice calmed with each word. "I mean both Cleveland and the agent. Sometimes, though, I could tell she thought she needed to take a step back that summer. Then she changed a bit afterwards. Seemed surer about herself." Jennie paused, and John sensed she was debating what to say. "John, tell me what really happened to that woman?"

Jennie angled her head, waiting, registering her husband's silence.

John lifted his coffee cup, and his next words ended the topic forever. "To Ruth, a brave child."

A Note from the Author

Although threats against President Grover Cleveland and his daughters are well-documented, we have no evidence Ruth was ever kidnapped. The events I portray are wholly figments of my imagination. We do, however, have evidence that Grover and Frances Cleveland kept newsworthy events in their lives from the American public. They kept their marriage engagement to themselves for a year and, more seriously, devised a scheme to hide the president's cancer. That scheme involved scores of medical experts and political operatives who kept the story to themselves for two decades. Given the couple's penchant for secrecy, and ability to persuade others, I consider it plausible that they could have hidden an attempt at kidnapping.

I wish I could write that Ruth Cleveland's early death was also a figment of my imagination. Sadly, she did die of diphtheria.

George Brinski served as a surrogate for Grover Cleveland during the Civil War. Research on him is complicated by the various spellings of his name: Brinski, Beniski, Brinske, Brinsky, Benninsky. He was injured in a wagon accident and died in poverty in Bath, New York, as I describe. We have a shred of evidence about his personal life—the 1860 census, which lists the one other member of the household, Mary, with the label "inferred spouse," and a note that she was twenty-one, born in Michigan, and illiterate. I took liberties with those facts, shaving four years off her age, placing her childhood in Buffalo, and giving her at least a rudimentary education. Mary's years in the Potter household in Pontiac, Michigan, are fictional. We have no record of Mary engaging in any unlawful activities, and no record of her death, at least not under the name Mary Brinski. In my mind, poor, lonely, forgotten Mary might plausibly harbor resentments that grow as she learns more and more about the Clevelands' life.

President Cleveland and his family summered at Gray Gables from the early 1890s until Ruth's death. The home no longer stands. The terrain of the area has changed since 1895, so I found it hard to calculate the time it would take to get from one location to another, or what route a walker, rider, or boater might take. I apologize for my mistakes. Red Brook Pond still exists but has changed a great deal since 1895.

Besides Frances, Grover, and their daughters, other characters in my novel who were actual historical figures include Henry Thurber, Joseph Jefferson, Frances Johnston, the Lamonts, the Gilders, Maria Halpin, Oscar Folsom, Emma Perrine, and William Sinclair.

We know a little about William Sinclair, the Cleveland's steward, but almost nothing about other members of the household. Newspapers mention many servants by their first names only, and either journalists were inaccurate in reporting those names or there was a great deal of turnover. I have on occasion seen the names Annie (described as a nurse, working for the Clevelands in 1893) and Susan. Lena, Bonnie, and Ingrid are invented characters. Stillman—known as "Bud"—and Effie were indeed a married couple working for the Clevelands, but under the last name Wright. I changed their surname to Wylie to avoid confusion with convicted criminal Cephas Wright. The Wrights had two living sons, neither named Ned. Another housekeeper may have been Mrs. Clinton, but I limited the story to one housekeeper in the interest of simplicity.

All the condemned criminals are historical figures. I simplified their stories, but each was condemned to hang.

Most of the places of business I mention in Bourne are fictional. The village police were known as constables. The two in the novel are invented characters. The Old Stone Studio in Marion is an actual place, still standing.

Almost all the newspaper quotations are part of the historic record, though I occasionally made slight changes for clarity and brevity.

The term White House was not in common use in 1895, which explains why I opted for Executive Mansion. Similarly, the term first lady was rarely used. For details about Frances Cleveland's life, I benefited from Annette Dunlap's book, *Frank*.

Most of the historic events I outline are true. Cleveland allegedly fathered a child with Maria Halpin. That child, renamed James King, became a doctor. The details of this story have been contested over the years. Readers wishing to know more can find a good summary in Angela Serratore's *Smithsonian Magazine* article, "President Cleveland's Problem Child." Workers did strike against the Pullman plant, with the participation of Eugene Debs.

The Atlanta Exposition did take place and was a major event. Cleveland did press a button, after the delays I describe, to start electricity in Atlanta. According to some reports, Ruth and Esther stayed up to see the button pressing, but accounts of the event were inconsistent.

John Nolan and Jennie Lander (aka Jennie Schultz Nolan), were historical figures. Jennie began working for the Clevelands as governess in 1894, not 1895. Jennie and John married on August 30, 1895, with the Clevelands hosting a reception at Gray Gables. The young couple did move to Mansfield, Ohio and had four daughters. We have no record of the details of their courtship.

Although there were Secret Service agents in 1895, their purview did not include protecting the president, and certainly did not include protecting the president's family. Frances Cleveland, almost single handedly, changed that in July, 1894. Curious readers can find the details of this story in Frederick M. Kaiser's article, "Origins of Secret Service Protection of the President."

Agent Hazen was indeed in the Secret Service, but I changed his name from George to Jeffrey to avoid confusion with George Brinski. Hazen was brother to the head of the Secret Service, William Hazen. Skylar Donnella also served as an agent. I could not pin down exactly how many agents worked at Gray Gables in 1895, and whether Hazen and Donnella were among them. I believe they worked at the residence for at least part of the time covered in the novel. They may have been joined or spelled by Agent William J. McManus. I decided that following the activities of three agents would add needless complexity to the story.

Emma Perrine did spend time with her daughter and granddaughters in Gray Gables, but I have taken liberties with the dates of her visit. The

Lamonts and Clevelands were friendly, and the Gilders and Clevelands were friendly. The particular visits I describe are imagined. Rumormongers suggested the relationship between Frances Cleveland and Richard Gilder went beyond friendship, but I found no foundation for those stories.

Frances Johnston was an accomplished photographer during the period my novel covers. She did know Frances Cleveland and photographed her at least once, in 1886, but we have no evidence that Frances Johnston visited Gray Gables.

We know little about Ruth Cleveland, in large part because her parents fiercely and understandably tried to protect her privacy. She is buried in Princeton Cemetery in Princeton, New Jersey, close to the graves of her mother and father.

Acknowledgments

I am grateful to many generous publishing professionals, family members, and friends. To keep this acknowledgments section from swelling in size, I am summarizing contributions, but please know that I could elaborate at length on the generosity and wisdom of the people whose names follow. Shawn Reilly Simmons and Deb Well, both at Level Best Books, have supported *First Daughter* and improved it in countless ways. My husband Mark listened to my fussing and provided historical background and plot suggestions. My brother, Robert D. Parker, undertook a superb critique, advised me on publishing matters, and perfected my formatting. My sister, Carol McConnell, offered crucial research, carefully reviewed a draft, and provided technical support. My writing buddy, Jeff Tanner, shared invaluable comments on drafts and taught me crucial lessons about writing. My friend from our publishing days, Dorothea Berkhout, provided encouragement and excellent suggestions. Historian Jacqueline Wolf assured me that Frances Cleveland was likely to have breastfed. MaryEllen Cecil, research assistant at the New Bedford Free Public Library in Massachusetts and Lucy Loomis, Director of the Sturgis Library in Barnstable, Massachusetts aided my research. Mary Sicchio of the Bourne Historical Commission made excellent suggestions, at least some of which I was able to incorporate.

About the Author

Marlie Parker Wasserman loves writing historical crime fiction. In addition to *First Daughter*, she has published *The Murderess Must Die*, *Path of Peril*, and *Inferno on Fifth*, all set around the year 1900. She writes from her home in Chapel Hill, North Carolina.

AUTHOR WEBSITE:
  marliewasserman.com

SOCIAL MEDIA HANDLES:
  Facebook: Marlie Wasserman
  Bluesky: @marliewasserman.bluesky.social
  Instagram: marliepwasserman

Also by Marlie Parker Wasserman

The Murderess Must Die

Path of Peril

Inferno on Fifth

9 7 9 8 8 9 8 2 0 1 5 3 1